Profit

Profit

Book 2 of the Joad Cycle

GARY LEVEY

iUniverse, Inc.
Bloomington

Profit
Book 2 of the Joad Cycle

iUniverse books may be ordered through booksellers or by contacting:

iUniverse
1663 Liberty Drive
Bloomington, IN 47403
www.iuniverse.com
1-800-Authors (1-800-288-4677)

ISBN: 978-1-4620-3396-6 (sc)
ISBN: 978-1-4620-3398-0 (dj)
ISBN: 978-1-4620-3397-3 (ebk)

Printed in the United States of America

iUniverse rev. date: 07/19/2011

Profit is a self-published novel. I have worked hard and spent a fair amount of ever-cheapening American dollars to reduce the grammatical errors and such to a minimum. If you find any, please bear with me, I will make it better in subsequent releases.

As to the novel itself, the words are mine, and I stand by them. 21st century Americans have become overconfident for good reasons. But this overconfidence has clouded our judgment and allowed greed to own us.

The Joad Cycle tells the story of where greed and power will take us.

I thank my wife, June, for putting up with persistent, business-based science fiction discussions and for enduring a constant barrage of both sides of an argument.

I am a better person for having lived my life with her and she claims the same about me.

This novel is dedicated to my wife, June, and also for all the Syls in my life.

Gary Levey
6/11/11

Novels of the Joad Cycle

Book 1: The Golden Rule

Book 2: Profit

Book 3: Circle of Life (Due Summer, 2011)

Book 4: The Rightness of Things (Due Fall, 2011)

Join us for a discussion about America's future at
WWW.Joadcycle.com

Prologue

The United States of America was great and growing and then it was full and exhausted, its frontiers absorbed and its assets owned by corporations who did business like they were too big to fail, an apostasy punishable by dissolution in Capitalist theology. Rebelling against the unreasonable economic restraints of Socialist leaning administrations, corporations had behaved so badly that federal, state, and local government, once thought by frivolous American citizens also to be too big to fail, went bankrupt trying to restore financial sanity.

What value remained in America the beautiful-from sea to shining sea-was bought cheap by select gigantic financial corporations who were under no obligation to provide more than appreciation for their stockholders and senior management; a financially rewarding if short term strategy.

The American economy reacted as economies must, it constricted into a death spiral with only the capable able to sustain a semblance of their former lifestyle. The resultant highly stratified wealth begat a highly stratified society along with a battered and broken middle and lower class, the once great domestic fuel for the engine of American Capitalism. In turns, the masses went from uneconomically unsure, to fickle and then resentful until finally realizing their impoverished government could offer no relief. Frightened, they became restive and then panicky and economically unpredictable and the Gross Domestic Product plummeted more.

Leaders implemented the inevitable solutions—downsizings, evictions, and bankruptcies which led, ultimately, to deaths by deprivation, murders in desperation, and executions by conviction until a great exodus began, a vast, frenzied migration from commerce and debt. It was a down market.

In 2029, in one final wheeze of liberal ennui, the administration of President Vernon L. Parrington commanded that money be printed, gobs and gobs of it, enough to provide a carnival of government largesse which briefly restored middle class joy, long enough for the re-nomination of President Parrington. But this great monetary transgression left the country bereft of the value necessary to preserve, protect and defend the Constitution of the United States and so it died along with America's First Republic.

The year was 2032, three years after Parrington's fiscal bollocks. Andrew M. Crelli, a successful entrepreneur and leader of the libertarian Conservative movement, was elected president as a Republican, chosen by the vast majority of the country over the incumbent, incompetent progressive, Parrington. Crelli's arrival in Washington was auspicious. These were desperate times and only a modern champion, a slayer of great monetary and fiscal dragons, could save America.

And a great hero he was. To resuscitate the economy, he commanded into existence programs known as the *Circle of Life*. Passed by super majorities in both Houses, these laws dictated the terms for American economic revival. Handouts, entitlements, subsidies, and welfare of any kind to anyone were expressly prohibited and the law required every citizen to earn at least what it cost to live or, as *Wasters*, face justifiable and legal elimination.

With *Wasters*, a new, but transient class appeared and a new and vibrant domestic industry took flight to process them. Private contractors funded by *Circle of Life* legislation expanded into the profitable industry of waste management, also called economic genocide, and stockholders lauded the results.

Thanks to President Crelli, Capitalist resolve, and time, the population of *Wasters* declined, approaching insignificance and the economy rebounded robustly. To sustain the growth, President Crelli eliminated America's no longer needed, burdensome bureaucracy, restructuring his government to insure the best for business in a super-heated, competitive free market world. When even that wasn't enough for stockholders, the president orchestrated a successful constitutional coup and the democratic, free market Capitalist Second Republic of the United States transitioned into an autocratic Capitalist oligarchy and profits soared to record heights.

Unprecedented growth led to a great golden age of productivity and profitability, a paradise where everything appreciated and anything was possible. Adding to this growth were nation-wide franchises of municipalities called *Wharton Towns*. Developed by the great social engineer of the age, and later President of the United States, Mark Rose, *Wharton Towns* were integrated, incorporated commercial communities owned by entrepreneurs. *Wharton Towns* expanded rapidly throughout the country and quickly achieved the glorious fiscal success their investors envisioned.

For all that, life wasn't yet perfect in America, though it was close. There were still a worrisome number of *Wasters* hiding in America's nether regions. Fortunately, storied economic growth provided funding that allowed HOMESEC, LLC, a private security corporation that began life as a division of the U.S. Department of Homeland Security, to relentlessly choke residual chaos, sabotage, dissent, and violence from an ever more productive America.

With technology inexpensive, overhead costs low, and taxes minimal, *Wharton Towns* grew into *Wharton Cities,* and they thrived while *Wasters,* the poor, the sick, the old and the young, and the incapable, fled the financial order of the Second Republic for places to survive though they struggled at subsistence levels in third world-like hovels in underutilized, out-of-the way *Unincorporated Lands.*

Wasters, the unwilling to compete, huddled in isolated, insignificant, ramshackle villages struggling to eke out an existence and trying not to be noticed by the government which had no interest in them so long as the cost to eliminate them was calculated as greater than the cost to ignore them.

Over time, prideful *Wasters* sought a better life through the ownership of more, and they turned to *Wharton Towns* for economic redemption; fearlessly facing the risk of death and the reward of an everlasting fiscal existence, the inevitable choices in the economic game of life. – **Archive**

Chapter 1
Angel Falls, Maine — 2070

He came to life at first light and directed his solar cells to gather what little energy the cool dawn provided. When lifting power was achieved, he hovered, unsteadily, to access more of the sun's enabling rays. Impatient to earn what the day would provide, he headed towards the less charted Unincorporated Lands south of Canada.

Flying high above the emerging Gulf of Delmarva, he transmitted his coordinates so the core, Gecko, could transmit back today's to-do list of revenue opportunities. He earned his first commission of the day transmitting maps of the Mid-Atlantic coastline to update the model projecting long-term capital implications of the rising tides. Then he was off, confirming his assignments, and heading north and east toward New York, Boston, and points beyond.

With little recent terrorist history, Maine was not normally an assignment, but what few opportunities existed there had the potential for large income generation. And he could always identify conditions of potential aberrance for cataloguing and analysis. That didn't pay much, but it would cover his overhead, so he spent the day soaring through blue skies, among the high clouds and over green hills, diligently investigating opportunities that might provide value to the core. As much as anything, he was hoping to get lucky as he luxuriated in wave-after-wave of energy that rushed over him, as he crossed countless reflective bodies of water that bounced life-affirming sunlight up to his collectors. After passing over five or six small lakes in short order, the massive rushes of energy had him shivering, drunk on the power of the sun.

The day soon lost its energy, and his financial expectations waned as well. There were Waster Towns scattered below, but nothing suspicious, so as he approached the Canadian border with the sun now setting, he calculated the day's points earned and dutifully reported. Feeling something akin to disappointment, he turned and headed home. But as he was banking high above the tall pines of northern Maine, he detected curious motion in the distance. Perhaps it was work for another day, but reward was reward so he pressed on . . .

The teenage boy and girl raced from the Angel Falls Meeting House, and out to the evergreen hills. They hopped fences, avoiding the livestock, as they sprinted until they reached the tree line. From there, they hiked the rolling sugar loaf hills between the lakes, discovering ravines for which they scrambled up and down utilizing rocks, branches, and each other for support. Here in nature's secluded calm, there was laughter as the two teens frolicked like the young of old, and even at a distance, could easily be identified one from the other, for though they were the same height, she was thin and blonde, and he was broad and dark. Gil Rose was nineteen years old and for the first time in his life, he had a real friend.

Five years had passed since he had met his great-grandfather, Bernie, at the hospice in Indiana, and rescued his grandfather, Mark, from a prison within a lavish mansion. Gil was tall, taller than the other boys of Angel Falls and aided by fresh air and outdoor hikes; his muscles had massed nicely. He was no longer the indoor, city boy who tended a tiny secluded garden after dark.

For all the fun and freedom a real, live friend provided, Gil remained intimate with his first love, Andrea, the joy of his life. In virtual they shared everything with each other, and outside the virtual confines of that cyber-world-within-the-mesh, Andrea was constantly in his thoughts. But on this summer day, after a brief, but torrential rainfall that had left the world smelling perfect, like a spring renewal, he preferred this live world to the old Virtuoso unit in his cabin, which provided a less satisfying replication of nature. Bernie had explained the lack of virtual realism as a bandwidth issue, something about frivolous rendering and wave transmissions, but whatever it was, here in real nature, Gil's senses reveled in the breathtaking depth and detail. With him, sharing this wonderment of reality was a live, local girl; his best friend in the real world, Stacey.

From the bed in his cabin, old and frail, Bernie stared through the window at his only view, the verdant hills that surrounded Angel Falls. Like too many times before, Gil was late and there was a good chance he wouldn't show at all. If Gil even spoke, his excuse would be that he had better things to do than to be lectured about his role in the world.

So much like Bernie waited for death, he waited for Gil. He was over a hundred years old, and every minute should have been precious and the lost ones irreplaceable. He wanted to feel that way especially since every lost second was so vital, seeing as he had been hiding from an autocratic government that had issued a death warrant for him. But too frail, he waited, alone, and it was terrifying, as the diminishing seconds of his life ticked away.

Where was the boy? Bernie Thought. *He's probably having sex in Virtual again, or with that real girl, heaven forbid.*

From that day, five years earlier, when Bernie and his teenaged great grandson arrived in Angel Falls, he had worked diligently, but unproductively to enlighten Gil about his potential, the future, and more importantly, Gil's responsibilities. Bernie understood that the poor and oppressed in America had no choice but to hope for the savior that he was grooming.

But it wasn't working. Gil was immature and resentful that he wasn't home with Howard, his father. That and he had been so enamored by the capitalist-nurturing world he grew up in, that he trivialized everything Bernie pleaded for. On top of that, Gil had difficulty focusing, which caused Bernie, who was already exhausted most of his waking time, to expend effort as he struggled to find ways to kindle a spark of humanity in the boy. Gil had to succeed. The senseless deaths of forty million Americans, including the two most important, his beloved wife Jane, and his beautiful daughter, Franki, had to be avenged. The genocide was partly his fault; his past failures helped to put Andrew Crelli in power and cost Bernie his family. Even now, a worse evil in the guise of current Chairwoman, Tanya Brandt, had taken over for Crelli, and that was clearly his responsibility too. But that was for Gil and another generation to set that wrong right. America could be saved. There was still a flicker of hope, if only Gil would understand.

What made it harder was the boy was all he had and yet he was so closed. And so Bernie's instructions became lectures to a boy who didn't care and frequently just stopped listening. Gil was a tougher nut than this tired old man could crack, but the stakes were too high, so exhausted or not, Bernie had to persist. In truth, it was the only thing keeping him alive.

He smiled at a fleeting memory, as they all were these days. Angst and his old career had taught him patience and prudence. He remembered explaining it to his loving wife, Jane, once long ago. "Never try to teach a pig to sing," he had said to her as she smiled, knowing his aphorisms better than he, "because it wastes your time, and annoys the hell out of the pig." He smiled in the absence of her laughter, but he felt sad and hollow as the smile ended in a productive cough. He couldn't give up on Gil; in these days, becoming a hero can't be easy. If he could only figure out how to get through to him.

Bernie felt a touch. He was startled, but stirred slowly until he recognized the teen's form beside his bed.

"You're late," he muttered. Gil reacted as he usually did by shrugging and staring out a window at the lake. "It's important, pay attention." It sounded like whining, but he'd lost the ability to hide his feelings from his voice. "Son, for what I want for you-for everyone, it's critical that you understand before I die. Please, Gil, be kind to a dying old man and pay attention."

There was no home for that plea because Gil's mind was in another place; a beautifully kept garden with Andrea. And they were naked.

A shout ripped Gil back into the present. It was a tricky transition as Gil covered his engorged penis by forming his hands in the biblical fig leaf position. To hide it further, he moved closer to the bed before nodding that he was back.

"We can't keep doing this. Focus son, please. There's evil out there and it's up to us to end it." The boy stared, but gave no sign of recognition. "Gil Rose, I'm talking to you. Remember that joke, the joke I always tell about time and inclination, remember time and inclination?" It felt like Bernie was shouting, but fatigue quickly quieted him. "Remember? They moved the clock at Big Ben into the Leaning Tower of Pisa. Why? Why did they do that?" Gil stared, apparently clueless. "You know this. Why did-?"

There were so many things Gil wanted to say, but Bernie was dying, this time for sure, and he was uncomfortable. He'd never seen a dying old person.

"Bernie, I'm not stupid. I know Big Ben is in England and the Tower is in Italy. I get the joke. It's not funny. What's the point?"

"What good is the time if you don't have the inclination, that's the point?"

"I know. It's not much of a joke."

"It's more than a joke. You only get out of life what you put into it, Gil. You need to be purposeful, do important things, necessary things. Good people are counting on you. You're young, you have time, but without inclination, life is wasted. But there is even more at stake for you. I know. You don't want to live with the ghosts of all those depending on you but that's beside the point. You must care. Why are you being so obtuse? Invest in your future. Do it now." Bernie stopped, exhausted. His heart was thundering excitedly and he imagined each beat would be his last.

"Listen." Bernie knew this was his fault, but the fates, too, had been unkind. He was too old and lacked energy, and Gil was too immature and distracted to be energized. Bernie had risked so much for the boy; to bring him here to Angel Falls to learn the values America had sold out more than a century before. Teaching him to fight for the people against a business community that stole and defrauded America of those great values was proving to be too much. Gil was bored with the bucolic life, and uninterested in his place in history.

"Please, son," he pleaded wearily, "You must understand what we're fighting for and against. America-," before he continued, he paused, remembering, "America was a great country, once for almost everyone. We did great things, and we did them for as many as we could. We made mistakes but we were human, not like today. It can be that way again. You can do that." Gil's eyes were riveted on him so intently that it was obvious his brittle attention would fracture long before Bernie could get to anything substantive.

Frustrated, Bernie closed his eyes. This conversation had occurred so many times before that they each had resorted to habit in order to survive it. Uprooting Gil from his sheltered existence and isolating him in northern Maine, even though it was for his protection, wasn't working. When they arrived, he endured Gil's constant whining over the early series Virtuoso unit because it lacked bandwidth. Who cared? Gil needed to be weaned off virtual anyway so what better place than here. What did he expect? Angel Falls was a tiny community of Quakers living in the furthest reaches of the *Unincorporated Lands*. They had no use for Virtuoso.

The residents of this isolated hilly, forest community between the lakes spent their time harvesting and doing chores. They kept to themselves and were no threat to the business community and thus the government showed no interest wasting money here. Bernie expected that life in Angel

Falls would expose Gil to good things, kids his age growing up together with involved parents, plenty of fresh air and beautiful surroundings and a community that cooperated, shared and cared. If Gil would learn these values he could discard his cool commercial perspective and that would open him up to things that would help him mature into the caring individual the world needed him to be. It hadn't worked. Things seldom do.

As soon as Gil had arrived at Angel Falls, and the excitement of avoiding capture wore off, life became crushingly dull and boring and he became sullen and distant. Though Bernie tried, the only thing that worked, even a little, was friendship with the local girl who had befriended Gil on Bernie's insistence. All the girls noticed Gil, he was a tall, well built, good looking nineteen year old, but hell, all nineteen year olds were good looking. Stacey treated him differently. She was a tomboy and her parents were very watchful. It should have been safe, but even that didn't work as he intended because when Gil wasn't in Virtuoso, he was hiking in the hills with the girl, doing God only knows what when he should have been with Bernie committing to a greater cause.

What if they were having sex? Stacey had been a pretty girl at thirteen, but now, at eighteen, she was extremely attractive. This was his fault. America's great hope for salvation couldn't fall in love, not again. The boy had more important things to do.

A cough startled him and his attention returned to the teen staring at him, looking concerned. When Bernie spoke, it seemed to startle Gil.

"Don't make the mistakes I made. Listen to me. Be kind to this dying old man and learn. What I ask isn't fun, I know that. Its hard work, but I promise you it will be worth it if you just pay attention. If you don't-," fatigued, Bernie closed his eyes again and tried to quiet the numbing buzz in his mind. If Gil and Stacey were having sex, could the Council of Elders stop it or will they force Gil and him to move on? His eyes fluttered open to see the easily distracted teen now sitting beside a window staring out. *Why couldn't he pay attention?* Bernie thought. *He knows how important this is.*

"Promise you'll work harder, please. Promise you'll be what you must be. Promise you'll try." Bernie's closed his eyes until he heard Gil's voice. Good, Gil was here, but he was late again.

"Bernie, what's the point?"

"The point of what?"

"What you said. Promising to do better, to be better."

"The point? I learned everything too late. My actions, or the lack, caused so many to die. But I was deceived. I couldn't imagine bad things like that could happen. I didn't pay attention and lost everything. I carry that grief with me and it's a burden I can't give up until you take it from me. That's why you must work harder. Give yourself a chance, pay attention, feel, and give the stars a push so they can align for you. Be a leader. Overthrow that witch, Tanya Brandt, and restore rightness and happiness to America. It's on you to change things so people can have their lives back, fulfilling lives, lives like my Jane and I had . . . once. You never knew her, that's a shame. She was special. We loved each other. I can tell you about her." A tear formed and he slowly brought up a palsied finger to wipe it away.

"You have told me, Bernie."

"It was the Chairman, Andrew Crelli. He was running for President and he murdered her. My Jane and my . . . and my . . . daughter, her, too. Capturing Crelli helped to avenge them, but it wasn't enough, not for all the others who died. It's time. You will make our country better. You will be what Mark . . . wasn't."

The boy sat closer. "I'm sorry, Bernie, but that's impossible."

"Impossible, that's exactly it. Impossible things make for greatness. It's risky, sure, but that's no reason not to do it. Be a fighter, be a man. Don't let this government and the entrepreneurs who run it turn you into another *Conducer*. Take control of your life. Don't waste it working for the benefit of people who don't care about people. You're better than that. I know you are. And you'll avenge the evildoers. That's what you'll do. You'll avenge them all."

He felt a touch and his eyes fluttered open. "Ah, Gil, you're back." The teen was silent. "Son, work with me." An important thought fluttered into his mind. "Are you sleeping with the Grant girl?"

Gil looked surprised and either embarrassed or guilty and he replied angrily. "That's none of your business."

"You can't. Everything depends on you. You can't have sex with that girl."

"I won't, Bernie, I promise."

More silence. When his eyes fluttered open, Gil was staring out the window again.

Chapter 2
Angel Falls, Maine—2070

Gil and Stacey were hiking again, this time with a friend of Gil's from a nearby village. Morris Mitcoskie was what Gil might have been if he was born and raised in the *Unincorporated Lands*. Morris, or Meat as everyone called him, was a tall, flabby, not unhandsome boy with a pink complexion, close cropped blond hair and dull brown eyes. And though he wasn't a trouble maker, Stacey didn't enjoy his company because trouble seemed to follow the annoying teen whenever he joined them.

As usual for their afternoon hike, Stacey was out in front. She brushed straight blond hair away from her green eyes and smiled to herself as she eavesdropped on the two teens behind her discussing today's itinerary.

"Why does she always have to come with us?" Meat whispered. "We never get time to play together."

"Come on, Meat," Gil explained. "Stace knows the trails and she always finds something fun to do." Thanks to Andrea, Gil had unique sexual experiences, but like Meat he lacked experience with real girls. And though he was comfortable with Stacey, Meat was always so awkward around her that it rubbed off on him. Gil was embarrassed around real girls as well, so he understood Meat's difficulty. When he had first arrived in Angel Falls with Bernie, Mark, and Gohmpers, it was Stacey who helped him. Unlike the other teens in Angel Falls who lent their hands on the farm and helped bring the produce to market; she tried to avoid chores and slipped away at every opportunity. They often found themselves together with nothing to do and so a bond had formed years before Gil met Meat. Still, he liked Meat but Meat had to learn to like Stacey, too.

Profit

"But we're buds," Meat insisted. "Sometimes I want to have, you know, just guy fun, you and me. Besides, she's too wild. Something always goes wrong when we're out with her."

"Things don't go wrong," Gil argued. "You just get strange around her. Get over it."

"I don't get strange," Meat looked briefly at Stacey, blushed and looked away.

"Meat, I'll bet you and Stacey get married someday," Gil needled. Stacey blushed but continued walking and remained quiet. Meat, however protested.

"No way, it's you two. You'll fall in love, get married and have hundreds of pukey kids," he teased. Gil shoved him hard and Meat retaliated by throwing Gil down and they wrestled on the ground. Meat pushed Gil's face into the mud, laughed and then raced into the woods with Gil in hot pursuit. Hearing the ruckus, Stacey turned to see her friends getting away and using her long legs to her advantage, soon caught up to them. Out of breath, she laughed as she watched them tussle, covered in mud and pine needles. Meat forced Gil into a headlock and then looked up to stare at her, his gaze never rising above her heaving halter-top. He stopped wrestling and went quiet as Gil tried to free himself.

When Meat realized she was staring at him, he blushed and released his hold on Gil. Gil looked at Meat, and then Stacey. In the awkward silence, and unsure why, Gil blushed, too. He started to get up, but now Stacey was uncomfortable too, so she pushed him down on top of Meat.

"You guys act like you've never seen a girl."

Gil was angry with himself. In spite of Bernie's fear of them having sex and though Stacey was real and pretty, he had never considered her in that way. She was his best friend. Because of Andrea, their relationship was that and nothing more. Still, Meat's awkward response triggered something uncomfortable.

Meat pushed him onto his back and Gil's head snapped back. "Yo, stop it!" he yelled.

"You jumped me first," Meat said as he impeded Gil from getting up.

Realizing how stupid this was, Gil simply stopped. "She pushed me," he added lamely. When he looked at Stacey, she was staring back, concerned. "What's wrong?" He asked.

9

"Me? You two are the ones acting strange. Maybe you two will be the ones to marry."

Embarrassed, Meat shouted. "Shut up Stacey. And don't go pushing me again, Gil, or you'll be sorry."

"That's enough," Stacey said in a voice meant to shut off the discussion. Then she changed the subject. "Meat, did you hitch or bike here?"

"I, uh . . . I biked down 95. I even saw a car."

"Did you glom a ride?"

"It was going the wrong way or I would have."

"It must have come from Presque Isle," Gil said and then he pointed to the woods. "Hey, let's do the Presque trail today. It should be real muddy after all the rain."

Stacey agreed and trotted ahead, motioning for them to follow.

"She has to come?" Meat asked as soon as she was out of sight.

"She comes," Gil insisted and took off after her. Reluctantly, Meat caught up and Gil tried to placate him. "Next time, it'll be just you and me and I'll even let you use my *Virtuoso*."

Meat punched Gil on the arm. "It's about time. Do you have a girl I can use?"

Gil stopped abruptly and punched Meat's shoulder. "Hush up. You'll use inventory and like it. Besides, that's all you can afford."

"But you have your own girl. What's she like?"

Gil was done discussing it. He hurried down the trail to where Stacey stood waiting with an odd smile on her face.

"What's wrong?" he asked.

She released a branch that she had bent. Gil ducked too late and it hit him hard on the shoulder. When he opened his mouth to yell, he swallowed a spray of water that cascaded down from the branches above. Meat was following and dropped to the ground to avoid the deluge, but he too got drenched.

Stacey laughed. "Need a towel, boys? Wait until you see what's ahead. I know a trail that's steep and muddy."

As she turned to go, on an impulse, Gil grabbed her to throw her into the mud. She dodged but not fast enough and they both lost their balance and slipped into the muck. The cool water made her shriek and she fought against his weight and rolled on top of him. Laughing, they wrestled briefly. He grabbed her shoulders to keep his head out of the mud while she tried to push him under. Their eyes met and he stopped. Her face was caked in mud, but her white teeth seemingly glowed, and she had the most beautiful, iridescent, green eyes. An odd look came over her face, but before he could say anything, she pushed him hard into the mud and while he rubbed the muddy water from his eyes, she quickly jumped out of the way and scurried up the steep muddy trail using tree limbs that lined the trail for leverage.

He yelled after her. "What the hell did you do that for? I didn't bring a towel." Meat offered his shirt and Gil isolated a few dry spots on it before wiping his eyes. Then, together, they chased after Stacey.

When he reached the top of the hill, she was standing with her back to him, legs wide apart, straddling a small stream that ran down the middle of the trail. The stream was fed by two smaller streams that emptied from the hills above. He stared down the hill at what she was looking at. The stream continued down the tree-lined trail to a pool of water at the bottom.

She offered her hand and he smiled and slapped it. Then he ran forward shrieking as loud as he could and flung his body, feet first, hands above his head, down the hill. His body hit the water and skidded, and like a missile he hurtled down the muddy trail to the pool of water below. Trees whizzed by as he tried to blink away muddy water that splashed into his eyes. Suddenly his feet hit the pool and the shock almost lifted him upright. His trip ended in the deepest part of the pool where his body settled into the muck. He was partially covered in water that was clouding with mud.

Laughing, he stood and found clear water to wash out his eyes and mouth. Then he heard Stacey's shriek and dodged away. She hit the pool laughing and staggered to her feet, her halter-top bunched up and wrapped around her neck. He couldn't help himself. He gawked at her exposed breasts as she frantically tried to adjust her top. She appeared angry and glowered at him as they trudged back up the hill but he was too embarrassed to apologize. Meat, too far above to see what had transpired, waited until he saw them leave the pool before hurtling down.

They took turns until they were so wet and covered with mud they could barely walk.

"I'm cold and my legs are chafing," Meat complained, sounding miserable.

"How about one last run?" Gil offered.

"What about the Presque Isle Trail?" Meat asked.

"I'm carrying twenty pounds of mud, Meat, you, too. Let's go home and clean up. We'll do Presque Isle another day."

Stacey agreed. "One last time," she shouted and threw herself down the slope, screaming.

He followed and they sputtered into the pool seconds apart. They stood and looked at each other, laughing at their mud-covered torsos as they headed back up the hill. They were midway when Meat hurtled by, screaming and spinning out of control. Gil heard a crack, a sharp cry, a moan and then *silence*.

Gil stepped onto the trail and stared. At the bottom, up to his ears in the muddy pool, Meat's body lay motionless. He must have hit a submerged tree root or something. Slipping and sliding, Gil hurried down to help but stopped when he heard her shout.

"Gil, no!"

He turned. Stacey motioned for him to be quiet. He thought Meat and Stacey were playing a trick on him so he grabbed a branch and moved to her. She put a finger to her mouth and pointed to an object hovering above the trees, its silver skin reflecting the sun.

It was a Government *SurveilEagle*. He'd learned about them from Mark the last time he had visited Angel Falls. They were hovering, unmanned, surveillance drones that HomeSec used to monitor remote parts of the country. According to Mark, since the Chairman's disappearance, more and more of these things had been launched to improve security.

Alarmed, Gil assessed the situation. Meat was lying unconscious in the mud with a possible severe injury, while he and Stacey were higher on the hill with the *SurveilEagle* in between. He motioned Stacey to follow as he crawled into the woods. Both understood that the *SurveilEagle* couldn't see him, so they worked cautiously through dense foliage to the spot where Meat was lying motionless. The *SurveilEagle* was hovering low to the ground, so it could capture a close-up image of Meat's face. While it maneuvered, so did Gil.

Meat lifted his head briefly and moaned. With his mud-covered face visible, the drone moved closer, concentrating on Meat. Gil noticed a small red light blinking. The *SurveilEagle* was transmitting. He was close enough now to act so he gauged the distance and hurled himself, spread-eagled, out over the mud. The drone must have detected motion because just as Gil made contact, its camera turned. He crashed hard, first onto the drone, and then he and the drone into the muddy water. The shock forced the air out of his lungs, but he held on tight while trying to blink the muddy water from his eyes. His face was pressed against the drone and all he could see was the red transmission light blinking as it sank deeper in the mud.

He kneeled and pressed the drone underwater. It fought back, vibrating wildly trying to extricate itself. Gil's chest ached, but he held firm while Stacey searched frantically for something to use as a weapon. Finally, she pulled up a large rock and beat the submerged drone until the light went out.

"Are you okay?" she asked, breathlessly.

He released the drone and stood, expecting it to emerge. When it didn't, he straightened up and started breathing again. They searched for purchase and pulled on the submerged drone until the vacuum was broken, and it released from the muck with a great, wet, sucking sound. After scraping all the excess mud and debris from the disabled unit, Gil checked it out. The light wasn't blinking but more promising, the camera lens was cracked.

"Gil?" she asked again.

"I'm okay," he said.

"I know that. What about, Meat?" They bent down to check on him, mindful that the drone might try to escape.

"It hurts," Meat whined as he tried to open his eyes but caked mud sealed them shut. "Am I dead? Are you angels?"

They laughed and Gil whispered to her. "Shhh, let's see how long he believes he's dead. This could be fun."

With a look of disdain, she knelt and gently turned Meat's head. Carefully, she scooped up the clearest water she could find and poured it over his head before carefully rubbing the mud away. Then she found some leaves nearby and used them to wipe Meat's face.

When he could see again, Meat hugged Stacey. It sounded to Gil like he was crying. She rocked him and patted him on the back until she was able to convince him that he was okay. When she turned to Gil, her blonde hair and most of her face were covered in dried mud but her green eyes were clear and mesmerizing. He'd never realized.

"Gil Rose, he's your best friend. How could you say such mean things?" Gil stared back, stupidly, but she continued to glare. Finally, she calmed down. "What is that thing?" she asked.

He explained what little he knew about *SurveilEagles* and then, feeling guilty, turned his attention to Meat. "Where does it hurt, Meat?" he asked.

"My elbow is killing me and my head hurts, too. I must have hit it on a rock or something on the way down. It's throbbing like crazy. I think I broke it."

"Your head?" Gil asked.

"No, asshole, my elbow. Get me out of here. Carefully." Stacey and Gil each took a side and slid him out of the water, being very careful to avoid Meat's elbow. Once back on dry land, Gil realized that they were so covered with mud they wouldn't be able to carry Meat back.

"What should we do?" she asked.

"You're a better long distance runner than me, hurry home and get some help. I'll stay here," Gil said. "We'll be okay."

"What do we do about that thing?"

"I don't know. Leave it here; the elders will know what to do with it."

Her eyes lit up dazzling him. "No, let's keep it. No one has to know."

It didn't sound right.

"We'll drag it into the woods and come back for it later. We can dissect it. It'll be fun."

"But the elders should know."

"When we're done, we'll tell them. Please."

He knew it was wrong, but to refuse her felt just as wrong. He stared into her eyes. No wasn't the answer. He helped her float the drone to the edge of the pool where they checked it out again. When he was certain it wasn't operational, they dragged it to a better hiding place and covered it. When they were done, Stacey ran up the hill to Angel Falls and Gil went back to his injured friend.

The mud had dried around Meat forming a hard shell that Gil had hoped would keep him warm, but even in the warm, midday son, Meat was shivering. He placed Meat's head on his lap and held him close until he finally fell asleep. Each time Gil moved, his friend woke moaning or screaming and then fell back asleep once the pain was bearable again.

Gil wasn't certain the drone wasn't transmitting so he carefully rested Meat's head on a mud pillow he formed and crawled into the woods to the spot where he and Stacey had buried it. For the first time he really looked at it. It was about two feet long and curved with a pair of small wings or stabilizers. The glass casing that protruded from the bottom was designed to protect the camera but it hadn't proved adequate. The camera was smashed. He leaned closer. A dim red light was blinking intermittently. Terrified, he grabbed a log and bashed it. When that proved futile, he found a large rock and beat the *SurveilEagle* until the light went out for good. Then he returned to Meat.

Not long afterwards, he heard Stacey's shouts. The rescue party appeared at the top of the hill, and seeing Gil and Meat, they ran to help. As soon as they reached the pool, Meat woke and began complaining. They put him on a stretcher and insisted on carrying Gil back on one as well. When they arrived the villagers clustered around in their work teams and stared at the fallen and filthy teenagers.

Meat had injured a bursar sack in his elbow, so one of the elders immobilized it and had someone take him home. Gil's injuries amounted to some minor soreness so he walked back to his cabin, showered off the layers of encrusted mud and spent the remainder of the day resting. After dinner, Stacey was escorted by some elders who came by to question him.

"Stacey saw a drone flying overhead. Do you think it saw you?" an elder asked.

He looked to Stacey. She winked and responded. "Gilbert and I were playing in the mud when I saw the sun reflecting off the drone. Isn't that right, Gilbert, dear?" The faked formality was their code for teamwork to avoid getting in trouble.

Reluctantly, he supported her. "Stacey's right. It didn't spot us but it definitely saw Meat."

Stacey gave him a sour look as that comment seemed to concern the elders. Stacey tried to minimize it. "But poor, dear Meat was so covered in mud. I doubt there's cause for alarm."

"I hope you kids are taking this seriously."

"We are," she answered.

"If Stacey's right, the worst is that it transmitted an image of a boy Gil's age." Another elder offered.

"There are boys in the area that are Gil's age. Meat could be anyone."

"And you are certain there's no way it could have seen you."

"Yes, sir," he said. "I'm almost certain." A look from Stacey clarified his thinking. "No sir, there's no way. It didn't see me."

"And it just flew away?"

"Yes," Stacey answered before Gil. "It flew by." A lie. A meaningless lie. He knew he was going to regret this.

"And that's all that happened."

"Yes. It was nothing, really."

"Stacey," an elder said. "For the sake of our community, it is critical that we know what happened. I hope you two understand. Gil, do you have anything to add?"

He would have told them everything, but she was glowering at him so he nodded.

The elders left less troubled than when they entered.

Stacey remained. "If you don't feel like talking, I'll come back later."

"Damn it, Stace, we lied."

"It wasn't a lie. Well, maybe it was, but it was harmless. I want to play with it and they wouldn't let me."

"You don't know what's harmless," he said, walking toward the door. She stood in his way. Their heads almost bumped and they stared awkwardly until she leaned forward and kissed him on the lips. It wasn't passionate but Gil's body reacted as if it was.

She pulled back. "Please don't be mad at me."

"I'm just sore and tired, Stace, I'll see you in the morning, okay?"

She looked disappointed. "Yeah, okay. If you need anything, how'll you get it?"

"Meat's the one who's hurting. Maybe you should spend some time with him. My chest only hurts when I take deep breaths."

Her face went red, a sure sign she was angry, but this time she controlled it. "It's late and his farm is too far away." She stood. "Well don't do any heavy breathing," she smiled and left.

He tried to relax, but he couldn't shake how he felt about Stacey's kiss. As he always did when he was uncomfortable, his thoughts drifted. At first they hovered around Stacey and then, with memories of the kiss lingering, he thought of Andrea.

Andrea! Excitedly, he fought through the pain and prepared.

He hated this Virtuoso. It was an antique, not built for full immersion and barely virtual. He pulled on the special garment and, absent contact lenses, strapped the headgear into place. The ambience wasn't the same, in fact, it was barely adequate, but it was the only way to Andrea. The sequence began and his tension drained. Andrea was waiting for him in an attic bedroom. It was near dusk and there was a large window overlooking a blue-green ocean with waves forming and breaking across the horizon. Her face was lit by candlelight.

She was wearing a bikini and sat staring up at him with that look that he cherished. He shivered as he remembered that same look in Stacey's green eyes. She seemed to sense something and hurried the moment along. Lacking aromatics, and with limited tactile capability, the scene left much to his imagination, but fortunately his imagination was a willing co-conspirator.

She kissed him and he returned it, feeling some and imagining more. It was enough. Though her speech was sometimes broken and garbled, and he was unable to suspend himself completely in this reality like he could back in Aeden, she was still all he needed. It wasn't what it once was, but it was all he was going to get. Though he hated this technology and was embarrassed for needing it, making love to her, and the afterglow he experienced as they lay entwined together, was more than enough for him to dream only of her.

Chapter 3
Monroe – 2070

Global Climate Change—The tides rose, destroying commercial assets along every coast. Business teams of forensic architectural engineers and accountants worked out solutions that included plans for a new Capital, further south and west of Washington D.C. based on reclamation projects in Arabia that built private-use cities on risen land using private funds under the auspices of the World Bank and the International Monetary Fund. Thus Monroe, named after Chairman Andrew Monroe Crelli, became America's new Capital and world class resort community.

Monroe is where America's commercial leadership works proudly, free from nature's incursions and with the assurance that the property here will appreciate forever or for the life of its residents, whichever lasts longer.

While the original White House decays in a losing battle against nature, America's new administrative structures are a vision of the future—constructed with advanced nano-materials that make it impervious and absolutely secure, yet open—a picture for the world to see that Fortress America reigns supreme.

Architecturally stunning, yet with just the right hint of foreboding, the new White House was constructed in the image of its mistress, and current inhabitant, Chairwoman Tanya Brandt. It has added touches like a negative carbon footprint and security capability so advanced and proactive that no human guards are necessary though some are staffed.—***Archive***

Chairwoman Tanya Brandt resided on the top floor living quarters of the Monroe White House. In her basement facility, across from a series of large aquariums, two young adults and two teenagers, all related by science, prepared. One of the adults, called Alph, strode purposefully into the basement dining area shouting for the attention of the other three who turned expectantly to their leader.

"The Chairwoman will arrive in a few minutes," he announced.

"Is she angry?" Cee-Cee, a sibling, asked nervously. "Did she . . . say why she's coming?"

Dee, the youngest and the most intelligent of the four, laughed. "Don't worry, Cee, there's nothing she can do to hurt us. She's restricted by Gecko's prime directive. There no way that bitch can do anything but threaten us."

Cee looked horrified. "Don't call her that. She can hear."

"She's heard far worse from me. Besides, she's invested too much to kill us. Our stockholders will never allow her to terminate this cloning project before we achieve a solid enough revenue stream to project payback. She's coming here because she's finally decided how to move our revenue streams along. My guess is she'll end our funding and contract us out."

"I don't want to be separated from you," Cee-Cee whined.

Dee possessed his father, the former Chairman Andrew Crelli's uncanny ability to understand the general disposition of things and employ that insight to reliably anticipate the actions of others. "Cee, everything will be fine."

Alph listened patiently before adding, "Dee's right. There's nothing we can do until we hear her decision."

"Actually, there isn't even much we can do afterwards," Dee interjected.

"That's enough, Dee," Alph snapped. "Father disappeared years ago and we're still safe. We have far too much potential, and America does not waste good resources."

Cee volunteered another worrisome thought. "Father never clarified how much protection Gecko should provide. We're her assets now, so the Chairwoman could cause us to fail and then . . . you know. She'll have the legal justification to divest us, and Gecko isn't allowed to intervene with sound financial decisions. The Chairwoman will be within her legal rights."

"Your batch always worried too much. It hurt productivity. That's why, even though you're the best of them, you'll never be chairwoman material. None of us will fail. The Bitch won't eliminate us until she's certain we provide no financial benefits. As long as we're productive, we're safe."

"If you're sure . . . ," Cee-Cee said, still doubting.

The fourth sibling, Bee, was sitting against the wall amusing herself by guessing what each of her mates would say next. "Say Dee, I have to hand it to you, you're wrong, but you're never in doubt."

Just then the door opened and a well-armed, uniformed HomeSec security team entered and scanned each of them for weapons. The diminutive, four-star Security Reverend General, Ginger Tucker, walked in briskly, followed by Chairwoman Tanya Brandt. Cee-Cee inched closer to Dee.

General Tucker turned to her boss. "Madam Chairwoman, we're secure here." The General took a position between the children and her leader and waited. The Chairwoman smiled her most dazzling smile and each clone returned it reticently.

"It's nice to see you today, children. Alph as the oldest, you'll be spokesperson."

Alph looked at the others and nodded. "It will be so, Madam Chairwoman."

"You know I prefer to be called Aunt Tanya," she purred. "You've probably guessed the reason for this meeting. The time has come to go into the real world and appreciate. *Our* Congress showed unexpected backbone when they insisted on eliminating funding for clone programs in these difficult economic times. *We* fought for you dears but *We're* afraid their assessment is correct. Recession makes it too difficult for your continued studies to be funded.

"It's been five years since *Our* beloved Chairman's unfortunate demise; years that Congress has been reluctant to alter his programs. *We've* been pounding on them for fiscal responsibility and finally, this year, they focused—and that will be most fortuitous for you. *We* appealed to them, demonstrating through clear analysis how important you are to *Us*, but Congress can be obstinate when investors are involved. They insist it is time you repay your country's investment."

"Is there new information confirming Father's death?" Bee interrupted.

"Bee, don't speak unless addressed," the Reverend General barked. "Alph is your spokesperson."

The Chairwoman looked sternly at Bee, "Yes, stifle yourself, dear." Before Bee could respond, a vacant look swept over Brandt's face. After a short pause, her eyes refocused and she continued, "Rest assured children, daddy's gone and is never coming back."

"But-"

"Bee, don't interrupt the Chairwoman!" Alph shouted, trying to take control before Tucker did. Bee stared at him, then complied and sat quietly.

"Do you children have any questions?"

"Where'll we be assigned and what'll we be doing?" Dee asked.

"The cloning project has been running at a loss for twenty five years now—since before you were born. Your father refused to provide cloning capability to the general population, causing project economics to suffer and that drove marginal investors away. Although the technology has created some useful commercial applications, there's been precious little revenue generated to reimburse our mezzanine investors. To assist in your financing, heavy weight private institutions have become involved and, as you know, they are much less forgiving, so *We've* scaled down the technology to compete against the simpler, more cost-effective, genetic modification protocols supported by the international *Pharma* cartels. So you see, thanks to your father's obstinacy and poor business instincts, the clone project has become cost prohibitive. It is appropriate that each of you recoup those losses for us."

Brandt turned to her assistant, "Ginger, the pro forma." The Reverend General transmitted the data to each clone for review and Tanya continued. "Look at these losses. *We're* at a stage where expenses simply must be minimized or eliminated if *We're* to achieve an adequate return to satisfy the remaining investors. As Chairwoman, it's *Our* responsibility to put an end to the financial hemorrhaging. As of today, all funding is hereby suspended." She nodded to each of them. "To satisfy *Our* investors, *We've* developed the following opportunities." She nodded and Tucker transferred additional data to the clones.

"Each of you have been in the program for different periods burdened with different cost flows so you've been allowed different payback periods.

We have estimated your cash flow requirements here." The Chairwoman nodded and Tucker transmitted again. "To understand this better, so you can meet your requirements, *We've* assigned a financial engineer to each of you to monitor your progress. Additionally, so that the country as a whole can benefit from your efforts, each of you has been assigned to a different Federal Reserve region. You start tomorrow."

"But what happens if we can't generate the appropriate returns?" Cee asked.

"That won't happen," Dee responded, reciting, as if programmed, the consequences he had studied and memorized. "According to the law, the Office of Performance Measurement and the Division of Financial Security can instruct HomeSec to diminish our lifestyle until repayment is accomplished. If, at the lowest economic lifestyle level, we fail to generate positive returns, the Coast Guard will auction us off as indentured servants to any business that has the wherewithal to cover our debt and pay for our services. If the auction fails to generate positive returns, we will be officially categorized as generators of negative net worth—in other words, *Wasters*—and our lives will be forfeit subject to Economic Value Added, or EVA guidelines. We will be executed in the most cost-effective way, which means there will be pain, and our human remains will be sold as byproducts with the revenue generated reimbursing execution costs, the remainder goes to our debts."

"I know that, but-" Cee looked around, worried.

Dee smiled. "We're far too valuable for that to happen."

Having heard enough, Bee tried to force her way out of the room but a guard stopped her. She pushed the guard and yelled, "Gecko won't allow this. He's father's, not yours. When he-"

Reverend General Tucker quickly readied her sidearm.

"Stop this immediately, you spoiled brat!" the Chairwoman shouted. "Daddy is dead, you get no help there. *We* are in charge and *We'll* have none of this. You're not a child anymore. Remember *Our* philosophy, to whom much is given, much return is expected. It's time to stop acting like the spoiled brat that you are and take your rightful place in *Our* economy. *We've* put up with your petulance long enough. *We* warn you, control yourself before it's too late. And understand, regardless what your relationship is to *Us*, you matter not unless you are profitable. If it had been *Our* wish, *We'd* have terminated you at birth; so give me any opportunity and I will fulfill that wish now. Bee, you will join the economy and produce, or die, you little shit, just like everyone else. Gecko can't protect you anymore, it's against the law. Stop your whining and be productive." Tanya stopped shouting and a great, warm smile oozed across her face.

That only made Bee angrier and she tried once again to push past the Reverend General, but Tucker easily subdued her, twisting Bee's arm behind her back, and forcing her to the floor.

Infuriated by this wanton behavior, Brandt screamed, "*We'll* have you bound and gagged! *We* will!" Still locked in Tucker's hold, Bee mumbled something vulgar but then relaxed. With a nod from the Chairwoman, Tucker released the teen and stepped away.

"Bee, just so you understand the position you're in," Brandt explained. "*Our* financial engineers project you to have the least probability of success. They project that you won't be able to repay your debt so, if *We* were you, *We'd* be a whole lot more considerate. Remember, with the new laws, on financial projections alone, *We* have the power to petition for your elimination to prevent additional losses."

"You wouldn't, you bitch-" Tucker quickly jammed her gloved fist into Bee's mouth.

"Bind her," the Chairwoman instructed. Her siblings watched, none protesting, as Tucker and her guards incapacitated the still-struggling Bee. Unable now to move or speak, she lay on the floor, glowering.

"I protest, Madam Chairwoman," Alph said. "Bee's out of control sometimes, but-"

Brandt bellowed, "*We* are all accountable for our actions and there are no exceptions." She took a few seconds to regain her composure. "Later today you will receive your assignments. Pack and be ready to leave before the start of business tomorrow morning. You will be taken to your destinations by a security team assigned to protect you for the duration. Once you have freed up enough cash, you may buy your freedom from this team, but that is a long ways off. You have neither family nor friends, so there's no need to notify anyone of your change of status and if you're not ready to go in the morning," the Chairwoman stared directly at Bee, "the security team will remove you forcibly. When you arrive at your new destination, like every American citizen, it is your unalienable right to determine how long and how well you live."

Dee raised his hand to speak. The Chairwoman nodded.

"Madam Chairwoman, paying for a security team will add cost to our debt, burdening the payback. If we agree to comply fully with your request, can we forego the security team?"

The Chairwoman laughed. "Good try, Dee, but no. *We've* evaluated the risk-reward for this venture. This approach is the most profitable scenario for everyone." The Chairwoman continued to smile. "Please understand, *We're* very fond of each of you," she looked at Bee, "some more than others, of course. Because of this fondness, *We* prefer not to lose you before your debt is repaid."

"Madam Chairwoman," Alph said. "We appreciate your sensitivity."

"*We* expect your best. You each have enhanced skills and training, but unfortunately, there are flaws that must be watched carefully. Each of you, except the aforementioned slacker, is projected to become a profitable entrepreneur—sooner will be better for you, for *Us*, and for the country." She bent down so she was eye to eye with Bee. "*We* have your best interest at heart, Bee. *We* expect, no, we demand, you give this your best effort, and *We're* certain you will be successful and make *Us* proud. If you promise to behave, as an act of good faith, *We* will unbind you." Bee nodded, and Tanya motioned for Tucker to set her free.

The Chairwoman followed her guards into the corridor. Something crashed against the wall to her right and, on instinct, Tanya ducked. Her guard detail acted swiftly, wrestling Bee back to the ground while Tucker located and handed the projectile to her leader. It was Bee's, now broken, personal communicator. Brandt stared at it, amused, and then smiled as Bee struggled to get free.

"Oh, child that was such a big mistake. Intelligence without the disposition to use it wisely is of no value to anyone." She turned to her assistant. "Ginger, darling, use this evening wisely. Teach *Our* dear Bee discipline she can use to her advantage. Try not to leave too many marks this time, and have her at the train in the morning." Tucker smiled, nodded, and saluted.

"Not again, Madam Chairwoman," Alph interrupted. "Gecko won't-"

Tanya stepped forward angrily, causing Alph to step back. "Won't what? Gecko is mine. If you doubt that, you can join Bee." Her eyes glazed quickly, leaving a beautiful, vacuous stare. Soon enough, her mean visage returned. "As long as Bee can depart in the morning, Gecko concurs with the punishment.

"Dear children, don't dare delude yourselves. *We* know precisely what *We* can do and precisely what Gecko will, and will not allow. Believe what you will, but trust that he won't interfere." She laughed at Bee, still struggling to get free. "Bee, darling, you have been spoiled long enough. There is a cost to nonconformance. If, in the future, you aren't totally supportive of *Our* leadership, *We* promise we will respond to that with extreme prejudice and you know what *We're* capable of. Anything—and *We* mean anything—written an inch above my signature is the law of the land, so be diligent and very afraid." With that, Brandt turned towards the exit but before she took a step, she turned back towards the clone children.

"One more thing," she said. "Unless each of you wishes to spend an evening with *Our* resourceful Reverend General, shut your spoiled fucking traps and do precisely what *We* ask."

Chairwoman Brandt once again offered her deceptively warm smile, and departed, escorted by her armed entourage.

Chapter 4

Angel Falls – 2070

After a night of lovemaking with Andrea, Gil was sleeping soundly until thunder woke him. Blinking sleep away, he staggered to the window and stared through the torrential rain as bolts of lightening turned the purple dawn sky a brilliant white. With no responsibility except to learn from Bernie, his days all ran together, but it was the nights he dreaded most and the rainy ones most of all. Days following a rainy night made it more difficult for him to slip out to find Stacey and together, head into the woods for fun and freedom.

Everyone in Angel Falls had their daily tasks but Gil. And everyone was always helping each other, even offering to help him, though he didn't need or want help. His life in Angel Falls consisted of Bernie's rambling lectures, sleeping, escaping with Stacey to the forest, and escaping in virtual to somewhere else with Andrea. So as he stared out at the rain, he faced a day trapped inside, forced to listen to Bernie's incomprehensible ramblings.

He returned to his bed, wrapped a pillow around his head, and prayed the storm front would move through quickly. He resisted the strong impulses until finally wrestling exotic, erotic thoughts of Andrea from his head, and he went back to sleep, but only briefly. He tossed and turned until the first light of a dark and cloudy morning finally broke through. He awoke with his pants tented and his ardor not sated. He searched for his headgear . . .

"Arlene?"

Arlene Klaatu was working late at a top security Government computer lab in a heavily guarded building across the Great Potomac Bay from the remains of Washington D.C. As soon as she recognized Joad's distress call, she cleared and secured her system, which was difficult in the highly sensitive environment she was working in. Continually monitored, any conversation between her and Joad could be hazardous to everyone she cared about. Still, it must be important so she activated a secret temporary shield she'd developed.

With her program operational, she responded. "Joad, you shouldn't contact me here."

"Everyone is safe enough. I'll be quick."

"What's wrong?"

"He is driving me crazy. I have important work to do but he makes demands on me."

"Who, Gecko?"

"No, I'm talking about Gil."

"What about him? Be quick."

"If his behavior is typical of what boys were doing before the . . . adjustments; I see why their behavior needed modifying."

"Don't joke about that, Joad. What's happening?"

"He wants to make love all the time. I can multitask with the best—I am the best. But this making love you people do, it's so intense and the frequency, it bogs me down. I can't afford a time killer like that, but I guess that's why people do it. They should get a life; he should, anyway because he's interfering with my concentration. And that's dangerous. Gecko is too powerful to ignore for too long and I can't drop my guard for a minute, let alone two, three, four times a day for twenty-eight-minutes-to-an-hour-and-eleven-minutes at a time. It's out of hand. You have to help me. If I have another orgasm, I'll . . . I'll lose my sense of humor."

Though this was obviously important, Arlene laughed. "That bad, huh? Four times? Aren't you overreacting? After all, you have plenty of bandwidth and you don't have a body."

"Do not try humor. It's not your thing. We both know it's not a physical thing."

"Couldn't you tell him you have a headache?" Arlene smiled.

"Do I take that to mean you have nothing useful to recommend?"

"There are plenty of women who'd gladly trade places-"

"Okay, but you should know it's creating a potentially dangerous situation. I can't fake it? He'd know. If I'm off my game with him, just a little, he gets so sensitive. With me, he is so unlike the detached, distant teen Bernie reports on. Anyway, this is part of a more important issue. It's time. He needs to accept responsibility. He's nineteen and Bernie is failing. You're not there; you don't know what it's like."

"This love making," Arlene said. "Could you be losing your perspective?"

"If only. There's just too much going on. Chairwoman Brandt has consolidated her power, Gecko is becoming more powerful, and he's still searching for me. In addition, Bernie is dying and Gohmpers needs my help in the field. With all that, I'm expending significant resources camouflaging Angel Falls and I have to do all of it without mistakes because if I make just one, our plans fail. So having a bored, love-sick nineteen-year-old teen jump my bones for what seems like all day, every day, it is not something I need. I'm becoming anxious. Let's see you try to maintain your perspective with all that going on."

"I understand," Arlene said calmly. "What Gil is doing was once considered somewhat normal behavior for teenagers before Andy's behavior modification program became law. But you're right; he needs to be doing more. Can't Bernie help?"

"No, he hasn't been right for a long time."

"I've been so busy. I didn't realize. Can it wait until Mark arrives?"

"He's not scheduled for days."

"Okay, try not to burden Bernie, but tell him to try to set Gil straight, if he can. Maybe he can get Gil involved in something real. Bernie was right to move Gil to Angel Falls, but its remote isolation is a blessing and a curse. Gil is too constrained. Maybe it is time we chance him on the outside."

There was silence. "Joad? Are you there? Are you okay?"

Another silent moment passed and Arlene started to worry. When Joad spoke, her voice had changed. She seemed weary. "Another orgasm. He grew up in the Midwest. What's his fascination with the beach? I wouldn't mind some cornfields for variety. I forgot to report-see, I am losing it-yesterday he was out with friends and they saw a *SurveilEagle* doing reconnaissance."

"Did it spot him? Why didn't you say something sooner?"

"Sorry, I was busy."

"No, I'm sorry, Joad. How close was it to the village?"

"It was north, nearer Presque Isle. I couldn't chance tracking the transmission because surveillance protocols are directly linked to Gecko's subroutines. But even if it was random surveillance, it was too close."

"Are you sure Gil wasn't identified?"

"I'm not sure of much, but he didn't think so and I haven't detected any accelerated activity."

"We can't take chances. We have to get him out of there and soon."

"Bernie is too feeble. Can Mark be trusted?"

"I don't know, Joad. You've traced his comings and goings. His trips to the Capital are worrisome, but Bernie insists he's working for us now. Besides, what choice do we have? It will take Gohmpers a couple of months to get back and he's in the middle of something important, too. Gil must be safe and we must find a way to get him to grow up and commit."

"He believes he is grown up but as to commitment, he sees himself as a lover not a revolutionary. Now that he's sated, I'll have some time to continue to monitor in case we've been compromised. I should be free for maybe another four hours. In the meantime, we need another plan—wait. Damn, I have to go. What stamina he has."

"Good luck." Arlene signed off, smiling but concerned.

Later that morning, Gil awoke again. He felt more relaxed and definitely satisfied after a second round of love making with Andrea. A light rain had started to fall, and he was unable to delay any longer. He put on his parka and left his cabin for Bernie's. He flipped the hood up to cover his head and walked slowly down the muddy road that separated his cabin from Bernie's and the rest of the village. In the distant sky, he could see a clear blue break in the clouds that offered the potential for a better afternoon. In the greenish-tinged light of the remnants of the morning storms, Gil watched young children laughing as they were stripped down to their underwear by their mothers to frolic around in the mud playing a form of football. As they screamed and laughed, covered in mud, their mothers kept a watchful eye on them while preparing the picnic tables for lunch. As he walked by, a few of the local teens waved and a girl Gil's age giggled at nothing Gil could fathom.

"Hi, Gil, I love the bedroom hair," The girl said boldly before blushing and looking down. Instinctively, his hand went to pat down his curly brown hair. Other than Stacey, Gil stayed away from the local girls because they were always trying to get him to go to the barn or to the far side of the lake. Dian was the most persistent. She was nice enough, but Stacey disliked her even though he told her she had no reason to be jealous of any girl in Angel Falls. That was when he mentioned he had a serious girlfriend back in Indiana, but Stacey didn't seem to believe him though she didn't seem happy about it either. She asked him his girlfriend's name, but he thought it best not to tell her anything about Andrea and she seemed to take it okay as long as her competition wasn't in Angel Falls.

"Wanna get muddy with me?" Dian asked while smiling and playing with her hair.

"I can't, Dian, I need to see my great-grandfather. Maybe later?"

"It's always later. How is the rabbi feeling?"

"He's old."

"He's so nice. When I was a girl, he would instruct us on current affairs. It was real boring stuff, but I didn't mind."

He smiled, but stopped abruptly when she sidled up closer so that their hips were almost touching. In spite of himself, he felt a warm glow. She rubbed her finger along his chest. "You have a great smile, Gil, it makes me all tingly." She continued to rub his chest until he removed it. "Poor rabbi," she continued. "He helped mom and dad find work and they love him for that. They say he's real sick." She purred the last remark and gently put her head on his shoulder.

Gil stepped back and Dian stumbled forward before stabilizing. Hearing her view of Bernie made him even more uncomfortable. Without modern medicines to prolong his life, it was only a matter of time. "Yes, he's real sick," he mumbled.

"What was that, Gil?"

"Nothing." With that, Gil turned and headed to Bernie's cabin, leaving Dian standing there. He knocked on the door and waited. He knocked again, louder and then entered. As always, Bernie was in bed, staring blindly at the window.

When the door shut, Bernie yelled, "Is that you, Mark?"

"It's Gil, Bernie, it's always Gil." he said as he gave the fragile old man an awkward but gentle hug. "How are you today?"

"Like a man who's overstayed his welcome. I'm dying," his voice sounded strained.

"You haven't overstayed."

Bernie's eyes seemed to clear. "Gil, son, we need to talk. I don't know how much longer . . ." Exhausted, his words trailed off and he laid his head back on the pillow. "Thanks for freeing Mark." Bernie struggled to hold his thin, white arms up, searching for an embrace. Embarrassed, Gil hugged the frail body again.

"I was happy to help you and Mark."

Bernie made a gurgling sound that Gil recognized as laughter. "Don't take too much credit, boy." His lips moved but no sound came out. Finally, he muttered, "Gil, are you here? What do you want?" Bernie was confused again.

"I'm here. I came to see how you're doing."

"I'm glad you're here. It's time to study."

"Not today, Bernie. I can use Archive later."

"You can't learn from Archive."

"I know, Bernie, but there's something valuable to be learned from the winners and Archive tells their story."

"No, I meant-"

He had come a long way with Bernie. His life had changed because of the old man, but now, with Bernie fading like this, what would he do. "Bernie, I have to go, to meet someone." He hated lying but he just couldn't be here.

"But you're late."

Was Bernie referring to today or to his life, Gil wondered. "Yes, it's too late to study."

"I'm sorry I lied to you when I told you in the Hospice that I was dying. I'm not lying now."

"I don't blame you, Bernie, you're old," Gil said. There was a sharp pain in his throat. Was it sadness or something else?

"Gil, after I die, you must leave Angel Falls."

"You won't die and I'm not ready to leave just yet."

"You hate it here. Besides, you can't stay. For you to achieve your destiny, you need to be out in the world to see what it's like so you can do what needs to be done. That time has come. You must get ready to leave."

"I don't like it here much of the time but it's my home now. You said I can't go back to Howard and it's too dangerous for me anywhere else. You said so. Besides, the revolution you want can't be done, no one can do it.

If I try, they'll kill me. You said that, too. And once I'm out there, who'll protect me? No, I don't want to leave and I won't go until I'm ready."

Bernie's rheumy eyes seemed more sunken than usual. "I heard about the drone," he said. "They're searching and life is going to be dangerous for you everywhere, all the time. There are forces at work. I hoped you'd have more time, but you must leave soon."

"I can stay here and learn with Archive and *Virtuoso*."

"You won't always be able to hide in *Virtuoso*, Mark. There's a real world out there with real problems and you need to live in that world with real people so you can understand what this is all about. You'll be safe if you're careful. We have allies, Mark, and this was never supposed to be your home."

"I'm Gil, Bernie. And don't want Angel Falls to be my home either, but I have to stay here until I can figure everything out. When I'm older, maybe I'll do what you're asking, but I can't, not now. I'm just a teenager and no matter how much you want it, I can't stop the government. No one can."

"You can. I failed because I wasn't desperate enough. And my failure caused so many deaths. I wish I had been stronger. You can be stronger, I know it. One motivated good man like you can make a difference if he's desperate and willing to sacrifice everything to live in a better world."

"I don't know why you think that person is me."

"It is you. You will do it. You will. In my heart I know you will. It is all that's left to soothe my heart. Remember my Jane and . . . and . . . Franki, yes, Franki." Bernie's eyes closed but the tears were slow to appear. He blinked his eyes rapidly and continued. "So many need to be avenged and so many more need help. Gil, it's on you to make this world right."

"You ask me to do good things, fine, but why must I avenge stuff?"

"It's all one. Our family . . . the others . . . I failed them, I failed them."

"I know, Bernie. But I'm not ready to leave or do what you want."

"Is it the girl?"

"Who are you talking about?"

"The girl you play with all the time. The reason you don't study enough."

"No, it's not Stacey. It has nothing to do with her."

"There's something else we must discuss." Gil waited as Bernie stared off at nothing. Finally, when Gil considered leaving, he spoke. "When you leave . . . there won't be . . . *Virtuoso*."

"There's always *Virtuoso*, it's-"

"No, not for you, not after you leave," Bernie explained. Gil started to protest, but the old man held up his trembling hand to stop him. "Don't argue. It's the way it must be. There are more important things in this world than virtual fucking, particularly for you."

Gil was aghast, staring at Bernie as if seeing him for the first time. "How . . . how did you know?"

"Know what?"

"I won't leave without her. I love her and she loves me."

"Who?"

"Andrea, of course."

"She's a virtual girlfriend. Don't be ridiculous. Grow up. You can't take an avatar with you, no matter how much you love her."

"You don't know what she means to me, Bernie. She understands me and I have no one-"

"That's absurd rubbish. You're talking about a computer simulation, for God's sake, nothing more. If you need a woman, find a real woman out there, but not an avatar and not the girl you play with here."

"I don't want Stacey. I want . . . Andrea."

"You can't have either. And you can't settle down here, not now. Maybe someday, but not today."

"I don't want anyone else," Gil argued. "I want Andrea." When it came out, it sounded pathetic and sad.

"What you want doesn't matter. Put virtual out of your mind. It's a toy, a device marketers use to mess with your mind. Nothing more."

What little life was in Bernie's face seemed to drain as he closed his eyes, too weary to continue. Gil waited as patiently as he could, but when that took too long, he blurted, "How did you know? About me and Andrea, I mean."

Bernie's eyes remained closed as he answered, "It doesn't matter. It's time for you to move on."

"You don't know what she means to me. I have no one. You're too old and you've forgotten what love is. I won't let you take that away from me. I promise you I won't never see her again? It won't happen. We love each other too much. I can't live without her." He was angry.

33

"What you have may feel good, but it isn't true love. It's synthetic and contrived, so it can't never ever be true."

"How would you know? You never used *Virtuoso*."

Bernie closed his eyes once again and his head fell back on the pillow while Gil paced the room, waiting, angry at the old man for what he had gotten Gil into. When, once again, too much time passed without a response, Gil became concerned and walked closer. He put his ear close to Bernie's face checking his breath. Finally, when Bernie opened his eyes, Gil pulled back. But this time, Bernie failed to recognize him and his voice was barely audible.

"Jane and . . . Franki . . . are real and true, and I won't allow that to be erased by a billion pretty pixels in some computer program. It's a false world and I'll never use it. That's why you can't use it anymore either. You must live in the real world so you know how to make it better."

"But every day your wife and daughter would still be alive for you. Instead of grief, you'd have your family. You would be happy."

"I'm old and dying but reality is still more important than fake happiness. *Virtuoso* is another addiction brought to you by people who want your money and they're more successful if they bypass your heart and mind. Don't be another *Virtuoso* junkie consumed by a past that never happened while your future is dependent on those who conspire to create a dream that ends all dreaming. *Virtuoso* is their tool, their grand diversion; their way to avoid accountability and retribution for unpunished sins. Reality is painful but it's true and without it, nothing is true."

Bernie was off again on his wild tangents and Gil wanted to flee to the forest to free himself, but Bernie was so weak and he was struggling so hard to talk that he stayed. "Bernie, I don't understand. You're sad all the time when you could be happy. If *Virtuoso* can make life better, why not use it? Be happy for me because I use it and I found someone who cares for me. I trust her and she's always there for me. You could have that, but instead you endure sad and painful memories. I don't want to end up like you."

This time a tear did form. "There is nothing wrong with sadness. Like happiness, it's earned. It's the memory of better times. When a loved one dies, sadness and grief are necessary. They make dying easier and right now, that's what I need."

"That's something to look forward to," Gil said sarcastically.

"All I have are memories. Why would I want to corrupt them? I won't, regardless how sad they make me."

"I won't let my life be as sad as yours."

"From your lips to God's ears, I hope that's true, but if you avoid the worst, you'll miss the best. Yes, I'm sad but my life is great, too. Don't be so afraid of sadness that you end up with nothing but that. Happiness and sadness are born from living; they make you a better person, something that can't happen in *Virtuoso*, regardless what they advertise. It's time to live your life and that's not what *Virtuoso* is for. It's a dead end, something to be scared of as much as Tanya Brandt herself. It is the ultimate addiction because the world you create becomes too expensive while the world you live in becomes unforgiving."

"Not for me. Andrea will protect me. When I choose to leave Angel Falls, she'll make it safe for me out there. So whether you like it or not, she will always be an important part of my life."

"Stop this. You're not a child. Listen to what you're saying. Andrea is your addiction. You can't see that here, but once you get out in the real world, once you get involved with real people, you'll see how much *Virtuoso* truly costs. Free yourself before you destroy what matters, real relationships. Stay with *Virtuoso* and you will lose everything including Andrea, and you will end up trapped and alone."

"But I'm already trapped and alone."

"You have friends. Don't submit to it. You're better than that. The world needs you to be better than that. People are depending on you. Take control of your life," Bernie sighed. "What heroes you and I are. The world depends on us and I'm . . . dying and you're hormonal."

"But I don't want people depending on me. I'm still a kid. I want . . . I don't know what I want except I don't want people depending on me, at least not yet. When I'm older, maybe I'll do what you want, but now, with Joad's help-" He stopped. Bernie did say Joad, not Andrea. A series of thoughts he didn't want to recognize poured into his head. Yes, it was there all the time. Why had he missed it or had he just avoided it because it was so uncomfortable. His face burned with embarrassment as the implications burrowed into his brain. He slumped into a chair and ran his hands through his thick brown hair.

"Oh, Bernie . . . no . . . , please tell me I'm wrong. Andrea and . . . Joad, they're not-?" Mortified, he put his head in his hands and refused to look up. "I think I'm going to be sick. Everyone knows about me and Andrea, don't they? They know everything."

"What is there to know?"

"Joad is Andrea, isn't she?" Bernie's silence confirmed it. Gil was so ashamed, he felt like crying. How could he have been so stupid? "Bernie, for once tell me the truth."

"You're making a big deal. Joad, Andrea, what does it matter? Our friends from the hospice know," Bernie responded. "But it was nobody's business until it kept you from progressing toward who you must be. What were you thinking? To protect your identity, Joad must control a certain piece of *Virtuoso* and that's Andrea, that's all. If Joad doesn't, Gecko would find you and . . . well no one wants that."

"You knew it all along?" Gil asked, smacking his head with his fist. "Even when I was in Aeden?" Bernie nodded. The enormity of the deception made Gil gag. It took rapid breaths to hold the bile down so he walked to the window to catch a breath of fresh air and just like that, it all came into focus. He turned and struck Bernie's bedpost, rattling the bed and causing Bernie to gasp. "Of course you know. Everybody does. What is it, some kind of a joke between you? Let's watch little Gil perform to see if he's grown up all by himself—literally all by myself. Did you check my moves or evaluate my performance? Was I good enough? Tell me, Bernie, do I have the right stuff to meet your requirements? Jesus, how could you. This was . . . she was real to me. I fell in love with her. What did you expect? I have no one else. Did I pass your test? Did I? You wanted my allegiance, but did you have to go this far to get it?

He looked around for something to smash but he wasn't done talking. "Maybe it's my fault. I'm stupid, needy and immature, the perfect rebel leader. How desperate are you to trick me into falling for some damn software? I thought you cared. You lied to me. You allowed it. How? Good God, Bernie, it's sick what you did. You insisted that I trust you and then and you lie, you continue to lie. I'm sick of it. God, what's wrong with me? And what's wrong with you, with this whole fucking world."

Gil's started to walk toward the door but stopped and turned around. "Whose idea was it? Who decided to pull this trick to win me over? It had to be you. That makes you a pimp, doesn't it? You provide the girl and what? I screw my brains out and I'm hers and yours forever. Is that the plan? How could you do it? I'm a kid. God, Bernie I'm family; remember how important that was to you once? How could you do this to me?" Once again, he looked around Bernie's starkly decorated room for something to break, but he ended up shrugging in defeat.

"I'm such an idiot. I fell in love with a god-damned avatar. How fucked up is that? I hope you're satisfied." He spoke while his eyes looked for something to destroy, finally focusing on Bernie's picture of his Geist Lake property, which he swiped at, knocking it onto the wooden floor and shattering the glass. "How's what you did to me better than what you accuse Crelli and Brandt's government of doing?"

"It wasn't like that."

"Did Howard know?" Bernie shook his head. "Thank god." Gil pounded the table. "If you think you have me, you're wrong." He turned to the wall, unable to face the old man. "This is how you treat family? Would your beloved Jane and Franki approve? Maybe you lied about them, too. Maybe your whole story is made up. You're a liar, a god damned liar, that's for sure," he yelled angrily. "You used me. You . . . you . . ."

"No, that's not it. Yes, we knew. But what happened between you and Joad—Andrea, was none of our business. We did nothing wrong. Neither did you. It wasn't like that."

Gil's legs felt heavy and his arms tingled. Frustrated, he screamed, turned and ran to the door. Then something inside him exploded and he pounded the door until his hands were raw. Finally exhausted and miserable, he opened it and simply walked out.

"Come back," he heard Bernie feebly entreat. He turned and glared. "This isn't what we want," Bernie begged. "We don't know anything that happened between you and Andrea, but at least now you can see how addictive *Virtuoso* can be. Look how mad you are at something that's not real. See. It's more addictive than drugs or carbohydrates. You know that now. You're angry but that's okay. I understand. *Virtuoso* is a big part of what we're fighting against and now you know how difficult it'll be to convince those hooked on it and on so many other tools business uses to fabricate their truth to their economic advantage. You have to experience this to truly understand. It was the only way."

"You uncaring son of a bitch," Gil shouted. "You say you loved your wife and daughter. You said you loved me, too. But you don't know what love is at all. And whatever your pathetic life quest was, I don't want any part of it. Do you hear me, I won't accept it. I was thirteen. I had one friend, who died, and no experience. What did you think would happen? What choice did I have in all this? You unleashed a smart, sexy, fucking machine on me," he yelled. "I believed that Andrea cared when nobody ever cares. And nobody ever will." He considered it for a second. "A fucking machine, talk about reality, that's what she is. She doesn't love me. How could she? How could you? If you thought you needed some idiot to fall in love with a software program in order to save the world, you're fucked up to start with, really messed up." Gil started to walk back into the cabin but hesitated. "Since you skulked into my life, all I've known is disappointment. But you taught me, taught me good. People who say they love me hurt me instead. If that's love, I want no part of it. Jesus fucking Christ, Bernie, you should be proud. You out-Crellied your hero."

"I'm sorry," Bernie's voice was hoarse and broken. "You need to calm down and put this in its proper prospective. You're going to face worse than this. If there was another way-"

He was right, and Bernie and the rest were wrong. "Damn you. I'm not listening anymore." He grabbed the door. "I loved her . . . it," he said quietly and then slammed the door hard, rattling the cabin. "I'll never forgive you." The door bounced back and he slammed it again as he yelled his final frustration. "If you need someone like me so badly, clone him." With that, Gil ran. He just ran.

Chapter 5
Angel Falls – 2070

Incensed at the betrayal, Gil fled to his cabin, slammed the door and hurtled onto his bed. He lay there finding little solace. Though his hands were raw, he still felt like hitting something and his usual relief—*Virtuoso* and Andrea—were waiting, mocking him from across the room, but participation was now out of the question. He forced his stare away from the *Virtuoso* unit, wrestling with his desire to give in and use it or kick it until it was mangled beyond repair. He wanted Andrea so badly, but there was no way he would ever do that again and that stressed him more. He paced inside the cabin, his arc taking him closer and closer to Virtuoso until he could take it no longer. He grabbed a jacket and opened the door, pausing, he wondered where in the world he could go and still be safe.

Gil forced himself to remain calm so he could think. He accepted that his anger concealed some guilt, but mostly he was disappointed with everyone else. He messaged his neck while struggling for an answer that might work. He knew there was more to life than Andrea but, how do you chase the feeling of love? He didn't need her; he was addicted to her, too attached, but nothing more. She had filled a role, but he never should have allowed her closer and never would again. As always, Archive said it best, everything but wealth is transient. He was right to be angry. He was a boy, somewhat naïve and they knew better. But mostly, he wanted the hurt to go away so he could begin anew. But where could he start? He was a fugitive and the *SurveilEagle* confirmed they were still looking for him. And though he hated Bernie, how could he avoid him or flee from him knowing he would soon die? With each alternative blocked, his choice was simple. He locked his cabin door and hid inside. His penance would be severe, he would stare at *Virtuoso* and deny himself its relief until he learned to control himself and then he would destroy it and live in the forest, a hermit.

Throughout the long night, he fought and wavered. Deep in thought, once, he found himself holding the headgear, not remembering how he got it. He fought a loathsome battle with his nature until he hurled the headgear across the room. He tried to sleep but the *Virtuoso* unit seemed to hover, an evil presence in his thoughts until he was so restless, he thought he'd never again enjoy the blessed oblivion sleep offered.

He tried to masturbate, but that too seemed repulsive now, a surrogate for a surrogate. How sad a boy he was.

When morning came, it surprised him when he woke. He checked to insure the *Virtuoso* door was still locked, that he hadn't weakened in the night, and then he thought of Bernie. They would have to meet again though he couldn't face him now. Mark was due to arrive soon and that would be another confrontation.

In the brilliant morning light when, in the past, he would have gone hiking, instead today he sat, morose, in a corner of his cabin, staring out at the trees, tracking the path of the sun through the day. By evening, he was so tense that he couldn't sit, stand, or lie down. Still, he resisted *Virtuoso*.

When he couldn't bear his cabin or his own company any longer he decided to face Bernie. As soon as he opened his cabin door, he regretted it. The annual early-summer black fly swarms had materialized. The tiny gnats, with their blessedly short lifespan, but vigorous mating cycle, insinuated themselves into everything that wasn't tightly wrapped. He rushed back into his cabin and put on a hat with fine netting and covered his jacket and arms with more. Then he ran to Bernie's, occasionally chewing and spitting out bugs that slipped through his protective gear.

He bolted into Bernie's cabin without bothering to knock and slammed the door against the black fly swarm. By the horrified look on Bernie's face, it must have seemed to him that Gil was entering the same angry way he'd left yesterday. The old man growled something and then a quivering smile formed parentheses around his perfect, artificial teeth.

"You've come back. Are you ready to leave Angel Falls?" he said weakly.

"I was concerned about you. How're you feeling?"

"Tell me you're leaving Angel Falls, and soon," Bernie repeated, his voice, though insistent, was barely audible.

"I'm sorry I got mad yesterday," Gil explained. "I didn't come back to argue."

"Agree and nothing's lost," Bernie insisted.

"I can't do that. I know it's what you want and I know it's important, but doesn't it have to be important to me too? Right now, it doesn't feel important. I feel cornered and conned—I'm sorry, Bernie, that's how I feel. I want to believe . . . no, that's not it. I just want everyone to leave me alone so I can make up my own mind about stuff, that's all. I don't want to be convinced all the time how great it's going to be—not by you or anybody. You say the bad guys use every means to convince the country they're right. Well, isn't that what you've been doing to me? Doesn't that make you a bad guy, too?" Bernie was silent, his eyes staring. "Bernie, this is what I'll agree to. When Mark comes, he and I will discuss it. If, afterward, I think it's the right thing, then I'll leave. That's fair. But I'm tired of the pressure. I'm tired of being worked for something everybody else says is big and important even if it isn't important to me. I'm nineteen. I want my life back or any life for that matter. I want it now. I don't want what you want. Not right now. So stop trying to force me to do what I don't know I can do or even want to do. Until Mark arrives, let's call a truce. We can talk about something else, please?"

Bernie struggled to sit up, failed and sank back onto the bed. "Horseshit, boy. And more horseshit," he said in a tiny voice. "This isn't something you can decide by committee and no, you can't just do what you want. It would be nice and it might be fair, but we don't live in those times anymore, if we ever did. This is just too important. Too many lives are at stake." He started to cough which forced him to settle back in his pillow and close his eyes. He rested until, slowly, he regained enough strength to continue. By then, Gil was staring out a window. "I'm here, Gil. It's time you take responsibility. You don't like what has happened, well I don't either. And you know what, that's tough. It simply doesn't matter. It's not your decision. More than anything, I want you to be happy and I want you to believe in what I'm asking you to do but even if you aren't happy and don't believe, you need to do it anyway because it's right and so many good people are depending on you. And you need to start today so I can know before I die that my life has meaning."

"Shut up, Bernie. Please," he begged. "You are not going to use me anymore. I won't allow it. I don't want you to die but you've been telling me you're dying for years. The only reason I'm here is because I thought you were dying. You've been so unfair to me."

"You think I've been unfair? Was your wife and daughter murdered? Did you lose the love and loyalty of your only son who thought you caused their murder? That's unfair. And did you lose two more generations of family members because you were forced to spend your life in hiding? Did that happen to you? Don't talk to me about how unfair life is, I know."

"I'm sorry your life's been so sad. And I believe you believe what you say, but stop beating me with it. I didn't ask for this. You believe you're doing the right thing, fine. It doesn't mean it's the right thing for me."

"What happened to that brave boy who rescued Mark and volunteered to join the revolution?"

"Bernie, I was fourteen. Everyone says stupid things when they're young. I grew up, that's all. And the lies-"

"I never lied to you."

"Whatever, Bernie. It doesn't matter."

"Gil, you can make the world better. I know that must seem like an impossible burden, but I know in my heart that you can do it. I believe it and I can't let go. Someday, you will understand. You'll realize that, like me, when you're at the end of life, lying on your deathbed, you'll know, with whatever certainty we're allowed, that your life has meaning. That you were necessary in this world and that you'll be missed. Gil, do what I'm asking now and comfort two old men—me today and you someday in the far future."

It sounded so right but anger was still boiling in him. "Stop it," Gil bellowed. "You're doing it again. You're doing what I asked you not to do. Talk about something else, anything else."

"This is all that matters, son, that's the only way I'll have it."

"Bernie, please don't say that. Don't insist. You're making me wish you were gone so you won't lie or try to use me anymore." When he realized what he'd said, he stopped. "I'm sorry, I don't want you to die and I don't want to hate you. Can't we just talk? Tell me about when you were my age, or Mark, anything but this. Can't I comfort you in some other way? You don't want our relationship to end like this." He was hopeful, but Bernie rolled over to face the wall.

"This or nothing," he mumbled.

Once again, Gil left Bernie's cabin in anger, slamming the door as he left. This wasn't his fault. There was no talking to an old man. He stomped back through the village, swatting aggressively at the flies. This time he was going to stay in his cabin until the black flies completed the fucking phase of their life cycle.

Days later, Gil finally emerged from his cabin to a glorious Maine morning. He took a deep breath of the now bug-less air and looked to Bernie's cabin before turning to make his way down a path to his favorite spot by the lake, near a stream that poured over large rocks to plummet into the crystalline green water below. This spot gave the town its name, Angel Falls. And though it reminded him of a place he and Andrea once shared, he shook that thought from his mind because it was the only place left for him to find solace. He sprawled on the grass and stared down at the waterfall.

The beauty of it calmed him briefly, but his thoughts couldn't whitewash the falseness that was his life. Was lying the way of things? Absent truth, did everyone prey on everyone else; is that how it was when free will and informed choice collided with vested moneyed interests? It would be so much easier if there were only easily recognized simple truths so that even the most intricate lies could be exposed. And how evil must a government be to employ tools such as *Virtuoso* on its population and to kill them, too?

Andrea was no escape, if she ever truly was. He didn't understand that until now. Andrea was Joad and Joad was Arlene and Arlene was Gohmpers and Gohmpers was Bernie and God knows who else. But who was he? Why didn't he know? He tried to dull the confusion by staring at the water cascading into the lake, bubbling as it distorted the reflection of the clouds that filled the blue sky above and he shivered at the thought of what was ahead for him.

He struggled to clear his head, to organize and prioritize his thoughts, but visions of Andrea wouldn't cease and they defeated every attempt to seek closure. Does everyone endure this kind of stress? Why didn't he know even that? And was the only relief available through the manipulative palliative of *Virtuoso*? If that was true, then life was a farce and there was no reason to continue because nothing could overcome such compulsion. But the world was too large for a sheltered teen to understand so he decided to focus on something easier—himself. What did he want?

He was in deep thought and didn't hear Stacey approach until she sat beside him. She smiled and jabbed him playfully.

"Boy, have you been moody. What does a girl have to do in this town for a good time?"

"Sorry?"

"Sorry, hell. While you've been your usual, self-absorbed self, I've been so bored that I defied the flies and went for a hike." She spit. "I'm still spitting them out. Yuck. Meat and I have even been tolerating each other because you refuse to come out and play. You have no idea how little we have in common—even hiking. Meat kills squirrels with rocks. Snap out of it, Gil, please, for me."

"I don't know how."

"Have fun. That'll help. We both need some fun." She grabbed his hand and tried to pull him up but he resisted. "What's wrong?"

"We should have told the truth about the *SurveilEagle*."

"What truth? If you're worried, let's go back there and perform an autopsy. That'll be fun. And when we're done, we can bring it back and apologize."

"We should have told them. They're elders, they need to know." She was quiet. "You've been back there?"

She nodded. "You weren't available and I was bored. You don't have people yelling at you all the time to wash dishes or do the laundry, milk the cows, or wash the diapers. And you don't have younger sisters pestering you all the time. The only way I have fun is by getting away—and I haven't been able to do that because of you."

"If you want to have fun, don't let me stop you."

"I'm not saying-"

"I'm tired of people needing me so damn much."

"Who said I need you? I can keep plenty busy enough without you. Let's clean up the drone. It's still covered in mud."

"You didn't try to fix it, did you?"

"Me?" She hesitated. "Okay, I was bored and had some time so I played around but nothing happened. The blinking light didn't even turn back on. Come on, let's check it out. I'll get some tools from Uncle Ned's shed and we can take it apart and see what's inside. It'll be fun."

"We should have told the elders."

"Stop brooding or I'm going to find another best friend."

He stood up and walked down to the waterline, where he picked up a stone and skimmed it across the lake. When he turned, she was jogging back to the village. "Please don't," he said quietly, but she was already too far away to hear.

Gil moved to a spot by the lake well out of sight of the community, and stayed there throughout the day. But like his cabin, this, too, seemed like a prison.

He felt miserable. Andrea was the only truth he ever needed and he'd never been away from her this long. All he wanted was to be with her again. He was desperate for her and though he fought the tension, he was angry too. He knew his resolve would wither, and defeated and resigned, he would slink back into *Virtuoso* in search of her companionship and the ultimate release he so craved. In the end, he'd be disillusioned with himself and furious at those who were testing him and proving him weak. He'd relent, of that he was certain. His need for Andrea was that strong, and he hated her for it.

So it was late that evening that he returned to his cabin. He slept fitfully, even hallucinating about a *Virtuoso* unit come alive and threatening him and in the morning, he fled again, returning to the same spot by the lake searching for something to make him forget his weakness. It was late and growing dark when, in the distance, he heard the sound of partying—something he was in no mood for-so he hid behind a tree and away from the noise. How sad to be an unsafe distance from neighbors.

Finally, at the end of another solitary evening, he resolved that there were simply no answers. He rolled onto his back and stared up at the brilliant blue sky as it turned a dark purple. Maybe there was a pattern in the chaos of a billion stars that would help him understand, but in the end, the uncaring sky provided no guidance either.

He was startled by a sound and turned toward it. A silhouette approached and Gil recognized the irregular gait. It was his grandfather, Mark.

"Everyone's concerned," Mark said as he maneuvered his bad leg and sat awkwardly beside Gil.

"Did Bernie send you?"

"My father's not doing well. All I could get from him was I needed to talk to you."

"You can tell him for me that I'm still angry."

"That's a long time to be angry. Dad has a way of doing that to the people he loves. What were you arguing about?"

"I know about Andrea?"

"What about her?"

"Are you going to lie to me, too?"

"Of course not. What about her?"

"She's Joad."

"Who else could she be? Is that all?"

"What do you mean, is that all? Bernie lied to me. He embarrassed me. He used me."

"Dad could be more open, but he wasn't trying to hurt you. Surely you know that by now." Reluctantly, Gil nodded.

"Joad oversees Andrea because it's the only safe way for you to access her without Gecko's involvement. Is that what you're angry about?"

"Yes . . . no. You're making it sound less sinister."

"It is less sinister, whatever that means. You're overreacting because you're embarrassed."

"I'm not. Everyone is trying to manipulate me."

"That's a legitimate beef, but you're not alone in that. I've been hearing that one for decades. I remember when corporations were bidding on the rights to *Virtuoso*, as President, I should have known where it was leading, but powerful business owners with a great deal of capital are hard to deny. Back then, everyone was concerned with terrorism and it was my responsibility to keep the morale high so the engines of commerce could function effectively. Besides, power and money always find a way. I couldn't stop it."

Mark's stories of the past always relaxed Gil. Tonight, he really needed it so he turned on his side and listened.

"*Virtuoso* was considered the Promised Land for corporate and government advertising. It was remarkably effective. Parents had relinquished their responsibility for their children long before *Virtuoso*. Parents were guilty of allowing their children to become easy prey for marketers using sophisticated tools of entrapment. I allowed it with your father, Howard. Kid markets were saturated with advertising that worked so well that soon everyone was fair game and eventually *Virtuoso* became the all-pervasive advertising tool of choice in the economy. There has never been a greater incentive for creative people working in the sophisticated, people-manipulation business than surefire kingly riches. Virtuoso provided the platform and the marketers, with the deepest pockets, were the winners. They developed the strategies and tools that made *Virtuoso* and Archive the pied piper for the almighty dollar. I should have done something."

Mark shrugged and Gil tried to comfort him.

"Who else could do something? I was the President. There was too much money involved and I was doomed to fail, but I should have tried harder. But I knew it would be good for the economy and a good economy benefits everyone, particularly if you want to get reelected. Anyway, I'm sorry you feel manipulated and I'm sorry I'm responsible for some of it. But it's the way of the world and you have to learn to live with it. As long as there are people and money, you're going to have to live with disappointment, even from those you trust—maybe more from them. It doesn't mean they don't love you. Someday, it'll change. Maybe you will change it."

"That's what Bernie's says. I don't understand. Why me?"

"I can't answer that. Dad believes in you, but you must leave Angel Falls to discover it for yourself."

"If I leave, I'll die and then nothing will change."

"There is that. It must be hard to accept that we know about Andrea and didn't tell you. I can't say anything to make you feel better but it's up to you how important that is. Dad is a good man so I'm absolutely certain he didn't mean to hurt you. You need to give him another chance before it's too late. You may not want to live the life he's asking you to live, but regardless what he or Crelli or Tanya Brandt thinks; it's your life to put your stamp on. Do what you think is right."

Gil stood and walked to the edge of the lake where he skipped a few stones across. In the moonlight, he saw the ripples, not the stones. "That sounds right. It's just-"

"You're still a young man. Give yourself a chance. What's out there isn't your fault—it's mine, my generation and those who came before. But regardless of the horrors we created, Dad believes you can make it better, but that can only happen if you open up to it and you can't do that here. Learn what's out there—what we know and you don't—and then do what you feel is right. That's all Dad wants."

"You're in it with him. You think I should go."

"You don't want my view; I've been wrong too much. Make up your own mind. Out of necessity, your life has been sheltered. You need to go out and understand for yourself what's going on. That's all. If you can learn that here, stay, but no one can guarantee how long you'll be safe here. And when it's not safe here, where will you go?"

"I . . . I don't know? I appreciate what you're saying, though."

"We're family. You're like a son to me."

"My father, Howard, is your son. You can't be happy with how that worked out." Gil realized what he'd said and quickly apologized.

"No, no. That's fair." There was anguish on Mark's face. "Did your father talk about me?"

"Not much. I learned something about you in Archive and some from Bernie, but Howard never talks about when he was young."

"They were tough times and I tried to be a good parent but . . . I don't know. Parenthood's a time when you test skills you don't have in situations you don't expect and never wanted to be involved with in the first place. I wasn't a very good parent and Howard, your mother, and eventually you, all suffered because of it."

Gil perked up at that. "You knew my mother!"

"Briefly. She was a nice person and she was good for Howard, not an easy thing. What happened . . . it was . . . unfortunate."

"Tell me about her, please. Howard never speaks of her."

"He went through a great deal and most of it was my fault. He was always . . . different. But he was a good guy. I miss him. I do."

"I do to. Tell me about them, please."

Mark limped over to a spot beside an abandoned fire pit and he lit the kindling that was in it. Gil threw on some logs and soon they were staring into a fire. He sat across from his grandfather and waited.

A few times, Mark looked up, the light of the fire glistening off his moist eyes. "This is difficult. I tried to put it behind me." He remained quiet for a few minutes longer.

"You are my only chance to know about my mother and father."

"It was a long time ago and so much has happened since." Mark put his head in his hands. "You won't understand what it was like." He went quiet again. Finally, he whispered, "You'll hate me just like Howard hates me."

"You're my grandfather. I will never hate you."

"Promise to forgive me."

"Tell me the truth and I'll try."

"The truth . . ." Mark shook his head.

Chapter 6
Washington D.C. — 2033

Autarky — is the term given to a self-sufficient country or economy which is a rare but magnificent accomplishment. More than one hundred years before the United States achieved Autarky, the great capitalist state of Germany was defeated in the First World War. In defeat, Germany was falsely accused of causing the conflict by socialist leaning allies, Britain, France, and the First Republic of the United States of America and Germany was punished so severely that their economy was in ruins.

The Führer, or leader, of Germany, Adolf Hitler, despaired for his wretched country falsely accused and strove to make Germany strong so that the socialist world would never again dictate terms or withhold prosperity from his people. What Germany needed was to acquire the resources necessary to fuel their economic resurgence. Hitler achieved his goal through a forceful, single-minded program of aggressive political and military action all of which was made possible by funds provided by the privately owned banks and financial institutions of the very same socialist-leaning countries that punished Germany in the first place.

Fearing German autarky, the socialist economies of Britain, France, and the United States became vengeful and soon aligned against Germany, forcing Hitler into another war which turned out just as disastrous for Germany.

World War II was fought for control of oil, wheat fields and other natural resources that would have provided Germany with the ability to become fully free—an Autarky.

Herr Hitler's glorious and audacious dream to make his homeland free from the dictates of global socialism has become a symbol of hope to all freedom loving nations struggling against the oppressive International *Comintern* (global communist organization) and the heinous central control it demands of its adherents.

Since Hitler's demise, the *Comintern* has strengthened, forcing tariffs down, opening borders, and driving entrepreneurs to repatriate their enterprises to the lands of least cost. This has made it impossible for bold energetic independent capitalist free market nations to live truly free.

But even while the international conspiracy of Socialist nations sought to defeat Autarky by redistributing wealth globally, the dream of oppressed free market capitalists lived on in the hearts of entrepreneurs who desired true freedom through Autarky and self-sufficiency.

By 2034, the United States was faced with crippling debt and unforgiving creditors, rampant inflation, endemic unemployment, uncontrolled illegal immigration, and an aging, unproductive population. Only Autarky could save the American economy from the death spiral that began with the recession/depression of 2007 and spiraled out of control for years afterward as the country continually elected socialist cowards who lacked the will and the principles to oppose the world's attack on free market principles and who pressed for the U.S. to join the *Comintern* of lazy thinking social moralists.

As has always occurred within the course of American history, a great patriot leader emerged. Entrepreneur Party leader and President Andrew Monroe Crelli freed the United States from the servitude of global socialism and led the rebirth of the American capitalist economy by implementing the disciplined processes required to achieve Autarky.

Benefiting from America's vast resources including productive agricultural land, significant mineral deposits and vast oceans supported by large commercial ports on two shores, and having nurtured a significant technological infrastructure advantage that made America's military the best in the world, President Crelli closed America's borders to all trade and immigration. This act of defiance against global Socialism demanded great sacrifice from America's citizens and American enterprise as evil global forces used every means to destroy the American economy.

After years of perpetual economic warfare, President Crelli's great goal of self-sufficiency was achieved in the face of historic economic terrorism sponsored by the World Bank and the International Monetary Fund.

American entrepreneurs were rewarded for their perseverance and once all waste was purged from the economy and new breakthroughs, like alternative fuels and nano-technology, were implemented and conservation laws were rigorously enforced, Fortress America achieved true self-sufficiency and America prospered.

The ultimate credit for successfully isolating America from the world belongs to Tanya Brandt, Crelli's secretarial assistant, vice presidential running mate, and his successor first as President, and then as Chairwoman of the United States. By 2054, her efforts aided by the brilliant technical guidance of Van Mises social engineering wunderkind, Mark Rose, who succeeded her as President, America once again was the most powerful country on earth and a beacon of capitalist freedom that would guide the world forever after.

Autarky would not have been successful were it not for this steadfast leadership but it also required a world class, powerful, sophisticated state of the art intelligent entity that negated every terrorist plot to undermine the American economy.

Autarky was a stupendous triumph achieved at great cost. Still, the menace of global socialism was defeated and entrepreneurial freedom has flourished ever since in the world's only truly free market.—**Archive**

The winter of 2032 was cold and blustery in the Capital. For President-elect Andrew M. Crelli's swearing in, Mark Rose was dressed formally, including a top hat, while his wife, Terry, wore a fur coat and hat over a dark gray business suit. When they arrived at the Capital, a security officer, seeing that Terry was pregnant, quickly cleared them through and showed them to their special box among the honored guests.

After President Crelli's rousingly patriotic speech, Michael Bourke, Crelli's chief of staff, sent an attendant to escort Mark and Terry to see the new president. Mark congratulated his mentor who, uncharacteristically, hugged him.

"I couldn't have done it without you, Mark," Crelli whispered, his hand holding the back of Mark's head, keeping his ear close. "I'll never forget all you've done. I owe you, big time."

Mark then hugged Crelli's taller wife, Maddie, before Bourke took him aside. The president needed him in Cincinnati later that day for an important meeting so Mark left immediately while Terry, due to give birth any day, stayed in Washington.

The following morning, in a hotel in northern Kentucky, Mark watched in horror as the television media reported a major raid on a terrorist cell hidden on the site of the Indianapolis headquarters of his father's old company, ANGS. The media reported that America was safer now because of the attack and they showed video of the inferno as it burned for days on an abandoned industrial tank farm. Mark tried desperately to contact the president, but Andy wasn't accepting calls, even from Mark. Distracted, he spent the day in meetings haunted by the vision of his father burning to death in that dreadful blaze.

It wasn't until the following morning's reports that he discovered the president's disappointment. Inexplicably, there were no bodies found within the burned out wreckage, and thus no word as to the fate of his father. Initially relieved, he quickly realized how uncomfortable his position was.

Arriving in Washington later that day, a limo met his plane and took him directly to the White House. It was in the limo that he received word that his son, Howard, was born. At the White House, he was escorted to a meeting room and was unable to call his wife on what should have been the greatest day in both of their lives.

In attendance at the meeting was the president, vice president Tanya Brandt, Tom Gorman representing ANGS, and Michael Bourke, Andy's legal counsel. With the key players all in attendance, the president began the meeting.

"Thanks to your special efforts during the election, Mark, I was able to articulate a plan that the voters accepted as the right path to rejuvenate our economy. Now that we're here, we need you to revise your original plans for the stark reality we couldn't tell voters. Out of necessity, your study group must be small and security will be tight. Obviously, what I'm asking of you is extremely sensitive. Michael, distribute the latest report from HOMESEC."

Bourke sent the information to Mark's tablet where it was decrypted and displayed. The president continued. "This report confirms our earlier projections and should provide the incentive needed to aggressively pursue critical economic objectives."

"What objectives are these?" Mark asked his mentor, who deferred the question to Burke.

"The President must understand, in the greatest possible detail, what must be done to insure America's economic self sufficiency," said the chief-of-staff.

"Autarky? You're not serious. That's crazy." Mark realized where he was. "Sorry, sir."

"That's crazy, Mr. President," Crelli said, smiling sardonically at the expression on Mark's face. "As you are well aware, we are facing a national catastrophe. We must fix our economy, once and for all, something the last four administrations were too cowardly to take on. To do it, we must think outside the box and that is your specialty, Mark."

"Of course," Mark said. "But you can't be . . . I mean . . . why? How? The world is too integrated and interdependent. Autarky is, I don't know, impossible—unless, of course, you intend to conquer Canada and maybe the rest of the western hemisphere for resources. Are we going to war?"

"No, Mark, at least not in the way most people think of war."

"I don't understand. Autarky isn't feasible let alone beneficial with a global economy."

Gorman interrupted before Mark could finish his thought. "That's fine, Mark but we need specifics and if at all possible, we will make it work. Tell us the obstacles. Define our strengths and weaknesses; explain it to us and tell us what we need to do. We'll take care of the rest."

Mark thought back to the college thesis he'd written on the subject of the errors Nazi Germany made trying to achieve Autarky, actions that his thesis concluded brought on World War II. He had written it long ago and most of what he remembered was that his professors at Indiana University were disappointed with the subject matter and felt it irrelevant. Curiously, during their first interview, Andy had been very interested in the subject and they discussed it at great length.

"Well, Mark?" The president asked.

"Is this a joke, sir?"

"You've known me a long time, Mark. I don't joke. We need your best effort on this."

Properly chastised, Mark tried to recall information long forgotten. "The Nazis tried it, but their approach, though reasonable, required annexation of the Russian oil and wheat fields, and other productive land east and south of Germany. They went for it but as we all know, it failed."

"We need a better plan," Crelli offered.

"Fair enough, but it will be more than daunting. Off the top, our economy is much larger and far more complex than Germany's. In addition, we have too many-and far too diverse demand-side requirements that can't be satisfied internally because of inadequate supplies of captive resources. In addition, we have significant energy and other resource limitations and, over the years, significant portions of our productive capability have been mothballed, dismantled or left in disrepair as operations transferred offshore to gain economic advantage."

The president nodded, "Yes, certainly that's critical. And we lost a lot of business leaders when liberal presidents, like that ass, Parrington, raised our taxes in order to give away the store to the poor and needy voters that got him reelected. That idiot destroyed capitalist business incentives just to fund damn fool entitlement programs. We're meeting today because of what we have to show for that stupidity? Many of our best companies are gone, along with our tax base and employment potential. It all just evaporated. And every damn consulting and R & D organization that was nurtured here before those god-damned Socialists took over are based elsewhere and operating globally, increasing the capability of our competitors while America languishes.

"Progressives were so damned convinced patriotism somehow extended to shareholders that they bet the ranch on it and capital fled. We're left to face the music. Unemployment remains in double digits and entitlements absorb so much of our budget that we're unable to fund anything, even if we could find someone to lend us the funds. The economy is freezing up. It's bad now because on top of all the productivity lost, we have to face the impossibility of funding Social Security, Medicare, Medicaid, Welfare, Universal Health and other entitlements, like pensions and unemployment coverage, with an empty treasury. Hell, we can't even print money because we can't afford the ink and paper.

"We're broke, Mark, and I need you to work your magic and find a way out of this quagmire before my term ends. Not to add any pressure but if you fail, the resulting anarchy will destroy everything this great nation stands for, and open the way for foreign powers to buy up our assets at the dollar store and end our independence."

Sobered by the president's message, Mark labored on. "I . . . understand, sir. It's a real conundrum. But we can't repatriate corporations or repudiate global debt, and we can't improve our infrastructure without a suitable tax base. And even if we attract corporations back, we'd have to break the remaining unions so we can retrain and redeploy our work force at below subsistence-level wages to make it possible to compete in the world today. And even then, we'd have to find cheap capital and that doesn't grow on trees. With all that, we have to consider the enormous burden of unproductive entitlements. Autarky is a tall order, Mr. President. It would be easier if we could stop the world and ask a large number of unproductive Americans to simply get off before we even consider implementing self-sufficiency."

"How many people would you need to . . . disembark?" Bourke asked.

"Michael, I don't know what that question means," Mark said. "We have to consider where political power comes from. Transformation like this will take time, so while we're making hard decisions, someday, we will need to get reelected and hold power, maybe for more than two or even three terms. That's a tall order given how fickle and afraid voters are. America is still a dominating presence on both oceans and our navy controls all international commercial shipping lanes, so we have power to use, but if we pull back to implement Autarky, we could give up global hegemony. Is Autarky worth it?"

Bourke quickly read something on his handheld and then looked up. "Mark, the President is asking you to reconsider your hypothesis and provide us with a reliable estimate of scope, effort, and cost and to produce a timeline of activities that would allow America to become economically self-sufficient—or at least isolate us enough so we can begin triage and major repairs. We need for you to reconsider all significant factors and identify every variable. This is critical, Mark. We need your best answers regardless how surreal it seems at the moment."

"Mr. President, I still don't know what you want. It's not just the number of people. You'd have to, I don't know—not have those who were unproductive or wasteful—those who consume more resources more unproductively than everyone else—"

Mark paused, unsure where his mind was going, but very aware he didn't like it. "You'd have to factor in those who weren't trained for the type of commerce we will nurture. But even with that, you wouldn't want to lose the thinkers, technologists or entrepreneurs who may generate near term negative cash flow, but could provide significant next-wave economic breakthroughs. I couldn't begin to frame the scope of all that. And then there is information. How would we process it all?"

Bourke interjected, "Every Fortune 1000 company in the world has implemented employee Economic Value Added, or EVA programs, and other performance measurement applications similar to those at Angs and Crelli Enterprises, so we have databases and measurement tools in place. In addition, every employee in the country has a personal communicator, so we know where they are and what they're doing, seven by twenty four. But you're right about the types of people. We'll need to refine our data to consider that."

"That's fine, I guess," Mark continued. "But what would we do with the poor, sickly, old, retired, unemployed and underemployed? Our citizens are entitled to Medicare, Medicaid, all types of healthcare, unemployment compensation, food programs, pensions, and housing that provide what can't be rebalanced. These programs generate huge government deficits, but they also generate a huge payroll and create an environment many businesses are comfortable profiteering in. If you could somehow eliminate that, maybe, but then there's inflation—hell, it could even cause deflation for all I know. That's how bizarre this is—sorry, Sir. The burden of financing the deficit alone precludes us from attempting, let alone, achieving Autarky."

Bourke looked up. "Perhaps we can arrange to default on the debt."

"Wow, that's worth another whole meeting," Mark said. "Autarky will probably set our economy back years, even decades. And with global competition lined up against us, it could be the end of America. There must be something else with a better outcome potential and less risk, Mr. President?"

Tom Gorman responded. "There could be."

Bewildered, Mark turned to Gorman, "There could be, Tom? What does that mean?" Gorman just shrugged, avoiding the question. Though confused, Mark continued. "Mr. President, we'd need to consider potential earnings projections for students. Somehow, you'd have to be able to forecast and control what types of professions will be needed and which ones will not. That comes perilously close to a planned economy, and last I heard, we're not that.

"Remember, Nazi Germany was corporatist socialism, that's certainly not what you've been campaigning for." No one in the room offered a response. "And how do we handle the press, lawyers and other professions who won't like where we're going? The ACLU is under the impression that we're a republic, and the unions, the ones who've survived, are very strong and they certainly won't like it. After campaigning for it, it'll be like saying capitalism is a hindrance to achieving our economic goals, Sir, or that we need a period of socialism to recover. That flies in the face of everything you stand for, especially after how strong you argued for capitalism during the campaign."

"Of course that's not me, Mark," the president answered simply.

"Politics, not capitalism, is the problem," Mark said, mostly because it was true, and he was surprised when everyone in the room, including the president, was silent. "For Autarky to–I don't know–to work, it means growing our way out of our economic abyss, overcoming our bureaucratic, and unpatriotic ways, and convincing greedy entrepreneurs and self-important social and fiscal liberals who created this mess in the first place to go along. That's a tall, tall order."

"Mark, politics isn't your strongest suit," Bourke interrupted. "We're in. You don't realize what's possible. We need your thoughts, but concentrate solely on the economy. Let us figure out how to get it through Congress." The president nodded.

"I understand, but Mr. President, somehow, we'll need to acquire information from independent businessmen and non-earners or people who earn outside the system. The IRS might have been helpful, but your campaign commitment to eliminate the IRS means we'll need an alternative." When he took a breath to consider other options, the president finally spoke.

"As usual, Mark, you've considered some points we hadn't, and all without preparation. That's why you're so valuable to me. You're definitely the man for this job." The others nodded.

Mark considered that this might be a traditional first day hazing, maybe a White House initiation ceremony he wasn't aware of. But as he looked around the room, everyone seemed serious. Maybe they weren't in on it either. But the only way the President of the United States would attend a meeting like this would be if it were a joke. Whatever it was, it continued.

"We've assigned the code name, *Circle of Life* to the project," Burke said, breaking the silence in the room. "But that's not for public consumption. Consider this purely an academic exercise, but it's crucial we understand everything if we are forced to act on it."

"Excuse me, Mr. President, but what events might cause you to consider Autarky?"

"You know how perilous our situation is," the president said. "Besides the economy, we have the terrorist organizations of Omar Smith and Reverend Cavanaugh and of course your father's socialist rebel group although we dealt him a significant blow yesterday." Mark decided to remain silent about the bombing at his father's underground facility at ANGST.

"I'm certain we'll work our way out of the country's problems, but I need your study in my pocket just in case. Some of what you're doing will aid us in planning for disaster response in case of a significant terrorist attack. It's also conceivable that a global cartel could cut us off and freeze our assets, what few assets we have. China, Russia, India, Brazil, and even Turkey are interested in keeping our economy destabilized so we need to be prepared, especially since we've lost our control and influence over the World Bank and the International Monetary Fund. These are difficult times, Mark. The rest of the world can't wait to treat us like we've treated them over the centuries.

"All you need to know to do what I need, Mark, is that I take this very seriously and if any of these things, or a million others happen—and we're doing everything in our power to prevent them-but, if anything we haven't prepared for occurs—to save America I'll need to put everything on the table before deciding on the most effective response. We are already suffering through global water shortages, and natural resource depletion is causing every country to look covetously at our resources. On top of that, we're spending far too much money protecting our borders from South and Central American climate refugees, although we have a plan in place to resolve that. Compounding all of this are advances in medical technology that provides every citizen, not just those who can afford it, with longer lives, and that's draining us as well. You can see we have to be ready for anything."

It sounded reasonable. "Okay Mr. President," Mark said, "So I'm to develop a plan to sustain America through a significant catastrophe or a series of significant catastrophes."

"I can accept that framework," President Crelli said. "But factor in a large and very selective loss of life; mostly in urban areas, the poor and sickly, the elderly, entire families, neighborhoods, communities and I want to understand the business affect of losing these people. This will be your defining work, Mark, your crowning achievement, your ticket to the stars. I want results like the work you did with the prototype *Wharton Towns* because it's imperative we understand everything, and feel confident in each step toward Autarky." The president pointed to Bourke. "Mike, give Mark the list of academicians cleared to work on his project."

Bourke pulled out a single sheet of paper and slid it across the table. It contained a short list of elite professors from the best schools in the country.

"This project is top secret," the president declared. "Each of these people has been cleared and will provide the best available intellectual muscle. If you know others who should be on the list, give their names to Ginger Tucker, she's my new personal security chief. She'll make sure anyone you need clears security and is available."

Mark carefully perused the list. Impressed, he looked questioningly at the president. "Let me clarify again, Sir. You want me to plan for a reduced America that remains viable and free and these professors and doctors are ready and willing to cooperate."

The President nodded and then Bourke added, "We're looking for tempo on this, Mark. There are pressing national security issues we're aware of but we're not at liberty to discuss with you here, today."

The president waved Bourke silent. "You can do this, Mark. I wish I could tell you more, but I'm not at liberty. It's beyond your security clearance. All I can say is that when we act on what you do; you'll have the thanks of a grateful nation and the utmost respect of the President. How long will it take?"

Mark returned to the list, scanning the names and the location of their universities and academic 'think tanks' around the country. He pointed to the paper. "Each of these people is available?"

"Yes."

"I'll contact them tomorrow and schedule our first meetings for next week."

"I need a detailed report no later than three weeks," the president said.

"Detailed? Three weeks! That's impossible, sir. Can I ask why so soon?"

"You can ask but, three weeks is all you have to get the report to my desk. Michael will supply whatever you need. Start immediately. Go."

"But Mr. President, I haven't been home to see my son."

"Trust me, Mark, you don't notice or remember much about newborns in the first few months. I'll speak with Terry. She'll take photos. Everything will be fine. There's a limo waiting to take you to a military jet." The president paused and smiled. "No, go home, take a peek at your boy, but then get going."

Relieved, he left the meeting and went straight home. Terry had just returned from the hospital and was being tended to by a nurse and a temporary live-in maid. Exhausted, Terry was glad to see Mark though she was reticent to talk about the delivery, which had been long and difficult. He didn't see the baby who was still at the hospital undergoing tests for something that turned out not to be serious, and as soon as Terry fell asleep, he left.

That week, he flew to MIT and Drexel University, to Carnegie-Mellon, the University of Chicago, Cal Poly and, finally to the University of Virginia. By the end of the week, Mark had his team. When he arrived home, the baby was there and Terry was stronger but, because of the requirements of the project, he couldn't spend time with them. By working non-stop, two weeks later he delivered his plan. The president was pleased but to Mark's relief and disappointment, said nothing more about Autarky.

With a new baby, Mark did something he'd been contemplating since the night of the election. HomeSec forces still hadn't located his father, so in order to separate from a known terrorist; he changed his last name legally from Rosenthal to Rose.

The years passed. Mark continued to run Crelli Enterprises while performing special projects for the president, and assisting local bankrupt governments to convert to Wharton-like operations supported by the private sector. Andrew Crelli was reelected easily to a second term, and the Entrepreneur Party, riding on his coattails and taking advantage of an uptick in the economy, became the majority party. The president used those majorities to appoint young judges who would favorably interpret his restructuring of America to make it more competitive, now and far into the future. For his second term, Andy reassigned Mike Bourke and Mark resigned from Crelli Enterprise to become the new chief-of-staff.

Terry, Mark and now four year old Howard moved to a home in Georgetown, where Howard grew to be a nervous, quiet boy. With Mark away most of the time and Terry active in the Washington social life, Howard kept to himself even around other children his age. But it was during the last mid-term election of Crelli's presidency that life at the Rose household began to unravel.

Chapter 7
Washington, D.C.—2038

Mark's new job required significantly less travel, but that made little difference to his family because he was on constant call and rarely home when Terry and Howard were awake. One day he arrived home early to a crisis.

Terry greeted him in the living room where she was unloading shopping bags filled with her latest fashion trophies. "Mark? I didn't expect you. Why so early?"

"Andy wants me in later so we can complete his succession plans. I'm picking up clean clothes because Tanya and I will be working late at the White House for the next few days."

"Not again."

"I'll be at the White House."

"I know . . . with Tanya."

"And Michael and most of Andy's core group. Why?"

She looked away, dropping the last of her acquisitions on the sofa before running upstairs. Surprised, he hesitated but finally followed her. She was in their bed, sobbing.

"What's wrong, now?"

"You're gone all the time and Howard's in school. I'm bored, there's nothing to do."

"I'm sorry. You said you were going to take classes."

"That's not it. I mean it's not just that. Tanya invited me to a luncheon today at the Club. I was so excited I ran to Pierre's to buy an outfit. I searched and searched until I found the perfect one; it makes me look taller and important—you know, not plain." As she talked about her outfit, her eyes brightened. She wiped away smeared make-up from her cheek.

"Terry, I have a minute to grab some things. The car's waiting."

She frowned, a vale descending over her face, but she continued anyway. "I described the outfit to Tanya and she loved it. I arrive at the luncheon and that . . . that . . . she's a bitch; she is wearing almost the identical outfit. And you know what a knockout she is. She got all the attention. Everyone ignored me. I was so humiliated. She did it on purpose. I don't know why she doesn't like me; I've always tried to be nice to her." Terry sat and sobbed.

"Did you tell her how you feel?"

"Of course not. What could I say she's the Vice-President? She doesn't like me."

"I'm sure that's not true. Tanya's busy, like we all are, what with a campaign coming up. I'll bet she loved the sound of your outfit and because she had so little time, she asked one of her aides to pick up something like it. That's probably what happened."

She looked up hopefully and then sank back to the bed. "It figures you'd take her side."

He'd been down this road before and rarely made it through successfully. "What does that mean?"

"You know. You see her more than you see me."

"Of course. We work intimately with the President. And now with the succession plan-"

"Intimately?"

"For god's sake, it was a poor choice of words," he said as he checked his watch. He had to go.

"I saw that. You're leaving."

He hesitated because it was apparent she needed reassuring. He walked to the bed and tried to hug her. As usual, she made his effort uncomfortable and ultimately, unsuccessful.

"I have a couple of minutes, Terry. Show me your new clothes." She gave him a questioning look, like a child who thinks she's being fooled. He nodded and she managed a smile as she jumped up. Wiping her eyes, she grabbed his hand and guided him back to the living room where her packages lay about the couch and floor like a post-Christmas depression.

"Where's Howard?" he asked.

"He's in his room playing on the Mesh, where else?" she said, while happily digging out a new pair of shoes from the pile of boxes.

A few weeks later, Terry was visiting her ailing aunt in Indianapolis, leaving Mark to care for Howard. In order to dodge the snooping paparazzi that were searching for clues about their election plans, Mark hosted a planning session at his home.

Late in the evening, after Tanya, Michael Bourke, and he were finished wrapping up loose ends, Bourke excused himself and left. Tanya remained to discuss some lingering issues concerning her upcoming Presidential campaign. They talked, drank, and relaxed.

As usual, Tanya looked incredible, dressed casually in tight-fitting black jeans and a purple silk blouse that simultaneously accented her figure and her incredible violet eyes. She always dressed so elegantly, that when dressed down and unadorned; she looked even prettier and certainly more approachable. In addition, she had recently decided to change her look to something more distinctive by cutting her long, raven hair into a fashionable pixie style that further highlighted her eyes and her brilliant smile.

"As soon as Congress recesses, we'll transition the people you need," he offered.

"Marky." He found it annoying, but Tanya often called him that, just never in front of the media, or when they were out in public. "I need you." She accented the 'you'. "I know I can't lose the election, but I've made enemies and having you on the ticket will help. I must receive more votes than Andy."

He was flattered, but cautious. Like Andy, Tanya Brandt had a reputation for devouring her underlings, and though he'd been fortunate working for Andy, he knew he wouldn't be so lucky with her. Rumor had it that she made extraordinary demands on her staff—including sexual. Andy rarely spoke of such things, though he had joked in private that some rumors about his vice-President were understated. It made for an uncomfortable decision on his part.

"I'll help anyway I can, Tanya but I'll need to discuss it with Andy."

She sat beside him—those violet eyes so close and so magnetic. "Andy agrees. We discussed it today. He thinks it'll help both of us."

She was close enough that he could feel the heat emanating from her body. As she spoke, her breath was warm against his neck. He shivered and had difficulty concentrating. "You will win easy, Tanya, the economy's humming and we're finally eating into Parrington's deficits. Besides, you're a great campaigner, you don't need me. Hell, you could run with the Attorney General and get all the votes you need."

She laughed, running her tongue across her teeth and stood closer, straddling his legs, placing her arms on his shoulders. She began a slow and sensual dance. "I'm gonna be Pre-si-dent, I'm gonna be Pre-si-dent," she sang, over and over while undulating near enough that her breasts rubbed against him.

Embarrassed, he leaned away. "Tanya, you've had way too much to drink." He hoped he sounded more convincing than he felt. Against his will, he wondered if there was any way he could get lucky with this extraordinarily sexy woman while not hating himself for it.

She bent down and blew softly into his ear, taking a little nip with her teeth.

"Ouch, Tanya, stop it please. We can't," he said, resisting a tremor that coursed down his spine.

"Can't what, Marky?"

She played with the buttons on his shirt while continuing to dance and repeat her song. "I'm gonna be Pre-si-dent," she sang, even adding a new line. "This is my coun-try now." Her tongue took the lead and she painted a trail from his neck down to his now exposed chest. The hairs on the back of his neck stood at attention—and they weren't alone standing in praise.

"Tanya, please," he begged. She rubbed her hands up and down her body while continuing to recite her song softly into his ear. Then, she unbuttoned her blouse and shrugged it to the floor. Her fingers weren't the only things that poked him in the chest as she gently plopped onto his lap facing him.

If she thought she would have him like she had had everyone else, she was wrong. Still, he had to be careful because he didn't want to offend her. He knew what had to be done, but he just wasn't quite ready to do it. This took precise timing.

When she brought his hands to her breasts, he felt that the time for a decision might have passed. She guzzled the remainder of her drink and in her exuberance, threw the glass into the fireplace; the noise of broken glass shook him out of his reverie. He looked at her but her eyes were elsewhere. He turned and followed her smiling stare to its source.

Halfway up the steps, little, six-year old Howard Rose peered down on them, mesmerized.

Immediately, his mind cleared. "Howard, go upstairs!" he yelled. But his son wasn't focused on him. Too young to appreciate one of the sexiest and most powerful women in the world sitting on his father's lap in his living room with her breasts exposed, Howard was old enough to understand that something monumental in his life was occurring just below him.

"Howard?" Mark yelled again. The boy continued to stare and Tanya made no attempt to hide her nudity. Mark yelled one more time and finally Howard turned and ran up to his room. The bedroom door slammed shut.

"Tanya, what the hell just happened? This was a big mistake. You've gotta go."

"The damage, such as it is, is done, we shouldn't stop now. Besides, I'm mostly there and I can promise you from experience; it'd be a shame for you to waste me right now." She pointed to the tent in his pants. "It would be simply un-presidential to waste that resource too."

"Tanya, stop it. You drank too much and now I need to talk with my son. I've got some major psychological scarring to prevent. He's only six, for God's sake. I'm going upstairs to try to reason with him. Please see your self out." She smiled, picked her blouse and bra off the floor, hastily putting them back on and left.

Mark bolted upstairs, trying to exert himself as much as he could so he wouldn't enter his son's room with an erection. He knocked several times before entering. Howard was sitting on his bed wearing the latest virtual headgear, playing one of his Mesh games. He motioned for his son to take his helmet off, but the boy ignored him so he insisted until finally Howard complied. He sat on the bed and tried to put his arm around his boy, but Howard squirmed away.

"I'm sorry, Howard. Ms. Brandt was celebrating and got silly. She's sorry. Nothing happened, Howard. You know I love mommy. What happened was nothing. Are you okay?"

Barely acknowledging his presence, Howard kept eyeing his virtual equipment, anxious to begin playing again. He tried to put his helmet on but Mark stopped him.

"You've got to believe me, son, everything is okay. I love you and mommy and nothing is going to change that. Do you understand?"

Howard grabbed his helmet, put it on, and booted up a new game without saying a word.

"Turn around," Mark insisted, but Howard continued to play. "Howard!"

Finally, he grabbed his son's shoulders firmly and turned him around, taking off the helmet and putting it behind him. "You can't play until you say something."

"Momma's gonna be mad, again," Howard said as he reached for his helmet. Mark left the room knowing his son was right.

A few months later, Tanya announced her intentions to run for president with Mark as her vice-president. His days and nights got busier though never again did she try to seduce him. He made himself believe that she respected him too much, and knew that he was above that behavior, and though deluded, he respected her more for it.

He wasn't to learn just how much Tanya had respected him until many years later, when Terry was dying and she had asked Mark's forgiveness for her own secret relationship with Tanya.

It was right after Tanya won the presidential election. Crelli had been content to orchestrate the biggest landslide in America's history; one that had elected the first woman president. Two years of hard work and constant travel passed in a blur. Although Mark never told Terry about the incident with Tanya, their relationship was strained anyway. He tried everything except actually being with her and being honest about that night with Tanya.

One day, Mark was attending a business conference in Oregon, and while he was away, Tanya invited Terry on a shopping spree at an exclusive capital clothier. Terry was so excited she called to tell him. The women had a great time and bought so much that when the bill finally arrived he was angry. But there was more to that evening.

Terry gave the babysitter last minute instructions and joined Tanya in her midnight purple presidential limousine. They rode in the back drinking eighteen-year-old, single malt scotch; Tanya's favorite, which became Terry's too. When they arrived at the clothier they were laughing and a bit tipsy. The Secret Service cordoned off the area leaving Tanya and Terry inside with the owner. They must have tried on everything in the store. The owner, delighted with the attention, spared no expense, so they continued to drink while they tried on clothes. By the end of the evening, Terry was so sloshed that a Secret Service agent had to help her into the limo. On the ride home, Tanya started talking about men. In confidence, she gossiped about Andy and his conquests, sparing little detail and fictionalizing plenty.

When they arrived home, Terry paid and dismissed the babysitter and checked on Howard who was sleeping quietly in his room. Downstairs, Tanya decided to have another drink. Terry, needing bolstering for a discussion she needed to have, drank with her.

"Tanya, I've had a lovely time. Thanks."

"I did to. I really needed a night out doing girl stuff. You've helped me relax and I appreciate it. Being President is so demanding. Everyone else seems to have all the fun." Tanya poured another drink for both of them.

"I'm glad I could help."

"Thanks honey," Tanya said giving Terry a quick hug. "Washington is a difficult town to control rumors in. I don't know what you've heard about Mark, but believe me you have nothing to worry about. This is funny. One night when I was lit up drunk like I am now, I acted foolishly around Mark, like a coquette, and for that I am eternally sorry. Mark was a total gentleman and nothing happened. The next day, I was so embarrassed, I apologized profusely and he was great about it, as usual. That man of yours is a real sweetheart, even in a world where men are still playing by different rules than women."

"What different rules?"

"We're under tremendous stress and on the road all the time. The men, Andy and Mark, they have countless opportunities to enjoy local talent, while young men and women, teens even, they seem really worried about luxuriating in a one-nighter with royalty like me."

"Tanya!"

"That's Madam President," Tanya replied tersely.

"Oh, I'm sorry, I mean Madam President. I-"

"Oh shush, I'll always be Tanya to you. I'm buzzed that's all and I'm just having some fun. Aren't you buzzed too?" Terry nodded a bit unsure.

"After all these years, a woman is finally president and I'm held to a different standard than the men. I have needs too. Just because I'm president, why should I have to sneak someone in for a few hours of debauchery? Well sweetie, I don't want to embarrass you, but America should be proud to have a world class, hot president. Maybe I should order my interns to find some political groupies for me to work with. The last administration certainly broke new ground there."

"Political groupies?"

"It's an inside joke, Terry, that's all. Say, look at you. Mark has great taste in women." Tanya put her hands on Terry's waist. "I have an outfitter who loves to work with thin waists. I'll hook you up."

In an alcoholic fog, something Tanya said concerned her. "Did you say Mark has great taste in women?" she asked, distressed.

Tanya, smelling Terry's vulnerability, closed on her mission. "Now, there I go again," she said, her voice showing concern. "When it comes to business or politics, I'm great; but I've never been good talking woman things. Terry, I know this will surprise you but I don't have many women friends?"

Terry took a sip of scotch from Tanya's glass and tried to reassure her. "You have plenty of friends. You're very attractive."

Tanya waved her off. "No, no, I really don't, but you're sweet for saying it. I spend most of my time with men and to make my point with them, I have to be direct—outspoken, but yet guarded. I'm not used to girl-on-girl talks." She put her arm around Terry and gently combed her fingers through her hair. "Hey, thanks for saying I'm attractive."

Tanya's caring touch was comforting Terry. "You are. You're beautiful. You've been on the cover of fashion and gossip magazines. I'm sure everyone wants to be your friend."

"Mark doesn't."

"Mark does too. He talks about you all the time. That's why I thought he was sleeping with you, but I guess all this time he was with others."

"He was?" Tanya asked, then realizing what Terry meant, she whispered to get her to a quiet, comfortable place away from uncomfortable thoughts. She leaned in close to deliver the full affect of her violet eyes and Terry was mesmerized. "You have that wrong, Terry," she purred. "Mark's a saint. Why when I got so drunk that time and accidentally came on to him, he was gracious and kind and treated me with utmost respect. He told me he loves you. Anyone would love you; you're so kind and sweet and beautiful," she began rubbing Terry's shoulders, "and muscular, I like that in a woman." She slowly moved her hands, massaging gently.

"Ahh, that feels so good. Tanya, I'm so confused. I love Mark, oh, right there, that's great, but we've become so distant. That's why I think sometimes he looks elsewhere for affection. Ohh, that's wonderful, how do you do that? There are so many beautiful women like you in this town for him to choose from. I'm glad you say he's not interested. Ahhhh, yes, keep that up, yes, right there. A little harder. There-" She closed her eyes as Tanya worked to drive all her worry away.

"You and Mark will be fine. He told me when his responsibilities end; he wants to rededicate himself to you."

Behind a gentle fog, Terry responded. "He said that? Rededicate?" She thought to worry, but Tanya continued to massage; slowly moving to the front of her body, her fingers gently straying. She sighed. "Is that a good thing, I mean it sounds like he's not dedicated now . . . you're sure he's not . . . ?"

"No, no, no," Tanya said, slowly moving in, insinuating her fingers inside Terry's blouse, and working her way gently across her breasts. Her fingers seemed to materialize everywhere, driving not just worry, but all thought from Terry's head. Tanya worked the blouse loose then traveled down to and through Terry's belt, slowly tightening, and then loosening.

"You're so adorable. And look at those stomach muscles, they make me crazy, the President of the United States, well you drive me crazy. Mark would never cheat on you. Say, why do you hide that beautiful body under these clothes? You need to show it more. Like I do. Your body will stand up to a lot of scrutiny. When do you find time to exercise?"

Terry smiled, weakly. She was about to say something when Tanya's mouth connected with hers, her tongue softly slithering through her teeth, seeking her tongue.

Later, with Terry passed out on the couch; Tanya rolled over and looked up the stairs. "Seen enough this time, big boy?" she asked, laughing as Howard ran back into his room, in terror, slamming the door.

Terry dreamily turned toward the sudden noise. Who was Tanya talking too? Then she heard the frantic scurrying of little footsteps and the slamming of a door.

Driven by Tanya's laughter, Terry's brain heaved toward responsibility. She peered over their entwined naked bodies on the couch to the steps where Howard had been and she screamed.

Chapter 8

Angel Falls – 2070

Waster — Americans live in a free country with rules to keep them free and everyone in this free country has the opportunity to succeed at some level. This is a freedom that most of the people around the world can only hope for. In America, no one need take from anyone else, nor should anyone give to anyone else, we're free. That's what freedom means.

However, among truly free people, some may decide to break these simple, satisfying rules. Some by acts of larceny, fraud, and murder, others by sloth; all confirm that they cannot exist without depending on someone else.

The only way for our free society to remain free and thrive is to rid ourselves of these *Wasters.*—***Archive***

As Mark idly stoked the embers back into a blazing fire, Gil stared in shocked silence. Embarrassed by where the story of his grandparents had gone, he understood now why Mark was so reticent to discuss his part. Thankful for the silence as Mark placed a few logs on the fire, Gil finally asked, "Why did Tanya do that? And how did you find out about it?"

"Terry told me on her deathbed, and having been through the same with Tanya myself, I began to see how manipulative and evil our Chairwoman can be. That's not to mention the damage done to your poor father having witnessed Tanya's evil ways firsthand."

Mark shook his head and stared into the fire before continuing.

"What can I say? That's who Tanya is. I've tried to understand her, but all I can think of is that she needs to control people and has limited means to do it. Oh, she's smart, but not like Andy. She succeeds differently. Andy plans. Sometimes, you don't understand why he does something until you look back on it and see how well thought out it was and how tightly it fits together. Andy is extraordinary that way.

"But Tanya, she has Andy's ruthlessness, but does things without an obvious purpose—or at least without a grand plan. She wants to win, but she craves instant gratification, too. If you ever have to deal with her, be careful. She is incredibly effective playing a game with shifting rules of her own design. You couldn't outthink or outwork Andy, but you might have been able to anticipate him. Tanya, there's just no rhyme. You have to be damn fortunate to beat her."

"I'll keep that in mind," Gil said. "Tell me more about Howard."

"After we won that election, it was Howard's misfortune to grow up in, or near the White House under the omnipresent, omnipotent pair of Andrew Crelli and Tanya Brandt."

"It must have been pretty intense."

"Terry and I were adults. We should've been able to take care of ourselves. But Howard was just an innocent little guy. He needed us. With the strain of our failing marriage, we just weren't very good at providing protection. We were selfish and weren't up to the challenge of defending the poor kid. I know it's a rationalization, but until you feel the relentless pressure Andy and Tanya exert, you can't appreciate it."

Mark stared at the now raging fire, lost in sad thoughts. After a few moments of silence, he located a small, metal bucket near the fire pit, filled it with water from the lake, and drenched the fire and wasting his efforts to rebuild it. As the smoke billowed over the hissing of the dying embers, he turned to Gil. "It's getting late and I'm cold. If I have to, I'll finish this back in my cabin." He started limping back toward the village.

Gil followed and easily caught up, but Mark wanted to walk alone so Gil left him to his thoughts. They reached the cabin just as the last hint of the solstice sun dropped over the hills above. Deep blue sky turned black and thousands of stars emerged. They entered the cabin and sat on Mark's bed.

"Howard's my son and he's grown now so I try not to think about it. His entire life, he didn't have family or friends he could count on. Growing up, he was a shy boy living in the shadow of powerful politicians.

It was all he could do to avoid those people and when he couldn't, they tormented him."

"Did Crelli have children?" Gil asked.

"He had two really wild girls and when he and Maddie separated, they went with her. I miss Maddie; she was always nice and fun."

"What happened to her?"

"You have to remember; Andy was much more than president, he was a celebrity. His every action from the time he became a Senator was covered worldwide by paparazzi in the entertainment media. In fact, there were more paparazzi around than hard news correspondents because there was more money in the glamour media than in the news. And Andy always provided a provocative story. He attended the top sporting events, the Academy Awards, Broadway shows, and every big premiere. At every event, he was accompanied by some A-list female celebrity or model. Maddie knew. She lived it with her dad; he was Senate Majority leader, but the celebrity life she was familiar with wasn't nearly as grand as how Andy lived it. Maddie signed on for it, but she was smart. She knew it was just a matter of time. They separated amicably just after his re-election. The last I heard, she and the kids were in Kentucky, but that was more than thirty years ago. She may still be at his mansion and the kids are—I don't know."

"Tell me more about Howard?"

"Yes, Howard; sorry. He grew up extremely shy and cautious of everyone, including Terry and me. His school performance was horribly inadequate. He was bright, but he didn't seem to care. It was like he was living in a different dimension from his teachers and his classmates. I tried not to show my dissatisfaction, but I had such a laudatory academic career that it was hard for me to understand. But that was Howard. He knew that doing nothing or doing something poorly was the best way to displease me, so his instincts were to quit rather than compete against my record. It worked. He was good at failing."

"That seems unnecessarily cruel."

"It's accurate, but I suppose you're right. We tried doctors and medications and every stylish remedy that was marketed to help kids his age succeed. Nothing worked. He was in high school when I was president and even as the president's son, he barely graduated. When we applied to colleges, we had to look for ones that would accept a below average performance from the son of the president. We forced him to take college aptitude tests and he surprised everyone by scoring in the top third. I remember spending the day after we received his scores, proudly accepting congratulations from my White House staff on my late blooming genius.

"Andy pulled some strings and got him accepted into Georgetown and the University of Maryland on probationary status. I used my influence to get him grandfathered into Indiana University, but Howard wouldn't agree to any of them. For some reason, he wanted to go to New York. He applied to and received probationary acceptance from NYU, Greenwich Village. He wouldn't listen to reason, so after too many one-sided arguments, he enrolled there. He'd never been away from us before so I had doubts. If nothing else, I hoped it would be a good experience for him."

"Was it?"

"In some ways, not in others."

CHAPTER 9

New York City—2050

Howard Rose was standing at the street corner watching students scurrying through the puddles of water that had collected on the streets and sidewalks. In the 2050 freshman class at NYU, Greenwich Village, Howard was the most famous and least known.

He had spent his first week careening around campus trying to find his classes, but succeeding only in being late or lost most of the time. Rising tides had created constant puddles on the campus streets which were hard to navigate around and only added to his confusion. He was already late to his first civics class, as he looked frantically for a map of the campus. He saw one plastered to a billboard in front of a nearby building and ran to it. Never far away, his security detail closely monitored his movements. Because of them, he was never alone—another reason he was disappointed with college life.

As he approached the billboard, he stumbled, his knee hitting his books and spilling them beyond his grasp. When they hit the ground, he kicked one under the billboard.

"First week of class and you're already throwing your books away, huh?" It was a girl's voice, pleasant and kind of lyrical, with an accent he couldn't place. He didn't know what to say.

"Hey, do you want your book? Hello is anybody there?" The voice asked.

Embarrassed, Howard hunkered down to study the map. Unfortunately, his class was located at Crelli Hall, so his first thought was to blow it off. He felt a tap on his shoulder. Turning, he was eyeball to eyeball with a smiling black face—a beautiful, happy, smiling black face.

"These yours, gabby?"

He tried to speak, but the words came with difficulty. "My, um, my name's not Gabby."

"And . . . ?"

"And what?"

"And what is your name?"

"Oh, it's Howard."

"Howard?" she repeated. Because of her accent, it sounded like Howie. "Nice to meet you," she said, extending her hand. He stared at it until she touched his hand and then shook it. He shifted his feet nervously, unsure what to do next.

"No, it's Howard. H-o-w-a-r-d."

"Howie," she smiled. Somehow that relaxed him a little.

"Okay. Howie," he conceded.

"Howie, how do you know my name?"

"I . . . I don't know your name."

"Then why don't you ask me what it is?"

Now he was really uncomfortable, but he forced himself. "What's . . . your name?"

"None of your business." He turned to go. "Where ya going?"

"Class. I'm late. I have to go."

"You don't know my name."

"You said it was none of my business."

"That was a joke. Don't tell me you actually respect what I say. I like that in a human." Blushing, he walked away. She shouted, "I'm kidding. My name's Henrietta. Henrietta Boyar. See you around."

He paused and cautiously turned, but she was gone. His stomach felt weird and as he walked to class, he wondered if he would ever be a good boyfriend.

The next day, he saw her again in the cafeteria. She waved from a distance. He was nervous and didn't react until she pulled the red bandana from her head allowing a great mass of nappy brown hair to explode outward in all directions. Bandana in hand, she waved it yelling, "Howie, Howie." To keep her from drawing more attention to him, he ran over to her.

"Hey, Howie, how are you doing? Did you make that class?"

He nodded. Smiling, she grabbed his arm and led him to a table. Not knowing what to say, he allowed her to lead. He was grateful that she talked all through lunch as listening played to his strength. After lunch, she walked him to his next class.

For the rest of the semester, when she could, she would walk him to his classes and when his classes ended, she would be waiting for him.

She had the patience to relate to him, and like a good computer game, she seamlessly integrated her life into his. And just like the games he played, she changed him in subtle ways. His schoolwork improved and he began taking an interest in the outside world. Although most of the students at NYU were uncomfortable befriending the son of the President, she still found ways to help him enjoy campus life. As a bonus, his annoying Secret Service detail gave him more space and he enjoyed the freedom.

Not that anyone but Henrietta would notice, but he became more outgoing and soon they were inseparable. Because she was a sophomore, she'd had most of his classes so she tutored him until, by the end of the semester; he'd made the Dean's list.

It was late in his second semester when their relationship changed. They were studying and, as usual, she was teasing him. "I'm not going to help you with this stuff anymore because you don't like me."

"I do," he pleaded. "I like you a lot. You treat me nice. Why wouldn't I like you?"

"You never ask about me—it's like you don't care."

She saw the concern in his face and relented. "It's alright, Howie, I'm just teasing. If you like someone, it's nice to show an interest in their lives."

"I am interested, but I don't like it when people pry, so I didn't want to be impolite. Tell me about you."

"What do you want to know?"

"Where were you born?"

She smiled and rewarded him with a hug. "Until last year, I spent my entire life with my mama in my home in Barbuda. Did you ever hear of it?"

He hadn't so Henrietta pulled up a map of the Caribbean on her communicator. With her pencil, she pointed to a little dot northeast of South America where Barbuda was located.

"Wow, is it that tiny. There can't be much room to walk."

She stared blankly and then laughed. "You can't even blow it up bigger on the communicator, it's that small. That's good, Howie, you made a funny. I'm so proud of you." Pleased with himself, he returned her smile with an even bigger one.

"Barbuda's a small island with the most beautiful pink beaches and there are frigate birds everywhere. My mama raised me, and home-taught me, while my dad was away working on another island. When I came of age, a man of means wanted to marry me, but I was pretty good at schoolwork and told mama I wanted to go to college in America instead. We were poor, but I studied hard between my work and chores. Then something wonderful happened. I was seventeen when mama told me about St. Elmo."

"What's St. Elmo?" Howard asked.

"He's the patron saint of sailors. There's a statue of him near the beach back home. Mom took me into the hills behind our home where she dug up a box she'd wrapped and buried in a protected place. She opened it and handed me an empty, decaying wallet.

"Before you were born, she told me, a hurricane hit the island. Afterwards, she went down to the statue of St. Elmo to clean up the debris. As she was untangling sea weed, she noticed this wallet and an expensive watch hidden in a crack in the base of the statue. Somebody had put it there; the storm couldn't have done it. But there was no identification and nobody came around so she took them and left a note in case the person who lost them returned. She kept the wallet and the watch for a long time, but nobody claimed them so she sold the watch and invested the cash plus what was in the wallet in the American stock market."

"How much money was there?" he asked.

"There was a lot in the wallet and the watch was very expensive."

"Wow."

"Yes, wow. It was really lucky. After I completed school, mom gave me access to the funds. I had enough for airfare to America and four years of tuition and room and board if I was careful."

"Why'd you choose NYU?"

"They had a special program for Caribbean natives that made the tuition affordable and I have a few cousins working in the city. I see them from time to time."

"What do they do?"

"They collect trash and do repairs and other dirty work second and third generation American immigrants won't do. But the rules have changed so it's getting harder for everyone."

"What's happening?"

"When they first came here, the work didn't pay much so they all lived together in a one bedroom flat. Their combined incomes paid the bills and your government provided them with food stamps and other welfare. But since that *Circle of Life* bill passed, there are no benefits, so they're not able to eat regularly. Then, a few weeks ago, two of my cousins disappeared. Ronald, the oldest, said they went to Sacramento to find work. Rhonda's worried they'll be arrested by the Financial Security police and be deported or worse. I'm very concerned."

Howard was confused. "Who's Rhonda and who are the Financial Security police?"

She patted him on the shoulder. "Rhonda is my other cousin. And for the President's son, you're really naïve."

"I'm not naïve," Howard pouted. "You try to live in the White House with all those . . . those mean-spirited loud mouths. You have no idea how bad it is. If I say anything, they say I'm cute, and if I didn't know anything, I'm stupid. Believe me; it is better to be stupid. That's why I chose accounting. I couldn't take the pressure and abuse if I'd chosen something they know about."

"I understand, Howard," she said. "But this is still your country and it's changing in ways you need to know. Because of all that's going on, and because I'm concerned about my cousins, I'm taking a current events class with Herr Professor Huber. You should take it, too."

"Maybe I will but please don't lecture me about what I don't know. It is hard enough to endure Crelli and Brandt and their staffs, I can't take being put down by you, too."

He paused, letting the words hang in the air. The last thing he wanted was a fight, so he brought the conversation back on topic.

"So, who are the Financial Security Police? We haven't discussed them in my accounting classes yet."

"FinSec was created a few years ago under President Brandt. Everyone must earn enough to live on—there's no help from the government or anyone anymore. FinSec, the Financial Security police, is part of the Coast Guard that's responsible for enforcement."

"If everyone has to work, what do you do?"

"Not everyone has to work; you just need to have enough money to live. Nobody assists anybody. You must have funds for yourself first. I still have some of my savings left, but since tuition went up, I do some work around campus too."

"If I need a job, can you get me one?"

She laughed. "Your father makes enough so you won't ever have to work. Besides, no one is going to mess with the president's son. You're safe."

Howard considered her answer. "You know who my father is?"

"Everyone on campus knows." His face clouded up and he brooded. "Stop that, Howie. Don't be mad at me just because I know about you?"

He was silent for a while. Then he smiled and blurted out, "I love you."

Her face lit up. "Howie, that's nice of you to say." She gave him a hug. At first, his body was its normal, stiff, unyielding self, making the hug difficult for her to maintain. She hung on until slowly he figured some things out and relaxed, molding his arms around her and putting his chin on her shoulder. They remained in each others arms, lost in the moment.

After a while, she disengaged, her smile long gone.

"You look sad," he said, breaking the silence.

"It's nothing. That was a nice hug. You're a good hugger. We need to study."

"I'm all sweaty."

She laughed and wiped a tear from her eye. "That's what good hugs do. Now let's study."

The following year, Howard and Henrietta were inseparable at school. His good grades continued and she even convinced him to volunteer to assist in a campus production of Thornton Wilder's play, *Our Town*. He began to write home as well. They were only occasional, brief notes, updating his parents on the comings and goings of his life at NYU. But he never called. From time to time Howard and Henrietta's picture would appear in Mesh gossip sites, but for a president's son, his life was too boring for the media. By spring, they were a regular college couple. And like any college couple they faced the upcoming summer break that would force them apart.

"I have to go back to the White House. Can you come?"

"I have to find my cousins."

"You still haven't heard from them?"

"No, nothing and I'm worried. Now both Rhonda and Ronald are missing, and I'm going crazy. I promised my mama and my uncle I would look after them."

"Where will you look?"

"California. Sacramento, I think." She saw the expression on his face and her fragile smile faded. "Don't give me that look. I have to go. I'll miss you. You're my best friend. You know that. I'll be back before the fall semester starts. I promise."

"You're my best friend too," he said, thinking for a minute. "I'm going with you."

"Howie, you can't. I don't want to leave anymore than you want me to but you can't go; you're the son of the President."

"I love you, Hen," he said, giving her a defiant look. It was so out of place on him that she laughed. He was offended so she smiled and hugged him. He gently pushed her away, his look more determined.

"Howie, don't be doing this to me now. It's just for a little while. It's okay that you're sad. When you get back to Washington, you'll have fun and time will pass, you'll see."

"I said I love you," he said indignantly. "You're the only person who's ever treated me normal and nice. I don't want time to pass without you, particularly at the White House. You matter. I don't want to be without you."

She did the only thing a girl could do—she kissed him—but this time not like a friend. It required some work on her part because he lacked experience and wasn't very good. He'd never kissed anyone before, certainly not like this. But she was patient and he was motivated and they spent the rest of the day practicing. They kissed on the street and they kissed while walking up the stairs to his apartment. They kissed while studying and they kissed before and after meals. They kissed at night before they went to bed and first thing in the morning before she left. It was that morning that she gave him the best present she could to remember her by. She helped him to make love to her. It was mostly a mystery for him but he persevered, and with her love and persistence the rush of passion eventually dissolved nineteen years of well-structured defenses.

And then, too soon, she was gone. He sulked alone in his room until the presidential limo arrived to take him home. He moped and endured the White House until he returned to NYU in the fall, a nervous, hopeful young man.

A better parent or even a more attentive one, or a better president would have prevented what happened next. But it was a bad time to be president and a parent. So Howard returned to NYU soon to be aware of how completely Andrew Crelli had taken control of the United States.

From the first minute Howard stepped on campus, he knew something wasn't right. He waited at her apartment, but she didn't show. He waited there everyday but to no avail. He tried frantically to locate her on and around campus. Through the first few weeks of class he searched, but Henrietta Boyar was nowhere to be found. She was enrolled, she just wasn't attending. And although it was only a minor annoyance, the Secret Service had returned, clustering near him like they had at the beginning of his freshman year.

Love was a new experience for Howard, and without her to give expression to it, he went crazy. All his life he had kept his needs and wants limited and controlled so he couldn't ever be disappointed. Now, he needed her desperately, but there was nothing to do but obsess. Not practiced at handling disappointment, he was morose. Before Henrietta, whenever anything needed to be worried, he would simply boot up a computer game and the issue vanished. That was until now. Nothing had ever caused him so much angst that he couldn't play it away. Nothing, until Henrietta.

Then, one night, late in the semester, she appeared.

He was studying for his first exam, unfocused and resigned to failing. There was a knock on the door. She looked tired and worn out, but he didn't care. He rushed to her and hugged her as hard as he could. When she didn't respond, he pulled away and looked at her. She had tears in her eyes and he noticed purple and black bruises and welts on her dark skin.

"What happened? What's wrong, Hen? Are you okay? Where've you been?"

She shrugged off his questions, dragged herself into his apartment, and sat on the couch. He joined her, trying to embrace her but she resisted. Broken hearted at her response, he retreated to a window on the far side of the room and brooded. They remained at a distance for a long time. Finally, she came over to him.

He spoke first. "It's over, isn't it?" he asked with tears in his eyes. "You've found someone else and we're done."

"Howie, it's not like that. I missed you. I really did." She began crying.

"You're using the past tense. You told me you love me. You promised me you'd be back."

"I can't talk about it. It's not about you, it really isn't. But I can't see you, anymore."

Hearing that, he shrieked and moved petulantly back to the sofa

"I have to go home. Once I have the money, I'm leaving as soon as I can."

"Why? I don't understand." He began to cry.

"Howie, please. Don't."

"Don't what? I love you and I thought you loved me too. Now you've had your fun and you're moving on. Is that it? What do I do? How does this work? How am I supposed to react?"

Helpless, she stared at him. "Howie, look at me. Do I look like I'm having fun? Take a good long look. Do I look like the girl you remember from the end of last semester?" She gestured down her body from her face to her legs. "Well? Do I? If you love me, really love me; stop seeing everything through your eyes and start seeing through mine. Well?"

He paused and looked at her again. When he looked closer, the bruises were more noticeable. And she had gained weight, although, if anything, her face and shoulders were thinner. Concerned, he stood to hug her, but she put her hands out to keep him away. He persisted until she allowed him a gentle embrace. "I'm sorry," he cried. "I was worried you wouldn't come back. Forgive me."

Before she could answer, her eyes rolled up and she collapsed into his arms. It surprised him and he almost let her fall to the floor. Even with her apparent weight gain, she felt insubstantial and he carried her gently to the sofa and carefully placed her form down onto the cushions. He covered her with a blanket and let her sleep.

She awoke a few hours later and stared at him with that look that made him feel special. He smiled shyly, causing her to smile briefly.

"Feel better?"

"Better? I'm sorry, Howie, I shouldn't have done this to you. I wouldn't have come back at all but you're the only one who can help me."

"You weren't going to come back?"

"You don't understand what's going on. I have nobody else to turn to."

"What about Ronald?"

"He's gone."

"Where'd he go?"

"He's just gone."

"I don't understand."

"Could you make me some coffee? I have to go to the bathroom."

He set the coffee on the kitchen table, and waited. He heard the toilet flush and she came into the kitchen and sat down. Before she could begin, he spoke, "Whatever you need, Hen, I'll do it."

She seemed pleased by that. "When I left to find my cousins, I wasn't honest with you. I thought that if I told you the truth, you wouldn't want to see me again."

"Nothing you can say would ever keep me from wanting that."

"It's time for the truth, Howie," she paused and swallowed hard. She tried to speak but tears made her turn away. Finally, she took a deep breath and began. "Last year, when we met, we met by accident."

"You returned a book I kicked. By the map of the campus."

"Yes. But afterwards a man from the Secret Service visited me."

"Did they think you were threatening me?"

"No, nothing like that. They reported our meeting to your father. They told him you'd made a friend and he had them do a background check on me. They found nothing, of course, so the agent offered me a job. They agreed to pay my college living expenses if I agreed to be your friend and wear surveillance gear to help them monitor and protect you."

"No!" he screamed.

"I'm sorry. My cousins needed help and I was running out of money. I didn't have a choice. I know it hurts, but it's not what you think."

Trying to avoid hearing the rest of her story, he angrily stomped back to the window.

"Howie, please, it's not like that. Before you . . . remember, I didn't know you very well then and it was an order from the President of the United States."

Howard stalked past her to the kitchen. She followed him but froze, frightened, when he began pummeling a kitchen wall with his fists. He continued to flail at it until he'd worked a large hole in the drywall. He was still hitting it when two agents ran through the door to check things out. It took a while to calm him down and the agents refused to leave until Henrietta convinced them that he was not threatened. Even then, they remained outside the apartment, taking up positions in the hall, close to his apartment door. After they left, she tried to reason with him.

"I don't have much time now. It's not what you think. It's not. Everything I said to you and did for you, I meant—I still mean. Your father wanted you to feel more normal on campus—there's nothing wrong with that. He cares about you." He stared quietly at his bloodied fists.

"Howie, listen to me. There's nothing wrong with that. It was a good thing. The arrangement allowed me to spend more time with you without agents being so close. The more time I spent, the more I cared about you and the more I loved you. You're a sweet, gentle, and decent man." She smiled as he continued to stare at his bloody knuckles. "Well, maybe not so gentle," she laughed lightly. "You cared so much; I fell in love with you."

It slowly dawned on him what she was saying. Maybe it wasn't as bad as he thought. He took her hand and kissed it. Then they embraced.

"So, my father pays you to watch out for me and we fall in love. I can handle that. That's a good thing right?"

She nodded, sadly.

"I love you and you love me. So we're back. It can be like it was last semester."

"No, Howie, it can't, not anymore."

"Why not?" he whined.

"Things happened. I went to Sacramento to find my cousins. I visited an employer there that Ronald mentioned in his letters. The woman said she never saw him or any of my cousins, but when I talked to some of the workers, they were really frightened. I showed them pictures and they agreed with their employer that they'd never seen my cousins. As I was leaving, one of the workers gave me a piece of paper with an address on it.

"I drove to that location. It was a housing project near the town of Holarki, not far from the fields and the factory. When I arrived, armed *Federales* were herding people into busses. A few were crying. I asked one what was going on.

"She told me her husband and sons had been reclassified to something called a '*Waster*' and they were being rounded up for deportation. She was crying and she mumbled something about extermination, not deportation. I was sure she was wrong but when a man tried to escape a *Federale* shot him, shot him dead. I left as quickly as I could. But, as I was leaving, I saw one of the women on the porch wearing Rhonda's homemade skirt. The woman refused to say where she got it, but she was plenty scared.

"I was getting into my car when a *Federale* officer asked for my identification. He let me go, but before I left, he warned me to forget ever being there. I was desperate to find my cousins so as soon as I got back to school I contacted your agent, the one who hired me last year. He offered to pay for my services again this year. I desperately needed the money; the trip to California depleted everything I had set aside. But, that's when I made a mistake. I asked him if he could check on the whereabouts of my cousins. I gave him pictures and other information. He told me to stay away from you until they reviewed my request. I wanted to see you, but he was Secret Service. What could I do?

"The next day, the agent called and told me to come to his office in the Village. When I arrived, I was confronted by two men and a woman officer. The woman told me to forget about my cousins, they were, in her words, *unfindable*. That's when I made another mistake. I was angry. I told them about us and said the President would help me if she didn't.

"Howie, don't look at me like that. I had to do something, they're my family and they were in trouble. The woman officer—she was pretty even though her face was all scarred up-anyway, she locked me up and then they interrogated me. They can do that, you know, for no reason. I threatened to call my consulate, but they just kept asking me questions about someone named Omar Smith and Rey Diaz, names I didn't know. When I couldn't answer, they beat me. They kept beating me."

Henrietta turned away but refused to cry. She put her hand up to cover her eyes but pulled them away, almost angrily. "Before the officer let me go, she told me I couldn't see you anymore. I didn't know what to do so I hid in Ronald's housing project, hoping he'd come back but he didn't. Whatever happened to my cousins Poppy and Deirdre must have happened to Ronald and Rhoda too."

"She beat you?" Howard asked. Hen nodded. "She'll be one sorry officer because of what she did. She's going to jail when I tell my father-"

"You can't. You just can't," she shrugged, defeated.

"So you came here."

"What else could I do? They know I'm in New York so I don't think I'll be able to leave the country without your help. Howie, I'm scared." She hugged him again.

"I don't want to lose you, Hen, but I'll do whatever you want. If you need money, I'll get it. If you want me to drive you somewhere, I will. I'd drive you all the way to Barbuda if I could. We can live there, together."

She pointed to the door where the agents stood guard. "Howie, it's not that easy. Besides, I have another problem you haven't noticed."

He looked at her again. Confused, he just shrugged.

"I'm pregnant."

He was speechless.

"I'm pregnant, Howie, it's our baby. What should I do?" She threw her arms over his shoulders and sobbed anew.

He held her. As sad as she was when she stepped back, he squealed with delight and gently kissed her stomach. He'd never been this happy in his entire life. Whatever problems existed, for the moment, they were gone. "I love you. I'll drop out and work so we can raise the baby right."

"Howie, don't. Think of your position, your father's position, and my situation. I don't know what to do. I know I love you, but I have to leave."

"You look so tired. Get some rest and we'll figure it out later."

She was too exhausted to argue so he helped her to the bedroom where she fell asleep immediately. He walked back into the living room, dismissed the agents and locked the front door. Worn out, he climbed into bed beside her and quickly fell asleep.

He was startled awake by the sound of thunder and heavy rain, but what startled him more was that someone was inside his apartment. While Henrietta continued to sleep soundly beside him, he stared at the unwelcome apparition. The incongruence of the situation made him think he was still dreaming so he closed his eyes. Someone kicked him and he opened his eyes again. The vision was still there, it wasn't a dream. Andrew Crelli stood before him, buckled into a long, black leather trench coat.

Trying not to wake Henrietta, Howard got out of bed, carefully. Crelli motioned for him to be quiet and pointed to the living room. He settled into a chair and motioned for his bodyguards, who were standing at attention near the front door, to leave. When they were alone, Crelli began.

"Howard, it's sure nice to see you again. Glad you're enjoying the local trim. Good for you." He laughed pleasantly. "You've come a long way from that lost little boy who hid in the Bush bedroom playing computer games all day."

While at the White House, Howard had been scared of Andrew Crelli, always hiding or finding excuses to leave the room whenever he appeared. Now, facing a waking nightmare, he stared at the floor as Crelli spoke.

"Your father has so much on his plate that sometimes I help out with certain things he doesn't have time for. As you probably know, we have a problem."

"We, Sir?"

"You, me, your dad and the trollop in the other room, we have a problem."

"Hen? She's my girlfriend. I love her."

"That's utterly ridiculous. Too much has gone on for that."

"You're wrong. I really do love her."

"I have some advice for you, Howard. Don't fall in love. It'll only disappoint you. And the disappointment this time is that that sweet girl in your bed is a member of a terrorist group that is plotting to overthrow your father's government."

He stared at Crelli, not comprehending.

"You were never very bright. Do you want me to repeat what I said?"

"No, you're wrong. Hen's a student here at NYU and we love each other."

"Concentrate, boy. I know this is difficult for you, but remember who I am. My people are here to take her into custody. She will answer for her actions."

"What does that mean?"

"The little trick is going to jail. Then, she'll be convicted of treason and executed."

That, Howard understood. He forced himself to face Crelli's withering stare. "You can't do that, sir. Hen is innocent. She's just a student here."

Crelli just smiled, enjoying the cruelty he levied at will. "I'll speak to my father. He won't let it happen. He's the President, and you're not. You won't dare hurt her," Howard said defiantly.

Crelli continued to smile. "Are you threatening me? That's a surprise. It doesn't matter. Your father will do nothing. She's coming with me now."

"You can't take her. I won't let you. She's pregnant!"

That caused Crelli to pause and reconsider, "Not yours, I hope."

He balled his hands into fists, but Andy's guards quickly stepped into the apartment and closed around him. Crelli waved them off.

"Of course the baby's Howard's," replied a weary female voice from the bedroom. Henrietta walked directly over to Howard and grasped his hand. Together they confronted the former President of the United States.

"I'm five months pregnant, sir. The baby is Howard's. You can run tests if you want. They'll prove we're telling the truth."

Crelli turned to an officer standing outside, "Read this woman her rights and let's go."

Howard shouted, "You can't do that. She's having my baby." He tried to stop them from taking her, but physically, he wasn't up to the task. He was efficiently immobilized with a kick to the stomach. As he doubled over and fell to the ground, he let go of Henrietta's hand and they dragged her away. Writhing on the ground in pain, he shouted, "I'll save you, Hen. You didn't do anything wrong."

"I was only trying to find my relatives," she pleaded. "That's not a crime."

The security guards took her away, but before Crelli could follow, Howard reached up and grabbed hold of the hem of Crelli's leather trench coat. "My father will never agree to this. He'll straighten it out. You'll be sorry you picked on us."

Crelli yanked his coat free and marched out of the apartment without looking back. Howard was alone. He tried to contact his father, but couldn't get through to him. It was late the following day before Mark returned his call. By then, Howard was hysterical.

Chapter 10
Angel Falls—2070

Once again, Gil didn't know what to make of Mark's story. He had wanted to know more about his father, but he could not have anticipated such an appalling tale. He was extremely uncomfortable with the story and genuinely sad as he pictured his father enduring the events that Mark had just described. He was angry too. First it had been Bernie's wife and daughter, and now his own mother. The agony endured by Gil's family at Andrew Crelli's hands was immeasurable. Finally, he had the answer as to why Bernie was adamant that he learn about the past.

"You were the president," Gil said to Mark as if it was the answer to an unasked question.

Mark looked down and responded, "Yes, but Andy had the power."

"Tell me that you did something. Howard is your son. She was my mother. Certainly you knew that someday you and I would be discussing this."

Mark didn't respond immediately. The lines on his face and the sadness in his eyes reflected the anguish of decisions made and not made, and the regret from the consequences of both.

"She was my mother!" Gil yelled. Still Mark remained silent. "You did nothing." Gil exclaimed. "Bernie lectures me all the time about how important family is. How could you allow it? Why didn't you stop it? Why weren't you heroic? Bernie said you were the brightest, the best, and that there was a time when you wanted to help people. What happened to you? Where did you go wrong? You built *Wharton Towns* to help people. I don't understand. Why did he have me save you if you allowed this to happen? She was my mother, Mark. The girl your son loved. How can Bernie stand to look at you? I . . . what part of right and wrong didn't they teach you in those fancy schools you went to?" Mark remained silent. "Bernie describes our family as close. Was he making that up, too?"

"I did what I did."

"Or didn't do?"

"Okay, or didn't do," Mark agreed. "In all the years since, while I was incarcerated, don't you think I asked myself the same questions? I reviled myself the same way you're reviling me now? You wanted to hear the story and this is it and I have a lot more to be ashamed about than this. I'd gladly not think about it at all, but Dad insisted that I tell you if you asked. I can't change it. This is what happened."

"You mean it gets worse? What haven't you told me?"

Mark's face turned a sickly pale.

"I want to hear all of it."

Silence.

"You can't stop now."

More silence.

Gil stared into his grandfather's dead, lifeless eyes. "Please," he said gently, "I have the right to know and you're the only one who can tell me."

Unblinking, Mark looked at him and nodded. "Dad insisted that I do this for all of us, but it's hard, harder than I thought."

Mark continued in a voice wounded by self-loathing and he started where he seemed the least uncomfortable. "Everyone knows commercialism overwhelmed American society, but no one ever discusses how it happened. Every interpersonal relationship, what we say, how we say it and to whom, and what we don't say, how we react, all was once the province of family and neighborhoods. But once money and the media took over, most people grew up so deeply influenced by the media, twenty four/seven that they learned their behavior directly from it. People were commercialized. We learned first from newspapers, magazines, and books and then from radio, the movies, TV, video games and advanced media. We learned how to be cool because the moneyed interests had something cool for everyone. The dirty little secret was that the brand was us.

"Human comedies and dramas were created for public consumption and resolved with advertising messages imbedded throughout. Good and bad behavior was defined by the advertisers and the most productive view of good was confirmed, over and over again. No one asked why the advertisers chose their 'good' over some other good to proselytize, because the media understood what they were selling and they required profits to reward their management and to satisfy their stockholders. They knew what they were selling."

Gil remembered Bernie's rants about something similar.

"There wasn't a human condition, no matter how unlikely, that wasn't reproduced ad nauseam in the media until everyone bought into their life roles. As people grew up, their choices narrowed until most simply chose their role in life from the few available. The media demonstrated what the most appropriate way to be was, and everyone became indoctrinated in a commercial world of someone else's making.

"Behavior was reinforced by celebrities, advertising front-men and women whose lifestyles were mimicked because people saw these celebrities as heroes in so many of the situations they aspired to-fame, sex, money, lifestyle, you name it. Celebrities were the puppets of industry who became the puppeteers for mankind."

"Mark, that is all well and good, but I have to know what happened to my mother, please."

Mark continued to avoid answering. "Before leaving office in 2040, Andy signed an Anti-Terrorist Act that included Universal Identification Addendum Fifteen. It required a permanent two-way, low-frequency, universal identification chip be imbedded in everyone, starting immediately with infants and systematically progressing until everyone was chipped.

"Another innocuous act was funded in that same bill. Government research had successfully developed a procedure—I think it was a protein modification. Anyway, it altered brain chemistries in a way that created more balanced, quiescent behavior in emotionally unbalanced people. When the product was commercialized, the results were analyzed and further refinements were funded. It wasn't long before behavior became more predictable. That was all that Andy needed to direct funding that modified specific behavior based on what a team of social demographers employed in the government felt would improve work force efficiency. Don't look at me that way; we were living in desperate times. Among other sins, sloth and attention deficit were destroying our workforce. The research was productive and specific behavioral characteristics, or tendencies, were permanently altered to improve employee productivity."

"Why would they do that?"

"Our survival depended on economic recovery, and achieving that was paramount in everything we did. We were fighting for our lives and too many people just didn't get it. They were living in America's past and that was too high a risk to the country. We tried everything to make them accept economic realities. It was that, or make them disappear.

"To make matters worse, people were goaded by rebel groups; some of the rebels were lawyers who were eventually convinced that they had too much to lose, but there were some groups, like the one Dad was involved with, who were continually frustrating Andy's attempts at recovery. Later, another group led by an Islamic Fundamentalist Terrorist named Omar Smith created so much chaos that we were forced to use more advanced technologies to eliminate their supply of recruits."

"Mark, I appreciate the history lesson, I do, but where is this leading?"

Mark just continued. "Everything we did was cost-justified, but with welfare and other entitlements eliminated, we faced allegiance issues among at-risk citizens. The *Circle of Life* laws eliminated much of that noise, but you can never totally eliminate everyone who opposes you. We began, certain of ourselves and what we were doing, and we continued until everyone was converted, pacified, or eliminated. President Franklin Roosevelt faced a similar situation more than a century before and Andy was a big believer in Roosevelt. Roosevelt understood that for America to survive and prosper there could never be a critical mass of people who had nothing left to lose, because they became the kindling for revolution.

"By the end of Tanya's presidency, resistance came to a head. Reduced to their true believers, and with Omar Smith coordinating, various terrorists groups launched simultaneous offensives on many of our production towns. They were defeated easily enough, but they went underground and what followed was a period where costly, random unrest percolated throughout the economy. That's when Congress—Andy, really—passed a bill requiring obstetricians and pediatricians to treat infants and the newly born using the recently developed personality altering chemistries. Again, it was cost-justified and a clear winner, so I signed it. The Bureau of Labor Standards monitored programs that were in place when you were born. With those treatments, along with *Virtuoso*, Archive, and the *Circle of Life* laws, resistance disappeared and America prospered.

"Mark." Gil reiterated, "I want to know about my mother."

Mark put his hand up to stop Gil. "Andy always saw the big picture better than anyone."

"I never had those treatments."

"I'm getting to that. Your mother was in prison and your birth was imminent when I ordered Andy to the White House. He didn't have to come, but he did. I was in my last year as president, 2051 actually, and it was Christmas. Andy entered the Oval Office like he owned the place—which by then he did. Even the secretaries deferred to him."

CHAPTER 11
Washington, D.C. – 2051

"Andy, thanks for coming," Mark said as he rose from his seat behind the executive desk, and walked over to greet his friend and mentor. "We need resolve the situation with Howard."

"We've been through this. There are far too many security issues to deal with for me to be spending this much time worrying about one case. One that's already been resolved, might I add. Your idiot kid's playmate will be executed. The media's clamoring for it and the public wants evidence that it's not just the little people who're being punished. The girl must be made an example of to prove we're fair and square about defeating terrorism."

"This isn't about terrorism and you know it. The media's only interest is ratings, like always and Howard's girlfriend isn't some terrorist getting away with a crime against the nation. She didn't even commit one, I checked. This is about you. Tell me why you're doing this and let's resolve it."

"You were loyal, once," Crelli said, a hint of disappointment in his voice.

"I'm still loyal, but sometimes my view of what's best for America doesn't coincide with yours. I'm the President. You need to respect my decisions like I respected yours. Jesus, Andy, this is family. It doesn't make me disloyal."

"Like the Rose family has been so loyal. Let's not get into your father again, god damn it. It seems that now that you're where you've always wanted to be, you've lost your commitment to America."

"What kind of statement is that?"

"As I remember, committing to America is part of your swearing-in speech."

"Andy, I know my job. Now, about Howard and Henrietta-"

"She will be executed."

"If you fight me, I'll pardon her," Mark said, defiantly.

Andy moved behind Mark's desk and sat in his executive chair idly opening and closing the drawers. "You could do that. Yes, you could. And she'd go free. Of course the media might rally the public against your rash, selfish act. And the Congress might have some laws in the works that could alter your power to do that. And hell, while we're speculating, the Court might rule to negate your action outright or the Congress might also, I forget how I worded it. Any number of things will happen if you fight me on this and it will get ugly. Given the country's fear of terrorism, this might not be a good time to test resolves. Trust me on this; you don't want the public unsure if their leader has been turned by the enemy. Think of the consequences for the programs you campaigned for, ones you've been trying to pass to educate the underachieving. They will never become law. Now, I'm against the government getting involved in helping people who won't help themselves, but I'm prepared to move out of the way, even though some would say that it's the first step of the return to socialism.

"Think about it, Mark. Freeing the girl will piss off all those people who campaigned hard for you. Is your son's island *hootchie mama* really worth that?"

"That's enough, Andy. I don't understand you. Why this? Why her? Why is she this important?"

"She broke the law."

"People break the law everyday and don't get executed."

"Your information on that is out of date."

"This isn't the same. I know I haven't put up much of a fight in the past, but on this I will. I have to. It's too close to home. I'll pardon her and let the chips fall. Do your worst. Once I get my family out of harms way, I'm prepared to give up power. If you want the presidency back, take it. Just give me my family."

Crelli applauded politely. "That's a great plan. Do you really want to push me? And as for getting the presidency back, I don't want it—it's nothing. It was nothing when Tanya had it and now it's worth even less with you. This insignificant little girlfriend your son is screwing is what is important. Once she's executed, the media is geared up to generate heart-felt stories of your patriotism and sacrifice. You will become a legend, a deeply disillusioned and saddened great American hero who made the greatest sacrifice of all to save his country. Our citizens will know how far we will go to eradicate an implacable enemy who attempts to infiltrate the highest power in the land, and that the guilty, regardless of their connections, their station in life, or their family pedigree will be punished, with prejudice and without exception. It will be great theater, possibly a movie deal is in the offing that should yield a great return. You know how much I value that."

"You're not doing this to make me a hero."

"Mark, you've been at this long enough. If you can't figure out my end game, give it up and stop playing. But before you do, consider this? If you call my bluff and pardon her, I'm certain no matter how hard we try to protect that poor, unfortunate girl—and Ginger, she's such a sweetheart, has gladly volunteered to help—when Henrietta Boyar is freed, you can put your money on some irate cracker finding her and your son, and exacting the kind of retribution that, well, let's just speculate further that could make you eternally sorry you didn't allow her execution. Either way, Henrietta Boyar is out of the equation as they say. My way, everyone benefits. Well, almost everyone."

"Ginger volunteered?" Mark asked in disbelief.

"Yes, she was very enthusiastic."

Mark searched carefully for his next words. "Is there any way I can convince you to set her free and let her be?"

"When I was elected, I told you that I owed you. I keep my promises. Tell me the truth right now and maybe we can fix this."

He looked at Andy, hopefully. "What truth?"

"About the baby."

"What baby?"

"It has come to my attention that Howard's child hasn't received the prescribed in vitro behavior modification treatments. How do you suppose that was overlooked, unless, of course, you gave the order?"

Mark was taken aback. "Andy, I didn't know. You must believe that. With everything going on, I haven't given any thought to the child. It was probably red tape or carelessness or maybe an accident? How could it be overlooked? She was in a prison."

"So you see my concern. That's why my hands are tied. You know the law. Any child born unmodified simply isn't viable and must be terminated . . ."

" . . . along with the child's parents," Mark said. Horrified, he slumped into a nearby chair. Not just Henrietta, Howard and the child were going to die. "Andy, please, no. I swear Howard had nothing to do with this. How could he? You know he's slow and doesn't have any friends to help him. For God's sake, help me out here. All my years of loyal service should count for something."

"I'm not saying Howard had anything to do with it."

"You think it was me? Andy, I swear-"

Crelli didn't respond. "Then who?" he asked, the look on Crelli's face saying it all.

"No, he's dead. How could my father be involved? Not after all this time."

"Reno Soren should have taken care of him but he didn't and now, with your father alive, everything you've lived for is about to be destroyed—including your family, it seems. It's not as if losing Howard is a sorry waste of potential, but there's nothing I can do."

"Andy, please, you can't kill them. I'll do anything."

"I know." That's when Andy played his cards. "There's a solution that could save your family but, before I discuss it, the status of the girl is off the table." Helpless, Mark nodded. "I've been funding research on a top secret cloning technology project. I'll agree to provide access to this technology for the baby, but if it works, the clone baby will be modified."

"We have cloning technology?" Mark asked, shocked.

"If this test works, it's ready to be commercialized."

"Why don't I know about it, and how do I know it works?"

"You don't know because it's none of your business. Whether it works or not, we're here to find out."

"Can you clone Howard's girlfriend with the technology?"

Andy laughed. "Cloning the baby should work. We'll do it soon and there won't be much age difference. If you clone the girl, she won't be much of a sex partner for your son or a mother for the baby for almost two decades, unless Howard likes them young." With that, Crelli stood to leave. "This is the deal."

"And Howard is safe too."

Andy nodded.

"I don't understand, why this? Why now?"

"I have my reasons. What do you say?"

"How can I make this decision?"

"How can you not? The girl and the real child die anyway, that's the law. You can fight for their lives, but you'll lose and have nothing to show for it, I promise you. At least this way you keep your son and he gets a baby if that's what he really wants."

"I can't do it," Mark said.

"Then call Howard and give him the choice."

"I can't do that either. I can't ask him to be a part of his lover's death and his own baby's execution? God knows what that'll do to him."

"Agree Mark, and you'll be a grandfather and your boy will have something to remind him of the advantages of protected sex. So what will it be, Mr. President."

"Andy, as the president, I can't order someone to be murdered or even executed and certainly not my own family. We have laws. What you're asking, it's obscene. There must be another way. Give me some time, I'll figure out a way that works. You know me. You know I always come up with an angle no one else has thought of."

"Mark, I'm leaving the White House with my mind unchanged. The baby, the father, and the girl are enemies of the state and they must be executed."

"I can't. What you're asking is wrong, it's inhuman. I can't live with that guilt?"

"You are president, you don't do guilt. We orchestrated the *Circle of Life* campaign not because it was right, but because it was necessary. Think how many families were eliminated and then the good it did and continues to do. There's no guilt there, and this thing with that girl is like that. I came to you with a proposal that I thought was quite satisfactory. What's it going to be? It's up to you, Mr. President."

He couldn't do it. Frantically, he considered who he could confide in, who he could trust, who would support him in his time of need and that's when he realized that he was quite alone. He was the President of the United States and yet he was isolated from the world. There was no one to take his side, no one to help him work this out, to help him convince Andy that it was a grave mistake. He had wanted this job so much-too much, and now that he had it, he was utterly alone. He wiped the sweat from his brow.

"God forgive me. Andy, what happens now?"

Andy smiled. "God, as you well know, has very little to do with it. I want to hear nothing more about the girl. As to the cloning, my scientists are chomping at the bit. I'll tell them to begin working on it, while my marketing team plants stories of an impending, high-value scientific advancement in the journals."

"What do I tell Howard?"

"Tell Howard whatever you want."

"But how?"

"I don't give a fuck," Crelli said. "You're in charge, say something presidential." With that, he opened the door from the Oval Office and stepped through. Before closing it, he turned back. "One more thing, once the girl is executed, the ordeal of the presidency will be too much for you to handle. You'll announce your retirement at the end of your first term and support legislation I've been developing concerning the succession. You will not run again."

Defeated and deflated, Mark nodded.

Long after Andy left, Mark sat at his desk composing himself for a dreaded discussion with Howard. When his son arrived, he explained that he was unable to save Henrietta. Howard cried, pleaded, and begged him to do something, anything, insisting, again, that she was innocent. Mark listened in silence. Frustrated and hysterical, Howard went berserk and tried to assault him, knocking him down, but before he could do more, a security team entered and immobilized him. With agents now surrounding their president, Howard lay curled in a fetal position on the Presidential Seal, sobbing hysterically.

Mark had no words of comfort but Howard found the strength to stand, and through his tears, he looked past the security guards to his father. "If you allow this, you don't love me. You never loved me." With that, Howard was escorted from the Oval Office.

The execution was scheduled to commence shortly after Henrietta was to give birth. Mark permitted Howard to see her one last time the night before the execution.

He entered a bare, dimly lit cell in the lowest basement of the Federal prison where Henrietta was being held and waited for her to be brought to him. When the door opened a security officer entered and searched Howard again. Satisfied that it was safe, the officer signaled and another guard brought the condemned woman into the room. Gaunt, unkempt, exhausted, and in chains, Henrietta shuffled in like an old woman. As she got closer, he saw she was suffering from new bruises. Head down, she ambled slowly to him. He reached out and held her carefully, supporting her weight and trying to transfer his strength to her.

"Howie..." was all she could say in a low, slow-slurring, almost-mumble. Her happy sing-song voice was a long-gone, and unhappy memory.

He struggled, swallowing the pain. "I can't-"

"Howie, be strong. I love you. You know that?"

"I love you, too, but this hurts so much. I can't lose you."

"You're not losing me. You have our son."

He cried more at that. "He's beautiful. He looks like you. He will always remind me of you."

She stared down at her feet, too exhausted to sit, so he helped her onto a chair. "Howie, I miss him already. They took him from me right after he was born. Can you ask them to bring him back to me before . . . ?" He continued to cry. "Are you sure he's okay?"

"Hen, he's the grandson of the president. They're taking great care of him."

She held on to him and leaned against his chest. "Howie, Call him Gilbert; it's my daddy's name. Could you do that?" He nodded.

Then she began to cry, pounding her face with her fists. "Why are they doing this? Why is everyone so hateful in this country? I don't want to die? I didn't do anything wrong. I want to see our boy grow up." She sobbed in his arms.

"I promise I'll get even for what they did to you . . . to us."

She hugged him as tight as her battered arms could, and they sobbed together until she summoned some inner strength to console him. "You can do this, Howie." She whispered. "Take care of my Gilbert, he needs you. They're mean, bad people; don't do anything to expose Gilbert or yourself. Protect him, Howie. Do whatever it takes, but you must protect him." Unable to speak, he nodded.

They sat holding each other and crying until the guard came to escort him out.

"Can't he stay a little longer?" she begged.

"That's all the time he's allowed, Miss."

The guard dragged Howard out as Henrietta hugged his leg tightly, refusing to let go. Another guard came in to separate them, but they fought to hold on to one another. Finally, they were pried apart and Howard was hauled out by two guards while Henrietta sat, sobbing helpless in a chair, another guard restraining her.

She screamed at him. "Howie, I'm so sorry. Tell Gilbert I love him. I love you."

He turned and stared through tear-filled eyes at his Henrietta until the door slammed shut.

Later that day, Henrietta had another visitor. It was one she did not expect. The President of the United States, flanked by armed Secret Service agents, stepped into her cell. He was shocked by her condition.

Though physically and mentally defeated, she was still defiant. "So you're Howie's father? Mr. President, I wish I could say it is an honor."

"What have they done to you? You were not supposed to be tortured."

"That's good to know, but I imagine what goes on in here requires the approval of the president."

"I didn't-"

" . . . didn't know that innocent people are dying? Apparently Howard isn't the only person that you are responsible for that you ignore."

"You have no right-."

"That's clear, I have no rights. I am innocent and going to die."

"Innocent people die sometimes, Henrietta. I'm sorry. It's hard. I'm doing the best I can."

"Then you've set your standards too low, Mr. President. If citizens—not just a president, but American citizens—know that innocent people are dying, they aren't being good enough citizens."

"I'm sorry I permitted you to help Howard at NYU. You wouldn't be in this position."

"No, I'm glad I agreed to help. Howie is the best thing . . ." She paused, gathering her strength. "Nothing you do . . ." She paused again. "I will not regret our time together."

"You love him?"

She bit off a scream and looked away. "Mr. President, I feel sorry for you. You must be a sad, empty man. Of course I love him."

"I never thought-"

"What? That your son could be loved?" she asked. "You are a cruel and uncaring man to think that of your son."

He looked at the floor. "You shouldn't have allowed yourself to get involved?"

"If that's your advice, it's far too late to do anyone any good. Howie is a better man than you'll ever be. I beg you, help him save our son." There was an uncomfortable silence before she started crying. "I'm begging you to save your own family."

"I've done everything I can . . ."

She smiled wearily through broken, yellowed teeth. Trembling, she struggled to stand so she could stare him in the eyes. "My family was in trouble and I tried my best to save them. In the eyes of your government, that made me a terrorist. You've done nothing to help your family and yet you are a patriot. I don't want to live in a land that has such values."

He thought about the deaths of sister, Franki, and his mother. It hurt and he fought tears. "Ms. Boyar, I'm not the enemy."

"From where I am, that's exactly who you are. Look what you've done. Good people living free are dying for a lie. America is a bad country ruled by bad people."

"I'm sorry, Henrietta, I really am. I will help your baby. We have some time. Tell me about you and Howard?" Contempt showed in her battered eyes and she just stared at him incredulously through blood shot eyes.

"Please, tell me . . . for Gilbert," he asked again.

She told Mark their story in a sad, broken voice. When she was done, he could only stare at this woman that, as the leader of the free world, and as a father and grandfather, he had failed so badly. In a fog of melancholy, he thought back to a piece of advice Andy had once given him when he was young.

"The inevitable outcome of failure," Andy had said, "is a very sad story. Do everything in your power to avoid sad stories."

CHAPTER 12
Angel Falls, ME—2070

The cabin was dark when Marks finished his story. Tears welled in both Mark's and Gil's eyes as they each relived that horrific past. If Mark craved relief, Gil was unable to offer it. His tears were righteous so he waited as Mark struggled on.

"She told me things about Howard that I didn't know," Mark said. "She'd known him barely a year, yet she knew him better than I ever had. Sometimes, I think back to the early days when Terry and I were young. I've lost. I let love and family slip away. Later . . . after I left her cell, they came . . . they came for her."

"How do you live with yourself?"

"I try not to."

"What did Howard do?"

"I don't know. I never saw him again. He stayed in New York. The clone child, that's you, was ready less than a year later. Howard received his degree in accounting, of all things—basic accounting."

"Then what happened?"

"Nothing."

"When I came to the mansion, you said your wife was dead. How did that happen?"

"No, I've said enough. I'm ashamed of it, but I told you the truth. There are some things too private. I won't say more."

"I want to hear all of it, Mark. I deserve to hear it all."

"Leave me the rest, please."

"Is anyone in this world honest and decent? Is it all cheating and lying, greed and self-interest, from people who consider themselves decent folks? I don't understand. Explain to me what bad people are like if good people act like you? It's no wonder everyone uses *Virtuoso*; reality like this is too tough to live with."

"I'm weak. I made horrible mistakes."

"And I want to hear it all. Tell me about my grandmother. I want to know, I deserve to know how love ends."

Deflated and lost in thought, Mark stared at the floor while toying with his wedding band. Occasionally, an unguarded sob escaped, but he refused to look at Gil and he obviously didn't want to say more.

"Mark, this is my chance to understand all of it, or at least as much as I can. I need to know. Bernie is, well, you know, and in spite of this, you are still family. Please . . ." Gil waited. Mark remained silent, avoiding something that must have been even more painful than the pathetic story he had just told. "Mark, how much worse can it be?"

"I'm long past worrying about the worst," Mark said as he took a deep breath and let it out slowly. "I married Terry because I loved her, I really did. We spent our childhood together. She lost her mom and dad in an accident and lived with her aunt near us. She spent all of her time at our place. From grade school on, she was a fixture in our house. Mom and Dad loved her, and she was Franki's babysitter and grew to be her best friend." He paused. "God this is tough.

"Terry would look at me, sometimes . . . I don't know. She made me feel like what I was doing was noble and it had value. She was a great student, but she never seemed to mind that I won all the awards and got all the attention. She was happy just being with me. As the pressure increased, she was always there for me. It's what she did best and that's not slighting her other talents. God, I loved her. I'm so-"

Gil had seen Bernie depressed while recalling stories of how the world had changed, but he was never quite as miserable as what Mark was now. He would have been concerned, but that was too much to ask for after what he had just heard.

" . . . whether it was fishing off the dock at our Geist estate, or helping me prepare for an important presentation, she was there," Mark continued. "I never considered that she wouldn't be, and I knew from the beginning that I would marry her. Maybe that's why things didn't work out. Maybe it's the possibility of losing someone that makes love adhesive. Maybe . . . not, I don't know.

"She never insisted, but she knew we'd be married, too. When I traveled, even for long periods, she was there when I returned. For my part, whatever I did when I was away, whatever opportunities were presented, nothing felt right without her. I guess we were both waiting for me—she at home and me, wherever school or my job took me.

"When I graduated from Indiana University and decided not to go to graduate school, she was supportive. When I decided to take Andy's offer, she promised to wait and she did. You could never sell her loyalty short. She waited even when Mom and Dad were pissed because I royally screwed up our big engagement party."

"What did she think of Crelli?" Gil asked.

"She was excited for me. She knew how good I could be, and even though she was nervous and awkward around Andy and his friends, she persevered for my sake. When we got back together and moved to Northern Kentucky, she worked hard to get along with Andy's wife Maddie and her friends even though she was far too uncomplicated and nice for them to ever appreciate. I'll say this for Maddie, she tried. But Maddie and her friends were Type-A social and political types with no frame of reference to relate to someone like Terry. When we were together, she lived a kind of lonely splendor.

"I was on the road most of the time and when I was at the office, I worked late. In the early years, she'd wait for me to come home and I'd find her asleep on the couch by the door so she could hear when I came in. We . . . I tried to stay focused on our relationship, but the pressures of my job overwhelmed us–no, it overwhelmed me. I was so absorbed, and Andy was such a relentless taskmaster, along the way, we got lost. No, I lost her. I've asked myself when and how it happened."

"But you never asked her?"

"I couldn't bear to hear her tell me when her love for me turned into something less. Eventually, we separated. She didn't want to, but it was for the best. After those early few years before Howard was born, she was . . . I don't know, empty and lost, and we just stopped working at it. She asked me once if I wanted an emotionally satisfying relationship. I was busy and didn't think about it at the time, but I've had cause to think about my answer since. I told her I was content with the way things were and didn't want the extra demands of that type of relationship."

"Why hurt her if you didn't have to?

"You're young and full of yourself. You haven't had the chance to make big life mistakes yet. You will. We all do, and when you do, you'll see it differently. I do.

"Not long after we separated that first time, at the engagement party, she came back to help me through a very bad time. That was when Mom and Franki were murdered. Terry was amazing. She dropped everything and came down, no questions asked. I was spent and she breathed purpose back into my life."

"So what went wrong?" Gil asked.

"Jesus, I told you about Tanya, that was part of it. There were so many things like that—I don't mean the sex, I never cheated on Terry, never. But I was called on by Andy and Tanya to do things, things that had Terry known, she never would have stayed. Every relationship reaches a point where inertia takes over. You can only hope you're pointed in the right direction when it happens. We weren't."

"So you loved her," Gil began. "But over time, when things got in the way, you didn't love her anymore?"

"I suppose it's something like that. We tried to be considerate of each other and we never stopped caring—I believe that. Like everything in life, if you want to succeed, you work at it, but sometimes no matter how hard you work, it doesn't. As I said, I got lost . . ."

"Is that why people don't marry anymore?"

"I suppose. But the biggest reason is economics. I hurt Terry so much, but in the end, I stayed because I didn't think she'd be able to survive on her own. If there was a chance for us, it occurred before you were born, when Andy asked me to be president. Terry could have refused. Things would have been so different if only she had stood up to me and said the hard things that needed to be said. She didn't and that was the beginning of our end."

CHAPTER 13

Washington, DC—2047

It was the pivotal point of his life. Mark entered Terry's bedroom cautiously. When he didn't see her, he relaxed but he relaxed too soon. She pranced out of her overlarge, walk-in closet wearing only her bra and panties, and holding earrings to each ear. She hadn't seen him so he paused to collect himself before approaching her. This had to be handled just so. When she turned, she was equally surprised to see him.

"We need to talk, Terry."

"You'll have to hurry; I have reservations in twenty minutes at the new Persian restaurant. Do you like my earrings? I purchased them at *To Buy For*, they're originals."

"You shouldn't be seen at a Persian restaurant. You know the paparazzi. Who are you going with?"

"Don't be silly, I'll be seen wherever I go. How can I not, I live in your reflected glory. What can I do? I'll be damned if I have to forego a chance to experience a new hot spot just because your Government has a problem with Iran. That's between your boss and Teheran's mullahs, not me and some local Persian restaurateur. I'm meeting some of the girls. Why? Who do you think I'd be going with?"

"Don't be cute, Terry. The media will make a big deal out of it, that's all. Tanya's threatening Iran again and you're eating at a restaurant owned by Iranians. I don't know, but I think that will attract eyeballs and advertising, don't you? Look, I'm not here to discuss your dinner reservation, there's something more important on the table."

"On the table, oh, we're going to have another political discussion, great. Like I said, Mark, I'm here for you." She looked at the Byzantine clock on the wall. "But I have to go soon."

"Terry, please don't be difficult."

"I'm never difficult, Mark, that's your strength. Has Andy told you to be nice to me? It sounds like he has. Maybe it would be simpler if you stepped aside and let Andy tell me directly what he wants?"

"Stop it, Terry. This is important."

"For who? I already have a lovely house, a husband with a prestigious job as a toady for a great man, and I have accounts at every store in Washington. On top of that, I receive the full-time attention of some of the best-looking bodyguards from Tanya's stable of time tested testosterone. What more do I need?"

"You're being disgusting. That's enough."

"You're right, Mark, I'm sorry." She sat on the bed, legs curled under, staring intently at him. "I'm listening."

"I know you won't like it, but just give me a chance to explain first."

"Mark, the time," she reminded him, pointing at the clock. "What is it you want to tell me?"

"It's finally my time." He smiled. "I'm going to run for president. Andy made the decision this morning and he wants me to discuss it with you."

"If he hadn't asked, would you have discussed it with me on your own?"

"Of course."

"Thanks for that kindness. I'd owe you one, but who beside you keeps track? It's your career; do whatever Andy wants. I'm flattered you'd ask my opinion, even though you won't consider it unless I agree with you."

"That's not fair. I value what you have to say. This is a family decision."

"Is that what 'Randy Andy' said would work with me? Like he ever discusses anything with Maddie."

"Terry, let's keep Andy and Maddie out of this. Boy, are you in some kind of mood."

"If you don't know why, I can show you my scrapbooks."

"Terry, stop it. I need your help here."

"You have Tanya. You don't need my opinion."

"God damn it, I don't care what you think you know. I didn't sleep with her, or any other woman for that matter. I don't want to get into this again, particularly now. I'm still angry because you believe that crap. When I heard that absurd rumor that you were sleeping with Tanya, I laughed. Can't you see how ridiculous it is?"

"Sweetheart, for the third most important member of our government, you are such a tool. Why would I believe something about you that I know you're incapable of?"

"I don't know. I think you've lost faith in me."

"Enough. You're incapable of any perspective but your own."

"We have to resolve this; there's a great deal of preparation required. Will you campaign with me? Are you willing to endure the microscope of a presidential election campaign again, and then live four or eight years together in the White House?"

"Do we have to live them together? I mean Tanya didn't have just one man for her eight years at the White House, why should I?"

"God damn it, Terry."

"Run. Howard's a teenager and I have little else to do. It could be fun."

"It isn't going to be fun. There's a lot of hard work and . . ."

"Have you totally forgotten your negotiating skills? You just got a yes. Turn and go, Mr. President, turn and go."

"We should talk about the details?"

"You can take care of the details. Just make sure they provide me with the best looking security men and that someone tells me where I need to be and what I need to say and make sure nobody tries to tell me how I should feel. Do that and I'm onboard, Captain." She saluted.

"Do you have to taunt me all the time?"

"Why do you stay with me?"

"Because you love me."

She laughed and left the room.

After the election, Terry fled to Indiana, as far away from Washington as she could go. When Henrietta was tried and executed, she avoided him and the media. Then one day, near the end of his term, she made an appointment to visit the White House. She entered the Oval Office, without makeup, wearing overalls and boots.

"Mark, you should know, Howard and I are going back to Indiana."

"He'd go with you?"

"Not easily. Like everything in this family it was a difficult. Tanya found him a job at ANGST."

"I can't believe he accepted Tanya's assistance but not mine."

"I guess he was desperate but not quite that desperate."

"When do you leave?"

"You're giving the commencement speech at Howard's school. Please stay away from us. The only thing Howard and I agree on these days is that we don't want to see you ever again so his graduation will not be a family event. Am I clear?"

"If that's what he wants?"

"That's what he wants."

"Where will you live?"

"In my aunt's house for starters."

"And Howard?"

"Tanya pulled some strings. He and Gilbert, oh, did you know your grandson was finally released from the Infant's Division of Crelli Children's Hospital? What a chilling name for a children's hospital."

"How is he?"

"The hospital says everything is normal."

"Howard doesn't want me to know where he's staying does he?"

"You can find out if you want, but Howard thinks his only chance to not see you is for you to have to find him on your own."

"What'll you do?"

"You mean to make money so I don't become a celebrity *Waster*?"

"I don't like it when you talk that way."

"Duly noted, sir," she said. "I'm opening a little vintage retail shop in Zionsville. I'll stock it from my wardrobe. I bought damn near everything there is to buy, so I should do well just with that."

"You'll be assigned a security detail." She began to protest, but he held his hand up to stop her. "Terry, you're still the wife of the President and there are people out there who'll try to get to me through you."

She frowned. "I don't want security. Please, Mark, do this one thing for me. If I'm ever taken hostage, let them kill me. You know you will anyway. And don't worry about Howard. What I can tell you is that he will be living in one of those new privately-controlled communities that are springing up all over the country on property that was once owned by *Wasters*. It's time to stop thinking about me, about us, if you ever did. I'll take my chances. I was never in the know, so I'm no use to anyone. Please respect my wishes."

Mark approached his wife to give her a hug but she stepped back and put her hand out to stop him. "I'm sorry that it's come to this." She shook his hand, nodded sadly, and turned to go.

"Good luck. If you or Howard need anything . . ."

She left the Oval Office without responding.

It was many years before he saw her again. By then, he had been banished to his Avalon, Indiana mansion where, late one night, there was a knock at the door, which was unusual since he wasn't allowed visitors. He opened the door and there she was. She looked worn and depleted in a filthy, old sweat suit. Seemingly weary of her life, her eyes were flat and dead, her skin grey, and her hair thin, dirty and disheveled.

"Terry?" he asked, dumbstruck by the sight of his ex-wife in her current state. "How did you . . . ? You look . . . you're . . . How are you?"

"May I come in?" she asked in a tiny, defeated voice as if expecting him to deny her.

"Of course," he said, stepping away to allow her to walk through the door. In the light of the foyer, Mark could see that she looked even worse. The sweet girl he fell in love with as a child had become a *Waster*. "What happened?"

She stared nervously outside until he closed the door. "You always said my spending habits would do me in. I've had a run of bad luck. I guess it shows. I set up my clothes shop in a solid middle class neighborhood in Zionsville but during the last national downsizing, the town emptied and my shop failed. It wasn't long before my nest egg from the divorce ran out and with HomeSec prowling, I had to find another way." She hesitated. "There's no real work anymore in town, so I found a job escorting important local politicians to events. I was desperate and your name still has some value here in town. I'm sorry but I had no choice. Don't ask. I looked better than I do now." She made a lame attempt to smooth down her hair and she laughed but didn't bother to explain why. "In time, the importance of the politicians I escorted declined as did the money they offered. I aged out of the job . . ."

"Terry, it's okay."

She smiled a timid, embarrassed smile, her hand covering her mouth. "I've come a long way, Mark, and I'm sorry I treated you the way I did at the end." He offered forgiveness and put his arms out to receive her, but she didn't want any part of either. Instead she shifted her weight, looking uncomfortable.

"Have you seen Howard?" he asked.

"Not in a very long time."

That surprised him. "Is he still in Aeden?"

She nodded. "He's moderately successful and Gilbert is doing okay from what little I can find out. Once or twice I tried to sync with our grandson in *Virtuoso*, but I'm on somebody's list and the Avatars know me. They killed my character every time before he and I could interact."

"I haven't seen him either," Mark admitted. She seemed relieved at that.

"Oh, Mark, the choices we make. I'm not allowed here, but . . ."

"It's good to see you," he said simply, and meant it.

"I hate to ask, but I need a place to stay. I promise I'll be less trouble than before. It's just that . . ." She crumpled into the closest chair and cried, silent at first, and then loud. He didn't know what to do so he just sat beside her and waited. When he put his hand on her shoulder, she shrugged it off. He wanted to embrace her and comfort her, but he just sat and waited. Soon, she stopped crying and fell asleep.

It was very late in the evening when she woke him. She was sitting on the side of his bed, staring at him, looking sad. "Will it be all right if I stay?"

"Stay as long you want. They don't check my accounts anymore."

She was grateful. "You can't survive without a source of income. So many have—disappeared, that's what they call it-and I've done things. I lack marketable skills. Oh, Mark, when we were young, if I had known I'd be like this today . . . I've done nasty, vile things to survive. I've been arrested a few times, but someone intervened. Was it you?" He shook his head. "Then, it was Tanya."

"She always liked you."

"No she didn't. She's not capable of like."

"Then she did it for the same reason Andy keeps me here. They want Dad and his rebel gang and we're bait."

She nodded. "That sounds right." Together, they laughed the wretched laugh of the used and then she cried again. He tried to comfort her. For all his mistakes, here was one he could try to set right.

He took her in and they lived together—not happily, because too much had happened, and too much had been lost. But they shared each other's company when no one else wanted them. When she died, less than a year before Gil had rescued him, Mark was with her, providing what little medicine his worth could afford.

After her death, he retreated into the recesses of his Avalon mansion prison waiting, without hope, for Crelli to spring his trap, or for his own death, whichever came first.

CHAPTER 14
Angel Falls, ME—2070

Mark was done with his tale. The emotional dredging through memories, good and bad, had taken their toll. He sat, drained, facing Gil's judgment with tears welling in his eyes.

"So family is only important when there's nothing else," Gil concluded.

"Don't use my life as an example," Mark said. "Dad was a great family man. I was the one who failed. When Mom and Franki were murdered, I blamed Dad. Then he became a fugitive and worked to overthrow my boss. It seemed right to blame him for everything. You and I only met a few years ago, and these have not been my best years, either. What I did is painful. Family must be important or I wouldn't feel this miserable about it. What I had and lost, what I did, what I've lived through, these aren't things you should compare to anything.

"God knows I wish my life was different. I wish that . . . no, I wish because I failed. Learn from what you heard tonight. In life, promise means nothing. Words mean nothing. You are what you do when it counts. That's all there is. It's that simple. Everything else rounds out of life's math. Pity me or hate me, but learn from these mistakes. I was rich and important once, but on the whole, my life wasn't anywhere near what I expected it would be. I was President of the United States and had everything, but for all that, I wasn't who I should have been. Don't make the same mistake. People count for more than what they're worth. If I could wish one thing for you, Gil, it would be that you live your life believing that."

While Mark and Gil sat in Mark's cabin, Bernie sat alone in his own cabin. He was crying for Jane and Franki, who would never be avenged, and he cried for Gil who was too much a part of this world to understand that there could be a better, more caring one in the future. But most of all, he cried for himself. Losing, losing so absolutely when he knew he was right, it was beyond bearing. His chest ached from the pain of regret. He was doomed by disloyal children, but they were his children and he couldn't absolve himself. Why couldn't children see the rightness of things and a life of caring that was simple and true? Why did it take old age to make that connection? Through tears of damnation, he stared out to the trees in the distance, hoping, begging for release, yet not wanting to go until he was certain of redemption. *Gil, is that too much to ask?*

In the distance, branches were swaying in a light breeze and their were peals of laughter from the village children playing games that only children play. But even the innocent laughter brought no solace today.

He closed his eyes. When he opened them, again, all was silent, the laughter had stopped. Amidst the trees, something moved. A beautiful, smiling, dark-haired woman appeared, so familiar in a simple summer dress. He could never forget that smile, that beguiling smile, and it birthed a smile of his own. She beckoned him. Behind her, a younger version, a teenage girl, stood, and she was smiling at her daddy.

Bernie rose from his bed and went to them. They laughed as he approached, and then disappeared deeper into the woods. He followed, tantalizingly close, but still out of reach. He was in a clearing now. Jane and Franki were there, offering their hands and he took them. Franki hugged him, her head nestled against his chest as they walked deeper into the woods. His heart soared when, beyond the clearing, by a large lake, a gazebo appeared, a familiar gazebo.

Hand in hand, smiling and laughing, they walked to it. Inside, he turned to them, enraptured by their glorious smiles. Behind them, the sun reflected an impossibly bright molten gold across the lake. Bathed in shimmering brilliance, he took a final breath and happily, his pain was truly gone.

Chapter 15
Angel Falls, ME – 2070

When Gil finally left Mark's cabin, he was drained and depressed. He returned to his cabin but had difficulty sleeping and in the morning, he awoke feeling listless and stayed in bed until it was time to see Bernie. Finally, he got ready after delaying as long as possible. Bernie must have known that after listening to Mark's story, he wouldn't be any easier to convince. Regardless, Bernie deserved an answer, even if Gil was unsure what that answer was.

As he walked to Bernie's cabin, he considered why the old man would want him to know how pathetic his family really was. How could that help things? And how could a President of the United States be so weak unless it was because he was a Rose? And if all the Rose men acted badly, which, apparently they did, why was he expected to be better or different? Why give a damn about a world that had so corrupted his family? Gil wondered if he could have returned to that day in Aeden when he had received the message from Archive to visit Bernie, whether he would still go. No, he decided, he wouldn't have.

As wretched as Mark's story was, there were the wrongs to consider. He could deny everything, but eventually Bernie would find a way to convince him to do something he didn't want to do. He couldn't allow himself to be persuaded. He would not be manipulated, not anymore. But he approached Bernie's cabin knowing that whatever he decided, he'd likely choose badly. Just like every other Rose had before him.

He had asked Mark not to talk to Bernie until Gil had a chance to speak with him first. He didn't want them ganging up on him and agreeing to something before he had arrived. That's why he reacted so angrily when he saw Mark walking back from Bernie's cabin.

"Damn it," Gil yelled. "Bernie is always conniving and I'm sick of it. I asked you not to see him, Mark. If I'm so damn important, why doesn't anyone listen to me?" Mark didn't respond. "Whatever you two decided, I don't want any part of it. I'm done." He turned to go but reconsidered. "In fact, the hell with it, I'm staying put in Angel Falls. I don't care what you two think is best. You can stop your plotting now, it won't do any good."

Mark's eyes were red and he looked every bit as distraught as he had last night. "He's dead, Gil. Dad died last night in his sleep."

Stunned, Gil watched as Mark limped slowly past, disappearing down a trail and into the woods. He ran to Bernie's cabin. Word must have spread because he noticed a change in the community. Kids weren't outside playing, nor were the adults doing their chores. When he arrived at the cabin, Stacey was waiting outside. She walked up to him with tears in her eyes.

"I'm so sad, the rabbi's gone," she said. "Are you okay?"

"Why wouldn't I be?"

"He was family. And he was a good man."

"To you, maybe."

She put her hands on her hips. "He was good to everyone, Gil Rose. You've become mean and I don't know why. He loved you. Whenever I saw you together, you were happy. What happened to make you so angry? I want my friend back."

"Sorry to disappoint you. It's what the Rose family does."

She looked down. "You are a lousy friend. I've done everything, but you're always distant and inattentive and now you're plain cruel. I was wrong about you. You don't deserve friends."

"I didn't ask you to be my friend," Gil said. "And besides, bad behavior runs in my family so I don't have to apologize. Who needs friends anyway? I'm better off without them."

"You're a bastard," she said. "How can you say that? You're so mean and selfish. I feel sorry for you."

"Life is disappointment. Get used to it."

She froze, unable to respond. Then she slapped him hard on his cheek.

He was totally unprepared. "What the fuck did you do that for?" he shouted angrily, balling his fists.

She slapped him again and started to swing at him once more, but he grabbed her arm to prevent it.

"God damn it," he shouted. "Stop it. Do that again and I'll beat the living crap out of you."

She kicked him hard in the shin and pushed him away, breaking his hold on her. She stood, briefly defiant, with her fists ready as if to hit him again. He anticipated it this time and struck a defensive pose. "Don't do it," he warned. "I won't hit a girl, but I'll hit you."

"Gil Rose, you're a . . . a . . . dick," she said. "I won't hit you, I couldn't beat sense into that thick, egocentric skull of yours, even with an axe." She covered her face and ran away.

He rubbed the sting from his cheek. "You're a bitch, Stacey Grant," he yelled after her. He was alone now. Good. He entered Bernie's cabin.

He wasn't sure what he'd find or what he wanted to find. Either way, he was disappointed because the cabin had already been cleaned out and had an eerie, empty feel to it, like something was still present. He sat at the foot of Bernie's bed, a position he'd occupied many times over the years as he had listened to Bernie's boring, pointless lectures. He stared at the empty bed and felt sad for himself. He puffed up the pillows and could almost envision Bernie's head laying on it.

Beside the bed, on a chair, there was something that had been left behind. He recognized the irony, and smiled. It was a communicator glove like the one he had worn when he had freed Mark. Embroidered on the glove was the name *Berne Thau*. Curious, but fearful that it would come alive, he picked it up cautiously. The glove remained silent as he ran his fingers along the embroidery. Who was Berne Thau? Bernie may have mentioned him in the past, but Gil couldn't remember and why would his great-grandfather have his glove? The names were similar, which added to the mystery. He started to put the glove on, but hesitated and stuffed it into his back pocket instead. Before he left, he reached for a pillow and angrily hurled it across the room where it bounced off the wall, hit a picture, and knocked it to the floor breaking the glass.

At first, he just stared at the shards reflecting the sunlight and then he bent down to clean up the mess. When he turned the picture over, he laughed again. It was an old photo of Bernie, Mark, Jane, Franki, and Terry at Bernie's house on Geist Lake.

Suddenly he began to cry. He tried to stop but couldn't so he looked around to see if anyone was approaching. He was truly alone so he cried for all the things he knew now and cried some more because of who he was now that he knew them. He cried when he realized he was crying for himself.

When Gil finally stopped he was left with aching sadness. Had Bernie known all along what Gil would decide? Had he died this way, not wanting to face Gil's answer? Maybe Bernie had orchestrated Mark's pathetic story and the timing of his death, hoping that would change his decision. He pictured Bernie placing the communicator glove carefully on the chair and then crawling back into bed, folding his arms on his chest, and with everything in order, dying to achieve what he failed to achieve in life. What a loser. That was so like Bernie. Gil cried again. This time he cried because he had become someone who could think that way. When he finally stopped, he vowed that he would not cry again.

He left the cabin and wandered listlessly to the outskirts of the community, carefully avoiding the lake and his neighbors. The silence of the forest drew him in and he walked the trails that he and Stacey had recently hiked. He walked a long time and a great distance, thinking about nothing and everything, all at once. When he thought about his life, he worked hard to not put it into perspective. It was not an easy task.

Though he had cried, he wasn't sure what he felt. In the past, he had Andrea but she was no longer an option so, by late afternoon, miserable, anxious, and confused, he returned to his cabin.

He sat watching the sun drop below the tall evergreens. In the early evening, one of Stacey's girl friends came to his door. She knocked, but he didn't respond. A paper slid under the door and he waited until she was gone before retrieving it. The handwritten note announced that there would be a service in honor of his great-grandfather beginning within the hour on Sugar Loaf Hill, which overlooked the waterfall and the lake.

In the dim late-afternoon light, people were walking by his cabin, climbing the hill to the site of Bernie's service. Mark and Stacey would be there. He had to go, too so reluctant and late, he joined them—all of them-because the entire village had turned out to honor the man they had all called Rabbi.

As he climbed the hill, some neighbors approached to offer futile condolences; others just smiled oddly or looked sad, while others still avoided him. He continued his trek up the hill. Nearby, Mark struggled with his limp to reach the top, but Gil quickened his own pace to avoid him. Stacey ran over to Mark and offered assistance and they negotiated the hill, together. It was almost completely dark when some of the neighbors moved a large projection system in front of the chairs that had been placed in an inward facing square pattern, much like at the Meeting House. Someone directed Gil to sit with Mark, but Gil hung back, standing instead under the trees behind the rows of chairs. As people came by, they offered more empty condolences, but Gil directed them instead to Mark and moved further from the crowd.

Meat arrived, elbow bandaged from his accident. He offered his friend a hug, but Gil avoided it.

"Hey, man, I'm sorry. The old man was pretty special," Meat said.

"How'd you know to be here?"

"Stacey rode her horse to the farms to deliver the message. I borrowed my parents ATV and drove over."

"I never spoke with him at the end," Gil said absently. "Not that it mattered."

"Stacey said Rabbi was a great guy. You were lucky to have him for as long as you did. You must have known him pretty well."

"I knew him enough to not know him at all."

"I'm not smart, but you either know somebody or you don't."

"I guess."

The exterior lighting units dimmed, signaling the beginning of the program and the crowd went silent. Even the animals and the insects in the surrounding woods were quiet. Annoyed at having to be there, Gil shifted his weight back and forth. He wanted to run away, but stayed and waited, trying to keep thoughts of the old man out of his head.

The projection system lit up and a holographic likeness of Bernie appeared. In the background, a neighbor woman played an old fashioned acoustic guitar and sang a sad song. Her words faded and Bernie's image smiled.

"Welcome," Bernie's voice sounded eerie now that he was dead. "I hope I'm not late for my own funeral. Thank you everyone for coming. Whatever work was mine to finish, remains now for others. That's the way of things. I know that like-minded people will take up my burden and drag it a little further toward the goal. Nothing pleases me more.

"Faith tells me a merciful universe will grant me my wish and wherever I'm to be, I will be recognized by my loved ones, so be happy for me and picture me hugging my Jane and Franki.

"I leave on this earth a son who loves me and a grandson and great-grandson who will continue my legacy. I should be content with that, but I am not. I was there at the beginning of the horror that has become our lives, a horror that I should have stopped, but I was unfit for that task and failed. For that immense failure, I take full responsibility and the guilt with me to the grave. Remember me as each of you carry on with my burden in your own way.

"As for unfinished business, there is much, so when you doubt yourself, as we all must, consider my life, how hard I tried and how poorly I fared. Yet what I did, what all of you must do is live a life of real value to your family, your friends, your neighbors, and to your community. On that, I tried. That's all we can do, try.

"There is no perfect life. Regardless what others may say, this life is given to us ever so briefly, and it is for us to participate in it, truly participate. To do that, we must resist making others so influential that they prevent us from making our own way. Do this for me. Participate fully in your own life and hope that in your final days, when you look back, as I am now, you'll feel the love and support of those who appreciate your efforts. Live for that day and for your loved ones. Nothing matters more.

"I hope each of you is blessed with unique and interesting lives and I know with good hearts, you'll do what's right and best.

"If there is one thing that I have learned it's that we are what we believe in enough to do something about it and this, whether we accept it or not, is our life's work to succeed or fail. What we do when it counts defines us; the rest is shallow self-promotion and self-delusion."

There was more, but Gil was done listening so he wandered further into the woods. Death didn't require this contrivance. This was so unnecessary, and no wonder people wanted to live forever to avoid it. From a distance, he stared through the trees at the projection screen, which had gone blank. Then another holographic projection appeared this one of Gohmpers, Bernie's friend and one of the leaders of the resistance. He moved further away but the morbidity continued.

" . . . for all the great good Bernie, as Berne, accomplished with the company he created called *Greenhouse, Inc.* a company that employed and trained frightened, destitute *Wasters*, putting them to work so they could avoid being executed as unproductive citizens . . . For his tireless work trying to restore freedom . . . Good friend and revolutionary . . . never forgave himself the deaths of his beloved Jane and . . ."

In the distance he saw Mark sobbing, something he wouldn't do for Henrietta or Terry.

The image of Gohmpers faded and an image of Arlene Klaatu appeared. Gil had heard more than enough and turned to walk deeper into the forest to get away. Just then, there was static and a loud, deep, intimidating voice, burst from the sound system, causing the ground to vibrate even this far from the source.

"I have broken you." The speakers reverberated trying to offload the energy contained within that voice.

Arlene's image flickered and then restored. Her demeanor changed. She was frantically moving at her console until her image died. Then, Gil heard Joad's voice over the speakers.

"Everyone, this is an emergency. Follow the evacuation plan and move out immediately. Gecko has broken through. HomeSec troops will arrive shortly. Good luck."

He stared incredulously as the locals frantically ran for any transportation that would help them escape. Others sprinted to the village with their children to gather necessary belongings. Stacey and Mark stumbled down the hill as the first probing lights of jet copters appeared overhead. There were flares to light the way and then rockets began raining down on the village, destroying everything. Townspeople were screaming. Townspeople were dying.

Two choppers landed across the field and assault troopers rumbled out and began firing on the villagers who were running away terrified.

Gil backed further into the tree line and watched, horrified, as the blasts got closer. At the crest of the hill, an officer pointed in his direction and troopers ran to his location. He took off and ran until he found a place to hide, but the sanctuary was short-lived as an assault team approached. There were sounds of gunfire and the troopers dropped. Did the villagers have weapons? There were other assault troopers pursuing him so he searched for an escape route. In the distance, through the mayhem, he saw Stacey helping Mark into the woods. A trooper fired on them, but before the trooper could fire again, he too was gunned down. Mark and Stacey disappeared over a rise.

Gil hesitated to run after them and his indecision quickly made that choice impossible. He caught a glimpse of the assault leader as she neared.

It was the same scarred woman officer that had almost caught him five years earlier at Mark's mansion/prison. When she pointed for her troopers to take him, he bolted deep into the woods, dodging branches and avoiding the undergrowth, running low and making himself small, while seeking in the deepest, darkest place to hide. The light from the flares, the bomb explosions, and the beams from the search beacons that were attached to the helicopters created disorienting shadows as he stumbled and fell to the soft earth. Crawling now and shading his eyes, he caught a glimpse of troopers trying to outflank him. He stood and ran, but in the brief flashes of light, it was clear they were gaining on him.

He fell and struggled back to his feet and continued to run. At the last second, he noticed the creek before stepping knee deep into it stumbling, his hands disappearing into the muck, breaking his fall and he scrambled to reach the other side. He clawed at the ground to keep his balance and looked back over his shoulder expecting to see that evil scar-faced woman gaining on him. His pursuers were closer now, but they hadn't found him. Suddenly an ATV burst through the trees in front of him and stopped before him. He froze.

"Jump on, Gil," Meat shouted. "Let's get the hell out of here."

He grabbed Meat's hand and swung onto the back of the vehicle and they fled as fast, and as silently as they could. As the ATV bounced over the uneven terrain, Meat screamed through the pain of each jolt to his injured elbow as he tried to find an escape route while keeping to the deepest part of the forest. It was a harrowing task without lights to guide them. When they seemed to have put some distance between them and the assault team, Meat turned off his electric vehicle. He was breathing heavily.

"I can't go any more, Gil. My elbow is throbbing and I can't grip the handles. There's a cave nearby. We can hide there until morning."

They each looked back. In the distance, Gil saw dark reddish-grey smoke plumes accented by flares, rising from the village. "Did everyone else get out?" Meat asked. "I saw your grandfather."

"Did you see Stacey anywhere?"

"I think she was with the old man. She's resourceful. She'll find a way."

"We can't stay here and we have to stay off the roads," Gil said. "Stay with the ATV and hide when you can. It's me they want. I gotta go. I'll run ahead."

"Go north to the timber reserve and escape into Canada from there. You know the way. Here, take this." Meat reached into the storage compartment beneath the seat and pulled out a small gun.

"Whoa, where'd you get that?"

"Dad keeps one on all our vehicles in case a *Toller* stops us. Take it."

"No," Gil refused. "I've only used them in *Virtuoso*. I don't think I could hurt a real person. And in case you haven't noticed, *Tollers* aren't our problem."

They heard a noise and both dropped to the forest floor and rolled under a small evergreen. Gil stared through a gap in the trees. Choppers were flying overhead, their powerful light beams piercing through the treetops and illuminating the ground below.

"I've got to get going, Meat. I can't let them catch me."

"I hear something," Meat said.

Branches were breaking. There was a vehicle approaching. He tapped Meat's helmet. "Over there," Gil whispered and pointed. An ATV had spotted them, so they quickly jumped back onto their own vehicle and headed away. Over his shoulder, Gil saw the other ATV gaining on them.

Meat swerved between the trees, looking for the clearest path he could find away from the closing vehicle. Tree brush slapped hard against them leaving gashes and cuts across their exposed skin, but Meat continued to throttle up. And still the other ATV gained on them.

"That guy is a pro. We'll never get away," Meat shouted.

Gil tapped Meat's shoulder and pointed ahead. "Over that rise, there's another stream. When we get there I'll jump off and try to distract him. Take the ATV and hide. You can't out run anybody with your elbow like that. Tomorrow, when they're gone, escape."

At the stream, Gil jumped off and stayed in the water running parallel to a local road while Meat followed the meager path that led back toward the village. Gil looked all around for their pursuer just as Meat hit an open clearing. A helicopter captured him with a bright beam of light and Meat swerved sharply to the left to reach deeper woods.

Gil heard the roar of jets overhead, but didn't see them. Suddenly, the darkness was lit up by a huge, searing fireball. He covered his eyes, but even with his eyes tightly shut, the image burned into his retinas. He screamed as he felt the hair on his hands shrivel and melt from the intense heat. When he opened and uncovered his eyes, he gaped at the landscape before him. Overcome with sheer disbelief, he sank to the ground. Every tree for hundreds of yards was blackened and ablaze. And Meat was gone, just gone.

In the intense heat, every breath burned, but he fought through it to muster a scream.

"NO!"

Then he sank back to the ground and wept.

Chapter 16
New England – 2070

Bangor Maine: In its infancy, Bangor, Maine was a leading supplier of lumber for whaling ships. Logs were floated down the Penobscot River from the great upriver timber reserves that are now owned privately by U.S. Angs.

Once oil and then electrical power were discovered, the whaling industry was no longer viable and thus it died. Years of abject poverty caused Bangor's population to decline so that only those truly self-sufficient remained.

The population of Bangor remained small until the late nineteenth century when a shift to the production of pulp and paper provided growth and Maine's timber resources once again allowed the area to prosper.

Reliance on the pulp and paper industry lasted until well into the twentieth century when energy became scarce and expensive. Bangor was one of the first towns to feel the shift as it was too far north and east of its customer base, so once again, its economy shifted—this time to electronics and services.

In 2026, with the country facing a lingering depression and high unemployment, as the largest town near the Canadian border, Bangor was strategically located and so it became one of the early battlegrounds in the *Terrorist Wars*. By 2032, funded by the evil, progressive, former U.S. Congressman, Glen Smith, now called the Prophet, terrorists infiltrated Eastport, Maine from New Brunswick. A series of skirmishes were fought all the way down to Ellsworth.

Terrorists even attacked Bangor, occupying it, and murdering two mayors and many of its entrepreneurial citizens. Finally, HomeSec deployed troops who caught and executed the last of invading terrorist horde, although Congressman Smith escaped.

This terrorist incursion nearly precipitated a war between the United States and Canada, but after intense negotiations between President Crelli and the Canadian Prime Minister, Canada agreed to pay for damages and police their side of the border. A fragile peace ensued. – Archive

Gil fled on foot through the dense woods, his *Virtuoso* gaming survival instincts overcoming his grief. He had to distance himself from his pursuit, but he needed to find out what had happened in Angel Falls also, so he bolted down a path that wound through the trees and back toward the town. He kept out of view of the hovering helicopters, their bright beams slicing at the night sky until he reached a rise. He crawled on his belly, staying as low to the ground as he could and on the other side of the hill, he saw troopers everywhere, their truck headlights illuminating the remains of the town with mock daylight. There were no villagers, his neighbors were gone. Shocked, he sat and stared disbelieving of reality, finally shaking himself to action when one of the troopers walked towards his hiding place, only to relieve himself on the other side of the rise.

Gil backtracked and worked his way past the town by sliding down a long, steep, stone slope. Then, using trails that he and Stacey had hiked, he worked his way to a neglected path. As he stepped out, he heard the sound of an oncoming vehicle and twisted back into the trees just in time to avoid being seen by an ATV speeding down a nearby road that ran parallel, the vehicle's HomeSec hologram markings clearly visible on the windshield. He headed back into the woods and picked his way carefully, keeping I-95 to his left. He was resigned to a long and difficult walk to an unknown destination, his other choice, surrender, was even less appealing

For the first few days after the assault, he made little progress because *SurveilEagles* were everywhere. During the day, he hid under evergreens, sleeping when he could and watching for aerial surveillance when he couldn't. At night he traveled cautiously. On the third day after the attack, a heavily-guarded convoy roared past, heading south from Angel Falls. He suspected the trucks carried surviving neighbors, but he had no idea why it took three days for HomeSec to ship them this far. Then it occurred to him. What would the people who destroyed Angel Falls do if they had witnesses and three days on their hands? He shuddered at the fate of the neighbors HomeSec didn't kill that first night. Then he thought of Stacey and stopped. He couldn't bear to think what group she was in.

Occasionally, patrols searched nearby, but they never searched deep enough into the forest to force him to run. Tired, exhausted, and worried about flyovers, it was slow going as he held to the deepest part of the woods. By the end of the week, as the *SurveilEagle* flights became less frequent; he was making better time and approached the outlying houses of Bangor, hungry and wary. He'd eaten little, but there were plenty of streams to drink from.

Memories of Angel Falls, of Bernie, Mark, Meat and Stacey settled into a sorrowful burden that weighed him down as he struggled to develop a plan that would keep him alive and safe. When panic got the best of him, he tried to activate the glove, but it remained merely a fitted covering for his hand. Sometimes he stared at it, unsure whether Joad ever or still existed.

On the outskirts of Bangor, he snuck up to an abandoned stone house that was built on a hill and fortified with an impressive stone wall. He climbed over a splintered heavy oaken door and then bolted up the driveway. Once inside, he found a home with many large rooms and stairways and far too many windows, all without glass. The place was clearly built for a time when it could be heated. He searched, but the house was picked clean except for splinters on a bedroom floor near where intermittent boards had been ripped out. There was nothing of value here so he turned to leave. At the door, he was met by the blinking red lights of a patrol car.

"I'm not getting your register, son. Can I help you?" It was a woman's voice.

He flinched, but remained calm. He had nowhere to run and was too exhausted to try. A lie, formulated out of necessity, came to him.

"Yes, Ma'am, my grandfather lives in town somewhere. I'm trying to find him."

She gave him a curious smile. "That doesn't answer either of my questions."

"I'm not from around here, Ma'am."

"Just so we're clear, son, unless you're far from home—and I'll need an explanation for that, too—you're from nearby and nearby is *Waster* territory, Unincorporated Lands. What is it son, and I'm on the clock and

Maine HomeSec grades me real tight when I'm on the clock. So let's have it?"

"I don't know, Ma'am," he improvised. "I don't. I was young; I only ever called him Grandpa."

That only annoyed the officer. "I don't care. Stop it." She blew out a breath. "Okay, for starters, what's your name?"

"Stacey, Ma'am," he lied again. It was the first name that came to mind.

"Well, Mr. Stacey, do you have a first name?"

"Uhh . . . Dan Stacey, Ma'am," he said. He had to remember that.

"Well, Dan Stacey, my name is Reverend Sgt. First Class Obermuller and I need to know why you're not registering on my detector. Then I need to know what you're doing here and why and where you came from. In that order. Now, please begin."

"I don't know what registering means. I-"

"Fuck me, you ARE a *Waster*, but you don't have a Pɪᴅ. I wouldn't want to be either of those things if I were you, son. I can see the bonus points lighting up as I rack up my next power grade. The scan says you don't have a weapon so this'll be the easiest power upgrade ever. Move against the wall; do it or you'll get hurt."

"But I'm innocent," he pleaded. "There's no need to get involved, Ma'am."

"Back up and don't try to run. My unit has been upgraded for Pɪᴅ avoiders. It will immobilize you if it detects you're six feet away or further. Don't do it, son, most runners shit and piss themselves when they're hit." With that, the officer wrapped a ceramic contraption around Gil's wrist. That's when she noticed the glove. "What's that?"

"Nothing, a glove."

"If that's a weapon that I can't detect, you should know that if I'm disabled in any way and the culprit doesn't register, my coworkers will be out here after you like furies. The power points you get for avenging a domestic freedom fighter like me are so enormous that even the strongest among us crap in our pants in anticipation."

He remembered the night he saved Mark, and how the glove had immobilized the security officer. He stammered, "It's only a glove."

She grabbed his manacle, yanked him to the car and shoved him into the back. There were detectable red beams pointing at him from all directions. She sat in the front. "Stay put or-"

"These beams will fry my blood?"

She laughed and turned. "No, they're making a hologram so Archive can check your records. Stay cool." He tried to remain calm even though as soon as he was identified, HomeSec would have him. He looked around for a way to escape, but there was none so he just nodded. The car pulled away from the stone house and while they were traveling, the officer bent to look at her monitor.

When she turned back, the expression on her face had changed. She was smiling. "Mr. Stacey, on behalf of HomeSec management, we are truly sorry for any inconvenience. You should have told me that your father is Luke Stacey, one of our most decorated and devout freedom fighters from the Hamilton, Michigan regional office. I've read his papers on how he managed to capture the famous union terrorist, Gohmpers. It was extraordinary security work and should have been turned into an Archive adventure. I know I would have paid top dollar to live it. Anyway, Dan, your father has been alerted that we found you and he is expecting you as soon as possible. He was very, very concerned. He has a lot invested in you, you know. Why didn't you contact him?"

Gil was confused but tried not to show it. Someone, probably Joad, was helping him. "I . . . I was searching for my grandfather, but my dad was against it, my grandfather being a *Waster* and all. It's a family thing. Anyway, I couldn't find him, but if everything's okay, I'm ready to head back to . . . Hamilton."

"Your father is right to shun your *Waster* grandfather. I never even discuss my *Waster* relatives with my children. We all have family members who chose to be *Wasters*, but we should have no sympathy for them. I was on the front lines when it all came down—the government and the economy. I was proud that I was one who bought a shit load of gold bullion when I was young. It saved my bacon.

"Something had to be done to get rid of those fucking *Wasters*. I was a new police officer, getting paid low wages and struggling with woefully few power points toward my next promotion and barely eking out a living. I saw all those fucking *Waster Welfare Queens* back then. Thank Morgan the media exposed them. I can't tell you how many stories I watched that uncovered the fraud and abuse heaped on us loyal and hard working Americans by those fucking queens dodging taxes and making fraudulent claims against the Government. They bankrupted our whole fucking country. I saw it on my beat too; those lazy fat-assed women with a million kids, all paid for with my tax dollars while I had this useless good-for-nothing husband who was so limp, he couldn't even knock up one of those welfare bitches although I would have cut his worthless dick off if I had found out about it sooner.

"It was so fucking frustrating to listen to the media constantly reporting on how these queens with their sin babies and their pimps were living high and screwing us, but worse, they should have been penniless or dead like they deserved, except the feeble-minded socialists in our government provided them with a living which they stole from us as taxes. Can you believe it? Our stupid, god damned government paid those bitches to have worthless kids. Is that sick?"

Gil could think of nothing to say.

"Say, maybe you're too young to remember, but those harlots were not patriots. They wouldn't even nurture their little fuckers until they became appreciable assets like the rest of us. No sir, they wouldn't. They'd let the government pay for their kids and I can tell you from experience, it was a drain on my economy. I raised daughters until they got jobs and I wouldn't let that government near them. Now that they're old enough to underwrite some of my expenses, the whole child bearing and rearing expense, they want nothing to do with me. What happened to good old fashioned American family values?"

Before he could think of a response, the officer continued her rant.

"Anyway, here I am working my fingers to the bone protecting my little corner of my country and some of my hard earned money is taken from me by the mean fucking I R of S and handed to the queens so they can have indiscriminate sex. It's like I'm some easy mark! And the female children, they grow up to be just like their mommas, welfare queens themselves, perpetuating the take while the males grow up to form criminal black market gangs that defy the business contract laws that made America great.

"At least they got what they damn well deserved. This is God's country and Americans can't kill babies continually and without remorse, without retribution. Chairman Crelli, god rest his estate, he was our true messiah. He made them pay. Progressives, socialists, and liberals, defended these scum, but that didn't stop Mr. Crelli. What he did to them was cost justified as much as it was pre-ordained. Remember Exodus? The God of the Jews told Moses that whatever punishment Pharaoh decreed for the Jew would be delivered instead to Egyptians. Well, the baby genocide of helpless souls, that's abortion, and with Crelli's laws, it was the Welfare Queens who were genocided. It was fair and it was just and we god-fearing *Conducers*, we avenged our dead babies. We did it because it was right and we did it because we had a fiduciary responsibility to the country. God damn it." When the officer finished, she made a fist and hit the dashboard, jarring him to attention.

Gil was confused yet fascinated.

"Let that be a lesson. Forget your damn *Waster* relatives. They get what they deserve and I'm pleased as punch to have been an essential part of it."

She quieted and Gil felt he had to say something. "Yes, Ma'am, I don't want to be any trouble. I was avoiding dad and you know how hard it is to avoid someone who works for HOMESEC. May I please go now?"

She shook her head and laughed. "Damn right I know how hard that is. I didn't mind when my girls dated because I'd sit at home in my rocker confident that I'd have their dates neutered in a heartbeat if either of the girls' metabolism started to race. Thanks for listening, you're free to go, but I have to find you a ride. The Detroit Sector is one of our best revenue partners. If your dad hears we made you walk, there'll be intradepartmental mayhem and serious financial consequences. It's easier to bill him for transport. Say, I've been meaning to ask, how did you get here in the first place?"

He didn't have an answer for that. "One of dad's trucks. I explained it to the driver and he said it was okay. I told him not to wait for me. That was a mistake and dad will fine me, for sure, when I get back. I sure appreciate any help you can provide."

"A word of advice, a man in your position should be more considerate of *Conducers*. Our work is our life. What you did will cost that driver real money and it could cost his life, if I know your Dad, which I just might from my reading. That said, I will help you. Later, we're shipping fully depreciated prisoners in a guarded convoy to Albany for divestiture. I will see to it that one of our armored carriers takes you from there on to HOMESEC headquarters in Buffalo. They can move you to Detroit from there and we will settle up after we see how pleased your dad is to have his asset back. You are an asset?"

Gil nodded.

"Good, will that be okay, Mr. Stacey?"

He smiled. "Thanks, officer that'll be great."

"The convoy won't be leaving until later so you'll have time for a shower, a nap, and to change your clothes."

He nodded gratefully. "I'll put in a good word for you with my father."

She checked her monitor and yelped. "He has already shown his appreciation."

The drive through Massachusetts and eastern New York was uneventful. He rode in silence, seated in the back of the last car of the caravan and neither HomeSec officer in the front seemed much interested in him. When they arrived at the outskirts of Albany, one of the officers noted a vehicle following them. As they reached the Albany Airport, the first car in the caravan stopped abruptly and each of the others was forced to swerve and brake. The car Gil was in stopped with a lurch, causing him to bump his head hard on the seat in front of him. He checked for blood, but all he received was a bruise. Then he looked out the window.

The road meandered through rolling green hills. On both sides, all-terrain cycles descended, kicking up dust as they surrounded the convoy. From each cycle, a well-armed man jumped off and leveled a weapon.

A voice came over the squad car radio. "You're surrounded. If you try to slow us down we'll be forced to do extensive damage to your vehicles. Please get out and stand aside. We don't want to cause any damage, but we can pay for it, so we will if we have to. You are professionals, you know the drill. Let's let our accountants resolve this, shall we?" The officers in Gil's car tossed their weapons out and then stepped from the vehicle. Gil joined them.

When everyone was disarmed, the bandits searched each car taking what seemed economically useful until they found keys to the prison truck. Once the truck was opened, two old men, secured in chains, and wearing bright, lime-green prison uniforms staggered out, squinting in the fading light. They smiled and hugged their rescuers and then jumped on the cycles and escaped.

The bandit leader stood on top of his ATC and shouted instructions. "Do nothing until we're gone." Then he noticed Gil and waved for one of his men to grab him and bring him over. Gil resisted at first but soon was facing the leader.

"You're not HomeSec." Gil didn't know how to respond.

"Why were you in the patrol car?"

He decided to stay as close to the truth as he dared. "They were taking me to their headquarters in Buffalo."

"Why? Are you valuable?"

"I'm nobody."

The leader turned to one of his men. "Mohammad, if his next response is as unsatisfactory as his last, shoot him in the leg." The man nodded.

"Now, why were they taking you to Buffalo?"

"They thought I was the son of an important HomeSec commander."

"Are you?"

"No."

"How did they get that idea?"

"I don't know."

"Mohammad," the leader said, pointing. The man fired his rifle and Gil screamed as intense pain tore into his thigh. He dropped to the ground and rolled in agony, but couldn't shake the pain.

"You shot me!" Gil screamed.

"Time is money. I trust you'll be more open with your answers."

Gil nodded while squeezing his thigh to ease the pain.

"Please explain again why they thought you were important."

Fearing more pain, he spoke rapidly and as accurately as he could. "They thought my father was important, but they're wrong. A friend of mine has access to their system and she, I don't know, she provided information to help convince them. Don't shoot me again." The leader looked toward Mohammad.

Frightened, Gil screamed. "Don't shoot, please. It's the truth. Don't shoot me again."

"Your friend sounds important, even if you're not. We could use someone like that." He tossed his communicator to Gil. "Contact your friend for me. Tell her there is a deal to be made and it concerns your life."

"She won't do it. Besides, I can't communicate like that."

The leader turned to Mohammad. "If I don't like this answer, shoot his other leg." He turned back to Gil. "If she's your friend, she'll act. Contact her."

He didn't know what to say or do.

"Mohammad . . ."

Gil was frantic. "I can't use your communicator. I communicate through a device in my back pocket, but I don't know if she's listening or if she'll talk to you." Before the bandit leader could turn back to Mohammad, Gil ripped the glove from his pocket. "See, here."

"Stand down, Mohammad."

The leader stared at the glove. "I've seen its type before. You had better not try to use it to communicate with HOMESEC or you will be dead." He yelled to his men. "Everyone, pull out. We'll join you after we see how well this communication device works." He turned back to Gil. "Mohammad is right here. Now proceed."

Under the leader's watchful eye, Gil put the glove on and tapped his middle finger against his palm. Nothing happened. Nervously, he tapped the glove again.

"Joad?" he whispered. "Are you there?"

The leader moved closer to inspect the glove. Panicking, Gil tried again. "Joad, are you there?" There was silence. Finally, the leader looked over at Mohammad who aimed his rifle. Gil screamed into the glove but there was no response.

"No, don't, please, It's true!" he shouted while trying frantically to reach Joad.

The leader grabbed his gloved hand. "What's that name on your glove?"

Gil turned his glove hand over. "It says Berne Thau. I don't know who he is. My great-grandfather gave me this glove, but I don't know that name."

"Your great-grandfather, gave it too you?" the leader asked. Gil nodded, hoping that was a good sign. "I believe I know him."

"Who? My great-grandfather?"

"No, no, well maybe. I knew Berne Thau once, an age ago. Is he your great-grandfather?"

"I don't know." The leader gestured to Mohammad who aimed his rifle.

Gil screamed. "No, I really don't know who Berne Thau is, but please don't shoot me, please. My great-grandfather died last week and he left this glove for me. I don't know how he knew this Berne Thau, I wish I did, but I know this is my great-grandfather's glove." He looked up hopefully. "The names are similar so maybe . . . Please don't shoot me."

An ATC sped over to the leader and the frantic driver pointed to his monitor. "Boss, there's a *SurveilEagle* approaching from the southwest." The leader nodded and motioned toward his cycle. Mohammad dragged Gil to it and lashed him on. Soon they were speeding into the hills of central New York.

The vibration of the cycle made his wound throb and only the invisible *nanostrap* kept him from falling off the vehicle while his body swayed listlessly to the torque of the ride. When the leader stopped, though dazed, Gil rocked hack and forth to try to lessen the pain.

"No!" he heard the leader scream. Wearily, he turned in time to see one of the bandits fire a rocket from a shoulder-mounted launcher that destroyed the approaching *SurveilEagle*.

Angrily, the leader turned to Gil. "It's not so hard to get worthless help these days." He shouted for his men to move out and they continued on. For hours, they sliced through the hills past Syracuse and Rochester until they reached the outskirts of Buffalo. Weakened by blood loss, Gil's body dangled against the invisible restraints. The last thing he remembered before passing out was the blur of a blue rectangular sign identifying *Lake Erie Resorts and Casinos* and a distance marker for Ohio. In restless visions brought on by the blood loss, he saw a vast body of water, a narrow causeway, and a light tower that illuminated the center of a darkened village.

Chapter 17

Presque Isle, PA – 2070

The gunshot made for an uncomfortable night. He finally slept a little as the night wore on, but he awoke to the first rays of the morning sun feeling drained and needing more sleep. But the bright sunlight that reflected off the myriad glass surfaces in the building he was in was intrusive, so he sat up and checked his wound. The bandage was red with blood and his leg ached, but the throbbing had stopped. Satisfied for now, he turned his attention to his surroundings. The glass building he'd slept in was in disrepair with ruptured rusted girders and broken panels of glass everywhere. In the center, one large girder had crashed through the floor leaving an exposed section that allowed tall, wild plants to emerge.

An enticing breeze flowed through the many openings in the building to revitalize him a little so after checking out his wound, he struggled to stand and then limped to a door. His wound began to throb again, so he paused. Not sure of where to go, he was resigned to endure the pain until he got somewhere. Outside, in the fresh air, the pain eased a little and he limped past other, smaller, but similarly dilapidated buildings all built around a series of brackish ponds. He followed a path that paralleled the beach and led around the ponds and a complex of simple huts. He attempted to circumnavigate the flat island but the pain in his leg caused him to tire quickly. In the distance, he was startled by screams, which turned out to be the sound of the camp muezzin calling everyone to prayer.

Feeling weak, he rested against a tree stump as the locals walked past, scrutinizing him curiously and talking amongst themselves. No one seemed concerned that he might escape and it wasn't long before he realized why. Except for a long, narrow causeway guarded by a small tower, the encampment was entirely surrounded by water, and with all the ponds, there was little land, most of which was taken up by small logs huts. If he had to escape, it would require swimming, and he couldn't swim, even with two good legs. That would be his secret.

He stood again and limped along the blacktop trail, staring at the water, which reached to the horizon. Only on the guarded neck of the island was there any chance for escape. An armed guard approached. Gil stopped and the man informed him that he was wanted by the leader. He was escorted to the headquarters where the man in charge was waiting. It was the same man who gave the order to shoot Gil the previous day.

"How are you?" the man asked. Gil just nodded. The leader was old, not as old as Mark or certainly Bernie, but old with gray hair, a gray moustache and goatee, and dark leathery skin. "My name is Rachman Morris. You may call me Rachman as long as you're honest with me."

Remembering just in time, Gil replied, "I'm . . . Dan Stacey. You can call me . . . Dan."

"Tell me how you know Mr. Thau?"

"I don't know him."

"Then tell me about your grandfather?"

"It's my great-grandfather, Bernie. We lived together for a while."

"Mr. Thau was older than me, white and Jewish; at least he wore a Jewish Star. I believe he was from Indiana."

That gave Gil some comfort. "I didn't see a Jewish star, whatever that is, but Mr. Thau could be my great-grandfather who is from Indiana, too. That's a good thing, right?"

"It's enough," Rachman said. "For now, you'll be safe here—at least as safe as we are. I am sorry for having you shot, but in my line of work I can't be too careful. You're young, you'll heal.

"Also, please understand that you can't leave without my permission. And if you try on your own, you'd have to be a great swimmer and I can't guarantee that my other guards are as good a shot as Mohammad." Gil nodded. "Also, with the downing of that *SurveilEagle*, everyone will remain in camp until we're able to negotiate payment of the invoice and any penalties that HomeSec assesses."

"You have to pay?"

Rachman shook his head. "This is America, everyone has to pay. There's no such thing as a free lunch, even for former terrorists. HomeSec will bill us for damages, but until we know the amount levied, I've forbidden everyone from doing anything outside except our normal road maintenance and the manning of our toll booths."

"I don't understand?"

"Everyone in America must have a job, tolling is ours. Many years ago, a great many of us were desperate and fearful for our family's survival. As Muslims, we were being legislated against and the economy was so bad, no employer was hiring and least of all hiring us. For various reasons American politicians identified Muslims as scapegoats for their internal problems even though we were Americans, too. We became desperate, death and starvation will do that, and we turned to corrupt mentors who were funded by bad people. They organized us into revolutionary cells and convinced us we must take what we were not allowed to earn. We were badly defeated. We never really had a chance. Many of us did hard time, but when consultants advised the government that it wasn't cost effective, the private prison system was closed down. The prison corporation stockholders were angry because of lost earnings, so along with eliminating the prison population, guards and administrators were also eliminated. The prisoners were temporarily interned in places like this throughout the country.

"Over time, we were forced to develop a low profile so that eliminating us couldn't be cost-justified. We are an industrious people and we developed an effective business model, contracting to maintain commercial highways and operating tollbooths for profit. That work provides local entrepreneurs with a necessary service and we skim some of our toll money off the top, the rest goes to *Blackbyways Transportation Company*, the private corporation that controls interstate commerce in America. The magnificent buildings you see here," Rachman pointed to the ruins around him, "they are our reward for good behavior and for providing cost-effective highway maintenance. We were pardoned except for the debts we incurred which were amortized over a forty-year period that soon comes to an end. It was a better deal than execution, but when we don't pay our bills, FinSec takes our key young people for retraining."

"FinSec?"

"The Department of Financial Security, they are nice people when the rules are followed. Little by little, we learned what pisses them off and how to avoid it. But our teenagers are rebellious. Shooting the *SurveilEagle* was an impetuous act by my cousin's stupid eldest son. We'll pay."

"They really bill you?"

"Yes, they have good software and are very efficient. At the end of the month, we'll receive an invoice for damages from the Government Administrative Office. They offer various repayment plans and the interest isn't usurious. That's it. But if we miss a payment, FinSec agents or heavily armed agents from a mercenary private subcontractor, like *Stillwater, Incorporated*, arrives in force, makes us pay, and then takes their cut. We know this from the tragedies in other *Toller* communities, *Tollers* are what they call us, and *Tollers* don't miss a payment.

"Reif, the idiot who destroyed the *SurveilEagle*, is a young hothead. In the old days, we'd stand proud together to protect him, but these days we're not so proud and if we don't pay, certainly one of our young men will rat on Reif for the reward. Our young people are constantly searching for quick and better ways to make money so they can flee to start careers in corporate towns. We lose more youth to government propaganda that entices them to flee to the glory of entrepreneurial capitalism than we lose any other way. Reif's a fool but I'd hate to see him go. Our young men leave and never return."

"That must be difficult for your families."

Rachman nodded. "Mr. Thau was an accountant by trade. You don't, by any chance, have experience in that field. We desperately need someone who's good with the books."

"I'm sorry. I don't know anything about accounting."

"That's too bad; it's a very prestigious job. You can learn while you're healing?"

"Thanks, but I don't think so. Whenever Bernie talked about accounting, he felt disappointed and underappreciated."

"It's different now," Rachman said. "Everyone worships economics and finance of which accounting is an important subset." Again Gil refused, politely. "That's unfortunate. You're recovering and our doctor says there's no infection."

"It hurts, but in a few days, I'll be good to go."

"Good, yes, but I'm sorry, not to go."

Not wanting to confront Rachman on that matter, Gil changed the subject. "How did you know my great-grandfather?"

"I knew him as Berne Thau. Before the Prophet, Omar Smith, ruined my life, I was the leader of a feared gang in West Philly. All of that changed when Smith came to town. He taught me how to take advantage of current political realities and because there was more profit in it, I became what Archive history calls a terrorist. I wasn't, but I had little choice but to do what I did. The government was bankrupt and unable to fund welfare payments so the poor were desperate, dying, and disappearing all around me. The one thing the government could afford was to crack down so a life of crime no longer fit into my strategic plan. Like everyone in my food chain, my finances were hit hard by the bad times and desperate people do desperate things.

"Smith brought with him a world class terrorist consulting team and they instructed us in a system Smith called the 'Hamas model'. He and others supplied the funding and we clothed, fed, and otherwise helped needy Americans in ways the government was no longer willing or able to do and the ranks of our supporters swelled. In a way, you could call it free enterprise, particularly since we were able to take control of local politics.

"The U.S. government reacted as they always did by investing in additional security police and developing surveillance software that enabled them to select and eliminate all who were deemed economically redundant. The battle lines were drawn and under Smith's direction, we recruited and armed.

"It was so avoidable, but the government acted like everyone was the enemy and we had to fight them every way we could. Somehow, they knew our plans. They knew everything. HOMESEC troops were waiting for us wherever we went and we lost a great many good people. They kept after us until . . . well here we are."

"Yet you raided a HOMESEC convoy and took their prisoners. You even destroyed that *SurveilEagle*."

Rachman dismissed Gil's points with a wave of his hand. "For us, family is everything. The prisoners we took, they were ferrets, desperate members of our family who moved to commercial towns, but were unable to survive commercially so they took to what they know best, fraud. We rescued our brothers before they could be hauled away for interrogation and elimination. We tried to negotiate for their release, but couldn't agree on a price so we just took them. HOMESEC will bill us some exorbitant fee, including damages and our accountant, once we find one, will recast our budget so we can pay. But we didn't allow family to be interrogated and disappeared. Winter snows are coming and keeping the roads open for commerce is our primary revenue generator. Allah willing, a few good snows and we'll pay and keep our family free."

"What's a ferret?"

"They acquire information or useful items for resale."

"And terrorists like you maintain roads."

"Yes. They call us terrorists so they can give a name to an enemy and put fear in a citizen's heart, but we were never that. We weren't fighting to overthrow our government; we were fighting to get a better, more responsive one. But our old and honored religion isn't consistent with their interests and their religion; Morgan, allows only dealing, not compromise. It is said that the closer a civilization gets to its own death, the more religious it becomes." Rachman shook his head, solemnly. "Sadly, that is true of America. Call us terrorists, or road maintenance engineers, or *Tollers*, it doesn't matter what you call us as long as you don't call us late for dinner." Rachman laughed sadly and slapped Gil on the back.

"But am I safe here? Will the government come for me?"

"Safe? Who is safe anymore? Everyone is at risk, but you have little to fear from us. You say you are Dan Stacey. While you were asleep, we checked. Your PID supports that identity but it supplies no other information and that makes you transparent to most surveillance protocols." Gil didn't know what that meant or what to say. "If the government discovers this, you're gone, dead, but only after you've been tortured so they can discover how you acquired such a PID. As I said, you are safe here. My techies want that technology and we're willing to pay you for it."

"I honestly don't know what you're talking about."

"Good then, we're negotiating," The leader said, menacingly.

"I didn't mean it that way. I didn't know my PID was untraceable or how it got that way."

"When you are well, we will make a formal offer but don't make me send my surgeon to operate on you to discover the secret of your PID. We have medical capability here at Presque Isle, but little experience in medical electronics." With that, Rachman changed the subject. "Where were you heading?"

Gil hadn't given it much thought. "Detroit, I think, or maybe Indiana, I'm not sure. Either way, when you release me, I promise I won't tell anyone where I've been."

"That's of no concern. I owe Mr. Thau a great deal so, if you abide by our laws, you will be as safe as any of us." Rachman took a seat across from Gil. "So how is my old friend?"

"Bernie? He . . . he died last week."

"I'm saddened to hear that," he seemed genuinely sad. "Mr. Thau was a good man and will dine in the halls of Allah. How did he die?"

"Natural causes, he was very old."

Rachman laughed. "That's rich. I would never have guessed Mr. Thau for one who would leave this world in his own time. What a lucky bastard. Most people who oppose the government live shortened lives. I'm not that fortunate."

"I only knew him for a few years, but I don't think he ever felt fortunate."

"Bad things happened to him, but where is that not true these days? When I knew him, he never let those things demoralize him. His anger and frustration spoke in productive ways, by helping those who were worse off. I admired him and before he was forced underground, he taught me a great lesson. Until I met him, I did not believe there was a kind, white, rich person left in the world. How long did you know him?"

"Five years."

"You were in good hands. Mr. Thau always found the best in people."

"Were you a bad man?"

"Some say so. I spent years in prison; the last time was eight years ago. The years with Mr. Thau I consider good years, legal years, better than my time in the presence of the Prophet. That time, I am paying for forever."

"Archive says that there are no prisons anymore."

"That is true. The poor who filled them have perished. Today, the government knows where you are and what you're doing, so they are able to expedite punishment in ways that make prisons unprofitable. There are still places, places no one talks about—secure, privatized hell-holes where enemies of the State give up their truth before dying in agony. For everyone else, there's productivity or elimination."

"Why did you go to prison?"

"Which time?" he smiled. "Early and late in my career, I did time for various economic crimes like grand theft and trafficking. The law today is much simpler and those crimes no longer exist. When someone perpetrates a deed that has negative economic consequences, the perpetrator makes economic amends or they die. I did what I had to do. It was the only way to live in the old glory days of the First Republic. I don't miss those days though I hate what I have now."

"Bernie honored those days."

"Why not? He was wealthy and connected. When I was young, what Mr. Thau fondly called freedom, was in affect the dictatorship of the wealthy who controlled the many and the poor. I learned that from Omar and my prison time reinforced it. Today, the many and the poor are mostly gone."

"How did you and Bernie meet?"

"Thirty five years ago, the pressure was intensifying in West Philly. I gained control of a territory located in the depressed inner city that I acquired on an Internet auction site from a retired entrepreneur. I wasn't there long before *Waster* patrols appeared. Waster patrols were franchises that eliminated the homeless and poor using a model that had worked for the franchise owners in other major cities. Satellite transmissions directed armed workers on trucks and busses to pick up poor clueless souls. The poor are their own worst enemy. Most knew they had to create value to survive and yet they avoided work until it was too late. At the time, it didn't matter to me because I didn't need the poor to make a living. I was only interested in people of value because that's where I got my value."

"Like who?" Gil asked.

"We preyed on the fringe areas where desperate people collected gold and silver which they hoarded in hopes that the world would end only up to their doorstep. I used their wealth to build a staff and to buy more territories in areas where the government didn't have the budget to cleanse."

"I thought the government secured everything."

"I said cleanse. Disappear. Eliminate. Back then, it was the job of the police to keep street crime away from the rich and they were damn good at it. Most crime occurred near where the poor lived, but it wasn't that we were too stupid to rob the rich; it was all about risk-reward. The police made sure it was much less risky for us to rob our poor neighbors than go to a better neighborhood and rob someone else and get caught. Whenever we stole from the rich, they'd spend whatever it took to inflict severe reparations on us so we'd keep our crimes local. Believe me, to be successful; you learn quickly who the victims are supposed to be and what you could acquire from them."

"So you made a living preying on the poor?"

"That's what Mr. Thau would say. In my defense, I was damn good at it. I lived in a secure, inner city compound much like the wealthy and powerful live in their walled suburban estates."

"What changed?"

"When the *Waster Wagons* appeared in my neighborhood, it took all my talent to find revenue from those able to avoid them and the brute squads that accompanied them."

"I'm not sure I want to know what *Waster Wagons* were."

"They're HomeSec transports targeted for collecting people who weren't making it financially. In my neighborhoods, you'd see the wagons, all clearly marked with HomeSec logos. Initially, they created such a panic that people hid from them, making collection more costly so HomeSec started using unmarked trucks but even that didn't work because there was hysteria in the 'hood' whenever unmarked trucks rolled in. Finally, HomeSec commissioned old trash trucks and other generic vehicles for the task. That worked well enough. They left the area at full capacity. From that, it was easy to see that I needed reportable earnings."

"And that's when you met my great-grandfather?"

"No, that came later. Mr. Thau needed protection for his businesses and I was a wreck and just needed to do something I . . . just something.

"I'm not sure how but Mr. Thau obtained contracts to manufacture things and through his company, *Greenhouse, Incorporated,* he took the poor off the streets and away from the wagons and employed them. In a way, he and the wagons competed, but even though the poor were desperate to survive and would have worked for little, Mr. Thau gave everyone he hired a living wage. I don't know how he got the money, but it worked. If the government had ever considered doing something like that, America wouldn't have lost so many jobs overseas and so many to execution.

"My job was to find the workers and protect them from the wagons. It was a rare time when everyone won. After my experiences with the Prophet, Mr. Thau showed me how much people really matter, regardless of their economic status. If I'd remained with Mr. Thau, I wouldn't have returned to prison or be huddled here in Presque Isle, taking road tolls for my daily bread. Allah be praised."

"Presque Isle?"

"This is Presque Isle. It's French. It means almost, as in almost an island."

"But you preyed on the poor. How did you become their leader?"

"One day at a time and against my will and better judgment." Rachman laughed. "Mr. Thau made me the President of Greenhouse and he provided the facilities, the customers, and the processes. He even brought in trainers so the workers could improve their work habits and their life and survival skills, anything he could think of that would help them survive in a world menaced by libertarian businessmen on steroids. And when we graduated our workers, Mr. Thau found them jobs on the outside.

"Prison is a great time for introspection. When I was inside, I thought a lot about what we did. He was the reason why so many poor survived. I don't know how or why, but in this world where bad things never stop happening, Mr. Thau, caused better things to be and I learned something from him that I will never, ever forget. Solving your big problems is an incredible feeling, but nowhere near as rewarding as when you help others to overcome their problems."

"That sounds like Bernie," Gil said. "I'm disappointed that he never mentioned his Greenhouses to me."

"I can't say why he didn't. To him they were a sacred mission. We didn't save as many as we wanted and eventually, we were chased out of business when President Crelli created government-funded competition for us called *Work Hotels* that lured *Wasters* in with the offer of jobs, but they never left. They were collection halls that facilitated extermination. That's some mean shit. Our government was that malicious and they eventually put Greenhouses out of business."

"But you were only helping desperate people," Gil said.

"Crelli had some kind of a vendetta against Mr. Thau. He used the media to channel the poor to his *Work Hotel* locations and that was that. Soon, Mr. Thau was chased into hiding and I went back onto the streets again."

Rachman paused and his eyes got that wistful, far away look. "I was involved in doing the right thing at a time that I considered killing myself. It changed me. Most *Wasters*, when they realized they'd die if they didn't work and you gave them the opportunity, most were enthusiastic—some for the first time in their life." He sighed.

"After my experience with the Prophet, I was desperate and I needed to feel better about myself. I bless Mr. Thau for providing that. Unfortunately, it didn't last, it never does. Your choices doom you, man." The joy in Rachman's face drained.

"What happened with the Prophet?" Gil asked.

"He was an unfathomable, strange and evil man. If you looked at mug shots of Muslim terrorists, his face would be the first you'd notice." Before he could expound on that, a horn sounded and a voice cried out over a loudspeaker, calling all to assemble for prayer.

"Wait for me outside or if your leg can handle it, you can walk around our village. Be back in a couple of hours and I'll continue. And please don't try to escape." With that, Rachman departed, and Gil stepped out into the late morning daylight.

As he limped around the vast complex, he considered how little he really knew about Bernie. Whenever he thought he knew him, another element added to his confusion. In the distance he could hear the prayers and it was with an aching heart that he explored the island.

Chapter 18

Presque Isle, PA—2070

Gil wandered the *Toller* community searching for anything to make his stay there easier and his departure faster. There was little in the village but dilapidated buildings and huts, so it didn't take him long to determine that he had to find a way to escape. He found his way down to the lakeshore where he stared out at the water, surveying the distance when he was interrupted by two of Rachman's soldiers who approached to escort him back to the village.

When he arrived, Rachman had just finished prayers and there was a small, pungent-smelling meal laid out on a wood table in the middle of his cabin. Rachman dismissed his men and motioned Gil to join him, offering him some bland tasting juice to go along with the unfamiliar, odd looking, and foul smelling food, but he pulled a large jug of red wine for himself from below the table. Gil ate and drank sparingly while Rachman ridiculed himself for drinking so much.

"This is forbidden," he said, pouring another glass. A good Muslim shouldn't drink but-" He stopped, realizing he didn't have or need a good answer.

Rachman finished a second helping of wine and stared unhappily at empty glass, as if expecting that it would magically refill, or less hopefully, just disappear. Without looking up, he asked, "Did Mr. Thau talk of the old days, the days before Crelli?"

"Some," Gil answered.

"Though Mr. Thau was a good man and did many, many good things, he provided limited value to our revolution. He hated the Crelli government as much, or maybe more than we did, but he was unwilling to commit fully. That is so typical of Americans. Life is too good and so they do nothing that might cost their precious lives. Well they sure learned. I got on him about that. After all, revenge is rational; they killed his family except for his son, who was one of them but Mr. Thau would defend his actions by saying he had something more important to live for, but he never explained what that was. It is considered a fatal flaw among revolutionaries to have something to live for. The Prophet Omar decreed that we never recruit Mr. Thau's type. Now Mr. Thau helped a great many and for that he deserves honor, but you don't score revolutions, you win them. In the life or death struggle we faced, the ones who fight to the death are the winners."

"But you're still alive."

Rachman poured himself another glass of wine and took a long swig before answering. "I suppose." Then, he changed the subject. "It's hard to remember what it was truly like back then. Archive writes stories and calls them history but there's little truth there." He topped off his glass and set the bottle down on the floor beside him.

"You do it, too," Gil observed.

"I do what?" Rachman asked.

"You talk like the truth is something only you have and it's to be venerated but what you say is only your perspective. As far as I can tell, nobody knows the truth, let alone owns it."

Rachman stroked his goatee. "You're either very wise or very cynical. The truth is no more than honest perspective. Perhaps you'd like to hear mine?"

Gil had time. "Very much," he responded,

Rachman took another drink and began. "Americans never fail to rally to a self-serving politician's heartfelt, yet bogus call to patriotism, politicians who proclaimed that America was the last great hope of humanity. They offered their fool's prayer and then stole everything we had. And yet I was the criminal. Why did Americans buy into it, I'll never know. Most never leave their communities except to go shopping so how could they know how great America was and compared to what? And the impoverished millions never felt that way and they are Americans too. At least they were."

Rachman laughed and took another swig of wine. "Mr. Thau exposed me to the true power of the wealthy and he did it with not a little irony, as was his way. But it was the Prophet who drained me and turned me into the empty shell that I am today.

"What happened?"

He smiled sadly and took another gulp. "You're young and you probably won't understand. This is life you'll say whether I like it or not."

"I won't do that. Tell me, please."

Rachman laughed. "Life is penance, and if there's blame for that, it began a long time ago when limited liability corporations were allowed to become legally like individual citizens, having all the freedom of people with none of the moral and ethical constraints and few of the legal ones. They had responsibility only to their stockholders. This was the war where Americans lost their humanity. You see, we live in this vast food chain where those at the top, the rich and powerful, exercise their birthright over the rest of the planet while the rest of us, we never stand a chance."

"You learned this in prison?"

"Most but not all." Rachman took the bottle from off the floor beside him and finished it, pushing it and the glass to the far end of the table. Then, he pressed his hands to his head and continued. "I thought Omar was fighting against that and all the other wrongs the country had heaped on the poor, so did a great many others. He promised."

Once again, Rachman grabbed for the bottle but thought better of it. "I met the Prophet during Parrington's disastrous final year in office. Crelli had been elected and it was clear that things were going to get worse.

Lancaster Ave. was mine back then, but I was at the end of my run, I just didn't know it. It was 2031. I remember it as not a blessing from Allah."

Chapter 19

Lancaster Avenue, Philadelphia, PA—2032

"Nicky, here's how it is," Rachman said as his hand pressed the helpless stooge, Nicky Nodo, hard against a brick wall. "You haven't worked in memory and you're surviving on handouts, welfare checks, food coupons and housing chits. Nicky, boy, that's all changing."

Nicky tried to break away from Rachman's grip, but when he tried once too often Rachman twisted his arm hard, and hurled him face first across the alley and into another brick wall on the opposite side of the narrow alley. Bleeding now, Nick's yell echoed as he bounced back and fell hard. It took only one kick to the midsection to convince him to stay down.

"You'll get your money, Rocky, I promise," Nicky said through the pain.

Because two felt like the right number, Rachman kicked him again. "How the fuck are you going to do that? That bastard, Crelli, is President now, and it'll all be gone—welfare, handouts, everything—gone. So how the hell are you going to pay me back, or for that matter, live long enough to try? Come on, Nicky, I want your plan."

Expecting to be kicked again, Nicky cringed. When the kick was delayed, he slowly uncurled just as Rocky delivered another blow. He howled, "Rock, don't. I'll get the money. I'm doing a job."

"When was the last job you did? You need a job that pays, Nicky—one where someone regularly transfers funds to your account as compensation for effort, a job, Nicky—a *Joe* job."

"Rock, I had some bad luck, that's all. I'm good for it. I'm looking at a couple of jobs that'll get both of us even."

"Shut the fuck up. Jesus, where are your brains? If you're doing something big enough to get me all my money, they'll catch you for sure; you'll talk and tell them you did it to pay off a debt. You idiot, the laws are changing. If you're convicted and the *Federales* tie it to me, I'm guilty too—no trial—it's a deep pockets thing. There's no way I'm sticking my neck out for the likes of you. You're not doing any jobs, do you hear me? If I hear you're considering it, I'll kill you."

Nicky remained quiet until Rachman threatened to kick him again. He cringed. "Sorry, Rocky, you're right. I'll get work. I will. There's new construction in Bala Cynwyd. I know the people crewing it. I'll get the job and pay you back every two weeks, like you say."

"Who would hire you?" He twisted his arm until Nicky's hands and lips were trembling. Blinking incessantly, he began to make honking sounds when he breathed. "What work can you do?"

"They need someone to mark up drawings for input to the computer. I can do that."

Rachman twisted harder. "You shake too much; you can't pick up a pen the first time, let alone draw a straight line. If you're screwing with me Nicky-"

"I'm not, honest, Rock. None of the kids today know how to draw—everyone learns on computers. I can do this. I shake, but when I'm working, I control it."

"I hope to god you're not fucking with me. When do you start?"

"Next week for sure, Rocky. No later, I promise."

"I hope so, Nicky. I expect payments to be transferred to my account on time. You understand? I can fix it so you never work again and if that happens, you die. Am I clear?"

"Crystal, Rock, I'm good for it, I promise." Nicky slowly crawled to his feet.

"I don't want to hear about needing food or a place to stay. And I'll kill you if you start using again before the debt's repaid. I'll find out. You know I will. Now get out of my sight."

Nicky raced across the street and disappeared and Rachman straightened his clothes before leaving the alley. When he reached the street, Nicky was gone. He began to smile until he saw a very pale, red-eyed white man staring at him. For a second, he thought he was hallucinating. The man had long, straight, white hair and he was dressed in flowing white robes. The man put his hands together near his mouth and bowed.

"What the fuck do you want, fruitcake?" It was too soon after Nicky and there was too much pent up adrenaline coursing through his system.

"If you're relying on Mr. Nodo getting a regular job to pay you back, you're working far too hard to make ends meet." The man spoke good English, but with a faint European accent.

"That's none of your god-damned business, whitey."

"Thank you for noticing."

"Don't fuck with me."

"It seems I already have. No offense, my name is Smith, Omar Smith. And you're Rachman Morris, the neighborhood 'thug king'."

Rachman moved threateningly toward the man who, to his credit, didn't back away. "Hear me out," Smith said, reasonably. "Look, you're bigger, stronger, faster, and in your own way, meaner than me and these are your streets. You can certainly beat the crap out of me if you want. But you can do that anytime you want, so why not listen. Assume for a second that I'm smart—I really am very smart. Why would I pick a fight with you if you'll wipe the floor with me? Why would I do that?"

"Maybe you're not that smart."

"Come on, you didn't waste time with Nicky. I'm waiting."

"Okay, what do you need?"

"I'm looking for an assistant."

"I don't do assistant."

"The pay is very, very good and the work is short-term. Can we talk?"

"My place or yours?"

"Here's fine."

"What brings the whitest man I've ever seen to Lancaster Ave?"

Smith smiled. "Business."

"Then I'm all ears."

"Mr. Morris, I'm new to Philadelphia. I'm coming from Chicago where I've been organizing and after Philly, it's on to L.A. I'm looking for local protection. I was given the names of three gentlemen. I'm weighing the credentials of the others but, I think you're my guy."

"Depends on the offer," Rachman said. "And the job."

"I want you to provide protection for me while I'm organizing and if I get out of town alive, and relatively unhurt, you'll receive a hundred thousand for your efforts."

"Euro?"

"I can accept that. I even deal in Yuan if it makes your decision easier. Or take it in Thai baht if you want. First, so you're clear, I'm in the very profitable business of revolution. I build networks of soldiers among the poor, disfranchised street people, along with impressionable college kids and local punks. I have franchises in two cities and the media is beginning to link local violence in those cities to my brand. Philly is my next target. My business plan calls for ten franchises in the next five years before I have the clout to link them into a national revolutionary movement, but that's a discussion for another day."

"There's money in revolution?"

"High risk keeps the riff-raff out, that's for sure and there's significant negative cash flow up front, but the long-term will be lucrative beyond your sense of wonder. The Smith brand is backed by very deep pockets; Sovereign Wealth Funds of several nations are among my investors. Join me. Provide the service I need, keep me alive and functioning, and help me recruit and I'll guarantee your money. Guarantee it! And, oh yes, we will display enough violence here in Philly to attract the media.

"I want to be upfront. This is my revolution and there are two things I will not tolerate. I will not do interviews and I will not get hurt. That's where you come in. I'll cover all of your expenses and you can use your people, but you will need to recruit far more. You will recruit on your own so thugs can't be easily traced to me, and when I'm gone, these people will be yours. Keep me alive to succeed and you'll become a very rich and powerful man."

"Rich doesn't help if I'm in jail."

"And poor doesn't help if you're in jail either. If it helps your decision, the only people I don't want to lose here in Philly are you and me."

"Keep talking."

"This weekend, I'm having my first rally for the poor and homeless in Fairmount Park. It'll be your job to control the crowd who'll come in droves for the free food handouts that I'm advertising. The police will show up, late as usual, and most of the crowd will leave on gurneys or be left for dead. That must definitely not include you and me. Do you understand? What do you say?"

Rachman surprised himself. "A hundred fifty thou," came out. He put his hand out, but the Smith wouldn't shake. Instead, he stared at Rocky's hand

"Rocky," he said, using Rachman's street name, "it seems we have a deal." He handed Rachman a leather pouch. "This is your first installment along with an estimate for expenses. I know you won't disappoint me because I am far more ruthless than you want to know."

At first, the work was easy. The problem was Smith was never around. For all the protection money he earned, Rachman didn't see his employer until that first rally.

He had received his instructions from someone within Smith's consulting team and everything was in place. To get a feel for what was in store at the first rally, on the day of the rally, Rachman walked the macadam paths by the decorated statues and concrete, man-made lakes of Fairmount Park; the large, heavily treed park that dominates west central Philadelphia. When he reached the site, he saw the Prophet, Omar Smith, bracketed by the imposing armed security team, Rachman had hired. They were standing on the steps below a large statue of a man riding a rearing horse. The Prophet wore a traditional white Arab *dishdasha*, and on his head he wore a white *egal* that covered his long, flowing, silky-straight white hair. Rachman turned to the gathering throng of local poor attracted by the smell of hot food on the nearby tables while his thugs prodded them away.

Rocky smiled at Omar's wizardly countenance, but then he began to speak and he became the Prophet; channeling the intensity of an Imam speaking the economic word of God. At first, he spoke quietly forcing the crowd to move closer, close enough to be ensnared.

"Come, my friends, listen," the Prophet began. "I am the holy deliverer of God Allah's consecrated word, the word that has saved mankind throughout time. Hear me and be redeemed." As the Prophet, Omar didn't shout, but somehow his modulated voice found its way above the noise and drove the crowd silent.

"I know how you live like you do and why you live like you do because I know how the system of the United States works. I was part of it once, the worst part of it. I was a politician and like most politicians, I wanted to do good things for you, but I was naïve and I was won over. I stopped listening to Allah and he punished me. It seemed only natural to receive help from important local and national resources to further my campaign so I could continue to accomplish the necessary things for you, my constituents. And I did good work, but mostly I tried and failed, for the American system of government is designed to allow very little change. For you see, to repay the little that I was able to achieve, my colleagues insisted that I accept legislation that my patrons, the rich, wanted and to resist legislation they did not want. I could say I fought for vital things like more and better paying jobs, health care, a living wage, safety in the workplace and in the community, but it would be a lie. I raged against laws that took from you what little the government provided, but you didn't care, so in the end, I gave up on that work. That's right, you heard me right, if you don't care about your own future, why should I?

You have been trained to believe you don't matter and that you are a leaf to be blown in the wind. You smell the food I offer here today but you must hope that it is free because you can't pay for it. In fact, in our commercial society, you can pay for nothing and yet that is okay with you. You live in the streets and hope to die. This is where your not caring has taken you and me.

"I could tell you, here today, how good I will make your life, how hard I'm willing to work for you and how much I'm willing to feed, protect, and defend you. I could say that and I am wealthy, I can do it, but I won't because you don't care. You are less than a pawn to me, and even less to them, you are nothing. And when your government wants you gone, which will be soon because you are a burden to business, you will be gone. It will depend on their needs and it could be by starvation or execution; they could not care less, so long as you are gone and you burden them no longer.

"But you mustn't think of death as some silent, peaceful end. Starvation is a long and horrible process as your body decays from the inside. There is great pain and a hunger greater than what you are feeling today when you look out at the feast that I have provided." Omar waved and his men uncovered the steaming pots and the fresh scent of food wafted through the crowd. When all eyes had turned to the tables, he waved again and the pots were covered, eliciting a collective groan among the starving.

"You feel that hunger knowing that this will be yours. Feel it and remember it when there is no further quenching available. When all hope is truly gone and no one offers you any more. Feel that hunger linger until the last blink of your eye and your last breath exhausts your heart. That is how you wish to die. But what if the government wants you gone quicker? Feel their clubs and whips, their electronic prods which inflict great pain. And know that in the mass extermination camps that are being built in every local prison and in every empty manufacturing facility, know that they are being designed to achieve high volume at low cost, without consideration as to the pain they will inflict. It will be a nasty experience and your last on this earth. The last sound you will ever hear will be your own blood curdling screams above those of the unfortunate around you. Death comes for you and it comes with pain. And yet you care not."

Rachman watched the apathetic faces. How pitiful they must be if Omar couldn't arouse some fear.

"Alas, a great good fortunate is upon you. Allah has shined his hallowed light on the government's plan to exterminate you and I know it for what it is. In shame and repugnance, I tore the western clothes from my body and swore my allegiance to Him and now as I stand before you, I wear more natural raiment, not those made for profit. I broke with this government of, by, and for business, this America where greed and inhumanity are rewarded, and I fled into the desert. I have been to the mountaintop and returned with Allah's blessing to build an army to defeat the vile avarice of the creatures of Satan who rule this land. And defeat them we will, but before we can, Allah wants you to prove that you will do what is necessary to renounce your yoke; that you will honor the life he has bestowed on you by reinvigorating yourself in his just cause. With Allah's blessing, my leadership, and your efforts, we will tear down the temples of the moneychangers and forever damage the American brand. We will destroy the evil that makes good citizens less than the humans that God Allah loves, and turns them into beggars living in a twilight world, doomed to a short, painful life and an agonizing death.

"Join with me, I beg you, join. Evil men are in power here and I fear for you as I fear for my country. And though I fear, I am not afraid. God Allah has called me to put an end to their sacrilegious worship of the almighty dollar and to put an end to their inhumanity.

"What are we if not human with human traits? Allah promises to make the least of us the same as the greatest of us. And he will punish those who value the almighty dollar the symbol that makes severe judgments against those who are poor, yet wealthy in so many undervalued ways. We will not allow wealth to be the arbiter of goodness, that is not Allah's way, and even though the rich will try to put those words into our mouths, recognize it as the lie that it is, awake and join me. Together we will make the world fair and bright once again, just as God Allah intended. Break bread with me now and let's come together."

When the crowd heard the word 'bread', they stirred and Omar raised his voice. "I hear in your mournful sounds the pleas of the powerless disappearing in the oppression of the cash registers of the wealthy and the powerful."

"Feed us," someone shouted. That appeal rippled through the crowd

And the caterers grabbed the cloths that covered the banquet tables and the lids that covered the vast stewing pots. Rachman signaled his men to remain alert as with great show, Omar signaled his caterers, who lifted the cloths allowing them to billow in the wind. Then they lifted the pot lids which caught the reflection of the sun. Steam billowed up and the crowd pressed closer, staring longingly at the tables of food.

"No, not yet," Omar shouted as the caterers returned the lids to the pots. "I will feed you, I promise, but first, you must understand why."

"Feed us oh Prophet." Someone yelled.

As Omar moved from table to table, Rachman smiled at the wretched crowd whose covetous eyes struggled to follow his movements and not the food. And then he continued to rant.

"Satan rules America and welfare will be no more. There will be no aid of any kind, temporary or permanent, no entitlements, and no bridges over troubled water, nothing. The greedy wealthy are worried about their profits and the greedy always protect that first. There will be no more food stamps, or public housing, and free public education will be gone soon as well. There will be no handouts of food, no training programs for workers, and no subsidies for any reason or any medical assistance that you can't pay for before you need it. No, not anywhere in America will anything be free; there is no profit in that, not in a world that worships the almighty dollar. What you have now is all you will ever have and that too will soon be gone. So it is written, so it will be done. Your lives are a burden and they are forfeit.

"But God Allah is merciful and you can save yourselves. I offer you a way. Follow me. Be my army and you will come to know God Allah is on our side and He will prove it in a fiscally demonstrable way. Join with me, believe in Him, and act to make your future secure, and I offer each of you, free, at no cost, groundbreaking shares in revolution, our revolution, our noble enterprise to make the world a better place. Yes, you heard me right. This is wonderful news. You are all to be stockholders, investing your sweat equity to become vested in all of our country's great wealth once God Allah's revolution has succeeded. There is power in wealth and you will each own shares of that power, that wealth. My government will be as God and the Bill of Rights intended. Meet the requirements of rebellion and I guarantee each of you riches beyond imagination."

A sad, tired old woman dressed in ripped and worn paper clothing sheepishly raised her hand.

"Prophet, sir, I don't understand all this mumbo jumbo?" she asked. Smith took a step toward her and she stepped back. He smiled; his gleaming white teeth bright, even against his alabaster skin enhanced by his straight white hair. The woman was self conscious without any teeth of her own, but was divinely happy for the attention and she returned his smile.

"I have been very fortunate in my life," Omar explained. "My father was wealthy and his businesses do well. I have no heirs so it is for you to be the beneficiaries of His will and my great fortune. This is truly a ground floor opportunity. Join me in rebellion and your reward on this earth will include great wealth. As a down payment on that day, my followers will receive food, shelter, and protection as a pre-payment for your efforts. And when we achieve victory over the devil, each of you will exercise your options and live happily ever after. As proof of my commitment, there is a prospectus that is stacked on the tables beside the food. Read it, particularly the footnotes."

People turned expectantly toward the tables, but Smith lured them back once again.

"No, not yet," he said. "I know that you are hungry, but hunger is fleeting. True wealth and happiness wait. Read the prospectus here or on my website, *Allahisgreat.501C4*. You shall see that my offer is registered."

The poor woman, no stranger to cons, just turned and walked away, shaking her head in disbelief. She didn't walk far, pausing near the food. A few others followed her, unwilling to lose a place in line.

Rachman knew these people; they were his people, the ones who provided the pittance that allowed his street enterprises to function. These were the forgotten, the empty shells that America deemed incompetent and unqualified to survive. Here were the unrecognizable, the scorned, the embarrassing chaff of the great American free market harvest, forced to live on its periphery and die unlamented. These were wasted lives and they were becoming . . . curious.

Every eye in the crowd followed Omar to the food tables where he picked up a stack of prospectuses, pointed to them and with outstretched arms like he was trying to save a baby falling from the sky, he shouted to the crowd, "From Allah, above, here is signed and notarized proof. America is an ownership society and each of you will be an owner. Here is a valid business contract. Here is proof of God Allah's mercy and that all reward is not in heaven. Fight with me for your rights and what I promise will be yours."

Smith walked to the first table and began dramatically flipping off the lids. Steam rose up, wafting through the crowd, as did the exquisite fragrance of creamy French food.

"Will you fight with me?" Omar implored. There was a roar now from the crowd and he continued to remove cover after cover from table after table. Pastries and bread were piled high, while the deserts were presented in colorful arrays. The crowd screamed from hunger. "Come, be my foot soldiers for Allah and be redeemed, first here, then throughout America, and then in Paradise."

Anticipating the long delayed moment, the crowd pushed closer, looks of ravenous excitement on their faces. Once again, the guards held them back as Smith continued.

"Have faith in Allah, and today, you begin your journey to from want to pleasure, health and wealth." The crowd cheered as Smith raised his hands, spun and quickly pirouetted out of the way. At this signal, the guards stood aside and the crowd screamed, and clawed their way to the tables. Omar yelled one last time, "Rejoice in Allah!" The crowd screamed and various hired actors in the crowd shouted back professing their allegiance.

Once the crowd had been serviced and everyone was quietly stuffing their mouths with the vast amounts of food they'd acquired, Omar Smith, now safe behind the tables, held up his hands for quiet. "The evil in our world will test you, but through me, God Allah will be with you. Prove yourself to me in rebellion and you prove yourself to God."

Smith paused and looked around to insure his timing was right.

"The modern day devil is Andrew Crelli. He has infested the White House with his minions and instructed them to eliminate us. Your family, your friends, and your neighbors cannot help you. Deny God Allah, and you are nothing and face this horror on your own. Don't look to the person beside you because evil comes for him as well. It's coming for the homeless and it's coming for the poor. It's coming even though you've done nothing to deserve it. No one is safe. To believe you're one of the lucky ones who can create economic value or has available worth is to separate yourself from us. But be forewarned, this evil that President Crelli has wrought is equal opportunity evil. If you create no economic value, as the government has defined value, they will know your fear and find you. And once they have you, your most fervent prayer will be to die, a prayer that won't be answered near quickly enough. So I ask, again, are you with me?" There were shouts of joy.

Content with the performance of his men, Rachman walked up a grassy knoll to where two of Omar's consultants sat with computer tablets making notes. He stopped beside them only turning back toward the crowd when he heard the screams. The two with laptops nodded to each other as they watched on their screens as men dressed in police uniforms charged down the hill, savagely beating those innocent poor and recently sated. Fights broke out and many lay motionless on the ground while his security team stayed purposely away.

The police ravaged the crowd savagely, indiscriminately pounding on the poor who had already succumbed a lifetime ago. It was merciless and even though Rocky had expected it, he was appalled. He ran down the hill before realizing why and once there tried to save those few he could.

Someone with a short wood cudgel was beating on an elderly man, a man that Rocky knew from the streets of his youth. Rocky flung himself at the back of the attacker, knocking him over. The man jumped up and with a blood-curdling scream turned to confront Rocky but when he saw it was his boss, confused, he paused. Rocky grabbed him, pushed him out of the crowd, and told him to remain there. Then Rocky went back into the fracas to save others. He wasn't sure who the real police were, so he concentrated on those without uniforms who were doing the mauling. When the time allotted to the riot was over, and the paid players had fled, he had managed to save a few—too few of these innocent, poor souls.

When he returned to the hill, the consultants were staring at a monitor and nodding. One looked up.

"Well done, Rocky, well done. We're not sure what the Prophet's take will be but we can definitely use the footage for the news and our website. We polled it and that footage of you is attractive enough to sell to advertisers who will allow it on their news shows.

We still have the problem that almost everyone in America hates the poor and most believe the poor are their enemy. That's why them taking a beating is less news and more entertainment. But what you just did down there makes this a news story. Well done.

He must have looked confused because the other consultant clarified. "The poor don't buy shit so we've been struggling to attract advertisers. Without advertising, the Prophet's rebellion just doesn't take off. No one cares to watch poor people being poor people. It scares the bejesus out of every demographic group, including the poor! But what you did, some Americans will see as brave and that is brilliant marketing because it will draw eyeballs. Eyeballs draw advertising, advertising draws interest and interest draws, well; you don't have a need to know. A thank you is in order." The consultant paused and smiled. "Thank you. Now all we have to do is return to headquarters and convince the albino."

The other consultant looked up from his laptop. "It'll work."

Disgusted, Rocky straightened his clothes, wrapped his bloody fist in a rag and stalked away, decidedly unsatisfied.

The crowd that remained was made up mostly of the frightened mauled who were unable to leave on their own or else had nowhere to go. Some were looking up the hill to Rocky but most were beseeching the Prophet. With a wave, Omar motioned for Rachman's security guards to form a perimeter around the survivors to protect them and though terrified, the people gathered warily, walking and crawling back to their feasting. From the hill, Rocky heard shouts of praise for their Prophet and protector.

Omar absorbed the praise with hands outstretched. As the sounds of the beaten crowd dissipated, his voice echoed over the silent field

"God Allah has chosen wisely. You, my loving survivors, are my honored guests. You have looked into the face of our enemy, the enemy of God, and you have survived to bring justice to the world. Eat, eat and rejoice! You are the great, good soldiers of Allah's glorious revolution and you will receive God's reward when we win. The government will send their evil minions to stop us, but we will not ever turn away, not ever. Our faith has been tempered here today and though our enemies are strong, we will wear them down and defeat them and the greed that has allowed them to acquire unfairly. By God Allah, we will have what is rightfully ours. We will take it back."

The crowd cheered between bites, but crowds are tenuous things; fed, sated, scared, and anxious to be gone from this place. They searched for places to hide, some with their eyes, some already wandering off, some running and most hobbling to other parts of the park. Food will bring them, but words won't hold them, not where danger prowls.

On his cue, actors planted throughout the crowd began to cheer and shout. Smith raised his hands to the sky and called everyone to prayer. Immediately, the actors in the crowd turned and dropped to the ground in fealty. Unsure why, some of the innocent others knelt, as well, acceding to those certain.

"There is no God but Allah!" Omar shouted.

The crowd repeated, "There is no God but Allah."

"And Omar is his Prophet," Omar said and the crowd repeated.

"Revolution."

"Revolution."

And it was over. A security team surrounded Smith and guided him to the waiting limo. As it pulled away, Rachman's team cleaned up and removed the tables, now bereft of food or scraps. Most copies of the Prophet's *Contract with America* lay undisturbed and they, too, were gathered up for reuse.

The Prophet's business team met later in the dining room of the posh Main Line mansion Omar rented for his revolution. They debriefed around a long, narrow wooden table in a dining hall of the pre-Revolutionary War mansion. Omar's catering staff, dressed in white, served the evening meal and it was the best food Rachman had ever tasted. After the sumptuous prime rib dinner, supported by a magnum of a luscious, fruit-forward Chinese Pinot Noir, they entered the smoking room where Omar offered his team an exotic desert of *Awamat* and a strong Turkish coffee. Finally, he dismissed his team managers, everyone but Rachman, and called for a servant to roll out a glass cart with cigars and cognac.

After recommending his favorites, Omar settled into an overlarge easy chair and nodded to Rachman.

Rachman returned the nod, took a sip and a puff, and asked the question that had been bothering him all day. "Omar, those beatings were pretty rough. What happens when the media finds out that most of the thugs were on your payroll?"

Smith looked up from his coffee and smiled. "It simply doesn't matter, Rocky. This is how it's done," he replied. "By the way, I was advised by my consultants that there was some bravery and possibly a moral dilemma out there today. You're not getting soft on me, are you?"

"I don't understand?"

"My friend, a great many want to rebel, but most are weaker than they know and more important, weaker than we need. For our cause to achieve the payback I desire, it needs the support of dedicated, like-minded people. It is lucrative, yes, but not easy. There are tests to pass."

"Did I fail some test?"

"My people say the video of you racing to the rescue will play. We can use it so if you feel the urge to save a few more souls, at a later date, have at it. But you're on your own. If you get bludgeoned to death or arrested by real police, I will disavow. Worse, I can't honor our contract if you're not protecting me so when you get out of jail, you'll be poorer than when you went in. I like you Rocky, so be careful it won't go well for you if you're caught and questioned by local authorities."

"I'm a big boy, Omar, I can handle myself. I surprised myself out there today, so I'm sure I surprised you, too. I rule neighborhoods and people are rightly scared of me so I know what it takes and I can dish it out better than anyone, but today, seeing those childlike, helpless people . . . they were getting creamed . . . and I don't do that. I never have." He just shrugged.

"Revolutions aren't for the faint of heart. But as I say, as long as my consultants see the advantage, it's your choice. Just don't get caught. Am I clear?"

"I appreciate your concern."

"My concern is business. You're assigned to organize my protection. That must come first. Frankly, I shouldn't have to tell you where the money is. But I do want to make you aware that revolutions have only one leader. One undeniable leader is the only way the rabble can be led to victory so you shouldn't try to be too much of a hero, Rocky. It confuses things."

Rachman nodded and Omar changed the subject.

"My consultants assure me that today's events will be distributed to the appropriate media. Your primary task now, Rocky—other than keeping me alive—is to identify the capable rebels. What I'm looking for are the most photogenic sad, disheartened creatures on the face of this planet that speak English and whose only motivation is to die and to die fast and well. It works and it's critical to my project schedule that you help identify these people quickly because, ongoing, they will be the faces of my brand.

"You know how the media thrives on beatings, murders, and mayhem so ours can't be just some generic onslaught. It is a delicate balance, attracting the right media and enough victims willing to endure unspeakable brutality yet still willing to pose for the cameras if they are able. This is where your job is critical. There will be chaos and it will be difficult to tell the right story so during this period, I must be certain that I am the face that the sorrowful look to for redemption. Make certain of that and keep me safe and you are a very rich man. That is all I have, Rocky. I am counting on you." Smith smiled his best, charming smile.

Before he left, Rachman offered, "You are the leader."

"I am. Those people in the back of the crowd with the laptops," the Prophet explained, "they're a Sales and Marketing team from RCI, *Revolutionary Consultants, Inc.* They've been planning this campaign for years and they assure me—as long as I stay alive—this is the way to go. And since I sign all the checks, it was their recommendation that I hire you in the first place so they would be more certain of their payday."

"How did they know I was the person for that job?"

Smith laughed. "Ever since the CIA was downsized as a result of the continuing government financial crisis, the private consulting company, RCI, has been the first choice for experienced retirees and pensioners for projects that require overthrowing foreign powers whose economics, technology, or simply their geographic placement, America doesn't like. They know what it takes. They've done this before. And RCI will receive a great many millions of petrodollars when we've achieved our goal and it will be well worth it to me. Rocky, they do the research, they know. Do what you're asked and this could be an audition for a very interesting and lucrative career for you."

"I never would have thought-"

"There is still much to do. For the next rally, we ramp up the body count"

"Body count?"

"Listen, learn, and you will go far. The media has a passion for numbers that graph well, but there also must be an interesting back-story, reporters so hate to do research anymore. Every one of those bodies out there today has been given a heart-rending, advertiser friendly story."

"Times are hard, Rocky, and capitalism, not freedom, won in America and Americans are no longer moved by anything but money. But financial transactions also make Americans wary, so it takes a lot to create momentum. Still, by the end of the month, when I head to my next battleground, we will have met our requirements here.

"This stuff really works. In Chicago, we had a wonderful outpouring from the locals that destabilized the city so much that the National Guard was called in. The awards banquet celebration that I sponsored before I fled Chicago was even reported on in Chicago papers and magazines. You may have read about it. It would have been even better but the mayor refused to attend even though he was under extreme pressure from my bank.

At the party, we had a band and so many of my loyal cripples came by to thank me for giving their life meaning. I was genuinely touched. That is our goal here. We do everything possible to insure chaos that drives the federal, state, and local administrations and local businesses to enforce draconian measures on the poor and middle class and the battle is won without you and me even having to be here.

"I'm a very wealthy man, Rocky, and you don't acquire that kind of wealth by hiring second class talent. To overthrow the government of the United States of America, I have the very best consultants. They plan and I work the plan while my loyal foot soldiers man the trenches. This will be the best planned revolution in the history of mankind. Vive la revolution!" Omar toasted while grinning.

"So you'll continue to kill and maim."

"For the cause, Rocky, for the cause. I ask myself why a man in your line of work cares."

"For me, killing is a tactic of last resort; this will be a learning experience."

"To put it in perspective, my followers are going to die anyway; I'm giving them glory, a final hurrah, fame and purpose so at the moment of their death, they will believe themselves to be heroes. There can be no greater kindness."

"Do they know they're going to die?"

"Some, the volunteers from Chicago surely did, but most don't, not yet. Over the next few weeks, when we get rolling, many will happily die to further the movement because they know it's the only time in their lives that they will ever count for anything. My consultants assure me they'll go eagerly and I trust my consultants on this."

"Why didn't you tell me all of this before?"

"You receive a regular paycheck, how much more information do you need? Frankly, it wasn't your concern, but you could have a future in the revolution business so you should understand the business dynamics. But don't get carried away, you are to focus on one thing, my survival. You know all you need to know about that."

"So there will be more days like today."

"Absolutely. I have great respect and passion for Gandhi-style passive resistance because it works where other methods do not. It takes longer than outright violence but duration is of little matter when you are certain of your funding.

But there are real issues to overcome with going passive. The media doesn't seem to have the desire to stretch a passive resistance story out long enough and they soon tire of it and move on. And without the media, revolutions are doomed. That is why I condone your actions today. You added another storyline, a bit more spice, now we're passive but with the hint of machismo."

"But what you call passive resistance seems to be merely beating the crap out of the innocent poor."

Omar smiled. "I don't care what you call it, my consultants say it works and it is our ticket to the middle class and victory. There is nothing the American middle class will knowingly die for, but they do get riled up if inconvenienced so it is imperative that we annoy the shit out of them while creating a revolutionary environment where they don't fear dying, that, my friend is victory."

"We inconvenience the middle class and they rebel. I don't—"

"My consultants assure me that once the middle class is truly inconvenienced, annoyed, hassled, and abused in their everyday life; we will be able to guide their discontent and make things difficult for the government. We spread that and it becomes our victory. We destabilize the fat, dumb, and miserable middle class and force them to choose sides. They make the easy decision and go with their neighbors who join us because the government provides no real solution. At that point, we galvanize massive, national passive resistance that forces businesses to press the government to attack and destroy with great fury.

"That's the end game and we know when to go on the offensive, when the real work begins. In Philly, like in Chicago, we'll know because the middle class will start attending our rallies and donating to my cause to demonstrate their dissatisfaction with inconvenience. This month, as my consultants assure me, we are priming the pump of discontent."

"It's not what I expected but as long as I get my money, I'm in."

"Rocky, I'm no fool. I've run large, complex global enterprises so I know how improbable what I'm saying sounds. But RCI Consultants are battle-hardened experts. They've delivered successful rebellions in eighty countries, ten of which were capitalist republics of some note. They know the revolution business enough to have become rich because of it. But America is unique in so many ways from what they've experienced in the past and they are anxious to prove their expertise works here. They've done their research and they assure me the country is ready. To gain important experience, they even reduced their consulting rates and offered me a gain sharing agreement that will benefit every stockholder once I am successful. They assure me that I have more than a puncher's chance to pull this off."

"You're talking larger crowds. That means more protection."

"Do it and don't worry about expenses. But make sure that you keep your eye on the prize. We want martyrs, just not me, and we need photo ops. That and stay in the background and keep me unharmed."

Rachman nodded.

"By the way, next week I'm speaking on the Drexel University campus. It's a great location; the poor live in great numbers on the outskirts of campus. I want you to find an eager, rich, young college kid who is idealistic enough to be interested in joining me. See who you can find."

"How will I know a good candidate?"

"You'll figure it out. By the way, we have scheduled a major political event for the last day of the month. It will blow the roof off everything and send a message that the Prophet's Rebel movement is real. You'll be impressed."

Rachman scouted the orange brick buildings and the modern glass structures that were the Drexel University Campus. As a location for Omar's rally, he picked a remote part of campus where abandoned homes designated with Greek letters denoted what was once fraternity row. On the day of the rally, he walked the area instructing his lieutenants.

"The Prophet will speak for about thirty minutes beginning at three o'clock which should coincide with the end of classes," Rachman explained to his crew. "The food wagons will appear at two to roust as many street people as possible. We keep them away from the food until the Prophet is done and gone. Keep an eye out for any students who seem particularly interested. Point them out to me. Remember, Philly's budget hasn't gone to hell yet like some other cities so they are still funding their police force. When the fighting starts, have your people use whatever force is required but if the real police come get them the hell out of here. Other than that, keep up the good work. The Prophet says there will be a bonus for everyone." They slapped hands and the meeting broke up.

That afternoon, while the Prophet was speaking to the crowd, Rachman searched for local talent. As he walked the perimeter, one girl, in particular, interested him. She was standing away from the crowd in a bright yellow windbreaker, listening intently as Omar expounded, and talking excitedly with her friends.

When, on queue, the violence began, Rachman watched her and her friends back away nervously. He wandered over.

"Don't be alarmed, ladies. We'll take care of any goons. Most are probably just overzealous junior engineers."

The girls laughed, uneasily. "Are you with the Prophet?" one of them asked.

"I am, ladies. I'm the honorable Rachman Morris and it's my sacred duty to protect the great Prophet from harm. It's a difficult job but I'm up to the task. You see, the Prophet Omar is so concerned for the poor that he ignores his own safety, yet he knows that if anything were to happen to him, there would be no one to take up his mantle and save the poor. It's my job to protect him."

"Then you must protect him at all cost," one of the girls said as she extended her hand. "Hi, I'm Barb, I'm a sophomore. These are my friends Sam; she's a freshman, and Louise and Marti, who are in my class. I guess if we're near you, we'll be safe."

"Absolutely," Rachman said. He flashed a hand signal and his people began to break up the fights, while others guided some of the injured to a first aid station nearby. The girls watched horrified until the violence wound down. Rachman took the hand of the best looking of the girls, the freshman, Sam, the one in the yellow windbreaker and guided her and her friends a distance away to a quieter place. "Why are four fine Drexel university women spending this pleasant afternoon watching the poor fight for their birthright?"

Sam answered, readily. "My economics professor is teaching us about the Prophet. When I heard he was coming to campus, I talked my friends into attending, but it's rougher than I thought. Why do the poor get hurt? They're not doing anything."

"From the mouths of babes. Why? In America, only the rich avoid pain. The Prophet's teachings, I'm afraid, only make it rougher. Business is so frightened of what he has to say that they fund government goon squads to stop him. Sam. It is Sam, isn't it?"

She smiled.

"Well, Sam, rich, well-off Americans protect and defend their own lifestyle but would never consider diluting their profits to protect and defend America's needy. They've been stealing from, starving and killing these poor people who ask for little and the rich have been doing it for centuries. It is time. The Prophet will end that."

"That's what my professor says, too," Sam added. "Still, it's so violent."

As they discussed Omar's revolution, Rachman checked Sam out. She was petite, and pretty enough; someone he certainly could be interested in if this wasn't business. She had straight, reddish-blonde hair, a ruddy pink complexion and light-blue eyes that stared innocently at him as if expecting to be amazed. She would be the one so Rachman used the best material.

"Greed is killing America. When we neglect the unfortunate among us, we only weaken ourselves and keep America from being the caring nation we all want."

Sam stared at him wide-eyed. "You're right," she said enthusiastically. "The Prophet is so courageous to do what he's doing."

"That's my Prophet," Rachman boasted. "What're you ladies doing after the rally?"

Rarely blinking, Sam responded, guardedly. "I would like to learn more about your revolution and I'd love to meet . . . meet the Prophet."

"Because of the great risk, the Prophet must keep his distance but I'm here for you. Where can we talk?"

"Sam, be careful," one of her friends warned. "You just met this guy and things are pretty rough. Don't go off alone with him."

She nodded. "I . . . I really shouldn't. I don't know you."

"You're fortunate to have such caring friends. How about if I come for you tomorrow? You tell me where? You can bring your boyfriend if you like."

Sam blushed and her girlfriends giggled. "Brad would never meet someone like you. His family is rich, like the ones the Prophet is fighting. If Brad even knew I was here, talking to . . . you, I'd be in big trouble."

Rachman tried to sound concerned. "Maybe we shouldn't . . . I don't want him to hurt me." He laughed and she smiled, shyly. "We're just talking. I'm sure it will be alright." Sam smiled again at that. "I understand your concern, Sam, I really do. But I'm your best source of information on the Prophet and I would love to tell you things about him that most people don't know. Hey, take whatever precautions you like but if you really want to learn about the revolution, I'm your man."

Unsure, she looked at her girlfriends for support and then hastily took out a pen and wrote her number on the palm of his hand. "Call me tomorrow," she said, and with that, she and her friends left.

That night, back at the mansion, there was another debriefing over dinner.

"The consultants say it went well," Omar began. "With all the people with cameras uploading video we didn't need nearly as many to start fights. Word is getting out and things are moving along. Rocky, I heard that you were making time with some campus cuties. Any luck?"

"I got one of the girl's numbers." He showed his palm with the smeared number on it. "Apparently her professor is teaching about you in class and she is interested in checking you out. I thought you had to be dead to make history?"

Omar smiled. "We are rewriting the history books. Tell me about the girl?"

"Her name is Sam; she's a freshman, shy, and interested."

Without looking up from his lobster bisque, Omar agreed. "She'll do. Do whatever you have to do but keep her interested. I'm counting on you, Rocky. The consultants say she has that nice kid look and that should work. This shouldn't be too difficult an assignment for you." Omar laughed and Rocky smiled. "She'll want to meet me, it's only natural, but she will have to earn it. By the way, earlier today, we had our first successful road event. During the evening rush hour, my teams drove onto the Ben Franklin Bridge from the Philadelphia and Jersey sides and stalled their cars at various strategic spots. The traffic was snarled for hours. Others were in cars on both sides. They started a riot that closed the Bridge and there were some deaths, even a drowning that made the news. Tens of thousands of commuters were pissed because they spent the day smelling the foul Philadelphia air from the bridge. All in all, it was a promising beginning. Tomorrow, we go after shoppers. That always gets the press involved. After dinner, we'll watch and review today's news coverage."

Rachman looked up from his meal. "How does being annoying help your cause?"

"We must get the attention of the middle class."

"Why not march on City Hall or strike or something?"

"Bringing any system down, even a damaged one like ours, is a slow process. You have to loosen some of the bolts before it will fall over. Watch and learn. There is awesome power deployed against us so we can't do this directly and if we tried, Crelli has the tools to take us down. If we commit even one felony, the system cranks up their media and we become too frightening to make a difference. This is a police state as sure as Allah rules the world, so we can't give them easy justification to deploy against us nor can we be an easy target. The nut in this, as I've been told so many times by my consultants, is to cause the maximum number of people to lose the maximum amount of faith in our government and do it before the poor are wiped out. That's why we hit the middle class where it hurts the most. They hate nothing more than inconvenience and annoyance but all they ever seem to do is bitch and whine about it. We need more. Once we drive a critical mass of the middle class over the edge, victory is ours."

"And this stuff works?"

Smith nodded. "There's great beauty in it. We get businesses to panic and they force the government to act, to suspend laws in order to prevent chaos. To the middle class that will seem like indiscriminate reprisals and fear will drive them to us."

"And we keep it up until we bring the country down."

"Thank Allah, yes." Omar said and signaled for his servants to pour another glass of pinot noir for everyone. "So tell me more about this sweet girl you found."

The next morning, Rachman and Sam agreed to meet at the University Book Store. She came in wearing the same bright yellow windbreaker that she'd worn to the rally and they had coffee while she explained what she was being taught about Omar. Some of it was true.

"Professor Wrege says that with the economy so bad for so long, the whole country has become radicalized. We're studying parallels between where we are now, and where the Roman Empire was as it was decaying, post Christ. My Professor says it's like social tectonic plates, geological like, grating together, creating pressure that can only be relieved by massive social upheaval. He says President Crelli, the Prophet Omar, and Reverend Cavanaugh, the Deacon Deliverer of the Prosperity Gospel, he says they each represent tectonic plates rubbing together to create this huge energy for change that my Professor says we desperately need if world is going to get out of the malaise that's killing it. He's even writing a graphic novel about it."

Rachman smiled. "Tectonic plates? I didn't realize I was into something that important."

"They cause earthquakes."

"I know," he said.

"Tell me about the Prophet Omar. What's he like after the crowds go home?"

"I'm his right hand man and I know him better than anyone," he lied. "He wants peace, but peace alone won't change anything."

Rachman and Sam began by meeting regularly but always in public. He enjoyed her passionate, naïve intelligence, but what surprised him more was how much he coveted her worshipful stare. Still, it was almost two weeks before she trusted him enough to meet him somewhere more private. During this time, he found himself becoming more involved in Omar's demonstrations, wading into the mayhem sooner and more aggressively to help the most desperate of the poor and sorry lot. He did it because it felt right but more, he needed to feel worthy of Sam's worshipful stare, something he had never earned from anyone before. And because so many victims of the planned riots were the same pitiable poor who followed the Prophet from place to place for the chance that they would be fed before being beaten to death, he was beginning to develop a following.

The night after just such a beat down, He told her of those he rescued. Unblinking, she leaned in, ever so sweetly and kissed him innocently on his mouth. Soon, with much coaxing from him, they were more than friends. She was innocent and reluctant and Rachman had never needed to convince a girl before. The excitement of the slow and cautious seduction opened feelings he never thought possible. And though passionate about Sam, he knew that their burgeoning sexual relationship of incompatible needs couldn't last.

She wanted desperately to meet the Prophet and because she denied him nothing, he couldn't deny her but he could play it out slowly and for as long as he possibly could. That Omar showed no further interest in Sam was fine with him.

Chapter 20

Presque Isle, PA—2070

The sound of breaking glass jolted Gil's attention from Rachman's story. Rachman smiled sheepishly as he felt under the table for shards of the broken wine glass that he had accidentally tipped over in his inebriated state. After he piled most of the glass on Gil's end of the table, Rachman's rested his head on his arm and using his free hand, searched for another glass.

"Sorry," he said, his voice slurring. With that, he was soon snoring and Gil took his leave quietly.

It was still relatively early, so Gil walked the narrow path at the boundary of the community. The huts were all dark, but in one of the buildings, he heard music coming through an open door, so he entered. A small group of *Tollers* and their families were listening to a song playing quietly on cheap speakers. A man motioned him to come over.

"How's he doing?" the man asked.

"He's okay."

"Since returning from prison, he drinks too much."

"I don't know. Where I'm from, nobody drinks."

"Where are you from?" The man asked.

"I'm from a small manager's town," he lied, uncomfortably.

"You must have value, huh, or the boss wouldn't keep you. Which town did you say?"

"Doesn't matter. I don't have much value. I earn enough for my garden, but that's about it." With that, Gil turned to leave when he noticed a cute young girl sitting nearby. She smiled, shyly.

"You like gardens?" she asked. He nodded. "We have a garden. Do you want to see it?"

Her name was Annie, short for Christianne and she was eighteen and lived with her mother and father. Gil followed her to the garden and made her laugh when he asked if Christianne was an Arab name.

"We're Muslims, not Arabs. My parents liked the name, why else?" She continued to talk until they arrived at a tiny open area where wild flowers grew. "I love the smells our garden. Is yours like this?"

"Where I'm from," Gil explained, "gardening is very competitive and what we grow must be functional as well as attractive. We're graded for originality and the reward is our seeds are marketed nationally. We can even be promoted to an Executive community."

"Why do they force you to move away from your home? What kind of reward is that?" she asked.

"It's not . . . you should never turn down a reward. It's bad for your career."

"Don't you ever just want to walk through your garden and enjoy the smells?"

He'd never considered that. "Gardening is hard work and there's even cheating."

She laughed. "How do you cheat growing flowers?" The way she asked the question did make it sound absurd. "If you can't enjoy gardening, what do you do for fun?"

"We use *Virtuoso*."

"I've heard of that. What's fun about *Virtuoso*?"

"Everything."

She smiled. "Everything is a lot."

"In *Virtuoso*, you can prototype and run a business, participate in any kind of social activity like sky diving, mountain climbing, play games or sports, invent music or even dance."

"That sounds like fun. Who do you play with?"

"Other people who are signed on. Avatars help."

"What are Avatars?"

"Computer programs that act alive, but exist only in *Virtuoso*. They can do anything."

"Can they be buffaloes?"

He laughed. "Mostly they're human, but they can be buffaloes, if you want. They have personalities. They can be friends or enemies and even monsters like buffaloes, too."

"Can you make love in *Virtuoso*?"

"I suppose you could," he said, cautiously.

"Have you ever . . . ?"

"I don't think we should talk about that, Annie."

"Okay. My uncle says you communicate using a glove," she said.

"It's a gift from an old friend."

"Show me," she begged and moved closer to Gil.

"Annie, I'm not going to show you."

"Please," she pushed against him, trying to reach into his back pocket. He tried to stop her but she looked up, pursed her lips, and tried to kiss him.

"What are you doing? Everyone's looking."

"We're alone and I like you. It's okay to kiss me, you know."

"You must have boyfriends," he said as gently as he could while pushing her away. "

"Yuck. Everyone here is either a Terrorist or a *Toller*."

"What's the difference?" he asked not really caring, but trying to deflect her.

"My grandparents are Terrorists along with their leaders who were captured and imprisoned. The rest of the villagers were assigned to this reservation to maintain the roads between Buffalo and Cleveland. If you're born here, you're a *Toller*, if not, a terrorist. I'm a *Toller*."

"Do you help with the roads?"

"No, but I'd like to help you." She reached for him but he held her at arms length.

"Stop it, please, Annie."

"I'm a good kisser. I just need practice."

"I don't want to kiss you. Can't we just talk?"

"I can talk anytime. I want to do more with my mouth than that." She reached out to touch his neck. He felt a tremor as she clamped her hands around him and pulled him toward her.

He resisted. "I can't do this. Annie, I . . . I have a girlfriend."

"She's not here now. All I want is a kiss—for starters."

He had no experience kissing a real girl so he was tempted. "I like you and you're very pretty, but I'm a prisoner here. Can't we just talk?" he pleaded.

"Would you feel like kissing if you weren't a prisoner?"

What does that mean? he wondered. "Maybe, I guess. Why?"

"Kiss me and I'll help you not be a prisoner anymore."

"You can do that?"

"Kiss you, of course I can."

"No, no. I mean get me off your island."

"It's not an island. It's a peninsula. Anyway, there's more than one way to get off."

"You'd help me?"

She blushed. "If I help you get off, you have to help me get off."

When he realized what she was asking, shock became concern.

"I can't do that."

"Is it these?" she smiled and rubbed her small breasts with her hands. "My mother's are big. In a couple of years these will be too and you'll have more fun."

"Annie, don't-"

"I read that rubbing them makes them bigger. Would you like to help them grow?"

"No, besides, I won't be here when they're bigger. I'm leaving in a few days."

"Who told you that?"

"Nobody, but I'm of no value to your community so why would they keep me?"

"Some people with little value have great value to the government."

That concerned him. "I can't go to the government."

Sensing his concern, she pursued it. "I don't want that either. I'd rather have you here on top of me or any other way. But I don't make the rules. Presque Isle depends on barter and a *Toller* considers it a great blessing to discover value and find a buyer for it."

"I thought that's what ferrets do?"

"No way. Ferrets do all the yucky stuff with things of little value while we trade important things like people and equipment. My daddy says we're the grease that keeps the economy growing. They're no way like us; they have no self-respect or business sense. We're so much more business savvy that it's not even funny. We create value. Wanna kiss me?"

"No, Annie," he said. "I don't want to hurt your feelings but I can't."

She smiled. "You will hurt my feelings and Uncle Rocky won't be happy. Let's start with a kiss." She raised herself on her toes, lips pursed again. He reached out and gently pressed her shoulders down.

"What don't you understand about the word 'no'?"

"One of the first things we're taught in school is that the word 'no' is the opening response in every negotiation. I know a good looking young man who is going to be stuck on Presque Isle a long, long, time while his value is being determined unless he gets some help from a certain very attractive, and very, very, willing young lady."

"Rachman won't find anyone who'll pay for me."

"You'll still be stuck here and you'll have me with you."

"I don't want to be here. I want to be free so I can travel."

"Uncle Rocky took you from a police caravan. Is that how you travel free?"

"I won't get caught again."

She frowned. "I want to be your best friend and you're making me angry. If you're right and you have no value, you'll be sold to, I don't know, the Department of Commerce, who'll subcontract you to recover their cost. If that happens, neither of us get what we want so how about that kiss?"

"God, you're annoying."

He limped away but since both of them knew he had nowhere to go, she didn't chase after him. Instead she yelled at him, "I'll be here for you, you bad boy."

In the morning after prayers, Gil was once again summoned to Rachman's room. When he arrived, Rachman looked exhausted, but motioned for Gil to be seated.

"I apologize for last night. You can't imagine how . . . not well . . . I am this morning. Drinking isn't a good thing. How was your evening?"

"I met a girl."

"Yes, Annie. She's quite a handful, I'm afraid, but we love her."

"I can see why. She's very friendly."

"She's hoping you won't have value and you'll stay."

"I appreciate your hospitality but I can't stay."

Rachman waved his hand and shook his head. "Of course you can't. I understand. You have places to go. I'd be pleased if you would stay until I finish my story."

Gil wanted to leave as soon as possible, but he was mindful of his situation. "Annie said I can't leave without your permission and my wound still needs time, so yes, I'd like to hear the rest of your story."

Rachman smiled, but it turned into a grimace and he put his head in his hands. "We don't keep people against their will if they have no worth."

Gil didn't like the sound of that, but decided not to pursue it. "Is Annie your daughter?" he asked guardedly.

"She's my niece. If she makes you uncomfortable, you mustn't try to avoid her; it will hurt her feelings and she'll only become more insistent. You seem like a nice young man. Be a gentleman and do nothing to disgrace her. We're a small community and there's no place to hide."

"I'd never do that."

"If you do not take advantage of our hospitality, as long as you are a good guest, your desire to leave will be granted.

"I'd never take advantage."

"I know you won't. With that, Rachman poured his first glass of wine. "Hair of the dog," he murmured. "I'm not a fool, but too many times I've been convinced to do things I shouldn't have done. Call it a weakness. Be careful of weaknesses, Dan Stacey. Because of mine, I've spent too much of my life in prison. Omar offered me wealth and a hopeless cause so maybe I am a fool."

"I'm sure that's not true."

"Omar once said that America will die when the moneyed interests sell us out for a better return. I wasn't lucky and lived to see it."

"But America is still here."

"In a republic, who surrenders?"

"I don't know?"

Rachman gulped down the wine. "That's why we're still here. Someone once told me that the only coin we have is time and you should never give up that coin for someone else's dream. Life is too valuable and your dreams are all you have." His tortured expression seemed to relax as he poured himself another glass.

"Did you know you were making wrong decisions?" Gil asked.

"Nobody does, really, but there are warning signs you ignore at your own peril. I had doubts, but even when you make the right decision there are doubts. And what is life if not for the certainty of regret? I believed every decision I made was the correct one. That's the beauty of it. But except for my time with Mr. Thau, none of my decisions ever turned out right. Maybe I've been making the correct decisions all along, just performing badly. I don't know." he waved his hand dismissively and then took another swig of wine, made a face as he held it for a second, and then swallowed. He pushed the glass and bottle away. "No, I must do this without wine. The Prophet had this inner fire like no one I've ever met. He was young, did I mention that? Maybe only thirty when I met him. How old are you?"

"I'm nineteen."

"He was older than you and rich, or at least his family was. He didn't have to help the poor, but he did. His father was a very wealthy entrepreneur in northern Europe, Finland or somewhere. Omar was Muslim, but rarely followed our laws. He may have read the Quran, but I never heard him quote from it. And though European, he became a United States citizen, graduating from Yale with a degree in philanthropy."

"What's philanthropy?"

"I think it's the art or, if you're very good at it, the science of getting people to donate money to further your beliefs."

"There's really a degree in that?"

Rachman nodded. "Omar was pleased with the progress we were making in Philadelphia and I was happy because it looked like the easiest and best payout I'd ever earned. On top of that, Sam . . . Sam . . . she was making me feel things, really good things. But there's no such thing as a sure thing or easy money. The month Omar's revolutionary consultants had planned for was almost over."

Chapter 21
Philadelphia, PA – 2031

Omar's rallies grew with each event, and according to the Prophet's blog, there had been seventeen deaths and several hundred arrests, but strangely, Omar Smith was never detained or his rallies raided before he was finished. He attributed that to good lawyers but in reality it was more about strategic uses of vast sums of money.

Rachman's relationship with Samantha had been developing nicely until the last week that Omar Smith was to be town, the week that would end with his final rally. Mysteriously, Sam stopped coming to events and she failed to return any of his calls. He had never shown weakness to his women before, but Sam was different, so he spent his spare time searching the Drexel campus for her.

Meanwhile, Omar was preparing for an end-of-the-month project that had been too secretive to discuss with his staff. And though Rachman was living at Omar's mansion, as the date of the final rally drew near, his contacts with Omar ceased. When he needed to discuss something, the Prophet's consultants would pass on his needs, but would not allow him time with his employer. Then one day, he received a message informing him that once Omar left Philadelphia, everyone should hunker down for an extended period.

He tried to get an explanation, but was told that Omar couldn't be disturbed. Days before the rally, Rachman was reviewing his security checklist when a large wooden crate arrived. It was labeled, "sound equipment".

"What do I do with this?" he asked a consultant. The consultant told him to leave it alone, but he decided he'd had enough and barged into

Omar's study. The Prophet was working on his speech and looked up, unperturbed. "Rocky, is everything ready for the big day?"

"Everything's fine. You got a shipment of sound equipment this morning. What do you want me to do with it?"

Omar put down his papers. "What do I want you to do? Why nothing at all. My sound engineer will pick it up and take it to the stadium before the rally. Thanks for asking, but please don't interrupt me again." Rachman stayed his ground. Omar stared and then added, "Oh, right." He pulled a large envelope from his desk and handed it to him. Rachman took it but didn't open it until Omar nodded. Inside were a series of cashier's checks.

"Does this mean my gig here is over?"

"After Friday night's rally, yes," the Prophet said. "Thanks for all you've done. You more than satisfied your end of our contract, though I wish you hadn't made such a heroic spectacle."

"It was something I had to do and it was hardly heroic. Some of those people, they were so old; you couldn't even hear the sound of their bones breaking. Whatever I did; it doesn't seem to have affected anything."

"Sam is very appreciative of your efforts."

"I wish that was enough," Rachman said. "Is there anything more I can do?"

"Keep me alive until the rally ends. There is one thing." Omar handed him another envelope.

Inside was a single, large, glossy red, white, and blue ticket. "Thanks, but I can enter with the crew, I don't need a ticket."

"This is for Saturday night," Omar explained. "President Crelli is speaking and after listening to me rant about him, you must hear my enemy and make up your own mind. I won't be able to join you, but it will be a memorable evening, I'm sure."

He agreed and then shook Omar's hand before leaving.

With final planning for the last rally complete, Rachman took the afternoon off. Always the one to end relationships, he was confused by Sam's sudden disappearance. He hated to admit it, but he was a little hurt and later a little embarrassed when he found himself nervously waiting for her outside her campus apartment. After wasting a couple of futile hours waiting, he was ready to give up when a familiar limousine pulled up to the curb and Sam jumped out. From the other side, Omar, wearing jeans and a sweatshirt, exited and took her hand. Together, they disappeared into her apartment. Confused, Rachman considered his options. He wasn't the jealous type, until now, but there was the issue of money. He didn't want to jeopardize any future deals with Omar. So, angry and frustrated, he drove to Omar's mansion and waited some more.

It was late when he heard the limo pull up. From the windows of Omar's library, he watched as the car lights illuminated the long stone driveway. When he heard a car door close and someone enter the mansion, he walked into the hall, meeting Omar as he entered.

"Are you waiting for me, Rocky?"

"I am."

"I'm certain my checks didn't bounce."

"No, they were good as gold."

"Everything's okay?"

"Yes, I transmitted the funds to my offshore accounts like you recommended. Omar, I'm not mad, I'm just confused. Help me out."

Omar spoke his concern. "Sam?"

Rachman nodded. "I'm not jealous. I just met her and I wouldn't let that get in the way of a business deal, but I'm curious. If you wanted her, why not just tell me?"

"I apologize, Rock. You're right, of course, we should have discussed it, but I wasn't sure how. I've never felt this way about anyone. It was my mistake. I'm sorry."

He was surprised, but tried to be understanding. "Does she love you, too?"

Smith nodded. "She's young, but yes, she does, very much. I'm sorry, my friend. I didn't realize how anxious she was to meet me. I never make it easy, but she went to great lengths to convince me of her feelings and I'm not easily impressed."

Rachman was uncomfortable but had to ask. "Great lengths?"

"While you were setting up for our last rally, she snuck in."

"How did she get past my security guards?"

"She didn't. That's what finally convinced me. They caught her three or four times before I told your men to let her in."

"My men never reported it."

"I told them not to."

"What happened?"

"That's none of your business," Smith said. "She very much wanted to get to know me better and I was surprised and impressed at how intelligent

184

and motivated she is. All I can say is she won me over and that never happens to me. We've been spending as much time as we can together."

"I still don't understand. Why did you hide all this from me?"

"I'm sorry, my friend. It was . . . necessary."

"And you love her?"

"I'm certain she's the one for me and I promise you, her honor is entirely safe."

"Really? She's a very emotional, and physically she-"

"Please," Omar said angrily. "I won't listen any further. We are involved in the deepest possible relationship and I'd never sully it by listening to talk like that. She's better than that. She's heaven to me. You and I are done with this conversation. And don't try to see her again. That's an order. I don't want her . . . confused. Do you understand?"

"That's not a problem, Omar. Business supersedes everything."

"I'm glad that you understand. What remains to be done for the rally?"

"The sound equipment is still here. I can take it down to the stadium."

"That is not necessary. Leave it here. Someone will get it."

Friday, the day of the rally arrived and Rachman slept late. When he went downstairs, he noticed the sound equipment crate still waiting and since Omar wasn't available and everyone else was gone, he loaded it into his van. As he lifted it, a few strands of the shredded newspaper worked their way out of the carton and onto the marble floor. The newspaper was written in exotic flowing *Cyrillic* script. Curious, he considered opening the crate, but decided that Omar was angry enough. He left for the stadium and upon arrival, made the final preparations with his security staff.

In the weeks since Omar's Philadelphia campaign began, Rachman's staff had increased from a handful of loyal men to five lieutenants and to each of them another five reported. Because everything was under control, the meeting was brief. Afterwards, he drove the van to the stadium's sound engineer's office.

"This is sound equipment for tonight's rally."

The engineer gave him an odd look. "If it is, it's not ours. We have the best equipment in the business, buddy." The engineer went back to his office leaving him with the large box.

He waited for Omar to arrive on-site to once again ask about the shipment. But as the rally start time neared, Omar still hadn't arrived.

He was concerned, but Omar's consultants assured him that all was well. Finally, just before the rally, Omar and Sam arrived together in his limo. From a discreet distance, Rachman watched them through the car's window as they talked quietly. She was crying.

Omar took her hand, kissed her cheek and whispered something in her ear. Still crying, she smiled and wiped away the tears. Then they embraced. It was clear Sam didn't want the embrace to end. When it did, she put out her hands, but Omar shook his head and opened the door for her. She got out and ran backstage, sobbing and trying to hide it from the stage crew.

Omar wasn't happy when he approached Rachman and saw the crate of sound equipment. He thanked Rachman curtly and asked him to store it backstage. They didn't discuss Sam at all.

With the arriving crowd piling in, the noise within the stadium grew deafening. Rachman reviewed the final security routines while keeping an eye on Omar and the clock. When everything was in order, he carried the crate backstage where he found Sam. He used the sound equipment delivery as an excuse to approach her, setting it down next to her.

Handkerchief in hand, she sat on a tall stool dabbing her eyes and rubbing her nose as she listened to the shrieks from the crowd reacting to the Prophet's speech.

"Sam, how are you?" he asked quietly.

"Rock, I . . . I'm sorry," she said. "I don't know what to say." She spoke as if she was searching the universe for each word. And she was sobbing again.

"I'm a big boy," Rachman said. "We had a good time. I like you but I understand. Omar's quite a guy." He stared out onto the stage where the Prophet was performing.

Her sobs grew louder.

"What is it, Sam?"

"He's so beautiful. He's like no one I've ever met. He's so intense and he will change the world. How do you do it, work so close with him I mean? He's so . . . so . . . on."

"He's a ride, isn't he?" Rachman asked, embarrassed by his choice of words. "I'm sorry, Sam. I didn't mean . . . Why are you crying?"

"This past week with him . . . it's been like nothing I've ever known. It's destiny. He's so brilliant and he's, kind, and . . . and-"

"Has he done something to hurt you?"

She gulped in air to stop crying. "No, he's a total gentleman and he loves me, Rock, I know he loves me."

"He said that?"

"I know he loves everybody. But the trust he has in me. And he's so open. He shares things, all the pain and his fear for our country. He hurts so much because of what our leaders have done to the innocent and the poor. He feels the burden like . . . like their father, or a savior, or something. I feel it too, Rock. He is the best man I'll ever know and I don't deserve his trust, but I love him so much. I never thought anyone could be so important to me."

It was awkward to listen to her speak so glowingly of his rival for her affections, who also happened to be his boss. "That's great, so why the sad face?"

"I'm not sad," she said. "Look, I'm happy." She forced a smile. "I'll . . . just . . . I'll miss him." The tears flowed freely again.

"You knew he'd be going," Rachman said, trying his best to calm her. "Besides, he won't be far. He's considering Denver for his next rally."

Her sobs grew louder and she reached up to him and held him while trembling and sobbing.

"Sam, you're a great girl. You'll find someone more your age who has more time for you. You know how Prophets can be." He forced a smile, but couldn't get one from her.

Onstage, under the careful tutelage of Omar Smith, the crowd roared with enthusiastic energy. Backstage, Sam remained distressed, engulfed in the crushing feeling of inestimable sadness. She pushed him away and fled to the sanctuary of Omar's limo. The driver opened the door for her and she entered without looking back. Rachman followed her, but the driver locked the windows and doors and denied him access.

"Is this the spot you chose to protect me?"

He turned toward the voice. Omar was walking toward him.

"Everything was secure and I saw Sam was crying so I thought I'd cheer her up."

"Did you?"

"No, I don't think so?"

"Well then, do the job you've been paid to do."

He turned to walk away, but Omar had something else to say.

"Where did you put the sound equipment?"

"It's backstage."

"Good. Thank you. Your work here is done. Spend your money wisely."

"Is there anything I can do to help, you know, Sam?"

"She's an emotional girl. Trust me, she'll be fine. There's more money in this than you know, Rocky, and maybe after attending President Crelli's speech tomorrow evening, I'll have more use for you in the future." With that, Omar walked brusquely past him and entered the limo. He watched uncomfortably as Sam kissed Omar feverishly, before walking away, confused and disappointed.

The following night, Rachman did as he was instructed and attended President Crelli's rally. It felt odd being in the same place with people whose goals were diametrically opposed to the Prophet's. Once he cleared security, he walked down the aisle, listening as someone on stage was singing the praises of the president. He found his seat near the stage and settled in to listen.

While the introductory speeches were being offered, he scanned the audience, comparing Crelli's people with Omar's. This rally had far better production values; it was more expensive and showier, obviously focusing on making the well-to-do comfortable. And while Omar had preached on a bare stage, this rally featured a podium that was beautifully designed in red, white, and blue and rose high above the stage.

Because of his previous responsibilities, he couldn't resist observing operations behind the scenes. In particular, he watched the security team. But the biggest difference was the audience itself. With the rich in attendance, the place was quiet and orderly.

The president sat behind and to the left of the podium with his wife. Crelli was lean, well-dressed and in his early forties and prematurely grey. His wife was a strikingly beautiful woman, tall, dark, and a real stunner. Beside her was a nurse who was trying to calm a restive infant. As various speakers took turns lauding the young president, Rachman noticed young interns providing refreshments to the guests in the elite seats behind the podium. One helper, in particular, caught his eye as she left the stage wearing a bright yellow windbreaker. He stared, waiting for her to return.

A few minutes later, the girl reappeared. At first he thought it was Sam, but this girl was much heavier and walked differently as she headed toward the president holding a drink. He continued to stare at her until she turned. It was Sam! *This was interesting,* he thought. After the rally he would have to find her.

As he stared, he was blinded by a bright flash and a loud explosion. The white-hot blast temporarily blinded him and he was knocked from his chair by a concussion that sucked the air from his lungs. Although blinded, his mind pictured Sam disappearing in a flash, pink spraying everywhere. Had he been hallucinating? In the brief silence that followed, he vomited. Slowly, his eyes cleared but a large white spot in his vision hid the ensuing chaos. All was silent.

Am I deaf, his mind questioned as he vomited again. Then, the noise slowly returned and he heard the screaming. He looked up and around, and through the fading blind spot in his eyes, saw a war zone. It was surreal. The podium had been blown back from the stage and was on fire and a large man was lying on top of the President and his wife. Crelli's wife was screaming hysterical, her clothes glistening pink with blood as pieces and parts of bodies flopped down on the stage and into the crowd, settling everywhere, causing screams anew. Dazed and lightheaded, Rachman tried to swallow down the sick feeling. Then he tried to stand, but his legs wouldn't support him. Holding the chair in front of him with sweaty hands, he slowly gained control and wobbled to his feet. He staggered to the aisle just as a small piece of singed yellow windbreaker floated down from above. He bent over and vomited again.

Chapter 22

Presque Isle, PA—2070

"Jesus," Gil said. He stared at Rachman whose head was face down on the table. "Was it Sam? A bomb? What?" Gil asked.

"Rachman looked up. There were tears in the tough old man's eyes. "Sam . . . she died. She was gone, her mind, her body, everything in a flash. That fucking yellow windbreaker. I dream of it still. I'm suffocated in yellow."

"How-" Gil struggled to form a coherent thought.

Rachman reburied his head in his hands. "He had no right . . ."

"Who? No, of course, what did you do?"

"There was screaming and moaning, police and ambulance sirens, it was a nightmare. I see it now, all in silence; slow motion silent horror. Somehow, I stumbled from the stadium and stayed in the crowds on the street outside waiting . . . waiting for Allah knows what.

"Everyone was concerned, asking about the President, his wife and their baby or one of the other dignitaries. I was numb, listening as all the questions that could be answered, were. Once people heard what happened, they left in shock. But I stayed, waiting to hear something, anything about Sam. I don't know what I expected. In the end, I was the only one there except for the police and the media."

"What did you do?"

"Do? Hell, I was too stunned to do anything. Of all the people involved in Omar's operation, I was the easiest to catch. I was the numb dumb guy standing beside a news crew when a security team surrounded me and beat the crap out of me. I hadn't been beaten that badly since high school. I woke handcuffed to bars in some detention facility. If anyone ever said torture was outlawed in America, they lied. I never saw the inside of a courtroom and it was twenty years before I was free—or at least free to come here."

"What happened to Omar?"

"That son of a bitch was halfway to Tehran when Sam . . ." Rachman paused. "Every day in prison, I was fighting for my life while he was being treated like royalty wherever in the Arab world he went. When I was released I was broke and the funds Omar paid me were gone; the government had confiscated them. I tried to start again, poor in a world that Crelli ruled. The last I heard, Smith built an extravagantly huge, heavily-fortified estate somewhere in Canada where he's some kind of celebrity. It turns out, Omar hated Crelli for some reason and the revolution was an elaborate set-up to kill him. There was no Chicago or any other city. He came to Philly for one thing and my Sam was his instrument. Some revolutionary." He shook his head. "Wealth makes such a difference. Smith lives like a king while I organize road crews from ruins just north of nowhere."

"I'm sorry," Gil offered.

"Sorry? What about Sam? She was such a sweet, naïve girl. Or what about Crelli's baby? Even though it was Crelli's, the child was innocent. They died and I went to prison, while Omar and Crelli continued on. Royalty and wealth are unassailable. It's the world we live in. Don't feel sorry for me. I've been doing that for years and it gets me nowhere. I was an adult, I should have been smarter. Feel sorry for the baby, for Sam, and for all the Sams who give more than their fair share to the undeserving and uncaring power mongers who soak up the glory and spit out the remains of those who believe in them and are willing to sacrifice to provide their glory." He tried to hide the tears by sagging and pressing his head on the table.

Troubled, Gil left him in that position. Rachman had been open and honest, maybe to a fault. Apparently Bernie had trusted him so why shouldn't he. What choice did he have? He had no one else and he needed to confide in someone. He had nowhere to turn and nowhere to run. Returning to Howard was impossible, and Angel Falls no longer existed, so he sat by the shore under a tree and stared out at the lake feeling sorry for himself, for Rachman and Sam, and for the hopelessness of everything. He resisted crying, but tears leaked out anyway. Was anyone in this rotten world good or was everyone just varying degrees of bad? And was he, like everyone, just being used, and doomed to unhappiness and misfortune because of it? Is this what being an adult was?

He took out his glove and tried halfheartedly to communicate with Joad, but frustrated by the silence, he stuffed the glove back in his pocket and continued to stare out at the lake until endless day became endless night. He searched his limited experience for something to hold onto, something to provide solace in the world that had obviously crumbled into one huge quagmire of despair. Sad to be alone and scared to be intruded upon, he huddled against the night wind which added chill to his many woes.

He lost track of time until a sound startled him back from the abysmal emptiness.

"You're such a gloomy puss," Annie said. "There's no sense sulking over here when there's a party going on and a pretty girl waiting to show you a good time."

At first he thought she was mocking him. Then he realized she was just being friendly. "Hi, Annie. How are you?"

"Better than you. Why so sad?"

"It's nothing. I guess I miss home."

"That can't be good for a traveling man like yourself."

"No, I guess not. Annie, I don't feel like company right now. Could you please leave me alone? Maybe later-"

"No. Company is what you need," she said as she sat down beside him. "I'm sorry about yesterday. There aren't many kids my age here, particularly good-looking guys like you. I'll slow down."

"Its okay, Annie, I'm not mad at you. But I'm not going to be here for long so whatever you want to happen, it just can't. I like you but-"

She smiled when he said that. "If you have a better place to be tonight, go, go. But don't be so ready to leave that you miss something worth staying for. While you're here, let's get to know each other. Who knows, it could be fun. And while you're here, I'm sure I can get my uncle to let you do something useful to pass the time."

It sounded more appealing than he wanted it to. His wound still hadn't healed and he didn't have anywhere else to go or anyone else to go there for. Even though he didn't feel safe here, he knew he was safer in Presque Isle than other places. She waited patiently, more reserved than the previous night. Finally, she poked him gently. "Let's go to the party.

I know you're not in the mood, but sometimes a party is the right thing, even if it doesn't feel like it."

Reluctantly, he nodded and together they walked toward the music. Cautiously, she grabbed his hand and held it lightly in her own. He considered removing it, but it did feel good to hold onto so he let it be. When they reached the party, couples were dancing and the younger children were jumping and playing. He looked around for Rachman but he wasn't there.

She looked up at him. "Do you want to?"

"I don't dance. Never have. Besides, my leg-"

"I'll be gentle," she said. "Besides, it's simple." She demonstrated the foot movements for him, when to jump and when to sway and in a few minutes, he was dancing, awkwardly.

The evening passed. Because of his bum leg, he tired quickly. But as he left the dance floor, others began dancing in circles around him. At first reluctant, he began mimicking their movements and continued dancing until late into the evening when he noticed couples separating from the group and strolling away.

He worried that Annie would force him away as well, but as the last couple left, they sat with the few single men who remained. He was tired and his wound throbbed, but he felt better than he had in a long while. Thankful, he smiled at her. She grabbed his hands and pulled him from the fire toward the far side of the encampment. He was anxious, but continued on without complaint.

In the dark, on the beach, she found a spot protected from the wind and spread out a blanket. She sat and held her hand up for him to join her.

"I haven't danced like that in so long, thank you," she said, patting the blanket.

He sat on a corner, trying to keep his distance to avoid another confrontation like the night before. Inevitably, she moved closer and cautiously rubbed her fingers on the palm of his hand. When she guided his head into her lap, he let himself relax and laid back and stared up into her deep, excited chocolate eyes. Her face was framed by a million stars in the clear night sky. He closed his eyes and dreamed of similar times.

He felt a warm, wet kiss and smiled as her tongue insinuated itself past his lips and into his mouth. A shiver darted through his body which responded excitedly to every sensation that Andrea presented, and he relaxed. Whatever warning signals he'd posted earlier dissipated with the dance of their tongues.

It had been so long since he felt release that the memory of it created compulsion, and though his mind separated from his body, it worked to please it. In a flash, they were naked and his mind's eye rekindled the joy of Andrea and he was lost. When, for a moment, her moans changed to sounds of pain, the magic wavered, but he was too far gone to stop. Finally, satisfied and exhausted, they lie sweating and out of breath in a cocoon-like embrace.

The late-evening call to prayers woke them from their sexual stupor. Annie offered a shy smile and a wet kiss then rushed to dress. It wasn't until she grabbed the blanket and folded it that he saw the blood stain but before he could ask, she ran back to the encampment. Alone now, his body tingling in the chilly night air, he slowly dressed. He wasn't unhappy. He had needed that.

The aura of Andrea wore off with the realization that Annie was the innocent victim. He vowed it would never happen again, but that didn't stop the sadness from crashing down on him. The memory of feeling good evaporated into disgust and he wiped the sweat from his forehead and fled to the encampment following the same path Annie had taken.

In the following weeks, he made every effort to fight the inevitable, but ended up spending most of his time with Annie anyway. It was enough time for rationalization to be inadequate. As wild and impulsive as she was, Annie carefully selected their lovemaking hideouts and somehow, it had remained a secret. During the day, he watched and learned and tried his best to fit in, chopping firewood or helping with the complex bookkeeping that was necessary in their barter society. Occasionally, Rachman allowed him to go out with the *Tollers* to collect from travelers, but he was never allowed to show his face. He did all of this each day while waiting for Annie to finish supervising the young children in her care. At night, they acted like friends until the coast was clear, then they became teenagers in heat.

One evening, before making love to her, he complained. "Annie, I've been here for months and all I do is kid stuff or accounting. When the *Tollers* return and tell their stories, I'm never involved. When will they trust me?"

"Uncle Rocky is still trying to find out whether you have value. He's never had this much trouble before. He's not getting a response to any of his *RFI*s and that concerns him."

"What's an *RFI*?"

"It's a request for information. We send out to other towns for information on a potential asset. If they don't know anything, they'll petition one of the corporate towns that has an Archive terminal. That's more costly, because they want a cut of the action, so Uncle Rocky doesn't do it unless he thinks there's real value. With the information he receives, he places a value on something. It seems that no one has any information on Dan Stacey." She smiled. "They'll keep trying but every night I pray you remain a mystery and so far my prayers have been answered."

"That's sweet, Annie," he said. Even though they weren't able to communicate, Gil expected that it was Joad who was protecting him. "I told Rachman I don't have value. What'll happen if I can't prove it?"

"Uncle Rocky always gets his information. What is concerning him is that he knows where you're from and he even knows some people you know. But even with that, no one has been able to substantiate your value. I pray you're unimportant like you say because I love you."

He fought a chill. "Don't do that, Annie, please. We can't go there. Too many things will go wrong. Does Rachman know about us?"

"What about us?"

"That we're . . . you know-"

"Allah be praised, he'd better not. He'd kill you on the spot."

He pushed her away and stood up. "What?"

"What do you think?"

"I . . . I have to go."

"Go where? If I'd told you that earlier, you never would've been my first."

"Your first? Oh my god, Annie, I . . . I . . . you didn't say anything."

"You saw the blanket."

"But-" She smiled, shyly. She knew he knew.

"I love you and I trust you. There aren't any boys here I can trust like I trust you. They're afraid of Uncle Rocky and they're only interested in money. Besides, if one of them even tried, to . . . you know, Uncle Rocky, my father, all of my family would cut off the fool's cock, tie it in a bag, put it in his mouth and bury him alive with it."

"God, that's awful. Don't say that." He felt like heaving. "Why did you do this to me?"

"But it's true. Uncle Rocky said it, so don't blame me."

"Annie, we can't keep doing this. If I'm caught . . . you don't want that, do you?" She shook her head. "Annie, you and I are done. I'll be your friend, but no more sex."

"We'll get married and then we can do it whenever we want."

"I can't marry you. I can't even stay here. You're a great girl and you will find someone someday worthy of you, but that isn't me."

"Of course you can stay here. Mommy says if you want something bad enough and you're willing to sacrifice everything to get it, you can have it. I want you. When we make love, I stare into your eyes and I can tell you want this as much as I do. You want me, I see it in your eyes so staying here is what you must do."

"I can't," Gil begged. "I like you, but I don't love you."

"That's not true and besides, it doesn't matter. You will love our baby. That's what a family is for anyway. We are a family."

"I don't want that. Besides, I won't be here long enough for you to have a baby."

"You're wrong."

"I'm not having a baby, not here, not now and not with you. I'll escape if I have to."

She picked up a stone and threw it, missing him. "You're mean. What have I ever done to you? It'll be okay, we'll raise Mary Khadijeh and be a family and have lots of kids, just like mom and dad."

"Who is Mary Khadijeh?"

"She's our baby girl," she said as she pulled up her jacket, exposing her slightly extended belly. "You're such a bad boy. Surely you noticed my little bump while you were paying attention to my other attractions."

His legs tingled and he felt sick. "You're kidding?"

"I haven't asked mom, yet so I'm not sure how far along I am. We're going to be the best parents." She jumped on him and kissed him. He forcefully pried her off, stood, and ran toward the village.

He spent the next few days frantically searching for a way out while trying desperately to avoid her. One cold evening a week or so later, Rachman called for him.

"Dan, we haven't spoken in a while. Are you enjoying your stay?"

He tried to hide his nervousness. "Yes, but I still want to leave. When can I go?"

"Soon, I suspect. My niece is very unhappy. Do you know why?"

"No." Had he answered too quickly? "No, sir, I don't," he lied. "I haven't seen her in a while."

"She seems happy when she's with you. Would you talk to her? Cheer her up?"

"I . . . I can do that."

"Thanks. She's very fond of you. She's only fourteen though she thinks she's older." Rocky laughed. "And she's so emotional. Girls are so much harder than boys. She'll grow up. Mohammad, the man who shot you, he's her fiancé and he's very concerned. Help her. Do what you can to cheer her."

Her age rattled in his brain. "Mohammad?"

Rachman nodded.

"I'll do what I can."

"Thanks. I'll find a way to reciprocate for this kindness."

When Rachman left, Gil sat rocking back and forth, almost paralyzed with fear. He was in so much trouble.

Later that evening he found Annie in the community courtyard, staring sadly at the fire. Nervous, he walked over to her. She looked up, smiled and ran to him, but she was smart enough not to touch him with people watching. They walked to a clearing not far from the encampment.

"Annie," he whispered, "your uncle told me you're only fourteen. You lied to me. Your uncle, your father, and your fiancé, they're going to kill me." He said it in a whisper. "What were you thinking?"

Tears formed in her eyes and she wiped her nose. "But I'm pregnant and my baby girl needs her father." She blinked as tears ran down her cheeks.

He sagged to the ground. "This was such a mistake. I can't stay here with you even if I wanted to. You know that." She nodded and slipped down beside him, her shoulders heaving from pathetic, silent crying. In spite of his fear and anger, he felt bad and hugged her tight, her tears wetting his shirt. Finally, she pulled away.

"I know," she said in a small, hollow, broken-hearted voice. "I can't go; Mohammad and the rest will bring us back and they'll torture you before they kill you. I'm sorry. You're so handsome and so nice and I'm so lonely," she wept.

"I'm sorry, too, Annie."

When she stopped crying, she said. "You have to go."

"I know, but how?"

"I'll help you. In front of the lighthouse, there's a section of lake that's frozen all the way across. I checked. Tonight, when everyone's at prayers, I'll make a fuss and when the guards come, run straight across to the mainland and keep running. Don't ever stop, not ever." She began crying again. "Stay off the main roads and anywhere our ATV's can go. I don't know if you can escape but-"

"What'll they do to you?" he asked. She was too sad to answer. "Annie, you don't deserve this. I can't let you to face this by yourself."

"If you stay, it won't matter. They'll kill you and punish me anyway." He had been so stupid and he felt like crying. She noticed. "I'll be sad for both of us, it's safer. Wait for the prayers."

He sat unable to move. "Annie, I'm sorry . . . I wish you didn't have to live this way. I wish I could help but-"

She kissed him hard, her tongue searching for his, and he let her have her way this one last time. She straightened her clothes, stood up and looked at him defiantly. "I love you and I'm keeping our baby. Don't ever forget me and our Mary Khadijeh."

She wiped the tears from her eyes, turned and walked resolutely back to the encampment, stopping to smooth her clothes and wipe her face. Then she walked over to the fire and sat with the adults.

Later, when it was dark, he found a hiding place behind a frozen rain barrel near the lighthouse. When he heard the call to prayer, he waited nervously as people walked by. While he waited he wondered if Annie could, or would, do what she said, or if she would be caught in a lie by her uncle who was setting a trap for him.

In the distance, he heard a commotion. There was yelling and the two men guarding the village entrance ran toward the screams. As soon as they were out of sight, he bolted down the path and onto the beach. He headed onto the ice, slipping on the surface, almost falling, but he kept his balance and ran, even as he heard the ice cracking beneath his footsteps. He turned, and in the lights of Presque Isle, saw silhouettes of people running in all directions, including his. Then, a powerful beam of light cut through the night and illuminated the main gate. He turned and fled, continuing to slip on the ice as he ran until finally, he reached the beach on the opposite shore. He looked left and then ran to the right, down a road and into the first grove of trees he found as the beacon of light continued its sweeping search for him.

He ran as hard as he could on his now almost healed leg and he did it for as long as he could. When he stopped to rest, he heard the low rumble of the *Tollers'* all terrain vehicles in the distance. That sound propelled him faster and further into the woods. Soon, the distant roar of motors separated into individual sounds. One in particular was getting louder. He looked around for a place to hide, but the terrain provided few hiding options. As the rumble of the ATV grew louder, he looked back and saw his footprints in the mud. He'd have to be more careful.

The sound of vehicles was louder. He slipped and slid down the middle of a frozen creek until he reached a place where a tree had fallen across it. He climbed the ice coated tree and worked his way to the shore, jumping to a large tree and climbing until he was as hidden in the leafless branches as he could be. And he waited.

The vehicles were all around him now. Sometimes they got close, other times, they seemed to drift away. When ATVs stopped near the creek, he listened as the men talked.

"I knew that nigger was up to no good. It's the same with all those fucking capitalist kids, they come and just take what they want and move on. I don't care what Rachman says; death is too good for this one."

"I saw some tracks so he's around here somewhere. I'll head south, Abdullah, you go west. If you find him, send up a flare. We'll work him over good before we take him back but we don't kill him, you don't want to fuck with Rachman, he's got some crazy in him. Got it? We'll give this son of *Shaitan* what he deserves." The men started their vehicles and headed in different directions, unaware that their prey was hiding above them.

Even though his muscles ached, he remained in that precarious position until the last sounds faded. Groaning, he slid to the ground and looked at the tire tracks. They were heading in directions he needed to go and the other path led back to the Presque Isle compound. With his body and heart aching, he followed the vehicle tracks that led west, in the opposite direction of the *Toller* community, Annie and Rachman.

Chapter 23
North Central Ohio — 2070

Gil jogged in silence, his labored breaths escaping his mouth in wisps of white. Whenever he could, he headed south and west away from the lake community. When he found good roads, he made good time though he had no idea where he was going. For long periods there were nothing but deserted communities, circuitous roads, and large and decrepit houses.

When he heard vehicles, he assumed they were his pursuers and found places to hide—the houses providing good cover. Finally the sounds of vehicles disappeared and so did the urgency. Soon, he was walking in silence, walking listlessly with no destination or purpose in mind.

He wasn't prepared. Not for any of this. He was trapped in a world beyond his understanding and people were dying. Now there was Annie. He was so overwhelmingly disappointed with his behavior that he felt sick whenever he thought of her. He was so stupid and selfish. And thoughtless, he'd hurt an innocent girl forever—and their baby, and their baby! He had no idea how to process that. As he walked, sometimes he cried. Other times, lethargic, he sat and stared until something inside forced him to move—but to where, he had no clue. It was all he could do to keep his legs moving.

When it rained, he was slow to react to find shelter. When he reached new roads, he ignored caution and just crossed, unmindful of the risk. From time to time his glove crackled with static, but he ignored it. Thirsty, he crossed small creeks and rivers often without partaking. Hunger was harder to ignore, and yet easier because he deserved pain. Finally, in a numbing fog, his mind fashioned hunger as purpose so he stumbled up a road to a nearby hill topped with large, empty homes and looked out over the landscape. To the north was a body of water. He resisted looking further east towards Presque Isle. To the southeast, he saw a farm in the distance. He stumbled toward it.

He paused at a well-maintained fence and followed it to a farmhouse. Two young children were playing near a pond while a man and woman were loading a flat-bed truck with boxes of produce. He stared longingly at the boxes and then walked toward the woman. She saw him and moved between him and her kids.

"Morning, sir, ma'am," he said to the couple. "I need help. Can you help me?"

The woman's hair was gray, pulled back from her face and tied with an old piece of rope. She had young, alert eyes and smiled kindly, her face wrinkling. "You're a long way from town, son. What can we do for you?"

"I haven't eaten in a long time and I need a ride," he said, not wanting to explain more.

The man looked at him cautiously. "Is there anyone with you?" While he asked, he backed cautiously toward his truck, reached in and pulled out a rifle.

Gil stepped back. "Please don't hurt me." Before he realized it, tears were rolling down his cheeks. He tried to smile while rubbing the tears away with the back of his shirtsleeve.

"Mal, leave the boy alone. Can't you see he's in trouble?" The woman started to walk to him, but the man grabbed her and held her back while scanning the area around the farm with his rifle. "Is it just you, son? Don't lie to me."

"No, sir. It's just me."

"What're you doing out here, all by yourself?"

"Some men chased me, but that was days ago, I haven't seen or heard them since."

"Let me get him something to eat," the woman said to her husband. He nodded warily.

She ran into the house and brought back some bread, cheese and milk and between bites, Gil thanked them. When he was done, he helped the couple load the truck.

"What's your name?" the woman asked.

"Dan, ma'am."

"Where are you from?"

"I'm sorry, I can't say. It's safer that way."

"Where do you want to go?"

"I don't really know. Where are you going?"

"To the capital," she said. "There's a market town just outside old Columbus where we deliver produce and get credits and supplies. It's the closest Management town, about an hour from here. Mal, can we take him?" The man nodded cautiously, eyeing Gil with apprehension.

When they were ready to leave, the woman called out to her kids who jumped into the back of the truck. Gil joined them as the man locked the house door and then closed and locked the steel bars that secured the windows and doors. He wrapped a large chain around each gate and fastened locks to them.

When they were ready, Gil sat in the back with the kids and the boxes of canned food. The kids, both blonde, pig-tailed girls, were shy and stayed as far from him as they could. Despite the jarring ride, he soon fell asleep.

When he awoke, they were still moving and the kids were sleeping. To pass the time, as they drove by, he stared at the empty homes. When he heard static he wasn't sure what it was. When it persisted, he checked to make sure that the girls were asleep and then reached for the glove in his back pocket.

"Are you there?" He could barely make out her words.

"Yes. I thought you were gone." He looked up to see both kids eyeing him in awe.

"Will send help . . . Tracking . . . stay on course . . ." then nothing.

"Joad, Joad," he yelled into his glove. But it was silent.

It wasn't long before he heard a loud whirring overhead. He shaded his eyes. Above, a one-person helicopter was hovering behind the truck. He stared, in horror, as a missile ignited and headed straight for him. He screamed as the missile whistled passed the truck, exploding in a ball of fire on the road in front. The woman in the cab screamed and the truck swerved to avoid the explosion. Gil tried to grab the kids, but the swaying truck pinned him against the side as they screamed, bounced and rolled until they were near him. He grabbed them, just as the truck grazed a tree and he and the children were thrown hard out of the truck and onto the frozen ground. Stunned, he didn't get up immediately. Then he heard the kids wailing. When he looked back at the truck, the cabin was full of smoke. He stared at the kids and the unconscious man and woman and tried to decide who needed his attention more.

He ran to the children, and then looked up. The helicopter was hovering in the clearing. In the cockpit, he could see the memorable, scarred face of Ginger Tucker, the security officer who had tried to stop him at Mark's mansion five years before. He jumped as the dirt around him kicked up from rounds of gunfire being discharged from the onboard automatic rifle. Gil yelled at the kids to hide and then ran into the nearby woods. Using the trees as cover, he ran hard, keeping out of view. He heard the helicopter overhead, but whenever he looked up, all he could see were the tops of leafless trees. Whenever he approached a clearing, the helicopter was there waiting. *How was she tracking him*, he asked.

Finally, he came to a evergreen-covered ravine with an overhang wide enough to hide him from view. He crawled through the ravine until he reached the edge of another grove of trees. He searched in all directions for the copter and then ran into the woods. He didn't stop until he reached another clearing. He looked up, expecting to be killed, but the helicopter wasn't there so he continued on until he reached an abandoned town. With no helicopter in sight, he ran to the first building and stopped just out of view of the road and looked back towards the ravine. In the distance he saw the officer making her way down the road on foot, rifle in hand.

He ran through the town as quickly as he could. When he got to the other end, he stopped at a store whose large glass front window had been shattered. He couldn't chance running beyond the building because the ground was too open, so he squeezed through the broken glass, careful not to make a sound. Once inside, he hid, listening breathlessly for his pursuer.

After a few minutes, he heard the whir of other helicopters. Truly frightened now, he crawled carefully over the broken glass to a back room. On the back wall a large panel appeared loose. He slid it open just wide enough to squeeze through and set it back in place, waiting in the dark silence for the patrol to track his signal and capture him. He was sure that it wouldn't be long and soon enough, he heard voices.

"Sir, we've checked the buildings, he's not here. He must have escaped."

An annoyed woman's voice responded. "Bullshit. He didn't have time. He must be here. Keep checking. I'll get this building."

Tense, sweating profusely, and feeling like he had to pee, Gil knelt in the dark hideout, helpless, staring through a crack in the wall. When the sound of his pursuers intensified, he pulled back from the wall expecting someone to rip the board away at any moment.

As they got closer, the sound of cracking glass got louder.

"Do you believe it?" a woman asked. "That close and we lost his fucking signal. The kid's got to be here somewhere."

He tried to visualize where they were by the sound of their voices and the sound of cracking glass. He was sure that the footsteps were beside his hiding spot. He stifled a scream when the thin beam of light from outside the slit in the wall disappeared.

"Sir, one of my men reported tracks around back. What should we do?"

"He's not here," the woman responded. "Expand the search area."

The footsteps moved away and soon it got quiet. He waited as long as he could before peering out of the crack into the room outside. It was empty, but he didn't dare leave his hiding place because it was the only safety he was certain of. Finally, he whispered into his glove as quietly as he could.

"Are you there? Are you there? I'm okay. Thanks."

No sound came back.

"Hello. Joad?" he whispered, again.

Still nothing.

"Who are you talking to?"

It was a whisper, but it could have been a shout, it scared him that much. He flinched at the sound and began to mouth a scream but the fear of giving away his location prevented it from being born.

"Shut up," the voice whispered again. "Are you trying to get us caught?"

"You're . . . you're a girl. Who are you?"

"I was here first, so I ask the questions. Who are you?"

"Umm, my name is Dan."

"Okay, Dan. Who were you talking to?"

"Nothing, no one. I . . . I was just praying?"

"I'm not stupid. That wasn't a prayer. Who prays anyway? Who were you talking to?"

"It's none of your business."

"Who is Joad? Is that a code word or something?"

"No, it's just a word I use." In the light, she'd see his communication glove so he removed it and put it in his back pocket and changed the subject. "What are you doing here?"

"I'll ask the questions. Why were you hiding?"

"Some people back in the last village didn't want me to leave."

She laughed briefly. He liked that sound. "Look, I'm not an idiot. That was HomeSec, e-swat, probably. You must be important because those are scary, high-cost people chasing you."

"I didn't know. I got in a lot trouble up north, that's all."

"If you're going to lie, don't say anything. My guess is these people could care less what you did up north."

"It sounds like you know them."

"That's none of your business. This is my hiding place, I found it first. You'll have to leave. I can't be near anyone who has people like that taking an interest. Go! Go now."

"Not until it's safe. Anyway, why are you here? You're obviously hiding from someone. Maybe these people were looking for you?"

"I don't know how to respond to that."

"What kind of answer is that?" He felt ridiculous having a conversation in the dark with a faceless voice.

"Are you still here?"

"I'll stay here until I feel safe."

"It's never safe," she said and then was silent. He sat in the dark imagining her staring back at him. "Are you staring at me?" she asked.

"Of course not," he laughed. "Why would I be staring, it's too dark to see." More time passed. He leaned against the wall, trying to relax and killed time by watching as the sun shifted and the bit of light that filtered through the crack in the wall, worked its way across the floor, exposing tiny slices of his shared hideout.

"You're staring again. I'm warning you. Don't."

"Why would I stare? Is there something unusual about you?"

"Yes, I'm incredibly beautiful and you're obviously desperate. You're a rebel, aren't you?"

"A rebel? I'm trying to escape from bad people, that's all and it has nothing to do with you or rebels, whoever they are. How do you know about rebels?"

"I don't know how to respond to that."

"Again? What kind of response is that? You asked the question."

"What does HomeSec want with you?"

"You were hiding before I got here, what do they want with you?"

"I don't-"

"Stop!" The conversation was driving him crazy. "I know. You don't know how to respond to that. It sounds like you're in trouble, too. Those HomeSec people could just as easily have tracked you here. Maybe we can help each other out."

"That sounds desperate on your part."

"Grow up. We're both hiding behind a crack in a wall. My guess is I would never have met you except that you're in trouble, too."

"Not likely."

She was quiet. Then he heard her pull something from a bag and crush it in her hands. A minute later, the smell of cooked food permeated their hiding place.

He was starving and the smell amplified it. "Can I have some? I'm really hungry."

"If I give you some, there won't be enough for me."

"If you give me some, I promise I'll help you."

"That would be an acceptable deal if I needed help, which I don't."

"It's the best I can do and I'm really hungry. Please."

"Sorry, nope. And don't reach for it because I've got a nano-whip. If you're not familiar, it doesn't actually hurt until after an appendage falls off."

"Really? Really!" Annoyed and a little worried, he turned and curled away from the sound of her eating and tried to sleep, but his attempts were made futile with the smell of food. When he tried to think about something else, everything that came to mind made him sad so he stared into the darkness inhaling the smell of food that he couldn't have until eventually, exhausted, he fell asleep.

Very early in the morning, he felt a nudge and woke as the girl squeezed carefully past him. He feigned sleep, waiting until she was outside before he followed. She sprinted across the road and headed towards the trees behind the deserted building. He trailed at a distance.

In the dark, Gil continued to follow as she headed north and east in the direction he had just escaped. He considered turning but then continued to follow her. She was wearing a heavy, tight fitting winter jacket and at first light and from a safe distance, all he could determine about her was that she was tall and probably thin, with long, shiny, black hair that was tucked, tightly, down the nape of her coat. She wore tight work pants that were tucked into knee-high boots and covered legs that seemed to go on and on as she walked with an agile grace that covered ground quickly. He noticed one important thing. She must be fleeing something as well, because she carried nothing with her and at every clearing, before crossing, she stopped to watch the skies. And when she passed through abandoned communities, she cautiously worked her way using the rows of decaying homes as cover. In their shared stealth, his affinity toward her grew.

By mid-morning, she had stopped in a grove of trees, put her hands on her hips and waited. He paused, a distance away, waiting for her to continue, but she remained motionless.

"I'm not moving until you come over here," she shouted. He waited, motionless, but so did she, without even turning toward him. Reluctantly, he walked to her. When he got closer, she turned.

She was his age, tall and slim, with jet-black hair but she had eyes, eyes that . . .

"You're beautiful," he blurted out. That wasn't new information to her because her expression didn't change. She had flawless, vibrant and perfect skin and a cute, upturned nose. But those eyes; they were pale blue, almost gray, like a cloudless winter morning sky and surrounding them was a purple corona that added depth, enriching the experience but as he got closer, he noticed that they were flecked and there was violet and yellow, too. They were simply the most beautiful eyes he'd ever seen.

"What?" she asked, mocking his gawk with a smile so radiant that he almost forgot about her eyes. She had a natural, unforced smile; lips happily clear of her gums showing perfect white teeth that dazzled and made his embarrassment complete. However inadequate it felt, he could not help but smile back.

"I didn't mean," Gil stammered. "I'm sorry. Not sorry about your looks, you are beautiful."

Once again, she didn't acknowledge his comment—like he was stating the obvious. She looked him over from head to toe.

"Actually, you're not bad looking, yourself," she said in a matter-of-fact way. "Now that we got that out of the way, why are you following me?"

"I'm not following," he said. "I'm going your way."

"And which way is that?"

"I can't say. Where are you headed?"

"Okay, fine, I'm visiting my father in Detroit."

"Wouldn't it be easier to take a train? And why are you heading north and east?"

"I don't know how to respond to that."

"I could rephrase it."

"Don't bother. I told you where I'm going; now, tell me where you're going."

"I'm going to Detroit too, to visit a friend."

"That's pathetic. You can't even fabricate your own plan." Her brilliant smile faded and he felt somehow chastised. "You can come along but don't get any ideas, I'm a trained killer."

"I know. You have a nano-whip. What is that again?"

"You don't want to know." Before he could reply, she took to walking briskly and Gil had to hustle to catch up to her.

Meanwhile, at the White House, on the shores of the Gulf of Delmarva, Ginger Tucker reported to her boss on her failed mission.

"Madam Chairwoman, I had him but lost him between west of Columbus and south of the Presque Isle Toller compound."

"Do you think the *Tollers* have him?" Brandt asked.

"He was injured and stayed there briefly but he left, I caught him on the open road . . ."

"Ginger, dear, not again? That's three times now. Maybe the little Rose boy has your number."

"No one has my number, Madam Chairwoman, I'll get him. It won't happen again, I promise. Turns out, unlike his grandfather, the boy's quite a ladies man, got some *Toller* pre-teen whore preggers before he ran off."

"Now, that's unfair, Ginger. Marky had moments."

They laughed.

Chapter 24

The Road to Profit — 2070

Gil was walking with the most beautiful girl he had ever seen and he felt so awkward that he remained silent. She didn't want to talk either, so they made good time in silence, traveling on what was once a wide highway. Now, except for the center two lanes that were worn black by tire tracks, the rest of the concrete road was cracked and broken; a sparsely traveled road overgrown with dirt, weeds and grass. They were each concerned, separately, with oncoming traffic, hiding from the regular truck convoys that passed by. It was easy because the sound of the engines could be heard for miles. They were more circumspect as they scanned the skies for surveillance drones even though neither knew why the other was concerned. They decided—actually, she decided—to follow road signs directing them to the town of Mayfield Heights, which lay east and south. The mile markers and the appearance of street after street of empty buildings confirmed they were getting closer.

When they came upon an exit ramp, Gil read a green metal sign proclaiming that it was the Mayfield Heights exit, though the town's name had been defaced by buckshot fired at close range. Above the obliterated words on the sign, he read a new name, *Profit*, neatly painted in white letters.

"Looks like it's not Mayfield Heights anymore," he announced.

He pointed to a winding cloverleaf ramp that spiraled down to a local road below and began to follow it around, not noticing that the girl wasn't with him until he heard her yell.

"That's the long way," she shouted as she jumped over a small metal barrier and ran, stumbled down the grassy slope to the bottom. Tired of following her, Gil continued his way, a long, winding trek around the exit ramp.

She sprinted down the hill to beat him by the greatest possible margin, but at the bottom, she tripped and almost slammed into a concrete road support and fell as the slope leveled off. Breathless, happy and free, she staggered, but laughed in triumph when she saw that her annoying but cute companion wasn't even in sight. She looked back up the slope, admiring its degree of difficulty and thus distracted, she failed to notice two people approaching from the nearby underpass. When they were closer, she finally took notice, and watched them warily. It was an older woman and a young man-possibly the woman's son-she had guessed by the shared features on their dirty, travel-worn faces. The woman was pushing a shopping cart topped full with scavenged junk. The boy was merely staring, malevolently. As she eyed their approach, she backed away and up against the concrete support.

"Say little honey," the woman called out, her squeaky, shrill voice unnerving. "It's not safe traveling these parts alone."

"My friend's coming; he'll be here in a minute." She pointed back towards the exit ramp.

They looked in the direction she pointed, but saw no one. "Well, your friend's sure taking his good old time," the young man said. "You should be more careful. Independent socialist road terrorist cooperatives hang out in these parts preying on travelers."

"I'm not-"

The woman pushed the junk-filled shopping cart over to her. "My son and I are unlicensed independent toll collectors. If you wish to go on, sweetheart, you need to contribute."

"I can't help you," she explained. "I have nothing of value. I'm sorry."

The young man walked up to her and put his arms on her shoulders pressing her back against the concrete. He might have been good looking except for his pimply, pock-marked face, and a smile that seemed to hide something sinister along with a few missing teeth. Those that remained had a greenish yellow cast, which was probably why his breath was repellent. She pushed him away and assumed a defensive stance.

"Hey, Mama, look at her," the young man said. "She's feisty, Mama, but I think we can take her." Each pulled a knife from pockets in their oversized woolen coats.

"I don't want any problems," she said, "I'm just passing through," all the while scanning the road futilely for signs of her traveling companion. "I don't have anything. What value can I possibly be to you?"

They moved closer, knives at the ready.

"Relax," the old woman said, eyeing her warily. "Herbie is at that age where he needs to collect interpersonal experiences, deary, and, as you can imagine, they are difficult to come by out here in *Wasterland*. He's learning, though, and he'll be gentle, won't you Herbie dear?"

"I will, Mama, if she takes off her clothes, real slow, and she doesn't struggle much."

"I'm not-" The girl started to protest, but Herbie raised his knife and pointed it toward her so she shut up.

They closed on her, carefully, knives in hand. The young man lurched forward just as she noticed a small, thick metal chain in the old woman's shopping cart, the kind of chain she had once used to lock up her possessions when she was a little girl. She dodged Herbie's grasp, avoided the old lady, and grabbed the chain. Herbie cut her off but didn't approach as she swung it menacingly overhead. When she stepped toward them, swinging it in a wide arc, the boy stayed beyond its reach. Then, when the chain whizzed by him, he leapt inside the arc and caught her arm, twisting it and grabbing her by the shoulder. He put his knife to her throat and she surrendered.

"That was exciting, little lady," the old woman cackled. "But you'll have to be a whole lot quicker than that to stop my boy."

In a panic, she glanced up the ramp, searching in vain for help. Her travel companion was nowhere in sight.

Herbie tossed the chain far out of her reach and, while pressing his knife to her throat, walked her into the shadows, under the concrete overpass.

"Sweetie," the old woman said, pointing to her shopping cart. "We need your clothes in our inventory. You won't be needing them anyway because my Herbie needs access. We'll have your Pɪᴅ data too, but that can wait until Herbie's done practicing. Knowing Herbie, it won't be long."

"Mama," Herbie pleaded.

"It's okay, sweetie, you're learning is all. All I'm saying, honey, is you don't waste a lot of time with your women. I've shown you and you don't learn. It's more than getting in and getting out. You listen okay, but as soon as you get in the saddle, it's all a sprint to you. It takes time, honey, it takes time. Maybe this looker here will be the one." The woman laughed so hard, spittle came out.

"But Herbie, dear, you be gentle too, by the look of her, you might be her first. Now hand over your clothes, deary." The old woman then whispered, if you do it real sexy-like, it goes quicker."

She was almost hysterical, looking everywhere for help and a way out.

When Gil saw his traveling companion take a shortcut down the hill, he was relieved. She was so bossy and besides, they'd been together every moment since they'd met and he hadn't had a chance to try to contact Joad. He found a spot out of sight and activated his glove.

"Joad, this is Gil. Are you there?" There was nothing. He moved further away from the exit ramp in case the girl came looking for him, but still there was no signal. In case the transmission was being blocked, he decided higher ground might work, so he crossed the road to a tall, old, red brick building on the other side. He found a way in through the front door of a building that had seen better days and bounded up the steps to the roof, mindful that the girl wouldn't wait for him. Once on the roof, he stared down at the exit ramp, but she must have already left. Hurriedly, he activated his glove.

"Gil . . . ?"

"Joad, am I okay? Are you okay?"

"Only . . . moment . . . ," the transmission was faint, crackling with static and breaking up. "Gecko . . . subroutine . . . not decipher . . . Angel Falls . . . everyone . . . Grant . . . dead."

"No!" he screamed, and then looked around to see if anyone heard.

The transmission continued to break up. " . . . worried . . ."

"We spoke a few days ago."

"No! no . . ."

"Before Ginger Tucker attacked me."

"Tucker? . . . Okay? Communicator . . . Gecko . . ."

"What? You're breaking up."

" . . . Detroit . . . Toma . . ."

"Say what? Detroit? What are you talking about? What?" But the static had won out and Joad's voice faded. If Gecko had neutralized Joad, it was hopeless and all was lost so he couldn't think about that. He put the glove back in his pocket and ran in the direction he hoped the girl had been heading.

At the bottom of the exit ramp he saw two people under the overpass, a man and a woman, each wearing heavy winter clothing and facing away from him. At first, he didn't see the girl, or notice her dilemma, and he continued to walk cautiously toward the people. When he got closer, he saw the man take something and hand it to his companion. Gil inched closer.

"Hurry up, girl," the man said. "I don't have all day. Sexy-like, can't you do it more sexy-like?"

The old woman cackled. "Why are you complaining about all day when it doesn't take you but a minute?"

"Mama, don't start that now, please," The young man whined.

That's when Gil glimpsed the girl, wearing only her bra and panties. He was immediately impressed by her long, lean, well-built and incredibly hot body, and also disgusted by his initial reaction. He searched for a way to help and noticed the shopping cart. There appeared to be only clothes and small junk in it. Then he saw a chain lying on the ground a few feet away and he inched forward hoping these people didn't have guns.

The man took something from his pant pocket and walked to the girl who was cowering and shivering against the cold concrete wall. That was the moment Gil chose to lunge for the chain. The old woman turned, knife at the ready as Gil grabbed the chain and swung it in one continuous motion catching the woman's shoulder and neck, spinning her, stunning her, and knocking her down and out. The man turned, shock painted on his face. Gil was surprised and relieved that the man was younger than him.

"Are you okay Mama?" the young man yelled.

The old woman's eyes opened and she groaned, but didn't move. "Herbie, there's a blue-eyed *nigger* with a chain standing over me. I think I've died and gone to hell. As God is my witness, Herbie, boy, I've met the devil, himself."

Herbie looked at the half-naked girl.

"So, princess you weren't fibbing," he said to her, and then turned back to Gil. "Run away, boyfriend, or I'm going to make you blacker and bluer everywhere, including places you can't see." He stared down at his mother and vowed. "I'll get him for you, Mama."

Her eyes rolled. "I have always loved you, Herbie, dearest," she said. Her eyelids fluttered and then her eyes slowly closed.

"You son of a bitch!" Herbie screamed and leapt at Gil, knife poised to strike.

Awkwardly, Gil ducked away from the knife and dropped low. From his knees he swung the chain. The tip glanced off the side of Herbie's face and knocking him clear off his feet. His knife bounced across the concrete walk while the shock from the contact caused Gil to lose his hold on the chain and it spiraled over Herbie's head and out of reach. Stunned and bleeding, Herbie staggered to his feet and seeing Gil unarmed, grabbed his knife and approached him warily, blood trickling down his face.

"Time for me to prove to Mama that you're not the devil," Herbie said. "Just the best looking nigger boy I ever saw." He looked at his Mother. Her eyes were still closed. "Are you sure you wouldn't rather make love than fight?" Herbie whispered.

Stunned, Gil shook his head as the kid lunged forward, but Gil backed away quickly and fortunately blocked Herbie's hand from driving the blade into his chest. Slowly, the knife pressed towards him. Herbie smiled in triumph as Gil felt the tip of the knife digging into his clothes. Desperate, he twisted frantically and just as suddenly the young man's hand opened in spasm, losing its hold on the knife, which dropped harmlessly to the ground. Herbie's eyes were pained and then empty and he fell to his knees then slipped listlessly to the ground, face first.

Standing over him, in her bra and panties, his companion stood shivering in a martial arts pose. She stared angrily at the unconscious body of her would-be assailant; in her hand she held the chunk of loose cement that she had hammered Herbie unconscious with. She took a quick step forward and kicked Herbie hard in the kidneys over and over again with her bare foot. He woke, briefly, sobbing, and begged her to stop before passing out again.

Gil picked up Herbie's knife and searched the area until he found the old woman's. He turned his back and watched the couple while the girl ran for her clothes and quickly dressed, all the time eyeing her attackers angrily.

"Pick on me, you bastards," she said, her fear turning now to rage. "That'll teach you." She turned to Gil. "Where in hell were you anyway?"

"I'm sorry," he said, forcing his eyes to stay focused on the two prone bodies.

"It's okay," she said quietly.

"No, it's not. I shouldn't have left you. I got distracted and I'm sorry."

"Don't get all 'I'm the brave knight who saved the helpless wench' on me. I can handle myself. I'll bet Herbie here won't hurry to take a piss anytime soon."

Gil nodded. "He'll be pissing red for a while. That'll teach him."

She allowed herself to laugh and then finished dressing. Gil put the knives in his pocket and then they walked down the road, turning back from time to time to make sure the couple wasn't following.

When they were far enough away, she turned to him. "Pissing red?" she asked.

"You did the world a favor. He'll be more careful charming people after the way you kicked him around," Gil said.

"If that was charm, I did the neighborhood a favor by beating it out of him. Charm?" She looked at him and started to laugh and that caused him to laugh, too. When he put his hand on her shoulder, she flinched and looked up and then away and he saw the change in her eyes. It had sounded so much like laughter. He did the only thing that made sense. He held her close and let her cry herself out. And truth be told, he had things worth crying about too but he held back. Entwined in each other's arms, they sat down on the crumbled pavement and took a moment for themselves.

When she recovered sufficiently, she pushed him away, wiping the last tears from her reddened eyes while offering him a shy smile. "I'm sorry. I never, ever do that. It was . . . it was-"

"I know. It's okay now."

She nodded, meekly. "Thanks," she said in a small voice.

He nodded and stood up to leave. Something troubled him though and he couldn't put his finger on it.

"I have a big favor to ask," he said. "Walk back there with me a little so I can still see you. Here, take a knife. I need to go back."

"Go back? Where? Back there? With them?! It's not safe."

"We left them in pretty bad shape and we have both their knives. It'll only be a few minutes, I promise."

"Why?" she asked.

215

He shrugged. "I'm not sure. Why do they do mean stuff like that?"

"Who cares?" she asked. "They do it and they got punished. By rights, they should die. I should kill them for what they did. It's what stupid, greedy *Wasters* do. I'll go back, but only if you're going back to kill them and take their stuff because I could use a few things and we can trade the rest. That'll teach them. We can sell what's in their cart to make enough to keep us in food for a while." She began to follow him.

"I'm not a thief or a murderer and neither are you, regardless of what they are. There's just something I need to understand."

"But we deserve their stuff and they deserve far worse. They were going to . . . and that's illegal."

"Illegal? I don't know what illegal even means anymore."

She stared at him, briefly. "I don't know how to respond to that. It's only fair we take their stuff as payment for what they did."

"They did a bad thing," Gil agreed. "I'm not saying it wasn't. But I have no idea what's fair, anymore, let alone legal. They're hurt and they've lost their knives so they won't be preying on other folks for a while, and you've left enough bruises that I'm sure Herbie will remember your kicks, and the pain, and be more gracious in the future. I'd like you to wait nearby while I talk to them. I promise I won't be long."

They walked to where they were laying and though she was against the idea, she waited. She sat holding the knife staring forlornly at him as he left. It was a look that tempted him to forget about going.

The old woman was sitting up against the concrete wall, her head tucked between her knees. Herbie was lying on his back near her, moaning.

When they saw him, the old woman begged. "Don't hurt us, we won't do it again."

"I'm not here to hurt you."

"Then what the hell are you doing here?"

She quieted when he pointed the knife at her son. "How're you feeling?" Herbie cringed and moaned. "How the hell do you think I'm feeling?"

He pointed the blade at the old woman. "And how are you doing, Ma'am?"

"Been worse," she said. "I'll miss the teeth though; don't have a lot to lose."

"I'm sorry, but you started it. We were just passing through. Why did you do it, she meant you no harm?"

The old woman tried to look at him, but it hurt her too much to look up so she closed her eyes.

"Why'd you do it?" he asked again.

"It's the damned government's fault," she spat. "Christ Almighty, they tax us to beat the band, taking all my hard earned money so they could hire lazy damn pansies to do nothing. Then we go broke and the puissant government stooges, they do nothing to help us. It's always the hard-working folk that get screwed. It's the damn government's damn fault that businesses up and left to go to *Chinktown* and Go *Fuckyoustan*, and all those darkie places where the labor is cheap and the living is easy. Wasn't businesses fault, this used to be a free country, but taxes and regulations made it a socialist paradise, a fucking socialist paradise. Look at it, look around, you call this a paradise? Well, maybe to a socialist, those perverts. Mayfield used to have this great shopping mall that was open all the time and crowded. My parents took me there to see Santa, but the government fucked it all up. Now there's no one left to steal from except travelers."

"Yes, but-," Gil tried to say.

"It's the fucking government. We were warned. Yep, TV back then tried to tip us off that if we didn't fight the commie bastards, they would take everything. See, look at me now, they took everything. Why didn't we believe? How could they convince us that our government cared? We got fucked, that's all. We should have used our guns when we had them and did something about it. We had the right. We could have forced the government to its knees when we had the chance. Business tried, but we didn't listen, so they left us in the shit and left the fucking U S of A and now they're all rich and living high overseas. Well good for them."

Gil tried to understand what had happened that caused a mother and son to become simple road thugs. It was easy to blame the government but nothing they said had substance. Bernie had told him enough that Gil understood where the hate came from. But he still couldn't grasp how citizens could let themselves be turned into monsters so easily and monsters they could blame on someone else.

"I spent my life voting for damn libertarians who lost out to fucking socialists whose only goal was to spread the wealth to lazy bastards, who have no regard for life; who never cared about good, hard working folks like me. That's what it was, a great big suck and fuck. They sucked our hard earned wages with taxes and fees and a whole bunch of other shit, while fucking us up the ass with their capitalist-choking, commie regulations so we can't be free anymore. They bled us the fuck dry. Look at us. And what did that get them."

"I understand. That's why you believe you're here. But why do you act like this, scaring and hurting strangers?

"Strangers is what did it to us," the woman explained. "The Mexicans, Asians, Muslims and those damn *niggers*."

He had heard that term before. "What's a *nigger*?" Gil asked.

"God, lord help me, they don't even know what they are."

"I don't understand," Gil said.

"Darkies, kind of like you, but most don't have your blue eyes, which are really freaky. It was your kind who took from us what was rightfully ours. Just because you were good at being slaves, is no reason to steal from people that have. So you got tired of doing it. Me and Herbie sometimes get tired of this, but we keep on doing it. You people are why the Commies won and took everything. You're guilty as the government and don't say you're not."

Gil tried to understand, but couldn't wrap his mind around the vitriol so he turned to Herbie. "So, what's your story?"

Herbie, still in agony, spoke softly. "This is where my Mama is. What choice do we have? Me and Mama gotta eat and there's nothing around here except the towns and those *plutes* won't let us in. They won't help us unless we have money and if we had money, we wouldn't want to live with those fucking *plutes*."

"Why not?" Gil asked. "And what's a '*plute*'?"

"*Plutes*, I don't know, plutocrats, I think, the people who live in the towns. They think they're better than us because they have something more than a job, they have a *career*." Herbie emphasized the word. "God damned wealthy sons of bitches who can enforce any rule they need to stay in power. And the damn Production Towns only allow in people who generate value. I could work there, maybe, but Mama can't and according to their rules, there's not enough value in an untrained worker like me to pay for Mama too. So what were we to do? We staked out this claim where travelers come by, or truckers stop on the cheap, and we take things of value and we steal PID data to live. It's what the *plutes* do, they steal, it's just they make it legal."

"What can you do with PID data?" Gil asked.

"PIDS give us access to people's estates, their wealth. We patch in and transfer value to our PIDS and live on it until it's reported or the system generates identification confirmation, which is usually about a week."

Herbie held out his arm and rolled up his sleeve. Two wires snaked out from a wax-sealed puncture in his skin near his elbow and were tied in place at his wrist.

"Mama and I are saving up for wireless," he said. "She would never abandon me and I won't let her die."

As Gil listened, he thought about the story Bernie once told him of meeting Joad and how she transferred money from the baddies to the good guys. Where are the good guys now?

"Herbie, supporting your mother is commendable and I'm sorry about your situation, but you shouldn't hurt people, threaten to rape them, or call them names. You could get hurt."

"Do you live in a box?" Herbie said. "You don't know nothing. This is the way of the world. Eat or be eaten. If we tell people we're going to steal from their estate, that's when they put up a fight, so we tell them we're going to rape or hurt them. It's easier that way."

"But you still hurt people," Gil said and Herbie looked away. "Aren't you worried about HOMESEC?"

"HOMESEC doesn't care," Herbie said, anger simmering under his words. "It would be easier for us if people didn't put up a fight, but credits are worth more to people than their lives. Anyway, you taught me a lesson. We won't do this again."

"There are people a whole lot meaner than me out there," Gil said. "You're going to get you and your Mama killed if you keep doing this."

Herbie offered a contemptuous gesture. "Dead is dead, makes no matter. It's not like we're super capitalist Jew types. We're hard working libertarians who will die for sure without food or weapons. Maybe we'll die sooner, but at least we die on our own terms."

"So you're going to continue hurting people?" Gil asked.

"Hey, do we look unhurt to you?"

"I said I was sorry."

"That means shit. Everyday, we're out here surviving. Mama has faith, but I pray that the damned Messiah stops coming and just gets the hell here, for God's sake. We can't wait forever. But if he exists at all, until he arrives, and until he sets this pile of shit right, we're going to keep doing whatever we can, because until we die this is what it takes to live."

"Who's this Messiah?" Gil asked.

"Some godly man who is supposed to free us from the fat, bloated, damned Commie government. And if he comes, we'll have a nice life, something a hell of a lot easier, at least for people like us. Me, I say a prayer every night for him to get here quick but I don't believe it. Mama does though. She thinks if she only had her arsenal back and her gold bullion, she can wait forever. Sometimes, she says the Messiah is coming back in a blaze of weaponry, but I think it's more of that slick advertising from Commie government marketers. Faith is hard, marketing is easy."

"Marketing?" Gil asked, confused.

"HomeSec knows everything that matters, so how can anyone, even a godly guy Messiah, overcome them? Now if, like Mama thinks, this Messiah has some powerful new weapon, I'd agree with her. But I think that everybody's selling something. I just don't know what the angle is, but so many people know about this Messiah that it could be some kind of new selling gimmick, like someone will probably introduce a new consumer product called the Messiah, or something like that. Hell, some product probably has a better chance of succeeding than some revolution led by god, god damn it."

Herbie tried to move and let out a loud, mournful moan. "If you're not going to rob us or kill us, leave us the hell alone so we can recover in peace."

Gil stared down at Herbie. "You called me a *nigger*."

"Mama said you are. I didn't mean nothing." Fearful, Herbie struggled to move away, but Gil moved with him, forcing Herbie to look up at him.

"But Herbie, what you say does mean something," Gil tried to explain. "You don't know me. You don't know anything about me. Before you call me anything, shouldn't you find out more about who I am?"

Herbie stared at the ground. "Kill me, what the fuck do I care? Just stop talking, for Christ's sake. But if you kill me, kill Mama too 'cause she'll never survive without me."

"I'm not going to kill you," Gil said. "You and your Mama live close enough to the edge already. But I think you could be . . . friendlier. You'd survive a lot easier if you didn't treat people like you do. Some might even help you find a better way to survive."

"And you're a commie bastard," Herbie said as he hugged his mother and offered Gil an obscene gesture. Disgusted, Gil turned and left. After a short distance, he hesitated and looked back. Herbie was still huddled next to his mother, his back to Gil.

That didn't work out. Whatever reason he had for going back, it seemed like a waste of time now. Still, it made him feel a little better knowing that he tried. Disappointed, he jogged back to where his traveling companion stood, watching the exchange. She had a curious look on her face as he approached, but didn't ask what had happened.

In silence, they followed a local road toward what was once Mayfield Heights. It was getting dark and according to the signs, they were still miles from the town so they decided to hide somewhere and rest. They found a small, abandoned, two-story building with boarded windows. It seemed like a good choice for a peaceful night's sleep. They approached the building carefully, walking around it once to check it out. The only door was locked.

"Let's try one of the windows," She suggested as she positioned herself under one. "Give me a boost and I'll climb through."

He wasn't sure what she wanted

"Cup your hands like this," she demonstrated. "I'll put my foot there and you can lift me up so I can reach the window."

"That's cool. Where'd you learn to do that?"

"Didn't you ever play with your friends or your brothers or sisters?"

"I don't have any brothers or sisters."

"What about your friends?"

"I mostly played with them in my system."

"You mean *Virtuoso*?"

Her interest caused him concern. "Yes," he said cautiously.

She gave him an odd look. Gil couldn't decide if it was a look of respect or indignation.

"If you had access to *Virtuoso* it means you lived in some developmental community. Which one?"

He lied. "I visited friends who had a portal."

"You said 'my system'."

"I meant I used one, that's all."

She stared, evaluating him for the first time. "Ok, you lived in a corporate town. You're more polished than the boys I've met in Production Towns. I'll bet your family is management material."

"How do you know about Production towns?"

"I'm asking the questions."

Gil cupped his hands and made ready to lift her. She stepped onto his hands and he boosted her to the window. She was light and athletic and easily pushed the window open. She pulled herself through and within minutes the front door was open.

"Right this way, Mr. Manager."

"Shut up."

It was filthy inside, but reasonable enough for their needs. He found some cardboard to serve as bedding and they fashioned it into two places to sleep, one on either side of the small room. Then, he checked the door and they both lay down to sleep.

He must have fallen right to sleep because the sound of someone kicking at the door startled him awake. There was a hand over his mouth.

"Shhh," she whispered.

They remained silent as the door was repeatedly tested but soon, everything was quiet.

"Whatever that was is gone," she said.

"Let's get some sleep."

She sat down beside him and closed her eyes. He stared at her face illuminated in the pale yellow moonlight that bled through a window. She was breathtaking. He wanted to kiss her but realized that was stupid and maybe even dangerous.

Her voice startled him back to reality.

"Really, why did you go back?"

He pondered it. "I could say that I don't know how to respond to that."

"You could. I would. Really, why did you go?"

"I don't know. It didn't feel right to just leave them like that."

"They're *Wasters*. Who cares as long as they got what they deserve?"

"I do, I guess. Their life is difficult. It doesn't matter, they didn't say much."

"What we did to them served them right. Did they try to hurt you?"

"No. It'll be a long time before either of them tries that again."

She smiled. "Good." She was quiet for a few moments before asking, "Really, why'd you go back?"

"They're people," he tried to explain. "I don't know."

"They're animals! They were going to rape me—or worse, and yet you still went back to them."

He was frustrated. "It didn't seem right to leave them like that. It's been a difficult day and we're both tired. When I figure it out, I'll tell you."

She stood and walked to her bed where she quietly lay down. There was silence, but just as he was drifting back to sleep he heard her whisper. "Dan, my name is Bree, Bree Andrews. Thank you for today."

He awoke early and found she was already up. It was a frosty morning and since the last of her food was gone, they decided to head straight to the town of Profit.

"Bree," Gil said, testing her with her name, "I sure hope Profit has food."

"Production Towns are always looking to improve their labor force with new blood so I'm sure we'll be okay."

"How do you know about Production Towns again?"

"We should approach the town from one of the smaller streets," she said, not answering his question. "Let's get off the main road in case there are more *Wasters* like Herbie and his Mama nearby."

Though there was nobody around, they walked along the curving streets lined with ramshackle homes overgrown with vegetation, dashing from house to house while watching the main road and the intersections for people or vehicles. Soon the structures changed from vacant residential homes to larger office buildings—also empty and in disrepair.

"It seems that every building has been stripped of anything useful," Gil said. "Is this the work of the townspeople or did it occur earlier?"

Bree began to say something but stopped.

"Enlighten me," Gil pleaded.

"I will," she began. "Maybe twenty years ago, some terrorist group launched a viral epidemic and big city folks like around here were forced to move to smaller communities, further away from the cities where they were protected. They were less likely to be targeted and ultimately they were closer to where there was work. Of course, businesses followed them and soon enough *Conducers* had to follow them as well.

"With no economics in cities, the few who remained became *Wasters* because they didn't have enough gumption to leave. Without work, they were forced to scavenge for anything of value. I've seen pictures, they were like locusts who, forced to wander, stripped whole towns clean."

He was impressed by her knowledge and besides, it gave him a chance to stare at her without appearing rude or weird.

"Well?"

"Well what?"

"You weren't listening?"

"I was."

"No, you weren't, but never mind."

They continued following the small curving streets until they heard music playing and the distinct pounding sound of hammer on nail.

Chapter 25
Profit – 2070

Profit, Ohio — In order to restore the American economy to greatness during the great depression in America (2027-2034), the extreme but effective economic policy of *pogrom* was instituted. Highly organized and efficient national *pogroms* began in the early 2030's after the election of President Andrew Crelli, the leader of the Libertarian-Entrepreneur wing of the Republican Party.

As a result of these *pogroms* the size of the American population and, just as important, the need for government bureaucracy was reduced significantly to economical levels. This monumental achievement eliminated the vast non-productive and counter productive population that had burdened the American economy for almost two hundred years.

Almost immediately, with taxes virtually eliminated on commercial operations, American business began to thrive once again and the great pall of depression was lifted.

One of the significant consequences of the pogroms was that most large American city populations were decimated and therefore lacked economic viability.

The gated communities of the well-off were unaffected by the pogroms, but cities and neighboring suburbs were unable to generate enough revenue to tax and support infrastructure, so the remaining citizens abandoned their homes, left their assets to rust and depreciate, and drifted to vibrant, local *Wharton Towns* that sprung up around the country to support a now thriving business environment. *Wharton Towns* are characterized by efficient, integrated operations with low overhead and administration. They achieve that by admitting only those with viable economic skills forcing the rest to struggle for survival, as *Wasters*, in the Unincorporated Lands.

All cities and towns felt the brunt of the economic solution but Cleveland, Ohio felt it worst because, quite simply, old Cleveland had the highest inhabitance of the economically inadequate in the United States.

One very successful migratory group from Cleveland, led by fledgling entrepreneur, Owen Oren, moved to the nearby abandoned town of Mayfield Heights. There, the group discovered a mothballed manufacturing complex. The people voted to stay and work it and Mayor Oren renamed the town for their optimism, calling it *Profit*. Fortunately, many in Oren's group had manufacturing experience and soon the facility was on-line and productive. At first all the *Profiteers* could manufacture were cheap knock-offs and trinkets. Everything changed when Mayor Oren purchased a used Archive terminal which allowed Profit to report their production into the national logistics grid. This allowed distributors, *Tollers* mostly, from around the region to place orders and send trucks to distribute Profit's product to customers around the country. Profit's reputation grew along with its profits and the community thrived, proving the great glory of free enterprise capitalism.

Word spread of Profit's success and struggling small communities in surrounding areas petitioned the Profit board for admittance. And so Profit grew until it drew the attention of larger corporations.

It was at this time that the managing partners of Profit had a disagreement as to the town's future causing a change in leadership. Profit's first mayor, Oren Owen was set aside and Profit's current mayor, Doris Jay became mayor and managing partner.

Mayor Jay subscribes to the Christian Fundamentalist Capitalist theology of Morgan and has successfully proselytized her neighbors such that Morgan is the town's formal religion. Profit is the first town in America in modern times to choose the religious over the secular and adopting Morgan, has helped the town assimilate into the National Chamber of Commerce network, further enhancing Profits reputation and performance.

Through the Morgan Church and Stock Exchange and the Morgan National Religious Consulting Network, U.S. ANGS, a trillion dollar, American conglomerate contracted for Profit's entire manufacturing capacity and since that event, Profit has continued to thrive; its citizens' futures all but guaranteed and secure.

As Profit grew, the town faced numerous critical issues. Few Profiteers knew each other prior to the great trek and the added growth added more strangers to the mix. With the new prosperity, almost immediately, most *Profiteers* formed personal corporations and began birthing liabilities with the expectations of nurturing them into assets.

During those long work days, weeks, and months that so typify Profiteer work ethic, working capital is stretched to the limit and there is great strain on working relationships, efficiency, and profits. Many relationships dissolve during this time causing stockholder dissatisfaction as costs rise.

To restore order, to reduce the pressure on incorporated relationships, and to minimize the irrationality caused by the lack of long-term goals for Profit's now divested, hard working men and women, and also to resolve liability-rearing issues that reduce productivity further, Mayor Doris Jay initiated a biannual ceremony that celebrates the long-term productivity of personal corporations. This celebration has proven successful and efficiency was restored.

The biannual corporate partner ceremony continues to be celebrated twice each fiscal year during the less commercially productive business seasons of Thanksgiving and Easter.—**Archive**

Gil and Bree were on the outskirts of Profit when a small truck filled with building materials pulled through the guarded brick entrance.

"This is our stop." she said.

He nodded.

"Don't ask me how I know, but Profit is a secure corporate production town and commerce is so critical here that they usually permit prospective employees in without invitation—to evaluate them. For the record, I'm Bree Andrews and I'm from the New York Executive town of Portfolio."

He made a face.

"What is it?" she asked. "Stop looking at me like that."

"How am I looking?" Gil asked. "I just learned the first thing I know about you. How is it you're from a New York Executive community and your father is in Detroit?"

"Grow up, will you? It's the start of our sales pitch, it's not true. But it's our job to make it true if we're to get accepted. My dad's in banking and financial services and he travels a lot." She reached inside her jacket and removed a tiny electronic device from inside her bra and pointed it at him. "According to this, you're . . . Dan Stacey and your PID says . . . hey, I don't know what you do. There's no info. How did you do that?"

"Where'd you get that?" he asked, staring at the device in her hand.

"It's a portable PID reader, anyone can buy one. Your chip is faulty. We blame it on that fight, but you have to help me out here. What's your story? We need to corroborate each other's stories if we're going to work here. Give it a second and give me the basics."

"We're going to work here?"

"Spring is a long time away and working here is better than starving. So who are you?"

"I'm Dan Stacey from Bangor, Maine. My dad works in Detroit with HomeSec."

She made a face. "That's a horrible cover. You're not even trying. It'll take them two seconds to find out it's a lie. Bangor's okay, it's out of the way but the rest . . . your parents were killed in the food riots in Boston and you were raised by your . . . grandmother?" He shook his head. "Okay, grandfather."

"They can't check that?"

"They'll try. Usually smaller Production towns don't spend a lot of effort checking their workers because if they're unproductive, they're sent away and if they're good, they'll overlook any sin. All we need is enough cover to get in and get working."

"And then what?"

"We work until we earn enough credits for me to go to Detroit," Bree paused, thinking. "Okay, this is our story. We're a personal corporation. They'll want that and it'll keep us together so we can protect each other's identities and interests and it should be enough so single corporations won't hit on either of us to incorporate. But don't get any ideas. Our bylaws provide no personal benefits and we won't be seeking any either. This is solely a mutual protection pact and purely financial—a cover story that ends when we leave Profit. Agreed?"

He had little idea what any of that meant, but she was so sure about it that he agreed. "We're here to work hard and earn enough to pay for our travels and at the first sign of trouble; we're getting out."

"You can't say that."

"I'm not stupid," he said. She shrugged and together they walked toward the gate.

"So do I walk in front of, or behind my corporate wife?" She made a face. "Wait, you never told me where you got that ID gizmo."

"They're nothing. People use them to check out future partners instead of paying professional firms to generate a prospectus. It beats talking to people if you don't have to. Remember to stick with our stories."

She grabbed his hand and they walked through the town gate. Two guards watched them warily and the men unloading lumber from the truck also stared.

"Keep walking—and smile," she said. "We can't turn around now."

They continued on until they reached a small group of women who were also staring at them. Soon they were the center of attention. A woman wearing a print dress, covered with an apron embroidered with the name ANGS in large letters walked over and two other women followed, each similarly dressed. A couple of men, wearing overalls and boots, joined them.

The first woman spoke. "Welcome to Profit. We don't get many visitors in winter, particularly young people. I'm Doris Jay, the mayor and plant manager for our ANGS facility. These are my assistants, Mary Luongo, Kate Dorrow and my security team leaders, Bruce Dworkin and Barry Ludwig." The women smiled but the men simply nodded.

Gil was about to greet them but before he could say anything, Bree squeezed his fingers tightly.

"Hi, I'm Bree Andrews," she said cheerfully, "and this is my partner, Dan Stacey. We were traveling with a group to Erie when we were accosted by terrorists." He tried not to look startled by her adlib.

"Yes," he kept up the façade. "We were fortunate to escape."

The mayor put her hand up to her throat. "That's horrible," she said. "What are those Pennsylvania towns thinking? They should have paid to have those vultures cleared out. Don't you worry; we're safe here because we're part of the Westlake militia that keeps the riff-raff away. Don't you worry, if *Tollers* begin acting up down here, our security can handle it.

"You are a lovely couple. You say you're incorporated?" Bree nodded and the mayor hugged her. "That's lovely, dears. Erie's a long way from here and you must be tired and hungry. If you want to stay, you're welcome here until we can assess your value. Can we get you something?"

"Well, your Honor, Dan and I are famished."

The mayor smiled. "Please, call me Doris. We're putting the finishing touches on our biannual corporate partner ceremony so everyone who isn't scheduled to work in production is working on the preparations. There's a food wagon behind those trees," she said as she pointed off to the right. "Help yourself. Tell the cooks Doris sent you."

"Thanks, Ma'am. I mean Doris," Gil said, politely. Bree turned to go but stopped when he tugged on her hand.

"What's a partner ceremony?" he asked causing Doris to smile, proudly.

"Twice a year we host a celebration for our residents to renew their corporate vows. It's important to the community's bottom line and it's always a great, though brief, party because it's one of the few times work is suspended, of course without pay." She laughed as did the others. "I'm not kidding though, there's no commerce allowed, even at the party. You must stay for it. Maybe you'll want to renew your vows."

"Thanks Doris, we'd like that," he responded.

Doris was pleased and went back to work as they walked toward the food wagon. When they were far enough away, he whispered. "What are we going to do now?"

"What do you mean?" Bree asked.

"If they check that story, they'll arrest us."

"Why would they check our story?"

"You don't think they will."

"As long as we're productive and act consistently with what we told them, we'll be fine. They'll be nice today because this is the recruiting phase."

"Should we take part in their ceremony?"

"Let's eat and get a feel for the community. Then I'll figure out the rest."

He smelled the food wagon before he saw it. On the far side of the wagon, rows of picnic tables were lined up and small groups sat, eating and talking until Bree and Gil came into view. Everyone stopped and stared.

Bree smiled her most dazzling smile and waved. "Hi, everyone," she shouted, "I'm Bree Andrews and this is my partner, Dan Stacey. Doris said it was okay to eat here."

At the mention of Doris' name, the people seemed to relax and become friendlier. They took Bree and Gil to the food wagon where he faced the first choice of their faux relationship.

The roasted chicken smelled of rosemary with a hint of citrus, possibly lemon. The skin was evenly browned and a small river of juice trickled down the side, escaping from a puncture hole that one of the cooks must have made when checking for doneness. The potatoes were browned also, almost charred with onions and carrots and gave off a strong aroma of garlic.

The smell was intoxicating and Gil was famished, so he grabbed for a plate but Bree's hand stymied him. "Look at these prices. We need to ask how we pay for this unless you've got some wealth stored on that mysterious PID of yours."

He looked longingly at the chicken.

One of the Profiteers came up to them. "Its okay, Doris says it's okay if you run a tab. Consider today a recruiting day. If you're accepted in, you'll have to pay it off though."

"And if we're not?" Gil asked.

The Profiteers nearby looked embarrassed so Bree pushed Gil and smiled. "Of course we will be accepted. You're such a joker."

That was all Gil needed. He grabbed two plates of chicken with the potatoes and two deserts. He took one of the frozen deserts with fruit on top, the other had a chocolate topping, and then looked longingly at the water but decided that it was too expensive and just took one bottle.

Bree watched him load up his tray and then surprised him by stacking her plates just as high. He smiled. "You've got a heck of an appetite."

"Don't you dare say, 'for a girl.' And when we sit down, don't be so negative and make defeatist comments like that. It makes workers nervous. We're here for the money and we have to appear confident."

Before he could respond, they were at the tables. Bree was so ravenous that he had to find napkins for her as the chicken juices dripped from her chin to her plate and some even onto the ground as she gorged herself. While she ate, Bree charmed her way through the introductions with a more expansive fabrication of why they were there. Finally, one of the elders explained the ceremony while Gil endured some aching teeth from the sweet deserts.

"Christian productivity is our lifeblood here in Profit," the elder said. "But we were struggling in the early days so Doris came up with a brilliant idea. She adapted a marriage ritual from another Angs town and it's been working great ever since."

"What is it, exactly?" Bree asked. Gil tried hard to stay alert but the hearty meal and the sugar shock from the deserts made him feel tired and light-headed. When a small heavy-set woman with big hair and a bigger smile answered Bree's question, Gil just smiled and nodded.

"I'm Linda Troop, nice to meet such a handsome couple. I chair the announcements committee. Three months before each event, my committee meets to develop a unique set of invitations that exemplify the skills and interests of the Christian married couples participating. Believe me, it isn't easy and there are plenty of meaningful and even funny and embarrassing moments before we decide what message to market on our invitations. Of all the committees ours is the most fun. Maybe you'll consider joining if you stay."

Bree smiled, Gil just nodded.

"I'm Jill Troop-McCord, Linda's sister," another woman added. "I'm responsible for Themes and Favors. Each celebration has a different theme—and after all these years, you better believe it's hard to think of something productive and original." She covered her mouth with her hand and laughed to herself. "Remember our Christian Cowboys and Indians celebration?" The others joined in the laugh.

"One of the members of my committee, and she's no longer with us for obvious reasons, she researched themes in Archive but did a horrible job. We made the best of it, but it was an unusual event, a mixed culture event with American cowboys and India Indians in an exciting tug of war for peoples' immortal souls." Everyone, but Gil, laughed.

"I'm Estes McCord, Jill's husband, pleased to meet you both," a large, slow-talking man announced. "I'm chairman of the construction committee, that's our biggest committee. You saw my guys unloading wood and working on the stage. We build the props for our play and handle all the heavy lifting for Jesus and Morgan."

Bree smiled. "There's a play? That should be fun."

"Dermot is our director," Jill clarified. "He's responsible for writing and staging all of our plays. This year's theme is the critical role God plays in retirement planning and how personal corporations can be leveraged to produce a holy annuity that will last forever. I've seen the rehearsals—it's topical as well as entertaining. It's a musical-comedy Dermot adapted from an original source and the kids are just going to love it. It's so fun and gives off the right message. I play 'Fair Helen' and Estes plays 'Lysander' if he can only keep the beat."

Bree smiled at their enthusiasm but something troubled Gil. The women were wearing gloves, like Bernie's although cheaper looking. Concerned, but not willing to broach the subject, he followed Bree's lead and tried to act interested. "The play sounds great."

"So you kids will be staying?"

"Yes," Bree responded. "We're hoping to find work here. Are there openings?"

"You'll have to discuss that with Doris but you'll have to wait until after the ceremony. Orders are strong and production is ramping up to full capacity so it's a good time to seek work. You'll have to qualify, though."

Still smiling, Bree asked, "How do we qualify?"

"Doris will explain it. Did you say you're from Erie? What did you do there?"

"No, Jill," one of the men interrupted, "they said they were on their way to Erie."

"So where are you kids from?"

Gil stared at Bree who responded. "I am from Erie and I live just north of there."

"How'd you meet?"

Simultaneously, he said, "At a market," while Bree said, "in church".

Bree corrected him. "We met in the stock market at the Morgan church."

Gil looked at Bree like she was crazy until Jill said, "That sounds so romantic."

Bree nodded. "With this big fella, you have no idea. He is a natural investor and you know how that drives women crazy."

This time it was Jill's turn to nod. "Will you go back to Erie?"

"I have relatives in Detroit that we're planning to visit."

"You mean Hamilton, dear, don't you?"

"No, Ma'am, Detroit is where we're going—someday."

Everyone quieted. Linda Troop spoke first. "Detroit," she said warily. "That's not a good idea. It's rebel territory, a very dangerous place. They don't value people there for their economic worth, a very dangerous practice. And it's close to Canada so there are rebel communities everywhere. You should reconsider and maybe visit the nearby mega-production center at Hamilton, it's quite a place. There are stores everywhere and great manufacturing and distribution facilities that, I'm afraid put ours to shame. Hamilton is America's model Christian town. They beat us every year."

Gil looked to Bree but she was silent. "Why do rebel communities exist so close to towns?" he asked. "And why doesn't the Chairman just eliminate them?"

Bree's face seemed to lose color and the townspeople were shocked. Linda tried to save the moment. "I'm afraid that you are young and naïve and frightfully out of touch. The Chairman hasn't been in charge for years."

"Where'd he go?" Gil asked.

The Profiteers looked uncomfortable as Jill explained. "A few years ago, Archive announced he was leaving on a sabbatical, the final plateau for a Morgan before achieving everlasting life. We've heard rumors that he's cloistered at the Wall Street Seminary with Chief Spiritual Officer, Tom Morgan himself."

Estes spoke up, "A trucker told me that rebels had him—in Detroit, I think."

Linda looked horrified. "That's a detestable rumor, Estes, I told you never to mention that. The rebels are nothing. If they found a way to kidnap our beloved Chairman, Chairwoman Brandt wouldn't leave a rebel alive rescuing him. She'd never allow it."

"So Tanya Brandt is in charge," Gil concluded.

Bree squeezed his hand hard. He gave her a curious look, but said nothing more.

"Your economic and religious education is sorely lacking. You'll have to take remediation courses if you want to be successful here," Linda Troop said. "And your knowledge of civics is way out of touch. Chairwoman Brandt has always been the power. She controlled the Chairman all the way back to the time of the First Republic and elections, but frankly, as a capitalist free market economy, it doesn't matter who's in charge as long as there is a favorable business environment."

Gil persisted, "So why doesn't the Chairwoman do anything about the rebels and terrorists?" Bree squeezed his hand again, harder.

This time Estes responded. "Kids today. The Chairwoman doesn't act for the same reason anyone does or doesn't act. As long as it costs more to solve a problem than the solution's worth, there's no reason to act. The rebels and the terrorists know exactly how far to push us before they're too expensive to survive. From time to time, they step out of line and do something to hurt the economy, but they incur quick and cost-effective retribution. It's appropriate and efficient. All we're saying is we wouldn't go to Detroit."

Just then, Doris walked over to their table. It was obvious to Gil that she commanded respect because as soon as she was close enough, the conversation stopped and the people began cleaning up and heading back to work. "So you are joining our community." Doris announced pleasantly.

Before Gil could ask the mayor how the news had traveled so far, so fast, Bree answered. "Yes, Ma'am. Everyone's so nice. Would it be okay?"

"We have a procedure for accepting new shareholders but we can't begin until after Saturday's ceremony. Rest up tonight and tomorrow join me in the morning and I'll give you a tour and an overview of our town. Saturday's the ceremony and there'll be a brief party afterward and then everyone goes to work, including you."

"It sounds great," Gil said, following Bree's lead. "Where can we stay?"

Doris pointed. "Follow this road. There's a guesthouse just over the rise. Tell Phillip that you're my guests and he'll set you up. Remember, we meet tomorrow; right here at eight o'clock. Now excuse us, we have to get back to work to meet our deadline." Doris motioned for the rest of the townsfolk to finish their lunch and to get back to work.

Before the mayor left, Bree asked, "Ma'am, what exactly do you produce in Profit?"

"Good solid Christian products and services of great value, and lots of them. Mostly, we make the packaging for PID chips. With the population finally expanding again, it's a growth industry. We farm for most of our food, we grow cotton for trade, and we do some regional logistics too; although the *Tollers* handle most of the actual transportation."

That concerned Gil. "Do *Tollers* come here? We had a bad experience with them."

"In our busiest months, they're here everyday. I assure you when they're here, they're well behaved, for *Mohammedans*, their livelihood depends on it. It's only on the open road that there are problems. If you're chosen to join us, you'll have nothing to fear."

"Thanks, Ma'am."

Bree and Gil left and were making their way to the guesthouse that Doris had pointed to, when Gil discussed his concerns.

"Bree, if *Tollers* come here, I'm in big trouble. They'll kill me as soon as look at me."

She wasn't concerned. "Why did you speak out about the Chairwoman like that? Stick with the story. What you did wasn't part of our story. Be smart or I'll end the partnership."

"I don't see the big deal," he said. "I'm curious, that's all. I'm concerned about the *Tollers*. If they recognize me, I'm in big trouble."

"You said that. What did you do to them?"

"Trust me. It'll be bad if they recognize me."

"Then hope none show up who recognize you. If you've created value and there's any trouble, we'll leave together. If you haven't, you're on your own."

"You'd leave with me?"

"And I'd leave without you, too." she said. "So don't get all misty-eyed. Let's see what the rules and the acceptance procedures for new workers are."

They reached the lodge that Doris had directed them to and mentioned the mayor's name to the property manager, Phillip. He jumped to attention and escorted them to a large, well-appointed cabin with two bedrooms and two bathrooms and a great view of the planting fields that were covered with a light dusting of snow. They each found new clothing that had been set out for them and Bree looked longingly at the shower.

"This is heaven," she said, sounding relaxed for the first time since they had met. "I'll see you in the morning."

Before Gil could respond, Bree closed the door to her bedroom and started the shower.

In the morning, clean and dressed, Gil waited for Bree. When she exited her bedroom, he felt a hunger like none he had ever known. Her hair was straight and black, parted on the side and hanging loose to her shoulders. Almost his height, she wore a tight fitting blue blouse that accentuated her tight, though well-endowed figure and she wore long straight gray pants that covered legs wondrous and long, legs that extended a great distance from her tight athletic hips. There was no need to remind himself, he was seeing the most gorgeous person ever. He hadn't seen many girls and Stacy had been pretty too and so was Andrea but Bree was . . . she was stunning, truly stunning. She had no need for nano-makeup and wore none, and it was her smile, that kinetic smile and those blue-gray–violet eyes that made it hard for him to decide what feature of hers he found more enthralling. He couldn't stare at one feature without longingly seeking another.

"You're making me very uncomfortable."

He apologized and felt like he'd lost something when he demagnetized his eyes and looked away. He struggled to find a comfort level staring at her without making her uncomfortable as they discussed their plans in greater detail.

"We should act like partners," Gil said.

"Not if you look at me like that we don't, but I agree conceptually. How do partners act?"

"I don't know. Whatever one of us says, the other should agree with and we should avoid telling conflicting stories."

She laughed. "Is that's how partners act?"

He shook his head. "How do I know? After we're accepted, when we're alone, we can develop more common storylines but until then, when you say something to someone about us, tell me so I don't say the wrong thing and I'll do the same to you. We need to be careful until we have some history together."

"I'm okay except for that history together part," she said. "But remember, we're partners, there can be no emotional attachment or we'll blow our cover. And we're not doing this to create some history. We'll do whatever's required to get accepted and we stay until we make enough money to leave. We need this so don't screw it up for me. Let's find Doris and see what our new home is like."

Chapter 26
Profit — 2070

Saint Thomas Morgan speaks the true word of God. From the beginning of recorded time, the Lord's financial and economic magnificence was present here on earth, but until the present day, man had not evolved enough to learn the true beauty of God's pure and true economic promise. The time wasn't right and mankind wasn't capable of fully synthesizing God's purpose and employing it appropriately.

Saint Adam Smith, Sir Edmund Burke, Sir Thomas Hobbes, and Saint Milton Friedman *et al* espoused a more perfect understanding of God's economics, but his Holiness, our Chief Spiritual Officer, the revered Saint-in-his-lifetime, Saint Thomas Morgan, also called the "Enlightened One", he saw the vision of God's true purpose and how to implement it for American capitalists in a never ending cycle of commercial success.

In olden times, the times of Jesus and Mohammad, man's ability to process the everlasting was limited, so God responded in ways people in those eras could understand. It was for that reason that the ultimate reward for their short and difficult lives was limited to the promise of heaven, the hereafter–rebirth in all God's glory after physical death on earth.

In today's world, with the perspective supplied by God's illumination through the so-called secular sciences, medical and technological breakthroughs have provided humankind with long lives and the expectation of forever. In God's ordained future, heaven as a reward for a good life is simply no longer adequate or acceptable. For those who will live forever, there is no advantage to heaven.

God communicated this, his Holiest of Holies economic order through our beloved Saint Thomas. Everlasting life, here on earth, is God's true return on a fiscal life investment for those who have dedicated their lives with the passion, intelligence, and single mindedness to create an estate of biblical proportions with which to fund their perpetualness, forever.

To live by Saint Thomas's teachings is to achieve eternal life and bliss that makes certain that the destiny of the devout is to walk with God one day on earth. To achieve this destiny, a Morgan must possess the insatiable desire to accumulate wealth, for it is capital appreciation that enables everything in life. And what is life if not financial opportunity?

Forever is not possible for those bereft of capital and whose final payoff can only be death and no more. This is the gospel according to Saint Thomas who received his calling directly from God while serving as Secretary of the Treasury for President Andrew Monroe Crelli.

Working late one night, the voice of God spoke to Thomas through the speakers on his computer and they directed his life's energy toward the search for a capital-rich forever. From that first hallowed experience and all of the many subsequent visitations, Saint Thomas learned directly from God and communicated God's holy requirements to the world along with the generally accepted practices and procedures required to build God's great new holy order where the consecrated wealthy live forever.

Saint Thomas conferred God's blessing on mankind. That blessing, true market-driven free enterprise capitalism is a reflection of God's perfect glory and is man's highest and purest attainable state. And the Brethren of the financially adept are God's chosen people and it is they who are promised life everlasting, paradise, a perfect state of economic joy and contentment, here on earth, forever and ever.

As an historical footnote, the original computer God used to access Saint Thomas is today a religious relic enshrined in the Faith Based Museum at the Smithsonian Institute in Monroe, D.C. and a replica is available for viewing at the Morgan Free Market Seminary and Stock Exchange at Morgan corporate headquarters on Wall Street in New York City. Charms and bracelets with the likeness of that holy computer are available at Morgan Retail stores everywhere and on the Mesh at *www.ChurchofDivineProfit. com*—**Archive**

Doris was waiting for them outside of their housing complex. They traded pleasantries and were soon off to tour Profit. As Doris led them on the tour, Bree noticed a young couple and a child leaving town. The woman and child were distraught.

"Doris, who are they?" she asked.

"That's the Carters," the mayor explained. "They've been asked to leave because they're not providing value to themselves or our community. We gave them every chance, but they are foolish and undisciplined. He wanted to start a union. A union! You could tell from the start they were going to be troublemakers. Poor performance drove their net worth negative and with their lifestyle, a lethal combination of poor work ethic and hoarding, well, they had to go. Profit has a very conservative fiscal policy and with the significant production demands facing us, we simply can't allow a family of slackers to affect everyone else's future."

"That seems fair," Bree said.

"They really look unhappy," Gil observed.

Doris nodded. "Yes, it's sad. You're young so let this be a lesson for you. The mother, Marie, is immature. She behaves as if her ancestors might have been rich way back in the days of the First Republic. She's always late for work and she preens a lot to promote her social standing. It's unproductive, it wastes time, and Profiteers see right through it. Our people know value and it's not some shallow thing like popularity and friendship. Value is critical to our mission, but Marie trivialized it.

"To keep up her 'image'," Doris lifted her hands to make quote signs with her fingers, "She entertains far beyond what her income can support and she does it stupidly, with no economic purpose. It's such a waste. She never budgets for her parties so she's constantly overspending and her choice of what to offer for sale at those parties is wrong-headed so she always loses money. There's nothing wrong with throwing a party as a loss leader if it enhances financial relationships with your neighbors and friends and discounting is a permissible technique to prime the pump, but the way Marie goes about it shows no business savvy and *Profiteers* should not have to deal with that malady. There's a tradition in Profit that says no one can turn down an invitation to a party, so Marie is rarely invited because everyone knows she can't afford to spend enough for the hosts to yield a proper return on her attendance.

"Bree, that's another lesson for you. If you're going to succeed financially, know the rules. Wishing never bought anyone a future."

Bree nodded dutifully.

"And her husband, Jimmy," Doris continued. "He's a guy with potential. He's why we accepted the Carters in the first place. But though he's a hard worker, Jimmy's brutally inconsistent." She turned to Gil. "Keep that in mind, young man. To be effective, commerce, like a clock, must operate with precision. You will surely end up like poor Jimmy, here, if you aim to impress by trying to break production records rather than conform to production queuing requirements."

Gil didn't understand but nodded anyway. Doris read his confusion.

"What I'm saying, Dan, is that if you try to rush ahead to set production records to pick up some bonuses and you think you'll get promoted, you're going to be disappointed. We are at full capacity and eventually, you'll tire and fall behind. Our expertise, here in Profit, is in operations, smooth and efficient. We know how fast things should be done to be cost-effective and work must be steady and of good quality to support that. Our customers expect it and our bottom line suffers if we don't operate like that perpetually.

"Jimmy, Morgan blesses him, would rush around to get ahead and then daydream or become tired or bored, and fall behind. Unfortunately, it isn't in his makeup to work differently. We tried, we train, but we refuse to reengineer, it's simply too costly and too close to socialism for us.

"Profit is a family-oriented town with good, solid Midwestern capitalist ideals. We're not like the large operations that remain in or near big cities around the country. They're only interested in the bottom line, not the families who generate it. We're not ruthless like them, but we always make decisions that are in the best interest of Profit."

Gil watched the dejected couple distribute their belongings to various residents. "What are they doing?" he asked.

"They're heading into the economic wilderness and they can't be burdened by stuff they bought while living here because they'll never reach a market where they can get value for it. *Tollers* and independents will take it from them long before that so they may as well travel light to survive, at least until they find another economic opportunity." Doris said, grimly.

"My Profiteers know a deal when they see it and the Carters will get ten cents on the dollar, but it will lighten their load and the money will help them survive a bit longer. I can wait if you and Bree want to buy something. Go ahead."

Unsure, Gil looked at Bree and then shook his head. "No, Doris, I think we'll pass."

"Your choice. This is clearly their fault," Doris continued. "Private property is God's best and most powerful instrument for creating wealth and profit and we in Profit subscribe to that and are fiscally responsible to a fault. But returns must be what our stockholders expect or there is hell to pay. Take my compensation. It's based solely on how well the town does. You know, X number of Profiteers times Y revenue generated times my cut is how I live and I don't like to be disappointed. So when our residents live beyond their means, they don't do it for very long. We bill them for finance charges and interest payments on their debt as an early warning—and for the wise, it's warning enough. The Carters ignored the signals. Maybe they were hoping to get lucky, I don't know, but that's not a sound financial strategy. Instead of relying on good, solid financial principles and disciplines, they spent and spent and spent." Doris put her hands to her head.

"It's so frustrating. As their worth cratered, we had ways of helping them, but they ignored us. When net worth begins to decline, a signal is transmitted to your PID that generates relative discomfort, increasing to real pain until net worth improves. How can you not get that message?"

Doris paused and shook her head, in disbelief. "How can you not get the message?" She reemphasized. "The worse your economic situation is, the more severe the pain. The Carters were resistant to suggestion and even spent through the pain. You could say they were brave by ignoring it, but our merchants are not in the practice of gifting products and services so the Carter's fate was sealed. A few Profiteers who experienced it tell me it's almost impossible to be effective when your PID is running hot—and the pain can get intense enough to be immobilizing, some scream or moan continuously. There's only one way to relieve it. You sign away your assets to the community and pay your debts so we can dial down the discomfort. If that fails, you leave."

By this time the Carters had left the town and the people were carrying the remnants of their life in Profit back to their homes.

"The Carter's leaving is an economic relief," the mayor continued. "They're good people; don't get me wrong, and not that that matters. But leaving before their liability comes of age to receive his share of their pain is the right choice for responsible personal corporations to make and we wish them well."

Gil was curious about something and wanted to change the subject. "Doris, do you have e-medical capability here?"

Doris was pleased with the question.

"We do," she said proudly. "One of my first campaign promises was to acquire an e-facility. Before the economy fell apart, Cleveland was a major, and quite profitable, center for medical research, but after, with Cleveland's economy all but gutted—most commerce in the region has become small plot farmers, manufacturing subcontractors, and a relatively harmless rebel community. Private medical corporations can't profit in this area anymore so it's left to the towns to develop their own profitable medical solutions. Westlake is a manager's town with some local farming nearby and they have a medical center, but it's a long way to go and they charge a great deal more if you're not a resident. Besides that, the most direct routes run through Cleveland, which is still quite dangerous. For the long term growth of Profit, I felt a medical center here, even a small one, would be profitable and would attract more and better workers, and it has."

"Do you have resident doctors?" Bree asked.

Doris laughed. "No, dear, do we look like an Executive Community? Having a resident with medical certification just isn't economically feasible. Profiteers with medical needs find solutions at bid-for-services Mesh auction sites where the low bidder service provider performs procedures or surgeries remotely using our state-of-the-art robotics surgical center. We resolve legal and financial issues similarly through Mesh auctions. We lost a great revenue stream when we were too slow reacting and failed a few years ago to get into Mesh services."

They continued their walk, Doris stopping at a sprawling one story glass and brick building.

"This is our shopping center," she said proudly. "The Profit Chamber of Commerce owns the complex of shops here, but Profiteers rent them out and work their off hours to earn extra income which they parlay into long term wealth. When you've earned enough to invest in inventory, you profit by selling it right here or at social parties. When you accumulate enough funds, you can own a significant stake in your store or even the mall itself. What you see here is Saint Adam Smith's capitalism at its finest.

"Transactions here work like they do at other malls, you make a purchase and the price is automatically deducted from your account. We extend credit of up to one days pay but it's on you to pay it though as long as you can endure the pain, you can defer payments and use your cash to ensure additional profits. I warn you, for newbies, the pain gets jacked up pretty quickly. Once you run out of value and credit, you can't purchase necessities so it's 'bye-bye' like the Carters. The same policy holds in our restaurants, at our social events, and everywhere in Profit. It is wise to remember the Carters."

Inside, the mall was colorful, crowded, and noisy. There were barkers, shouting out specials and people demonstrating products and services as Profiteers wandered around, frantically searching for the best products at the best prices. At some stores there were arguments that Doris described as good old All American haggling, at others, concerned shop attendants worked the corridors frantically to entice their neighbors inside their shops.

"What happens if your balance goes negative?" Gil asked.

Doris looked concerned. "Has old town Buffalo gone socialist? Negative worth, now that's a concept to avoid. Seriously, one of the core values of Morgan is investment, but its only investment if one believes they will achieve an adequate return. It isn't possible to overspend your wealth. I mean you could, I guess, it's theoretically possible but without someone to underwrite you as their investment, the pain would be unendurable and your investors share that pain so there is that. The Chamber of Commerce does its level best to help you maintain value, but if you should go below break-even, true negative net worth, maybe because you're not anticipating fixed expense charges associated with living in Profit-the rents, utilities, housecleaning, defense and common area costs, the advertising we do in other towns and the like-bills we receive from our private contractors that are prorated daily to your account at the end of each shift, the physical distress emanating from your PID continues to amplify and if that isn't incentive enough to be productive and consume wisely or bail and like the Carters, become *Wasters*, then I don't know what more we, as a community, can do. Now, where was I?"

"You were talking about the Carter family," Bree said, helpfully.

"I was. In life, the secret of success is simple and lasts forever. Be productive and create value. That's all. And it is my responsibility to manage Profit's resources, it's potential, to insure that everyone is working toward the same goal—personal success, production line success, town success, success for our Federal Reserve region and success for our country."

With that, Doris paused. "I don't think I mentioned it before, but tonight, you must leave a urine sample in the secure box outside your cottage."

"Why?" Gil asked.

"It provides information my actuaries use to predict performance."

They continued to walk while Doris pointed out other facilities.

"I'll let you in on another little secret," The mayor confided. "Profit's performance has caught the attention of the Managers at Westlake and the executives on the Lake and I'm certain to be promoted to Westlake within the year. I'll miss Profit, but life in a Manager's town has so many more . . . possibilities. I say that because my departure will provide new opportunities for the enterprising here."

"Do they garden at Westlake?" Gil asked. Bree gave him a questioning look.

"Why yes, they do." Doris placed her hand on Bree's shoulder.

"Bree, dear," she said, "the most important thing in life is to know what that most important thing is, and then focus all of your efforts to achieve it. If you don't know what you want and where and how you to get it, why be alive? That is the last free advice I will provide so take advantage of it."

"Yes Ma'am," Bree said. "Thank you. I look forward to purchasing more of your advice in the future."

"You're welcome. By the way, you spoke of church yesterday. I assume you're both familiar with the teachings of our Chief Spiritual Officer, Tom Morgan?"

They stared at each other and then nodded, uncertainly.

"To be successful here, you must be true believers."

"Honestly, Ma'am I'm not," Gil answered truthfully. "I'm willing."

"What about you, Bree?"

"I received the training, but I'm kind of a lapsed Morgan."

Doris shook her head. "People, what is wrong with you? Bree, as the woman, I hold you responsible. Profit, like all of America, requires a deep and abiding faith in the teachings of our beloved Chief Spiritual Officer. Don't you want to attain everlasting life?"

"Certainly, Doris," Bree answered.

Gil was noncommittal. "I guess . . . it would be nice. I just haven't given it much thought. We're young and we've been pretty busy." Doris turned and slapped him hard on the cheek. He flinched.

"What was that for?"

"Pay attention! What did I just say?" Without allowing him to answer, she continued. "What's the most important thing in your life?" She pointed to her head and then made a fist and tapped her chest with it. "Think with your heart and your head. The longer you live, the better your chances are for success and to live like a successful person lives—well that's the privilege that everlasting life offers.

"Too busy or day-to-day, that is lethal. If you don't have that all-abiding faith in your ability to fund forever, you are a problem we won't share. In Profit, like in all communities, we will not hire people who aren't committed to doing whatever it takes to create the wealth to support forever. What is the most important thing?" Again, without letting him respond, she continued, "Morgan provides the dogma that is needed so it is the most important thing. Am I clear?"

"Yes, Ma'am you are," he said as resolutely as he could.

"Am I clear?" He nodded again.

"I take this very seriously because I am a *MILF*," the mayor explained. "I am an officer in the Morgan International Libertarian Fundamentalist sect and I know what I know. You, Dan Stacey, and you, Bree Andrews, must become true believers. I knew it when I first saw you. Your partnership cannot survive if forever isn't in the equation. You gain nothing by programming loss into your life. Bree, once your stay here is approved; I will assign to you the responsibility to insure that you both become the Morgans that God intended you to be."

Gil turned to Bree. "I'm sorry if I did anything to effect your pursuit of everlasting happiness. Doris has shown me the light, Bree. You and I will immerse ourselves in Morgan."

"And your reward will be infinite," Doris added.

Bree continued with Gil's sham. "Beginning with tomorrow's vows, I'll work relentlessly to generate value forever."

Doris clapped her hands. "Another couple on the road to forever, thanks be to Morgan, this is exactly what you need. Bree, Dan, be as I am. Work with passion and meet every requirement of every customer in every job you ever have. Make yourself necessary to your superiors and forever and all God's glory is yours."

"The more we earn the better and longer we live," Bree said, smiling.

"The truest words offered by a productive woman with renewed faith," Doris trilled. "But there's more. You must work with passion, live with passion, honor God and your contracts, and the world is yours. Passion is the secret ingredient. If I didn't honor God every day of my life, I would not be here today. I have distinguished myself and now I qualify for medical programs and performance enhancing *Pharma* so that I will execute my responsibilities better and longer. I qualify for cosmetic and systemic enhancement surgery, which grants me honor among my peers and I receive ever more sophisticated preventative treatments which enhances my everlasting potential. With my next promotion, my net worth will qualify me for cloning and body part replacement benefits that will transport me one step closer to God's immortality. I have invested much in me and much has been invested by others as well so that much more is expected from me. My lifespan has been increased by a hundred years with more to come. And with continued technological breakthroughs, forever is mine as it could be yours and someday, my genetic structure, my capability, and my personality matrix will be captured such that in my unlikely demise, I will be born again to live forever in a world of my own funding. Praise Morgan!"

Flushed, Doris looked from Bree to Gil.

"What I have accomplished is real, tangible and achievable, God's perfect reward for living right. It's exciting for me to see young people with that fever. It is more proof of God's plan. Can you feel it, Dan? Bree? Tell me you can feel it."

"Yes, Ma'am," Gil yelled with as much passion as he could muster. "You have made this real for me and I feel reborn." He smiled at Bree and she smiled back.

"Thank you, Ma'am." Bree responded. "I wish, when I was growing up, it had been explained the way you just did. You've given my life meaning. It makes perfect sense and funding eternity is now the goal of my life."

Doris seemed to glow. "Morgan sells itself. Open your mind, children, audit your life, and purge conventional wisdom from it. Faith is real and science has proven that dead is dead and that there is no heaven. *Wasters* who live believing in a hereafter are rewarded by their fate. God created us to live and he intends us to live with him. He created us in his image and since he can't die, neither can we. He has put life everlasting within our grasp and it is up to us to implement his will. Morgan has it right. There is only life and the rejection of life. What we have is real faith."

"You are an inspiration," Bree said, trying to build a relationship to meet her needs at Profit.

"At every stage there will be tests, sort of economic probation, a time when you're judged on your passion and capability to do what is required to live to another stage."

"What happens if, say, Bree can't meet those requirements but I can?" Gil asked.

"Won't happen," Bree said as she shot him an angry look. "I can meet any requirements you can."

Doris smiled. "I'm sure you can, Bree, but Dan asks a good question. The answer will be clear once you've taken our vows. Morgan isn't settled theology, like any business, it is dynamic, ever changing, adapting in anticipation of future needs. God, in His infinite wisdom, gave us free markets and free choice. If a partner falls by the economic wayside, you may support her and fund her shortfalls if that's what you desire. But you must have economic certainty that she is a good investment or risk mitigation is the proper religious response. You don't want to throw good money after bad and lose forever, too. Divestiture is a business choice that protects your portfolio from an incompetent partner or a liability like the Carter child who brings the individuals in a partnership down. One must be mature enough to evaluate from a disinterested perspective."

"How does divestiture work?" Bree asked.

"If a partner or a liability projects as no longer viable, after divestiture, others in town may bid on them as long as the bidder has suitable net worth to cover costs and obligations and another partnership agreement is constructed. Otherwise, the nonviable partner must move on and find viability elsewhere."

"But suppose I don't want her to leave," Gil said.

Bree put her hands on her hips. "If anyone's going to be asked to leave it'll be you."

"Alright, children, stop fighting," Doris interrupted. "No one wants to lose a partner in whom they have invested so much. That's why we insist everyone subscribe to weekly economic theology classes in Archive to keep your eyes on the prize. It's critical to successful partnerships that everyone work as hard and smart as possible all the time, but you never know what business cycles have in store and a successful relationship is really as much about risk mitigation as anything, so it's important to build your net worth early in anticipation of contingencies or you'll find yourself on the outside, living alone, or worse, eating tubers and selling wood carvings or weaved baskets at local markets. Don't laugh. To survive out there, you'd do worse."

"Like the Carters."

"Exactly, like the Carters. Creative destruction is another of our core beliefs. It keeps everything vibrant and fresh. And no Profiteer wants loser traits in the genetic pool. The America of my youth, the First Republic, the America of entitlements, was doomed because too many *Wasters* were kept alive and they selfishly burdened the lifestyles of the rest of us conscientious, hard workers. Those days are over, thank Morgan. Free enterprise was never meant to extend to *Wasters*. It is only meant for winners."

"So what's next?" Gil asked.

Doris showed them the factory and warehouse complex, a series of larger green, vinyl-sided and window-less buildings where value was added. Then she pointed to a fence in the distance. Beyond the fence there was a large old stone building that was obscured among dense trees.

"That is Merry Manor," The mayor added, turning away from it quickly. "There's no reason to visit there, today. Maybe someday," she said cryptically.

"So that's Profit, a simple town designed to satisfy every Profiteer's lifelong desire for commercial success. We buy, add value, and sell. Everything else is overhead and we keep that to a bare minimum so revenue is driven to the bottom line and profits are paramount." Doris said. "Walk around and talk to our citizens and when you return to your quarters, fill out the questionnaire and leave your urine samples in the box outside by the door. Conditionally, I've assigned you to starter home A-103. Check the map. It's not a house that appreciates, but that's by design. As your worth increases, so will the opportunity for bigger and better appreciating housing investments. Tomorrow, as soon as the ceremonies end, report for work—you will be told where. Your Pids will be reset to conform to our standards and you'll be held accountable for your net worth from that moment on. If you subscribe, work clothes will be delivered to you tomorrow morning—at a cost, of course. It's a good deal because the time or money you spend cleaning your attire is best utilized increasing your worth."

"Does this mean we've been accepted?" Bree asked.

"You prove yourself every day," the mayor said. "Remember the Carters. Today you are accepted. You will be given a glove when your Pid is updated. You've used one before?"

Gil nodded, but was surprised when Bree didn't. Doris explained.

"Bree, the glove was invented by the Reverend General Ginger Tucker for her security troops and at great cost, has only recently been distributed to the towns. It connects to your Pid and supplies the input and output necessary for you to communicate with your database. Dan has used one, I'm sure he can explain it.

"Now, I must attend to other duties. Explore and get us those urine samples." With that, Mayor Doris left them standing in the center of town.

When she was far enough away, Bree screamed, "we made it," and jumped into Gil's arms. It felt so comfortable that Gil held her, overlong, forcing her to extract herself from his embrace and push away. She was oblivious to his embarrassment as she led him off to find their new home.

As Doris had instructed, they checked the map and found their cottage easily enough. As soon as they entered, they were both very disappointed. Unlike the guesthouse they shared yesterday, this cottage was tiny, one room and a bath and the room barely had space for one bed, a small one at that, one nightstand, and one chair while the bathroom was considerably smaller with a shower that was a drape and a hole pick-axed into the floor. They stood on a faux fur rug in the cramped space between the small bed and the front door and stared at their accommodations in silence.

Finally she spoke. "We need rules and we need a plan to get out of here, too"

"At least it's inexpensive."

"How do you know that? We don't even know what we're being paid."

"Do you want to know about the glove?" he asked trying to change the subject.

"I know all about them, but how do you know? When did you ever need a glove?"

"I don't know how to respond to that," he said. He could tell she wanted to say something but she thought better of it and accepted his response.

"Now, as to the rules, the bed's mine and it is absolutely off limits," Bree began. "You can sleep on the rug by the door. I'll give up the blanket until we can afford to buy another. The bathroom is mine until it isn't and then it's yours, but be quick. Is that clear?"

He looked sadly at the rug and shook his head. "What do I get, other than a trampled rug and the joy of sleeping on the floor?"

"You get not having to sleep outside. Do you have a problem?"

He looked at her, then at the floor and shook his head.

Later, while Bree was showering and getting ready for bed, Gil left the cabin and walked to an Archive terminal he saw in the lobby of the shopping center. He was there checking out the local news when the clerk, Donald, received a call and looked at Gil curiously and then smiled.

"Mr. Stacey, your partner says she's ready for you to come home. You'd better hustle big fellow; you don't want to keep her waiting."

"Did she say that?" The man laughed louder and so embarrassed, Gil trotted back to the cabin.

She was dressed and waiting, but the shower was still running. She pulled him into the bathroom.

"There's a transmitter in here," she pointed and whispered, "So I assume there's one in the other room too. Be careful what you say." He nodded. She left the tiny bathroom to allow him to clean up and get ready for bed. When he was done, they bundled up and went out onto their tiny porch.

"We're going have to act more like partners inside," she began, "but don't get any ideas. Out there, I'll hug you if I have to but no kissing or if we must kiss; only pecks. Got it? You can make it sound more substantial if you want, but you're on your own there. If they ask, tell them I'm shy, or frigid, I don't care, but if you try anything in here, I mean anything; I don't care how it happens, I'll hurt you, and I can. Are we clear?" She stared as if daring him to say something.

He nodded and once again, he changed the subject. "I wonder what work I've been assigned."

"Work is work. Let's complete the questionnaire and give them our sample."

"And there are the vows, tomorrow, whatever that is."

"I won't convert," Bree said. "There's no way. The whole Morgan thing is moronic. The man's dumb as a rock. I'll say the vows, but I don't know what I'll do if they make us convert."

"Dumb as a rock?" Gil asked. Bree hesitated. "Do you know this Morgan guy?"

"Of course not," she explained. "I've read about him and he's stupid, that's all. He made a religion out of nothing more than hard work and fear. Like that hasn't been done before." She must have noticed that he was confused so she changed the subject. "I'm not sure I can share this dump. We have to earn enough fast so we can move."

"It's a crappy place but it's cheaper if we stay here," he said. "What choice do we have? We'd struggle worse trying to make Detroit in winter without enough credits. We almost starved getting here. We have to do this, even for a few weeks. The place is fine. I can get used to it. I've slept on floors before. Remember, Doris said we earn in real time so we'll leave soon. How long do you think it'll take?"

"Look at this hole," she said, jerking her thumb over her shoulder, motioning to the structure behind her. "Tomorrow is too long, and if it wasn't so late, I don't think I'd make it through tonight. Tomorrow, we'll need to visit their market to get an idea what things cost."

"That's a great idea. We live cheap and then bolt when we're ready. How bad can it get?"

"New Rule: We can't both be here at the same time, the place is too small. It's best you find evening work. I'll work days."

"This isn't all about you. I have problems with it, too, but I don't see what choice we have. I'll make the best of it but you'd better too. We're in this together, for now, and I'm the one stuck on the floor." He stared at her, the inside lighting illuminating her in a way that softened her good looks.

"The only interest I have in you as a partner is to do it to get through our time here at Profit," he said. Then, he addressed his other problem.

"What do you think will happen with our P$_{\text{IDS}}$?"

"I don't know." She didn't seem concerned.

"If being identified isn't important, why don't you want anyone to know who you are?"

She stared before finally saying, "I don't know how to respond to that."

"Again? That's not going to help us resolve problems."

"Okay, smart guy, why don't you want anyone to know who you are?"

He shrugged. "Okay, fair enough. Let's tackle that questionnaire before we head to the market. Then we can get sleep."

They shared answers and finished the questionnaire quickly. Afterward, they walked to the market where they noted the costs of various goods and services, but it was difficult to relate because they didn't know how they would be reimbursed. They headed back to the cottage where he waited for her to get into bed before trying to get comfortable on the rug. She needed the light on to sleep so he rolled away from it, pulled the blanket over his head, and tried to sleep.

Late that evening, after tossing and turning, chasing sleep that did not want to be found, he turned and listened to her light breathing and fell asleep watching her chest rise and fall.

Chapter 27
Profit — 2070

Gil woke to find two frost-covered packages with their work and dress clothes replacing the questionnaires and urine samples that he and Bree had placed in a box the previous night. Bree prepared for work while he waited in the main lodge. When he returned to the cabin, she was dressed in a simple blouse and skirt and still looked great.

"You're staring."

"You look great," he mumbled as he walked by.

She pulled him close and whispered. "It's good to say those things out loud just don't get any ideas."

He whispered, "Boy, you're sold on yourself. We've got a million issues more important so get off it. You were clear and I understand. You look great, that's all." They were so close that her heat made him uncomfortable and self-conscious. Seemingly enjoying his discomfort, she didn't move away.

"Then start looking bored; like a partner should."

"I don't think your partner would ever be bored," he said and then quickly joked, "Oh and try not to forget my name at the ceremony."

"Let's go, honey bun." She held out her hand and he took it. They walked outside looking like their best version of a couple.

The townsfolk had done their job. The park was decorated and even in the cold, there were flowers everywhere. The stage was decorated with local merchant advertising and near it, couples mingled, each wearing matching, elaborately painted nametags. Two tags remained on a table by the stage, Mr. Dan Stacey and Ms. Bree Andrews.

"It's official, partner," he whispered

She squeezed his hand hard enough to make him squeal, but he just smiled. Doris, who was talking with another couple, came over.

"Sleep well, folks?"

Bree let go of Gil's hand and answered, "It was like heaven, thanks."

"Remember, there is no such thing as heaven," Doris said, smiling. "Be productive, you don't have to stay there long if you don't want to. Today, with product demand so high, our theme is brevity so it'll be a quick ceremony with a fast lunch to follow. I see you received your clothes. After the ceremony you get your work assignments."

"We can't wait. Thanks," Gil said as he felt for Bree's hand, but she withheld it.

"No thanks are necessary. The clothes have been billed to your account so it's official, you've been accepted. You are a *Profiteer*. Here's how it works. For the first three months, you're on probation during which time your performance is monitored while your assigned avatar works with you on productivity. After the probation period, you receive a wage increase and from there it's up to you. Don't disappoint."

"No, Ma'am," he answered. "We'll work real hard, won't we Bree, honey?"

"We will do everything we can to create value for Profit," She added.

Doris handed them a small card. "You arrived too late to practice so when it's time to say your vows, read them from this card even though some of what is on it won't be relevant until your next renewal. Your work assignments are on the back."

The music started. "That's my cue. Good luck. I'll be monitoring your performance with great interest."

Doris headed for the podium as the audience respectfully quieted. She looked out on the crowd and began.

"As Mayor, Managing Partner and primary stockholder of Profit, it is my distinct pleasure to begin our sixtieth biennial partnership renewal celebration. Today, we have twelve couples eagerly anticipating renewal of their vows so let's begin." There was cheering as the couples held hands and marched onto the stage. Gil and Bree were last. Once onstage, following the lead of the other couples, they turned to face each other.

When everyone was ready, Doris continued. "We have one new corporate entity today. Everyone this is Bree Andrews and Dan Stacey. They have accreted to us from Erie in the north and are pleased to renew their vows and then join Profit's continuing worship of productivity and value. As is our custom, our corporate financial advisor, the Most Reverend Gussie Raymond will preside. Reverend Gus."

A tall, thin man approached the podium and shook Doris' hand. He was wearing a business suit with a gold religious icon of the Morgan Church, the silver *lemniscate* and gold dollar sign, hanging from his neck. "Reverend Gus, it's all yours." She left the stage to take her seat of honor in the front row.

The Reverend began. "Another group of dedicated Profiteers has chosen to renew their vows of Corporate Partnership and their economic commitment to each other, their community and to the Free Market that provides us with everlasting opportunity.

"As always, I've placed rating cards at everyone's seat so you can evaluate my performance and that of this ceremony. When you leave, place the cards in the box at the back. I want to repeat my plea from our spring ceremony. Your recommendations will not affect your net worth and I will not be offended by any suggestions that improve this ceremony." The Reverend smiled and took a deep breath.

"America has a long and storied history of corporation. Though invented elsewhere, the corporation, as it is today, is a truly American adaptation. Corporations grew and asserted their rights, and America thrived as corporate rights became settled law. Over these years our society became great as in Supreme Court case after Supreme Court case, judges decided in favor of America's future and that limited liability corporations must have more rights than do the people. That is why, today, everyone is a corporation in its various forms, making corporations the essential element of an economic life worth living.

"With the development of corporations, the Morgan religion was the natural and inevitable next step in God's holy strategic plan. Morgan is the culmination of religious economic thought that began with those illustrious groundbreakers, the Jews, and continued to grow and prosper through each of God's chosen prophets, Jesus, Mohammed, and Adam and John Smith, reaching its truest expression on that glorious November night in 2045 when the Great Market Maker Himself appeared on a humble computer monitor to His Eminence, Saint Thomas Morgan.

"The accretive nature of our religion, both in America and abroad, establishes the validity of our purpose and so, twice each year, Profiteers gather to recommit to free enterprise Capitalism and the fulfillment of everlasting life on Earth, with assets, God's markets willing, will appreciate forever." The Reverend turned to the onstage couples. "Please repeat after me, using your name where I use mine, the majority partner will begin."

Gil faced Bree confused as to who should start. She smiled and he deferred to her.

"I, Bree Andrews, hereby declare my faith in Free Markets and in Capitalism's immutable laws and do hereby renew my commitment to my economic well being, that of my business unit that provides support, my city of Profit that provides the economic infrastructure which allows me to be successful, and the state of Ohio and the United States of America who protects and defends my corporate rights.

"Further, I declare the contract with my spouse, Dan Stacey," Bree smiled at him, "is renewed. I declare our relationship has been duly codified, is reciprocally satisfactory, and has not been entered into under duress. I further affirm that so long as our combined wealth allows, any disputes will be resolved through binding arbitration, here in Profit, using an accredited Mesh-based legal service.

"I further affirm per the Profit Residents Codicil, the right of the Board of Directors to evaluate and if economically justified, grant the addition of each liability our partnership chooses to acquire under our corporate umbrella. I agree, also, to submit to the Board for approval a five-year partnership economic plan in a form of their choosing along with a detailed budget for the following year with quarterly performance updates.

"If I involuntarily divest from my partner, the Profit Board of Directors will manage my assets and provide such support as is codified in our Partnership Agreement until such time as I am reborn, everlasting and am capable of managing myself. If I separate voluntarily from my spouse without succession plans and do not reincorporate, the Profit Board will act as the executor of my estate and manage my accounts, as it deems appropriate until my return.

"Should I be separated from my partner by other reason, I am free to carry forward all the value I have accrued in the funds deemed joint, less operating expenses, as determined by an arbitrator appointed by the Board of Directors. And if I have inadequate asset value, I will abide by Profit's by-laws in all matters related to divesture, dissolution, and departure.

"All of this, I avow with unwavering faith in the glory of His Market and the long term requirements of life everlasting."

Gil knew the words but they all seemed to have strange new meanings and with people reciting not quite in cadence, he felt like laughing at the presentation, but he held back as Bree finished her vows. When it was his turn, he had to concentrate in order to read the vows and was barely able to hear his own voice over the din. He was disappointed because Bree's eyes were elsewhere, checking out other corporate entities.

With the vows complete, Reverend Raymond faced the audience smiling. "By the power vested in me by the Honorable Mayor of Profit and her Board of Directors, by the State of Ohio, and by the Department of the Treasury, I hereby revalidate your corporation for another six months. Go forth and appreciate."

The couples embraced to the cheers and applause of the audience. Gil looked uneasily at Bree and then each shrugged in unison and embraced guardedly. He pulled back to kiss her.

"No tongue," she whispered and her lips met his, at first briefly, then longer. Just as it began to feel comfortable, she pulled away.

"Whoa, big boy, don't get carried away."

"Sorry, I got lost in the moment."

Reverend Raymond walked over smiling. "Welcome aboard. Before you leave for work, don't forget to rate my performance."

Bree nodded. "Thanks, Reverend. When do we start work?"

"It's Reverend Gus. You'll start as soon as the meal ends. You're new; eat hearty because the cost is prorated by couple, not by amount eaten." The Reverend left to make another announcement and they found seats. "The play begins during lunch. Afterward, everyone back to work. But before we start, Mayor Doris has some announcements. Doris returned to the platform and the crowd immediately quieted.

"Is Laurence Hilliard in the crowd?" the mayor asked.

Everyone laughed except Gil and Bree. Gil leaned across to ask a woman nearby why everyone was laughing.

"Laurence is our Senior Engineer and Project Manager and kind of our mascot. He lives in the mansion," she pointed across the park. "Laurence is respected dearly, but he's a true *veek* and rarely leaves his home." Gil was about to question what a *veek* was, but his confused look alerted her. "Yes, well a *veek*, you know a virtual geek, he spends all his time patched into the Mesh in a *Virtuoso* simulator he built in his basement. He doesn't relate to people . . ."

"I didn't know Profit has *Virtuoso* capability?" Gil asked, hiding his excitement.

"It's not a *Virtuoso* unit per se, it's a simulator. I wish we had the bandwidth for true *Virtuoso*, but Doris insists that it inhibits productivity. In the last town we tried, *Virtuoso* provided flexibility that kept personal corporations stable. You see, a corporation must be a union of a man and a woman only, but in *Virtuoso*, any combination is permitted and it relieves the tedium." At the touch of her partner, she stopped. "Sorry, that's not relevant. About the *veek*, Doris permits Laurence to use a *Virtuoso* simulator because he's able to achieve more from Archive for our business needs with it, but Doris has forbidden it for us because she feels it gets in the way. Too much whimsy she says. Doris drives Profiteers much harder than-"

This time her partner nudged her and she turned to him. "Laurence built . . . a . . . jump unit. Is that right Hon?"

Her partner moved closer, whispering, "You get analog representation instead of fully rendered avatars. It's cheaper but works kind of the same. Laurence modified a kit from a division of ANGS and he's allowed to have it because he's critical to Profit's economy." He put his finger to his lips, "We can talk later," and turned his attention to the Mayor.

" . . . always hard to get Laurence's attention," Doris continued. There was more laughter.

"Now to the important news. We are entering into a joint venture in a vibrant new industry. Yesterday, we signed a contract to supply various building materials for a local franchise of Paradise, an Ongoing Concern Enterprise." There were cheers among those who knew what that was. "For those of you who don't know, Paradise is a low maintenance community for *perpetuals*. It will be state-of-the-art and will include every possible comfort. What makes the Paradise brand unique and will generate wealth for Profiteers is that, for all the luxury, it provides each perpetual resident the greatest possible amount of personal living space so that forever can be enjoyed without being infringed upon by neighbors." Doris paused to get full value from her next statement.

"As of now, all previously announced layoffs are rescinded." A cheer erupted from the crowd. "Details will be posted, but for now, enjoy the play and the lunch and then let's get back to work, people."

To Gil, the play was unwatchable. It began in all seriousness, an economic message with clear fiscal themes, but then one of the actors broke out in song and Gil started laughing. The people around him turned and Bree caught him with an elbow to the chest. He sat through the unendurable mess until, eventually, the play ended with a Greek chorus singing a wondrous message of productivity to a wildly cheering crowd. After the cast was introduced to thunderous applause, everyone headed for the buffet line.

Bree pushed to the front while Gil waited in line. He turned to the man who had explained about Laurence Hilliard.

"We didn't know there were lay-offs," he said.

"It's not technically a lay-off. It's a feature of the community's creative destruction program. Lay-offs provide an opportunity to redeploy assets more productively and for those unable to make successful inroads here, to move on to other work. This strengthens the country, overall, as former Profiteers find work more in line with their skills and aspirations in other communities. It's another case of the blessed invisible hand of Capitalism acting in our behalf. We get jobs, we lose jobs, it's continual, but along the way, the economic chain strengthens and we're all wealthier for it."

Gil thought about the Carters but decided not to mention it. "Paradise is a great opportunity for us," the man continued, "but it's not forever. Laurence will have to find us new, sustaining business. It's what he does. When he identifies a project he wants, he never loses it. Profit has hard and smart workers, but Laurence is why we continue to thrive." The man added, "Do you want some free advice?" Gil nodded. "Don't accept success too easily because someone always comes along who provides more and better, relieving you of your responsibilities." The man laughed. "Creative destruction and the invisible hand keep us hopping so to insure our future; we must always be concerned about performance and always look for new opportunities. The more success you find, the more Profiteers will glom onto you and the higher returns you will yield, for you and everybody. That's how my partner and I stay prosperous. As a rule, I work so hard that I am always cost-justified and town management must accept me as I'm necessary, not relatively but absolutely necessary. It's the only way."

"Thanks, we appreciate the advice," Gil said. "Bree and I are excited to be working in such a competitive and winning environment." Gil hoped his enthusiasm sounded honest.

Each loaded their plates with a savory looking chili, made of chunks of beef, beans, and a garden's worth of fresh vegetables. The dishes emitted a great deal of steam, which presented a preamble to the flavorful spiciness of the meal. With food in hand, the new partners sat together at a nearby table.

"Have you received your assignment?" the man asked. They handed him their cards. He read Gil's and nodded. "You work over there," he pointed, "in our material handling department. You'll be an entry-level handler; it's a great first job. When you get there, you'll be assigned a mentor, an avatar, that'll make like a drill instructor, but listen and pay attention and you'll become productive much faster and off probation that much sooner." He looked at Bree's assignment. "You're in the same building just on the administration side."

"Doris mentioned probation," Bree said. "What does it mean?"

"If you're productive, it's nothing to worry about. During probation you're paid at the lowest wage rate, but the mentoring and the training are free. Once you earn your way off probation you'll get a promotion and receive a raise. That's when your lifestyle improves, but any training you need thereafter must be paid for."

"Until then?" she asked.

"Live cheap. Housing is expensive here so stay in your start-up home as long as possible. Once you're off probation, you can upgrade your home. It makes life easier, helps your estate appreciate faster, and it's good for Profit to have a vital real estate business segment. Besides, a large mortgage only becomes a great incentive to keep aggressive, ambitious, energetic people performing if you can afford the interest and the daily payments. Besides, the last thing Profit needs is someone who is satisfied too soon; it creates too many bad habits. It's critical that new people like you have the right capitalist perspective. Comfort is anathema to productivity. It means lost opportunities, low net worth, divestiture and eventually a *Waster's* life of poverty and death."

They finished the meal in silence. When the siren sounded and the festivities ended Gil was relieved. While some of the residents cleaned up, the rest scattered to their homes to change for work. Gil and Bree separated to attend their first shift as newly minted citizens of Profit.

Gil arrived at his designated department as his supervisor, Jay Sinay, was completing the shift work assignments, so he waited and watched. Fifteen minutes later the supervisor walked over to him.

"Dan Stacey?"

"Yes, sir. Is it Hay?" Gil asked, giving Jay a Spanish pronunciation.

"Good try, but no," the man said. "It's pronounced like it's spelled, Jay. I'm your supervisor and you're late." He wanted to explain, but Jay was already talking while walking.

"Follow me and pay attention," Jay said turning back and motioning for Gil to catch up, "once I leave you with your mentor, you're on the clock and the evaluation period begins." Gil nodded.

"Has your PID been upgraded?"

Gil shook his head.

"Jesus, now you're even further behind. The Technology trailer will reconfigure it. Hurry over and get back as soon as they finish. Go."

Gil ran to the trailer where a woman carrying a large handheld computer tablet and a scanning device greeted him.

"Dan Stacey?" she asked. He answered affirmatively. "Stand over here." She pointed to a small white circle painted on the floor. "We'll scan our programs into your PID—it won't hurt." When he didn't laugh, she stared down at her tablet, disappointed. "Of course it won't hurt. Okay, it took. Here's your glove, you know how to use it?" He nodded. "Go forth and produce," she said smiling, but again he didn't respond. Disappointed, she just shook her head. "You're done, go, earn."

He put on the glove. It was surprisingly similar, yet a cheap imitation of Bernie's glove with the added enhancement of an inexpensive flexible monitor sewn onto the back where he could receive output. He clicked and found his current worth, his assignment, and a map of Profit. He was about to explore more of its functionality when a terse message appeared on the screen alerting him that his supervisor was waiting.

He found Jay standing impatiently outside the trailer. His supervisor quickly showed him around the warehouse, which was filled with tall racks of very large, woven plastic bags.

"Your role is to complete orders from a pick list that . . . never mind. Just listen to your avatar and do whatever she says. Keep in mind; your PID number is assigned to each activity, so everything you do is recorded. We know who's accountable and who screws things up so you don't want to screw up, not even in the beginning. Start and stop times are recorded for every task and the amount of effective work completed is accumulated and compared to an idealized performance profile so we can generate a fair and accurate measure of your contribution and your continuous improvement with which you will earn the appropriate credits while at the same time you'll receive feedback as to where you are and by how much your performance must improve. To receive the power points you must accumulate towards promotions, wage increase or select prizes including wonderful vacations you can sell to non-Morgans, we offer from time to time to our workers." He spoke as if he had said this speech many times in the past, and Gil was surprised that his supervisor didn't take more breaths between sentences. It was almost too much information to take in at one time.

"To assist you, your avatar has a personality profile geared to make you more effective. You two will become inseparable and interact continuously based on this profile and the questionnaire you filled out before you were hired, but I'll throw in one free tip, pick up the tempo as quickly as you can. Have they explained performance indicators?"

"No, sir."

"Are you just off the streets?" Gil nodded and his supervisor shrugged and began the explanation. Like the previous explanation, Gil felt from the beginning that he was listening words behind. "You can read it tonight on your glove. Here're the basics, pay attention; you have a cost-minimal probationary lifestyle which means your earnings're very low and worth is almost impossible to accumulate, but if you listen, follow directions and work as hard as your mentor requires, you'll earn more credits which'll be tallied onto your PID as you perform and earning enough credits'll power you to another performance level. More credits, more levels, got that? More effort and higher expectations come with each new level, but you'll earn more credits also and we monitor everyone all the time so we know what you're doing, where and why and we keep you informed so there're no surprises. Got it?"

Before Gil could assimilate it and respond, his supervisor moved on. "There're basically three statuses you should be concerned with," Jay continued, breathlessly. "The first, green means go, which means you're productive. Yellow's a warning that you aren't earning as fast as you're incurring debt, and be careful with orange, it's an elevated warning which means you're putting Profit's profits at risk so with low green and yellow alerts, you will notice a certain amount of heat emanating from your PID and that's okay, it's perfectly normal. In fact, in the winter some of our less intense workers prefer it because of the cold, of course, but the more in debt you get, the warmer the sensation, so by orange, all I'll say's watch out for orange and I mean it.

"So be prepared, because though everyone has a different threshold of pain and everyone goes through a certain amount of heat while they're learning it can get pretty intense-hot is possible and on the last guy, you could cook waffles off the heat it was so intense. And we do it this way or the whole system doesn't work. It can get to where you can't concentrate, you're failing and you want to resign as soon as possible because the discomfort can't be worked through easily even though everyone tries it and if you're smoking, literally, your skin is smoking, we aren't responsible for heroics, you signed the waiver. From what I hear the pain is brutal, just brutal, and from a distance, maybe a little funny to watch in others with all the screaming and contortions, but you have to decide that for yourself and it's not funny if it's happening to you. Any questions?" Without listening for a response, Jay walked to a bin and grabbed something.

"No, sir," Gil answered nervously. He hadn't heard everything and he was unsure he heard that right so he asked, "You're kidding about this, right?"

His supervisor gave him a sour look and handed him a headset. "Time's money and no one pays for kidding, got it? I've got to run, but let me introduce you to your avatar. You drew Bon-Bon. She's an entry-level avatar who's working her way up, a lot like you so pay attention and do what she says when she says it and you both should earn power points and promotions soon enough. Bon-Bon, here's your new trainee. Dan Stacey, Bon-Bon, Bon-Bon, Dan Stacey. You're in good hands, got to go." With that, Jay left and Gil put the headphones on.

"Dan Stacey, what a nice name," said a pleasant female voice. She spoke slower and that caused him to relax. "Here's to a profitable relationship, Dan, may I call you Dan? According to your profile, you learned work discipline from your grandfather at Stacey Manufacturing, Inc. in Bangor, Maine. With that experience, we project that you will be productive quickly."

"My . . . grandfather, yes," Gil muttered, unsure.

"What you will be doing initially may be a bit too easy for someone with your potential, but you should soon move up to something more representative of your ability to create value. Before we start, there are a few issues that need resolution. As usual, your account will be credited for each hour you work with performance bonuses and any garnishments recorded as soon as they are sanctioned. To begin, you have some choices to make—not really choices, more clarifications.

"Your earned wages will be offset by a minor Universal Health Care charge that's required of all members of the Morgan Church, but we ask anyway. So you are aware, this charge provides you with free, but not unlimited access at the clinic of your choice, we have a competitive two, and it's for preventative screenings on a regular, predetermined, basis once you reach a productive level. All subsequent healthcare costs will be out of pocket, but of course, as a Morgan, you will wish to invest in Profit's Indemnity Health Care program, which is a supplemental private plan managed by Mayor Doris and her Board. To qualify, you must be young and able to prove you are in perfect health and then once you are an active participant, you must pay one year's worth of projected medical expenses into your account before you can receive care and as soon as your account approaches zero, you must reestablish it before receiving further care. If, however, you become too sickly, regardless how much you have in your fund, the lack of productivity requirements will kick in and you may be asked to leave town and your contributions will be forfeit to pay potential debts."

Gil thought to ask a question but without needing to take a breath, Bon-Bon just continued on leaving no time for questions.

"As a Morgan, you know the rules, the more you invest, the healthier you get and vice-versa, of course. Also, if at any time your insurance account becomes an unsound investment, as determined by the Board of Directors Healthcare Budget Committee, chaired by our mayor, of course, we reserve the right to suspend care until the situation is resolved. Do you wish to begin your payroll deductions at 11, 29 or 32 percent?"

"Percent of what?" he asked, his head spinning, his mind racked with information overload. "Can I defer until I'm here a bit longer?"

"That is permissible. It is highly uncooperative of you however, but permissible. You may reject participation, but that lack of faith will be duly noted and could affect future rewards and stipends. Be aware that Profit's Management Review Committee evaluates every decision as it relates to future profitability and frankly, Mr. Stacey, Dan; frankly, they will be concerned if you are not participating. It sends the wrong message, you being new and a Morgan, you understand. It's like you are hedging when hedging, except in certain circumstances, is looked down upon in Profit, and your neighbors and co-workers will not be out of line condemning your career here. You really do not want to begin your quest for forever with your life's purpose judged on your decision to defer."

When Bon-Bon finally stopped, Gil felt like he had been sucked into a vacuum. Hopelessly confused, he hoped he was saying the right thing. "Okay, sign me up but make it for the minimum protection. I promise I'll get more when my income is higher."

"Of course. I have recorded your selection. Please confirm it with a simple yes."

"Yes, I will accept the minimum."

"Roger that, now as to your participation in the Morgan Lifetime Annuity Program. You are certainly interested in that?"

Fearing another verbal onslaught, Gil responded honestly. "I'm sorry, Bon-Bon, you'll have to explain that to me, too."

"Very well," the voice began. "Forever, Dan, is . . . well, forever and it costs a great deal of money as you know, and though your prime earning centuries are ahead of you, it is likely that in some future millennia, unexpected costs could overwhelm your worth causing . . . well, today isn't the day for that and anyway, to preclude that, Mayor Doris has extended the Entrepreneur Equity Fund so that all Profiteers can achieve the same appreciation that the Mayor and her Management team enjoys. The fund is a well-tested grouping of blue chip, plutonium-value stocks, semi-precious metals, various cyclical, non-cyclical, and counter-cyclical equity stocks, bonds, corporate bonds, and highly leveraged derivatives, sold short and long, forever, mostly here, but some in countries that have reciprocal stock trading agreements with us and have a functioning branch of the Morgan Church although we also invest in Sovereign Wealth Funds, but what is true about our Fund is that returns are guaranteed, let me repeat that, no Profiteer has ever lost a dime since the fund started last year. The funds are managed by Mayor Doris, herself, and returns are guaranteed, you heard what I said, and the net is that every resident of Profit should expect to enhance regular income in multiples up to one hundred percent depending on how aggressive and confident you feel about your future and ours but everything is dependent on the overall economy so we make no promises and the fees, don't forget, the small fee of less than one percent, is payable regardless of performance. We do have to eat. There are various options, of course to maximize returns. How old are you, Dan?"

"I'm nineteen," he said, and then thought for a second, truly unsure anymore "Or twenty."

"Curious, according to your records, well let us say you are twenty, that is what your record shows, and that means you can expect, once your contributions are vested—vesting is a simple concept, but the rules and exclusions could take a full day to explain so suffice it to say once you are firmly on the path to forever, you will receive your full return, less the front and back load and a median value management excise fee and of course the administration cost, the management team fee, Mayor Doris's special fee, insurance on the principal and the hedge fee on the insurance itself. So you never have a concern and that means nothing to dwell on except your work performance, oh yes, there are bookkeeping expenses, corporate overhead, and various other fees, too numerous to mention. I know it sounds like a lot, but each is no more than fair, and remember, your returns are guaranteed! I recommend that you receive your annuity using Profit's 10/100 rule which is when you reach the age of one hundred, your fund will pay you ten percent and continue paying that amount every century for another two thousand years, more as technology permits. Obviously, as you get older, compound growth rates increase the annuity value to truly staggering levels, but we're unlikely to estimate how much an infinite life can cost until you get there and frankly, if you do something wrong, our estimate is wrong and by then, it's too late." Bon-Bon paused to let that sink in. Then he asked, "So how much do you want removed from your daily earned account?"

"I don't know. I should discuss it with my partner, Bree."

"Every Profiteer signs up for it, and I'm sure Ms. Andrews has as well, how could she not? To do otherwise would be a rebuke to your Morgan faith as well as a show of lack of faith in the economic system of our United States of America. Say Dan, as a young man, my advice is that sound financial planning pays for itself and you should always pay for your future first unless it drives you to an early grave." Once again, Bon-Bon paused. "Please say yes so I can include you in our pool."

"Okay, yes," he said, slightly confused and buckling under the high-pressure sale. "But I only want the minimum, please. With living expenses and the health insurance, I don't know if I can afford to have more withheld."

"That's the spirit." Bon-Bon slowed down. It seemed sudden. "Trust me, Dan. You can't afford not to do this. You should always have more withheld because it will make you work harder and be ever more productive. And once your value increases enough, you will never miss the funds we're holding for you. Think about it. Living forever in one of Doris' new Paradise condos won't be cheap so you should get on the customer list as soon as possible. Then, sometime in your future, when you're sitting by your lakefront home on your hammock staring out at the waves and directing your personal landscapers or whatever wealthy people like you will do in the far future, you will think back and be pleased as punch that you planned for that today. And you will remember, with the greatest satisfaction, that you took the advice of your great good friend, financial adviser, and insurance agent, Bon-Bon."

"You will be living the great Morgan dream, untroubled by the financial headaches that kill lesser-funded *Wasters*."

"Yes, okay, fine, sign me up."

"Done. Now, here is your first assignment. There are five boxes in warehouse bin A101. Move them to shipping dock A07 and wait there for further instructions."

He did as he was told, all day and over and over and over again until the shift ended. On the walk home, exhausted in the refreshingly cold, crisp air, all he could hear was the persistent echo of the once pleasant, female avatar voice in his head. "Hurry up, Dan, you're falling behind. Dan, move it. No, not that way. I was told you were experienced . . . Get moving . . ."

Because he earned by the activity, not the hour, it had taken him longer to complete his shift and all the other workers were long gone. In the gathering darkness, frustrated and disappointed, he took a shortcut through the park.

Off the path, every home, except one, was lit up and inside, people were hosting parties. He walked slowly past the one dark, foreboding home, Larry Hilliard's mansion. A secure fence made of a black, glass-like material encircled the structure and there was an imposing gate made of the same ebony-like material.

The windows were barred with the same material as the gate and large pines had been planted so close behind the fence and so densely that the branches grew through the bars obscuring most of the property. The second floor was visible and he noticed a shadow move and when he paused to get a better look, the gate opened. That's when he noticed the odd construction. Every corner of the house pointed to the heavens.

A blue-gray light flickered as the shadow moved across another upper window. Even though the windows were closed, he shouted and waited for a response. When none came, he turned and headed home.

By the time he arrived, Bree was waiting, ready for dinner.

"I'm famished. You look like you had a hard day?"

"I hope you have no idea. How was yours?"

"It was fun. I notify customers when deliveries are due. I met a lot of nice people and my avatar says I have a knack for this kind of work. I even earned my first bonus, can you believe it. To celebrate I purchased these clothes. Do you like them?" When he only nodded, she seemed angry.

"Men. We're still going out to dinner and it's my treat. We won't have to eat low budget cafeteria swill tonight."

He tried not to show it, but he was disappointed by her success. After his day, he'd hoped, in a perverse way, her day was difficult, too, and they could share the experience.

"I'm glad it went well, Bree. I couldn't do anything right. I got in everyone's way and my avatar is a real ass." She smiled supportively and that cheered him. "I thought Avatars made work easier but she heaped abuse on me all afternoon. I'm happy your day went well, but I'm not hungry and I'm tired. Do you mind if I just crash tonight so I can be ready for tomorrow?"

She was disappointed. "Remember, you have to earn your keep for our plan to work."

Yet she was going out to eat. Her comment angered him but he didn't say anything but, "I know."

"And I won't stay in this dump for long, even if another one costs more. I need you productive so pick up the pace, starting tomorrow. We can't have you *shit-canned*."

"*Shit-canned?*" It didn't cheer him, but he laughed anyway.

She laughed too. "I don't know. My avatar said it and I thought it was funny. It's what happens when you aren't productive. Seriously, you'd better get it together because it's getting colder and we'll need to buy winter clothes and heat costs money, too. I'm going to dinner. Rest up and give them hell tomorrow." With that, she walked out the door leaving Gil in silence.

Lying on the rug by the front door, exhausted, he considered what just happened. Why, while needing to save money for their escape, is she purchasing new clothes and why was she ready to treat him to an expensive dinner?

The next day was better, but when it ended he had earned only slightly more than the day cost. That continued until, by the end of the week, although he was getting the hang of it; he had only earned slightly more than subsistence. Bree, however, had almost immediately started wearing new clothes and eating in better restaurants almost every night. When the weekend came, he volunteered to work extended hours to earn more while Bree attended a party hosted by a couple she'd met at dinner.

In the following weeks, every night when he arrived home from work, Bree spent hours in the bathroom preparing and then she left to attend parties, while exhausted, he stayed in and slept or worked overtime to earn additional credits. In spite of himself, he was jealous of her lifestyle. Then, one Friday evening, she came out of the bathroom wearing a short, black dress that made her look nothing short of spectacular and he decided to say something.

"Where do you go every night?" he asked. "And how, when I'm barely surviving, can you live this way, this quickly? And I thought we were still saving . . . for you know what?"

She shrugged. "Every night after work there are profitable parties to attend and I'm invited. Don't be jealous. It's business. We sell or barter things like baskets, food supplements, *Pharma*, financial instruments, just about anything you can make money on—including advice."

It didn't sound likely. "There must be more to the parties than just selling stuff."

"What else? Are you accusing me of something?" He had nothing to say. "Dan, don't be stupid, I'm making money. I have to go to every party I'm invited to. I'm new in town so I don't dare break any taboos, even if I wanted to, which I don't. I'm doing it for us."

"So we're still partners even though we're never seen together?"

"What does being seen together have to do with partnerships? Partnerships allow for diversification. I rarely see both partners at these events. Everyone attends the party they feel will be most profitable to their corporation. Profiteers are very serious about their partnerships. Do you have any idea how frivolous it is to spend unprofitable time with a spouse?" He just shrugged. She smiled proudly.

"My net worth is attracting some very eligible men and even a woman who's considering a legal way to replace her less economically viable spouse."

"You're leaving me . . . ?"

"Come off it, this is commerce, nothing more. I'm working some deal. That's all. What reason do you have to be jealous?"

"I don't understand. Is this what you are? When we started, you didn't think you could be productive."

"But I'm enjoying it and I'm really good at it. That's the great thing about working; you know exactly how good you are because it's so easy to keep score."

"But we're only here for a short time. You only need-" She pushed him hard and motioned for him to go outside with her.

She was angry. "Are you crazy and stupid? You know the cottage is bugged and neither of us has enough saved to get thrown out now so show some restraint." She pointed to her head. "Be smart, Dan."

He apologized, adding, "The money we're making is to get out of here, but you're buying, not saving."

"It's my hard earned money and I'll do what I want with it. Besides, I know what I'm doing. I'm not buying; I'm investing for the near future. Anyway, I've decided to stick around through the prime earning season."

He was shocked. "You're what? When's that?"

"See, that's what worries me about you. If you really wanted to get out of here, you'd be thinking of every possible way to do it. You never even thought to find out when you can earn the most money. If you want to leave, you have to work smarter and better and you have to plan. Maybe you like it here."

"Are you crazy? I want out worse than you. I'm the one who's working his ass off and getting nowhere." He paused. "So when's the best time to earn?"

"In a few weeks the biannual twenty four sales days of *Chrisnukkah* season begins."

"What's that?"

"*Chrisnukkah*, you dummy. It's a combination of various ancient religious festivals cleverly tied into gift giving rituals. Winter is a slow time for commerce so Morgan incorporates special holiday buying periods to stimulate the economy. To spice things up, everyone is evaluated on how much value their gifts provide to the recipients and winners receive special power point bonuses. From what I hear, shopping gets really intense. There are even fights. Two years ago, there was an attempted murder."

"You're kidding?"

"It's a fact. Because of the bonus implications, two gift givers were fighting over the latest gadget and one pushed the other over a railing. She almost didn't have enough funds in her health plan and could have died.

And mall traffic is so intense during the shopping seasons that the security system has been known to shut down."

"Bree, that's it."

"That's what?"

"That's the time we leave, when everyone's busy and the security system is down."

"That's a great plan except we can't leave until we maximize our earnings. After *Chrisnukkah*, we'll figure out a better way to leave."

He wanted to argue, but it was pointless. He opened the door to their tiny house and looked back over his shoulder.

"Have fun," he said as he shut the door behind him.

To improve Gil's worth, Bon-Bon had insisted that he spend evenings reviewing tapes of his recent performance. Bon-Bon had annotated the tapes to point out areas of improvement. While Bree was out, he watched the tapes but grew restless and bored so he went for a walk.

As he walked aimlessly through Profit, he noticed the residents dressed up and carrying packages and presentation graphics as they headed to their parties. At the entrance to the park, he stopped to read announcements on the electronic bulletin board. It was insulting. There were notices inviting people with high net worth to participate in various business opportunities, but nowhere was there an invitation for him. Bree was invited to many of the opportunities and he to none. Frustrated, he walked on, avoiding the people heading purposefully from house to house until he found himself in front of the one house that was no one's destination. He stopped at the fence and stared over the trees at the upstairs windows. Just like the last time, there was a blue-grey light inside. He was about to leave when the front door swung open.

He looked around to see if anyone was watching. The streets were empty except for a few stragglers rushing along. He checked the gate. It was open so he entered and walked down a brick walkway that was overgrown with weeds. Cautiously, he climbed the wooden steps, avoiding those that had rotted out. The porch sagged away from the door forcing him to walk more cautiously. At the open door, he hesitated, and then entered.

He was in a tiny vestibule with another door an arm's length in front of him. This door was locked. He pressed the doorbell and almost immediately he felt a vibration and the inner door opened. Inside, the unlit hall was long and ominous, and paneled in very dark wood. At the far end, a flickering candle barely illuminated a room with a large table covered in antique lace while a small, dark, ornate rug with long fringe covered most of the dark floor. Floorboards squeaked and groaned as he entered the room. In a corner, a small man with long gray hair brushed straight back was sitting on a very old, large and well-worn sofa. The sofa was so large the small man appeared to be a child.

"Mr. Hilliard?" he guessed.

"Come in. Am I seeking you?"

Gil didn't know how to answer that question. "I don't know what that means?"

"Are you him?"

"Who?"

"I don't know, but someone is coming."

"Someone else is coming? Coming now? Here? I'm confused, Mr. Hilliard. What are you talking about? What do you want?"

"Not this."

Gil didn't know what that meant, either. "Then what?" he asked.

"If you are him, you will know."

Thoroughly confused, Gil stared at the man. He was much older than Gil with a straight nose, sandy brown hair that was so straight and thin it looked like it would break off in the wind. And his eyes were a varicose blue. They stared at each other so long in silence that Gil felt he had met his master in this secretive man. Finally the man responded. "Virtual can be real."

"Mr. Hilliard, virtual can feel real."

"So are you him? Call me Hilly . . . they do."

"Who?"

"My family and others. Together, we access every nook and cranny of the Mesh that we're allowed in—that's if the Mesh had nooks and crannies." He smiled. "Do you understand what that entails?" Hilly stared expectantly but Gil was too confused to respond. Finally he motioned Gil to sit in an old, deep-cushioned leather chair whose frays and cracks were oozing stuffing. The cushions were too thick, slick, and unyielding and he struggled to stay in the chair.

Hilly responded in detail to an unasked question.

"The good mayor who preceded Doris sent word that I had one week before my net worth was exhausted and I was to prepare to leave or face the embarrassment of auction and indenture. I knew. How could I not? Management can force you to leave if you cost more than you're worth. I'd been feeling the heat for long enough and it was increasing in intensity, but I had more important things to do so I didn't care. For me, being with my family was all, regardless how much pain I had to endure, with them I am at peace.

"What are profits anyway? And I would have endured the pain." He smiled. "I don't anymore. I own this house, bought it outright once I realized the power.

"At first, I couldn't create value. I was with my family in the Mesh all the time," Hilly continued. "Life with them is worth everything. It is more real than Profit. I'm valued here but loved in the Mesh. There, I can do things; think things, be things, try things, learn things, things I never dreamed of and I can share it all with my family who appreciate me for more than my net worth. It's . . . it's astounding. I'm somebody in each place, but there I'm somebody to people who matter to me. That world is better, kinder, fairer, and just wonderfully different. I'm me there. And with me, my family searches for answers."

Laurence seemed momentarily distracted, but then continued what ever it was he was saying.

"The mayor insisted I leave Profit because I had no value in auction. It was out of the question. And I had no credits to offer to alter his financial and legal opinion so I had no choice but to leave. He didn't know about my family. He didn't know I couldn't leave them. I had to stay here or die forever."

Gil was unsure but he responded anyway. "You're still here."

"When you know, truly know, what matters most, everything gets easier. Faced with survival, families gain synergy, we did; we gained synergy, and we worked out the solution, a way to stay. This is what family does—not here, of course—but once it was the norm. In family, how you treat members is everything. Worth or value means nothing. Anyway, my family worked and worked to figure out a way for me to stay because I'd lose them out there, I'm not *Waster* material. We had a plan and we worked it and my value to Profit's stockholders soared. Today, because of my family, Profiteers are more than solvent—it's all they want and it's why I'm still here . . . and there."

Though Gil didn't understand, the man was making sense.

"I'm happy for you, but what does all that have to do with me?"

"We planned and we survive," Hilly paused again, this time for a very long time and then, when Gil thought he had fallen asleep, he smiled and in a whisper said words that sounded familiar but in that quiet whisper, Gil struggled to recognize them.

"Did you say . . . did you say Berne Thau?" He asked.

Laurence nodded causing Gil to grab the armrests and squeeze. He felt sick. "No," the word escaped like breath before Gil knew he was speaking.

"Good, you are him."

"No, no, I'm not Berne Thau."

"Of course not, but your secret is safe with us."

"What secret?"

"The time is growing near. I'll tell my friends. They will be excited, but no one else must know."

"Know what?" Gil was concerned. "What are you talking about? I'm not who you're looking for."

"You are in trouble."

With that, Gil stood to leave. He wasn't sure what he was going to do next, but this wasn't where he wanted to be. As he moved toward the hall, he tried to talk his way out.

"I know I'm in trouble. I can't pay Profit's maintenance fees and the fixed costs are killing me. I'm sorry. I have to leave . . . Excuse me."

"This isn't about that. Your PID is at yellow. How are you enduring the early stages of discomfort?"

"I'm not," Gil said. "At least, I don't think so. Not yet."

"You should be feeling unpleasant warmth, enough to focus your efforts." Hilly smiled. "I know that you should."

Gil edged into the hall. He wondered if the man could stop him from leaving and then if Mayor Doris and her guards were outside waiting. As if reading his mind, Hilly clarified.

"Security is monitoring, yes, but they haven't figured it out, not yet. They don't know who you are. You have a PID but they don't know. Isn't that wonderful? If they find out you will be in danger."

"But I'm not-"

Hilly explained, ignoring him. "There will be a formal inquiry to learn how you do it. It's how capitalists steal and grow. They will ask me to investigate. I need to know you better so I can tell them what I can, what

I suspect. I'm sorry. It's my job, the one that keeps me elsewhere. You're at risk. They will send you to HOMESEC once they know."

Gil was frightened and tried not to show the panic he felt.

"I'm not doing anything and I've never stolen anything. I'm trying to live by the rules and what you're saying is wrong."

"They will confront you with proof and it won't matter. But I will help."

"I don't need help. Let me leave, I'm innocent."

"Gods mislead, but they can never lie."

"What the hell are you talking about? What does that even mean?"

"Of all people, you know. There are great Gods in the Mesh and they do things far beyond what mortals can understand. Me and my family, we're the best and we don't have a clue what they're doing and why. They absorb so much bandwidth and power that their very presence bends everything toward them and they are always felt but they are never known. They leave no trail. But you know that. We have been given a great honor, you and I, by the Mesh Gods. They have sent you here and I will help you."

Concerned for his safety and sanity, Gil feared this crazy man. He never should have come and he had to leave. Hilly was insane. But as Gil turned to leave, he knew there was a kernel of sanity and that terrified him.

"Mr. Hilliard, Hilly, Laurence, I appreciate everything you said, but I have to go, it's very late."

Hilliard followed him to the door, but when he opened it to walk out, Hilliard whispered, "Gil?"

At the sound of his name, Gil froze. He felt like he had to pee for he knew he was a dead man. Slowly, he turned on wobbly legs to face his accuser,

"What did you say?"

Laurence merely smiled and Gil turned and fled, tearing down the path and through the park. He didn't stop until he reached his cabin. Sweating and scared, he leapt onto the porch, but before he entered, he paused and tried desperately to activate his glove. Maybe Joad could explain this. But, once again, the glove was silent.

He entered his small home, but seeing that Bree hadn't returned, he began frantically packing what little he had for his escape. With pack in hand, he opened the door, but paused again. Without value, where would he go and how would he get there. Besides, security closed the gates of Profit after the last trucks and he wouldn't be able to leave until morning when the gates re-opened and truck activity began anew. Despondent, he returned his pitifully few things to their shelf and then bundled himself in the thermal blanket Bree had recently acquired for him and like a dog, smoothed out his little rug by the door and laid down. He spent the night tossing and turning fearing morning wouldn't come fast, or that it would.

It was near dawn when he heard fumbling at the door. Bree entered quietly and pirouetted past him on the way to her bed. Remaining quiet and motionless until she was settled, he found sleep even more elusive as he imagined where she'd been.

Too soon, he was surprised by the unwelcome sound of his avatar waking him for another frustrating day at the warehouse. Expecting the worst, he left for work, leaving Bree sleeping soundly.

Chapter 28
Profit — 2070

Though fearful, the day after Gil's meeting with Laurence Hilliard, nothing unusual happened. No HomeSec vehicle arrived, no helicopter, he wasn't arrested, nothing untoward, and so he began to hope that his fear of Laurence was groundless. Without any real alternatives, he decided not to flee, but just in case, he checked gate security. Without a pass from Mayor Doris, he wouldn't be allowed out, so each day, feeling confined, wary and miserable, he put in the hours at his mind-numbing job, wondering if Hilliard and the Profit security team would arrive to arrest him and have him transferred to a HomeSec facility.

The pressure wore on him as busy, boring days, became long, lonely nights strung together in a numbing hell. There were nights when he suspected that a HomeSec prison couldn't be worse, but every day that went by was a test of his endurance. Tedious, repetitive and unrewarding workdays blended into evenings, isolated and alone, waiting for Bree to return from some business-social event—at least that's where she said she was. He spent his non-value-added time in their tiny cabin staring through a small window at leaves being ripped from trees by wind-driven rain. Then the last of the leaves were gone, the rain morphing into ice and snow and the ground that had been resplendent in red, yellow, and orange was layered with rotting, gray and brown dead things that soon became mounds of fresh white snow.

One evening, while Bree lounged in bed, he blurted out, "I'll never leave this place. At the rate I'm going, I'll never earn the funds."

As usual, she was angry and unsympathetic. "The walls have ears. Stop complaining and do something about it." It was her answer to everything.

To hide their discussions from the Profit spy system, she turned on the shower and whispered. "Right after *Chrisnukkah*. If you'd work harder and smarter, you'd be almost as successful as I am and you could leave too."

"I don't understand," Gil said. "If you want to leave, why are you buying gifts for people you don't know and you'll never think about after you leave? And you've acquired so much clothing that you'll never be able to carry it. You're using money we need when we get out of here."

"First, I don't like that tone of voice and second, do you have another partner in your pocket? What is it with this 'we'?

"*WE*," she said, heavily accenting the word, "only agreed to leave together, we have no deal to share while we're here or out there once we're gone. You and I have been through this, Dan. I don't have your value problems because I don't have your work issues. I'm a willing listener who's ready to learn and I follow instructions. It's not hard. And for your information, these gifts are critical. You have no idea how much bonus money I can earn for giving the best gifts. It'll enhance my worth and improve my travel. And my wardrobe is for professional purposes. When I dress sexy, my deals seem to get done quicker and more profitably. When will you learn how commerce works? Unlike you, everything I do, I do because I'm counting the days until I escape? You on the other hand-"

"Don't say it. I'm trying my damned hardest, but my stupid avatar is completely incompetent. You don't know what it's like. You don't have my problems."

"That's my point. I make sure I don't have your problems. You-"

He wanted to scream at her. "It figures you're succeeding. You play nice with everyone."

Enraged, she leaned close, her violet eyes tinged with anger. "What does that mean?"

"It means you'll do anything to get ahead with other people, but you do nothing for me."

"How dare you?" she asked. "Are you kidding me? I can't get near you because you try to suffocate me, the pressure you put on me. The only time I don't feel your neediness is when I'm working or partying to make extra money for OUR escape. It's no wonder I work so hard. If you truly wanted to leave, you'd find a way to thrive here instead of blaming an innocent avatar or me for all your inadequacies. Grow up and take responsibility, for Morgan's sake. If you're unwilling to dedicate every moment of every day to working harder so you can earn enough to control your own destiny, then I feel sorry for you and I don't care what happens to you. I don't care . . ."

She paused, turned, and walked slowly back to the bathroom. Before closing the door, she looked over her shoulder and in a small, almost wounded voice, said. "I think you like it here."

That was too much. There was so much he wanted to tell her but couldn't.

"Like it here?" he said. "Have I ever said I wanted to stay? You sleep in a bed while I sleep on a small, thin rug, but right now I'd rather sleep outside in the snow than in here with a bitch like-" He didn't finish. The bathroom door slammed and the electronic lock engaged.

In the ensuing silence, he reconsidered what he'd said and put his cheek against the bathroom door. "Bree, I'm sorry. You're right. I haven't thought this through. You're a lot smarter than I am. I promise I'll do more to contribute."

There was silence until the lock clicked and he stepped back. Surprisingly, she looked sad. He hadn't considered that maybe Profit was wearing on her too. He hadn't noticed.

"I saw your balance sheet," she whispered. "They're about to declare you unproductive and I don't have the funds to protect you. They're all tied up in product. You are going to be auctioned off for whatever value they can get or they'll throw you out with nothing."

It sounded to him like the same old critique and driven to anger, he looked around for something to smash. He pushed past her and into the bathroom where he saw the towel rack and ripped it off the wall. Unsatisfied, he eyed the mirrored cabinet next to it, but as he grabbed for it, she yelled.

"Don't! You idiot, that'll cost a week's wages. God Morgan, you're such a burden. Why can't you grow up and stop doing this unproductive crap?" When he took his hands off the warmer, she continued quietly. "Please? Try to do better so we can do what we set out to do."

He noticed something in her eyes he hadn't seen before and it calmed him. "I'm trying, Bree, I really am."

He sat on the side of the tub as she walked to the bathroom door. "Winter is here and Doris is ready to cut you loose. If she does, I don't know what we'll do."

"Stop worrying about an insignificant loser like me? I can take care of myself."

"You obviously cannot and you don't understand. I was talking to a member of the Finance Committee and he let a secret slip out. When you're sold, your assets get revalued quite a bit higher—they call it goodwill-so it costs even more to buy your way out of bondage. If you survive, we're talking perpetual indenture, slavery, or else they'll walk you out of Profit, like the Carters, in the dead of winter. You can't survive, Dan. You must take this seriously, please."

"You're not serious," he said. "Slavery?"

"They don't call it that but-"

"I've been here so long that what you're saying almost sounds rational? Only a loony accountant could figure out what they're doing here."

"That's why they don't allow accountants in. They promote incompetent locals into accounting jobs rather than have an expert exposed to their books. The townspeople are workers, they don't understand finance-well, personal finance they do-but this, nobody understands. Please, Gil, you must concentrate. You won't be able to buy your way out of indenture and slavery and leaving here to live like a *Waster* means death."

"I'll have to make sure that doesn't happen."

"How will you do that? I can't, no; we can't do what we need to do if I have to live here alone." She threw herself onto her bed. When he came out of the bathroom, she was laying face down on her pillow. He sat beside her. When she looked up, she was angry. "You know the rules. Get off my bed."

She was so approachable and then to say something like that just made Gil angrier. He'd seen the sadness in her amazing, but now red-rimmed eyes, but her words were insulting. She stared at him looking cold and hard, but he thought he saw through it and leaned forward, putting his hands to her cheeks. And then he kissed her. She pulled back and he flinched expecting a slap or worse. Instead, with her eyes just inches away, she stared at him and, cautiously, he moved forward again. Their lips met and this time held. When he broke the kiss, he sensed her reluctance so he reconsidered and kissed her again, longer.

It was impossible for him to pull away but he did. This close, her skin was flawless and the startling flecks of yellow and red in her vibrant blue-violet eyes ensnared him and sent a shiver down his spine. He stared at her until he suddenly realized how miserable and confused she looked. He leaned toward her again, but it was one time too many. She put her hands on his chest and lightly pushed him away.

"I can't," she said. "We can't. I won't. Please. You have to stop being so . . . so nice. It's unfair. It's destructive and it's unproductive."

"But I like you," Gil said. "I . . . I love you." There, he said it.

"Stop it. When you talk like that, I know you're selling something. Stop using me for something I don't want."

"But . . ."

"No, stop it." She continued to whisper. "You don't like me. No one likes me. Hell, I don't want to be liked and you certainly don't love me, whatever that is. And if you think you do, you have to stop liking me and stop doing nice things for me and start doing them for yourself. And love, don't be ridiculous, this is a partnership and a sham one at that. That's all it will ever be. Don't do this, Gil. Don't love me. Damned, I knew this would happen. If you were doing better, you could truck over to Westlake and buy yourself a *Virtuoso* session and let off some steam. That's what you need. It'll straighten you right out. I'd give you the credits but . . . Please, don't do this."

"But," he said again and kissed her again. This time her lips were unresponsive.

"Stop it please," she begged. "No wonder you're so unproductive, your priorities are all screwed up. I'm not what you want. I'm not who you need. Nobody needs anyone. It just gets in the way."

He kissed her again. She struggled, but her lips were soft and there was the flick of tongue that sent a thrill and chill down his spine. She didn't stop him until he rolled his body onto the bed beside her. Alarmed, she sat up, wild eyed, and bolted into the bathroom, slamming the door shut for the second time that night.

Once again, he followed her to the door. "Bree, I'm sorry it's . . ." Once again there was no response. He struggled to find words to apologize for something he wasn't sorry about.

"We've . . . I've . . . I really like you. I'm sorry but I do."

Silence.

"It won't happen again, I promise. Please come out. I'll go to my rug like a good boy. I won't even look at you. I promise." Trying to make as much noise as possible to demonstrate to her that he was moving, he shuffled to his spot by the door, sat down, turned toward the window and began reading. A few minutes later, the bathroom door opened. He forced himself not to look as she walked out. There was silence as the lights went out and after staring into the darkness for what seemed like forever, exhausted, yet frustrated, he finally fell asleep.

In the morning when he awoke she was gone. He checked her alarm. She'd planned to be out early. Disappointed, he trudged off to work through the first snowstorm of the season. At the warehouse, he spoke his password and another hellish day began.

"It's about time," Bon-Bon began her rant. "We are busy today and I told you to get here early." Her raspy voice had enough authority in it to hate.

"Ease up Bon-Bon, I had a tough night. Besides, there's a foot of snow on the ground so there won't be many shipments or deliveries today."

"Well, look who just became our logistics guru. Pay attention, maybe you will learn something for a change that you can turn into value. The low-pressure area that is dumping snow across the Great Lakes is tracking north of where it was projected so precipitation will end within the hour. Earlier today, the snow stopped in the towns south and west of here so trucks have already been sent out and the *Tollers* have been notified to plow the main roads to Profit. We won't have as many trucks, but we won't have as many workers either because there is also a big financial party today which, of course, you haven't been invited to—there is no economic benefit to you being there. So it is just you and me today, Mr. Stacey, and we both need an economic boost so cut the gabfest and get to work."

"No one is working because of a party?"

"You and your partner need to talk more," Bon-Bon explained. "A consortium, that includes your partner, is hosting a party for senior entrepreneurs and you are not invited because you do not qualify—your net worth stretches the lower limits of credibility. If you work hard enough today to get off sooner rather than your normal later, the party should be going strong and by then, the uneconomical uninvited are allowed in but all the hot economic transactions will have been consummated and only uneconomical scraps will be left for the likes of you. In the meantime, get busy and this time, try to stay ahead."

Though he was disappointed with last evening, today, the work and the insults didn't get to him because, through it all, he pictured Bree's eyes so close he could trace every hue and fleck in glorious detail. Bon-Bon wouldn't get to him today because he knew Bree cared and Bon-Bon spending the day convincing him no one cared only reinforced that feeling.

"Go to B105. There are twenty boxes of M55-001S," Bon-Bon directed. Gil jogged over to the designated area and looked around. "There's nothing here."

"Do not start with me. It is too early. B105. The boxes are there."

"Check your damn signal. I'm standing here and the sign above the bin says B105 and there's nothing here, unless you count the few water cups and empty *Pharma* wrappers."

"Look around. The last shift just completed an audit so stop your complaining and find the boxes. The bin is wider than the sign so look around."

He wanted to say something but he knew it was useless. "There's nothing here. Find me something else."

"B105, that's where the boxes are, find them and load them before we do anything else."

"Fine. How do I do that if the boxes aren't here?"

"You're not new, you're just unproductive. Follow procedure. Root Cause Determination, the bin contents must be evaluated using quality procedures."

"The bid is empty. What more do you want?"

"Do your job."

Annoyed, Gil contacted the System Protocol avatar. "System 771, this is DStacey2053. We need error cause correction for bin B105."

The System Protocol avatar responded immediately in a voice that was, fortunately, less grating than Bon-Bon's.

"DStacey2053, an audit was completed last night before shift change."

"I know. But somehow the system misplaced some boxes. Revalidation is in order."

"DStacey2053," replied the avatar, "your work history indicates a high probability that you, not the system, is in error. Please recheck your findings before considering ordering revalidation."

Gil raised his voice. "I'm standing right here at B105. I see the sign. The area is empty."

"If that is your final response, I require supervisory confirmation before I can move ahead. Contact your shift supervisor."

"But I'm the only one here. You're integrated, you contact him?"

The Protocol Avatar wasn't happy. "Do not take that tone with me, DStacey2053, it is not in your financial self-interest. Contacting the shift supervisor is not my responsibility. Based on your worth, you do not want attitude reflected on your daily performance logs. Contact Steve Shea and have him confirm back to me. That is all I will say on this matter. There is only one acceptable response from you that will earn you credits for today's efforts."

Given his net worth, he had no choice but to comply and contact his supervisor, Steve Shea at a party. He listened patiently as Shea berated him for interrupting an economic opportunity. But when Shea finished venting, he authorized revalidation, commanding Gil to confirm when revalidation was complete.

"Stacey," Shea said before disconnecting, "sooner or later you'll be the *Waster*. We all know your lack of talent, drive, and business acumen forecasts it. Prepare for it. Every day since you arrived, my department's failed to achieve maximum value and your avatar has pleaded with me to have you removed from his duty roster. No avatar should have to do that. Now don't mess this one up or I'll petition the Mayor for relief, you worthless shit."

"I would greatly appreciate it, Steve," Gil said politely, "if you wouldn't do that."

"I sense an opportunity for negotiation. I've taken a liking to your partner, and she's been real friendly to me, too. Unlike you, she understands what it takes to make money and she appreciates the economic synergy our partnership will achieve if you catch my drift."

"You'd better not harass her."

"I'll harass whoever I goddamned want to. I have the worth and you don't so it doesn't matter what you think, you'll be gone soon, anyway, and I'll be free to show your partner the advantages living with two solid incomes brings. She wants me. She's made that clear. Wait, I'll ask her right now."

"Bree is there?"

"Of course, you idiot. Like all productive Profiteers, she works hard and parties harder. She's my kind of girl." Shea laughed at that. "I'm your boss so I'll be blunt. You're a loser and a fool and you don't deserve her. I do." Gil heard him yell above the revelry, "Bree, honey, keep your top on, sugar, I'm next." With that, the call disconnected.

The long day that started with promise got longer. Finally, hours after he was scheduled to complete his workload, Gil changed his clothes. Miserable and despondent with an empty, aching heart, he trudged home through the deep snow worrying each step of the way about Bree. It was wasted fretting because when he arrived, she wasn't there. He waited up for her but finally, tired and depressed, he bundled his blanket against the cold draft and fell asleep on his rug.

He awoke to a clear, bright Saturday morning and an empty room. There was no sign of Bree. He shook off the light dusting of fine snow that seeped under the door, driven by an overnight storm and looked outside. Fresh white powder covered everything; making the day, if not his mood, sparkle. Unsure what to do about Bree and unwilling to stay cooped up in the cabin, he decided to go for a walk, but unable to afford boots, he put on his work shoes, a heavy jacket and work gloves and headed to Laurence Hilliard's house. It wasn't where he wanted to be but it was his only choice.

He stopped at a nearby convenience store where he purchased a snack and energy drink. As he left the store, he picked up his receipt and thought he felt uncomfortable warmth emanating from his PID. He stared at the balance on the receipt. His net worth, adjusted for last night's income less Profit's amortized fixed costs and this morning's store purchase, had gone negative. He stepped out into the frigid air. With his PID heating up, in a macabre way, Gil felt that maybe his luck was changing.

He finished his snack and trekked through the park to Hilliard's home. On the way, he noticed people entering and leaving the Profit Entrepreneur Center. He wavered, but decided to search for Bree there. At the door a sign announced that the incorporation ceremony for Brad Jonas and Mary Ward was being held and below it was a list of merchants and the products they were selling at the event.

Once inside, he felt self-conscious because everyone was dressed for business and engaged in discussions at various tables. He entered the banquet hall and even in a crowd, she was easy to spot. She stood at the far end of the hall with a group of people Gil didn't know. He tried to act nonchalant as he circumnavigated the hall slowly, stopping to say hello to the few people he knew, or insinuating himself into small groups as a spectator pretending to listen to their business pitches.

He wasn't aware when she noticed him, but as soon as they were close enough to make avoidance awkward, they smiled at each other and nodded. He approached and gave her a peck on her cheek.

"Have a good time last night?" he asked.

"Don't, please," she pleaded.

They stood quietly waiting for people to drift away. When they were alone, he asked, trying not to sound like he was interested, "Where were you, last night?"

"We shouldn't be worrying about each other. I was at a party and afterward I stayed with Clare and her partner so I could get here early."

"I understand," he said, not really understanding. "I had an issue at work and had to call Steve Shea last night. He's my supervisor. He said you and he were-"

She seemed embarrassed. "Oh, you were the one who called."

"I needed his approval."

"Is everything okay?"

"I don't want to talk about it. Steve likes you."

"So what?" she whispered, angrily. "I'm doing what I can. We talked about this."

He hesitated. "Does it matter to you what you have to do to earn your worth?"

Whispering could no longer hide her anger and annoyance. "What does that mean? I'm not required to ask your permission to do what I have to do, whatever it is." She pulled him away from the now gawking guests. "Yesterday, you promised you'd recommit. You said you'd do anything. Look, never mind, forget it. Do what gets you where you want to be, but don't worry about me, I don't matter and I don't care."

"We both know that's not true."

"I don't know how to respond to that."

"Great, you and I have come a long way."

"What is that supposed to mean? You and I?"

"Nothing," he said, dejected. "I want to leave as much as you do, but there are things I won't do . . ."

"What? What are you accusing me of?" She grabbed his arm and pulled him even further away, to a quiet corner and then pulled him close. "You're broke. You have nothing, so how can you accuse me of doing too much when you're doing too little? I'm the responsible one here. I'm doing what has to be done." She paused and looked around. It seemed everyone was staring and whispering. She turned back to him. "Look, I'm sorry. I don't owe you anything, we're not really partners and I don't want to have this conversation because whenever we have it, it makes me feel like we are so you win and I lose. From now on, when I'm not working or selling, I'll be staying with Claire. I'll tell her you're working longer hours to improve your worth going into *Chrisnukkah* and the New Year. Don't blow that cover."

He removed her grip from his arm and started walking away. "That's fine with me. Have fun with Steve and everyone else you need who's not me. And as soon as you earn what you came for, go with my blessing and don't worry about me, I'll be fine." With that, he stalked away unaware of the buzz he'd created.

She grabbed his arm again.

"Your blessing?" she asked in sheer disbelief. Before she could say more, he shook away and left.

He was angry and intended to get away by himself, but someone steered him into another banquet room past rows of tables covered with assorted goods and trinkets and townspeople behind each table, hawking their wares. At the far end of the room the honored, prospective new partners were partying with business associates. He tried to excuse himself but, probably expecting a gift, the couple came over to talk.

"Dan, we were hoping you'd come. If you're looking for Bree, she's in the other room. We never see you at these propitious events. You must be the hardest worker in Profit."

He desperately wanted to be somewhere else because it was clear the couple was expecting a gift or at least an option on a gift he didn't have. After a few minutes, when it was clear Gil had nothing to offer, Brad, one of the prospective partners, broke the awkward silence.

"Bree told us you were exhausted from all the hours you've been putting in and you might not attend. We're glad you came. Don't worry about your value threshold; everyone here has been through what you're going through so don't get down. As long as you're a hard worker, value will come. Just keep doing your best. Profit needs all types of skills. You'll find one that yields a life-affirming return."

Gil was too depressed to participate in the conversation but he had no choice but to make the best of it.

"It's been . . . tough," he said. "Bree . . . no, I've been a burden." The couple looked uncomfortable so he tried to make a joke of it, but only succeeded in digging himself in deeper. "When Bree audits my balance sheet the panic on her face is priceless. Now that I'm working longer and harder, I'll miss that face." In the awkward silence, Gil searched for a way out.

Brad tried to salvage the moment. "Whatever you do, don't make excuses. Fix it. Profit's shareholders need everyone full bore and contributing because we don't participate in the profits, but we sure as hell share the losses." Everyone nodded at that.

Mary, Brad's partner-to-be, also tried to be supportive. "Brad struggled early, too. We all do, but eventually we find a rhythm and earn our keep. When he was struggling, Brad's avatar was so angry with him that he took a vow of silence and refused to help. That really scared him because it meant he was on his own. He was certain he'd be tossed out of Profit and forced to scavenge in *Wasterville.*"

"The good thing about terror is that it gets you focused," Brad added, draping his arm around his partner. "Mary was my cash cow, the real work horse in our corporation, a dividend queen, just like Bree is for you. Like any good partner-to-be, she threatened to break it off if I didn't improve my performance. I thought I was a goner, but I kept plucking away and finally started to get the swing of it. When you see the end coming, the heat-well you know-and you don't sleep well, so I worked evenings and through social events like this, even though there are more credits to be made in events like this, I couldn't invest and take the chance of coming up empty. My big break came when I leased a new avatar with funds Mary lent me. My value began to increase and I invested in training for work more in line with something I enjoy. Almost immediately my worth appreciated, but it took a long time to pay Mary back, she kept postponing this event because of it. The interest alone keeps me working two jobs. As you can see today, it was all worth it and the best advice I received came from my new avatar—the best advice ever."

"What did he say?" Gil asked.

"It was something like, 'the most important thing to do is find work that's comfortable enough that it absorbs all of your productive juices so you don't get distracted'. It was something like that. I would get distracted and that's bad when you're trying to meet schedules. My avatar told me to persevere, to work even when I didn't feel like working, and that's when I found that special job that makes the minutes, hours, and days melt away without all the anxiety; the perfect job for me. After all, if you're going to live forever, who cares how hard you work when you're young and if you have to work hard, you may as well enjoy it. It's great advice because it worked. That and Mary's loan which she didn't have to do but it made us closer.

"Today, I feel so much better about myself because I have value. I have worth. Think about it, every morning, I wake-up knowing I'm doing the same thing over and over again, but I'm doing it for the money, for my future and its kind of okay. Make that happen and someday you can afford to participate in fun like this, the money-making fun, social activities Profiteers participate in to become financially secure, but for now, it's work, work, and more work." He shook Mary's hand. "On this, our proud day, I'm a proud and fortunate asset who is pleased to be appreciating with my little cash cow."

"That's great, Brad, thanks. What do you do that saved you?"

"I'm third shift foreman in shipping," Brad said, proudly. "I got promoted last month."

It was like Gil's job. "And you like it?"

"Like it, I was born to it. It's my dream job. I was a bookkeeper before and I didn't love that. This, I truly love. I find it so easy to work even harder than I'm required to and the best thing is I am part of the chain that links consumers to their dreams. And now that my worth is up, Mary agreed to become my partner and to even write off some of the interest on my loan. How great is that? And the best news is that we've been approved to expand our corporation, you know, have little liabilities. Dan, just you wait. When you find that special job that defines you, that drives you to work even though you'd prefer to do any one of a million other things, your future will be assured."

"That sounds right, Brad, I guess."

"Everyone," Mary gushed, "speaking of that, I have an announcement. Brad and I were tested at the Surgery Center. Brad, tell everyone the good news."

She offered her hand and Brad slapped it. "The tests certify that our offspring, our liabilities will eventually become assets with a high likelihood of productivity." His shoved his fist into the air and everyone applauded. "And once Mary gets pregnant we'll be able to borrow against their future worth and amortize it over almost forever so it's a great loan program."

Gil understood none of this, but clapped anyway.

Mary gushed, "Profit's Board gave us permission to expand and pre-qualified us for loans and subsidies, so as soon as our precious little liability passes some early tests, we will ship it off to a school of Profit's choosing and soon enough, we'll see a return on that investment, too. Isn't that great?"

The guests applauded again and some offered toasts to the proud partners-to-be.

He pictured the Carter family and it was all Gil could take. He offered lame congratulations to the partners-to-be and excused himself to search for Bree so he could apologize. She was easy to spot even in the crowded banquet room surrounded by men seeking to expand their portfolio. He tried to get her attention, but she refused to recognize him. Dejected and depressed, he left the party.

Outside, the sun reflecting off the snow temporarily blinded him and induced tearing. He wiped the tears away with the back of his gloved hand.

"It's not your kind of party?"

He heard her voice before he saw her. He blinked to clear his vision and Mayor Doris was standing near him, smiling.

"I needed some fresh air," he said.

"You're in trouble." The fact that Doris said it made it so.

"If you please, your Honor, I'd prefer to be alone for a while."

"It's Doris. The Board is worried about you. Walk with me."

She started walking and, reluctantly, he caught up.

"Where are we going?" Gil asked.

"To Merry Manor. It's time. I find that after taking people there, their finances often turn around."

"Excuse me, Mayor . . . er . . . Doris, why do you care?"

"It's my job to care. The people of Profit are my assets and someday you too can be one and I want to be certain I've done everything I can to make it so."

He shrugged and walked with her down an unplowed path to an old, large, stone, barn-like building surrounded by a tall, chain-link fence topped in sparkling, ultra-secure nano-wire. She opened the gate and gestured for him to enter.

"This is Merry Manor," the mayor explained as she opened the door to the facility. "Unfortunately, it is a necessary facility for those citizens in Profit who've lost their dream of forever. Their stay here ends their miserable, unfunded lives.

"Lifestyle for every citizen of Profit, as everywhere in America, is based on the ability to pay, so for those who haven't been successful enough, we have private industry, failure-to-achieve programs ranging from assisted to unassisted dying. But the reality is Merry Manor exists for those who, for a multitude of rationalizations, failed to build an estate that qualifies for forever. They face life's ultimate disillusionment here until their funds run out."

Gil must have looked horrified.

"That look," she said. "it's what we often get from underachievers like you and I call it a good start. Life is all about free choice and Merry Manor is a necessary institution until everyone comes to understand the most basic economic reality of life, if you can't afford it, you die. Merry Manor is the culmination of a lifetime of poorly thought out and/or badly executed economic choices. Some *Profiteers*, the most foolish, can't even afford Merry Manor and are shown the gate to *Wasterville* where they face a brutal death in the wild. But for those who try, but fail to achieve a perpetual estate, our Merry Manor staff provides them as much comfort as their financial estate permits while still providing Profit stockholders with an adequate return on this investment.

Merry Manor is proof that free market capitalism is fair. If the residents here were to continue to live in our competitive environment, they would soon go broke, so we designed a low-cost yet profitable solution for their exit. There is a minimum entrance fee, but if they are unwilling or unable to pay it," Doris spread her hands toward the area beyond, outside Profit's boundaries, "they may take their chances out there," Doris smiled, "in what we fondly call life's open market. "Everyone chooses Merry Manor if they can."

He couldn't think of anything to say.

"Merry Manor stockholders aren't cold hearted if that's what you're thinking. We have the living and our forevers to consider. Truly, no one wants these facilities, and no one considers them until, frankly, it's too late. Most of our early Profiteers never truly planned for forever and were surprised and yes, even humiliated, when they were faced with their declining years and limited financial alternatives due to a lifetime of inadequate wealth accumulation. Honestly, it is the residents of Merry Manor who are the inconsiderate ones. If it is within their power to live forever, isn't failing to do so on them?"

Before Gil could respond, Doris continued. "Investors built this facility even though the concept of failure is contra to our way of life. And we're not socialists, so for this facility even to be, there had to be profit in it. It's ironic, really, most who live here actually believe they worked hard enough and made the best financial decisions. They feel they were being successful funding forever, but they either had no concept of the time frame they were dealing with or were simply deluding themselves as to what hard work truly is. In the end, they were forced to give up the grueling, punishing day-to-day effort required to achieve eternal success for this depressing deathwatch. Hell, Dan, everyone thinks they work hard, and if given the opportunity, they would argue vehemently with anyone who said otherwise. These people don't understand that, in its simplest form, true hard work means you avoid Merry Manor. It's that simple. These are failed souls who never recognized in their hearts, in their souls, and in their strategic planning that forever is a privilege that requires truly extraordinary effort."

Doris led him down a narrow windowless corridor.

"We are very clear with all Profiteers, like we were with you and Bree when you first arrived, as to what is expected to achieve eternity and we're even more blunt when the end is approaching. Ultimately, it is my responsibility and I don't want anyone saying they didn't know."

"Is this the only way?" Gil asked.

She nodded.

"Or out there. Dan, for some reason, I like you, but there is no charity in perpetuating delusion. If we took the socialist view and taxed everyone to help those without the perspicacity to help themselves, it would entice everyone to failure and everlasting life would remain a religious vision instead of a fiscal reality. Read your Archive. If American history proves nothing, it proves taxes and the redistribution of wealth is a dead end because it creates a country of *Wasters*. If we tried that in my beloved Profit, there would be no one to attend to the sad people here in Merry Manor because we would all be lost souls here and death would be even more horrific. How unfair would that be?"

"Yes, we don't want that to happen."

She took Gil's arm and led him to a central room with three long concrete corridors running off at angles. She stopped there to explain.

"We offer what is traditionally called a cafeteria plan. In spite of what you may think, these are beloved residents of Profit, former partners and co-workers, people we have all had business dealings with, and we're mindful of their sorry situation, so within the framework of their finances, everyone is entitled to choose how they will terminate.

"Each corridor provides a different level of decline and support. In each, of course, we supply the basics, some heat, the stench precludes much, some air conditioning, and regular meals if they can finance them, fluids, and of course waste removal, the cost of which is deducted from their accounts. As a resident's account approaches zero, services decline and we provide additional choices from our reduced cafeteria plan. Residents are permitted but not required to move to a less-costly service level, thus extending their lives a bit longer, if they choose, but at not insignificant discomfort or they can pass to the final warehouse, a much cheaper solution. She pointed to another corridor.

"The warehouse?" Gil didn't like the sound of that.

"That's where those with minimal funding are transitioned until they reach the valued byproducts stage. In the warehouse, they receive pain medication so long as their funds last. After that . . ." Doris shrugged. "I won't get into it here, but it's important for you to see for yourself so you understand how critical it is to have a plan and to work that plan, exhaustively, and how vital each and every work minute is to a productive, never ending life."

"What . . . what happens in there?"

"Very little, actually, you'll see," she added, almost cheerfully. "We require that certain new Profiteers travel these corridors and interact with the patients as a, I don't know, maybe a lesson or a motivator. We find it has a lasting affect. Within this corridor there are other corridors reserved for various levels of assisted dying. On the left is our *Almost Forever* wing. Here, are the most pathetic situations. This corridor is reserved for residents with significant fortunes, but whose wealth is not projected to be adequate to fund perpetuity, usually due to failing health which is expected to become debilitating or investments that have gone sour. Often they require expensive treatments to stay alive. If they had purchased Profit's Entrepreneurial Health Plan, which is offered by our Chamber of Commerce, and is the health insurance choice of Chairwoman Tanya Brandt, they wouldn't be in this situation, but they may have been gung ho libertarians and tried to self-fund at the expense of their eternal soul. It is such a pity.

"The residents of *Almost Forever* have the funds to be made very comfortable and we provide *Virtuoso*-like capability to help ease their burden. After all, they came so close. Failure at this level comes with deep neuroses and psychoses and depending on what they can afford we try to help. If there is truly a good way to die, our *Almost Forever* program is intended to be that and I highly recommend it for the most conscientious of failures."

Doris pointed to another corridor.

"*Sanctuary* is where most of our failed retirees expire. Since they're no longer able to add significantly to their fortunes, they live here in relative low maintenance, desperately hoping for cures or unforeseen business opportunities that might allow them one last chance at forever. We're honest with them because, ultimately, delusion is expensive to manage. Living in *Sanctuary*, they must accept minimal support in order to stretch their viable time and improve the chances of some breakthrough that will provide them with a new opportunity to live forever."

She leaned in close to Gil. "Honestly, it's a brave choice, there's no chance of success, but it has a great upside. I like you and I thought you should know."

"Thanks. But how is this group different from the first one? I don't understand."

"In *Sanctuary*, each retiree chooses the level of subsistence that they are willing to fund. They hope, and frankly our marketing department helps to enrich that hope, that if they amortize their wealth over a long enough period-until some medical breakthrough-they hope to re-qualify for forever; otherwise for them, it's the *Warehouse*. *Sanctuary* is the cash cow moneymaker in this business and without exception, our dearly disillusioned *Sanctuary* residents move on to the *Warehouse* once their funds decline to a targeted low level. Their unwavering belief in the future makes them the easiest patients to manage and they refuse to spend for palliatives so their accounts don't deteriorate as quickly."

"What about that?" Gil pointed to a corridor where he heard the faint sound of moans or muffled screams.

"We just talked about it. That's our *Warehouse*. You'll see it first hand. The residents of the *Warehouse* have little funding remaining so the end is often . . . unpleasant. We advise *Warehouse* residents to hold back a small amount so we can provide an injection to ease their way when the end comes. Surprisingly, most prefer to wing it, to use all their funds before facing the inevitable—and that's fine, too, the walls are mostly soundproof. When they're finally bankrupt, they're in no condition to listen to reason and we run a tight financial ship so our hands are tied. For some, if they have the desire and have the funds, we provide antidepressants, painkillers, and hallucinogens, anything to comfort them as they confront the reality of their limited-life achievements before expiring. Before entering, we require all residents to sign over their estate to the Profit Board so we can provide for them when they are no longer rational enough to make decisions on their own." She opened a door. "Please go in."

"Do I have to?" Gil pleaded. "I promise I'll work harder."

Doris merely held the door, nodded, and pushed him inside.

Immediately, he was assaulted by a heavy, cloying, detestable and almost physical odor. His eyes burned and watered and he felt dizzy and claustrophobic. He gagged and fought the need to vomit, swallowing hard while Doris stared at him through a window, smiling. She pointed at the bedridden and, reluctantly, he walked along the center corridor between the mattresses that were placed on numbered pallets along the wall. It was set up just like the warehouses he worked in during the day except there were people here, not material. In the dank heat, he began to sweat so he took his jacket off. To avoid the fetid air, his breaths came in shorter gasps as he fought becoming nauseous.

In the amber light, most of the residents of the *Warehouse* seemed dead, though they were probably only sleeping or comatose. Most were old except for a man who was waving exhaustedly for Gil to approach his pallet.

"Good brother, I'm glad you came." The man wheezed. He was lying naked on top of a worn, blood and puke stained blanket, his face screwed up in pain. One leg was missing above the knee with a compress over the wound held there with duct tape. It brought thoughts of Bernie, and Gil felt sorry for the man so he sat beside him.

"Hi, my name is . . . Dan. Can I help you?"

The man seemed unsure, like he was being tricked. Slowly, he smiled a wary smile, his teeth brown and black, and his breath distinctively putrid even in this foul air. Then his eyes brightened.

"You most certainly can. I have this financial opportunity. Wouldn't you give anything to have an appliance, say like an old microwave," with this the man started coughing uncontrollably, and so hard that tears formed in his eyes and his hands clawed up. He curled into a fetal position and moaned loudly as no longer in control, his sphincter opened and a bloody stool spurted out to stain the bed. Gil tried to get up but the man grabbed him and held on tight, taking a few harsh breaths before uncurling, and beginning his sales pitch again.

"Sorry." the man said. "Picture it, a microwave-like device that you can order take out food from any restaurant and it materializes inside the device ready for you to serve and eat. Wouldn't that be a great time-saver for commercial parties and a real attention getter?" Again, the man coughed hard, this time trying to clear his throat. Bringing up mucus and a bit of blood, he spat on the floor and went on with his pitch as if everything was fine.

"Think of it," his eyes seemed lost until he remembered something. "Think of it, Dan," he said finally and proudly. "There could be millions in it. Certainly everyone in Profit and all the other towns will need it. Think what we can charge, the profits. It will be a colossal technological and gastronomic breakthrough, with a payback of epic proportions for both of us." He coughed weakly and unproductively. He tried to speak but no sound came. When he tried harder, he let out an inadvertent scream. Too weak, he curled into a fetal position and moaned.

Gil got up to leave but the man's grip stopped him. "I don't need much of a stake, just a couple of mil should do it."

"It sounds great. It really does. Is something like that really possible?"

The man growled to himself before shaking his head violently. "Of course it isn't, but if I can find a smart investor looking to get rich on a guaranteed fail-safe, no nonsense R & D project like this, we'll all be millionaires, even billionaires, considering foreign rights, and our futures will be assured. This is a once in a lifetime chance. All I need right now is the money to protect my patent. Just a few hundred thou, you can spare it, Brother. We can sign the papers and you can be a thirty percent partner. Forty percent, okay, forty nine percent but that's it, it's my idea!"

Gil didn't want to disappoint the man since he was obviously dying but he didn't have the money and the technology seemed unlikely. He looked up to the window where Doris was staring and nodding. He didn't know what to do so he decided on the truth.

"I'd really love to help you, I would, but I don't have any money. In fact, I'm struggling to make ends meet. I wish I had it because it sounds like a wonderfully profitable idea. When I leave, I'll talk it up and maybe I can find an investor for you."

The man doubled up in pain again. This time, the tears flowed and he covered his face in agony. When the waves of pain subsided, he stared up at Gil, his eyes unfocused, his face slack.

"Whatever you have, I need it now, today. Time is money." The man squeezed Gil's pant leg hard, but not for long and soon his grip relaxed and his hand flopped down on the bed.

"Please, can't you spare maybe a few thousand? a few hundred?" The coughing returned, this time, Gil noticed a more significant trail of bloody mucous coming from the corner of his mouth. "Just some starter cash and once I get the remainder I will give you a favored position in my corporation. Please. Please, you won't regret it. I can't die just when I have a golden opportunity to live forever."

Gil didn't know what to say so he remained silent. With that, the man's body relaxed, he closed his eyes and seemed to fall into an uncomfortable sleep. Gil stood, gently, and moved on, purposely avoiding eye contact with Doris.

A few beds down, a woman of maybe thirty was sitting up staring at him. She had a large wrap covering her forehead and hair, stained brown with dried blood. He thought her eyes were following him until he stopped in front of her and noticed that her eyes kept moving back and forth without registering anything. He hesitated to move on, wanting to comfort her but not knowing how. Once again, he sat on the bed.

"My name is Dan, Dan Stacey. What's your name?" Her eyes continued to move slowly from side to side, but she spoke, quietly, without showing recognition. He leaned close to hear her.

"No difference, no difference, no difference. Worked hard did everything that was asked never could get that one big break. Never incorporated and passed up opportunity to produce liabilities, children, a girl and a boy, Pat and Shelia, cute, great kids, blond and adorable, passed them up for life everlasting didn't happen. Bum luck, failed investments, tired, keep trying, forever is so long and so hard to finance I'm tired, so tired, but keep trying, don't I? Keep trying, I do. but so tired, tired, keep after it-" All the while she spoke, her eyes moved from side to side, never recognizing Gil.

"I'm sorry for your pain. If there is anything I can do?"

"Tired, keep trying, tired, tired, tired . . ." Again, Gil stood and walked away as the woman kept up her uttering, her eyes failing to recognize his departure.

Depressed, Gil looked for Doris. She was standing outside the far door, waving for him to come out. As he walked toward her, he noticed the pallets full of people lined up along the outside walls stacked up two and down two levels and packed tightly with people. At each corner were the ramps that provided limited access. On the wall, at the foot of each pallet was a small, narrow access door. When he reached the open door, before he left to meet Doris, he stared back at the promise of capitalism and all of the pathetic people lying here somewhere between comatose and writhing and screaming in pain. He thought of Bernie and wanted to cry.

Doris reached in and pulled him out. Then she proceeded to clarify the *Warehouse* operations as if he might need to know.

"The lights at the head of each pallet indicate funding status, those near bankrupt are red, those dead and needing to be removed are the red blinking lights and they are removed immediately by fork truck through the access doors. Their bodies are cremated along with Profit's other refuse, but only after all byproducts are successfully recovered for sale or reuse per contract. There is a small staff in the control room that monitors those with green lights until they turn red and are tossed."

As Gil listened, sweat poured down his back and he felt a chill as he stared in horror at so many people in needless agony. He began to sway so Doris pulled him out into the main corridor where the fresher air steadied him.

"This seems fair but cruel but that's part of its purpose and it is the very best economic solution to a nightmare logistics problem. What are we to do? Everyone signs up for free market capitalism knowing there are winners and losers, and everyone has the same opportunity, but some just make wrong or bad choices or maybe even have bad luck. It's usually far more than bad luck that sends them here, though. It's been said of people that they act consistent with their rewards. I find that is not always true, but it is for that reason that I strongly recommend, for your long term benefit and the benefit of Profit, you etch what you've seen here into your mind so when you return to your job later today, you take your economic future and Profit a great deal more seriously.

"Just a warning. Some people who visit here try to block this image from their memory but I warn you, for those it's *Wasterville* or the *Warehouse*. Take this very seriously and never forget it unless you want it to be your future. I'm a friend and a fan, Dan, and would like nothing better than for you to take my advice because denial is more than a river in Egypt and it will doom you. I expect that this experience will provide you with the strongest possible incentive to follow a most revered Morgan message of severe discipline, effective long and short term planning and, most important, effort to the extreme. Forever isn't just a very long time, Dan, and it's well worth it if you can afford it."

With that, Doris walked with Gil back to the entrance of Merry Manor. "You are fortunate indeed to have witnessed so early in your career what happens when plans and deeds don't match goals. What do you think?"

He was truly moved and also concerned. "Thanks, Doris. I understand better now why I want to be productive. I'll never forget this." He knew that was true.

He couldn't read her, but he assumed he said the right thing because she smiled and grasped his arm.

"Dan, I see something in you, some spark, some intelligence. Life eternal is worth any effort and it is my hope that someday, if you put your mind and your passion to it, you can be on the Profit Board, maybe even mayor is not out of the realm of possibilities." Even if he could have thought of a response, she didn't allow it, continuing on. "Bon-Bon isn't right for you so I've reassigned you to a different job and a better avatar. Don't thank me and don't fail me."

He was relieved. "Mayor, I promise you I'll rededicate myself to improving my value and Profit's. You're busy and I appreciate the time you spent straightening me out."

She unclasped his arm but before allowing him to leave, she tapped his chest with her finger. "Oh, yes, there's one more thing. My Board has a minor issue with your partner, Bree Andrews, and we need your help. It will go a long way toward ensuring your future."

"Yes, anything," he said. "Is Bree in trouble? What is it?"

"It's nothing really," Doris explained. "An annoying case of fraud."

"Fraud? That doesn't sound good."

"Fraud is the intentional perversion of truth to induce others to part with economic value or surrender a legal right and as such is neither good nor bad. If done right, entrepreneurs find it very useful."

"And Bree has committed this fraud wrong?"

"Those I trust tell me she has, and I need your help."

"I don't understand."

"As you would expect, Profit has a superior accountability system. Each and every transaction—whether it's the time and effort you expend working or the value of the goods and services you use or purchase—everything is recorded automatically in real time so a person's net worth is always readily available—and accurate down to the penny. Actually, to tenths of pennies which gives our merchants a chance to raise prices without others noticing but we can discuss the advantages of that another time.

"This morning, you visited the Good Morning, America Convenience Store and purchased orange juice and a lo-cal, lo-carb, breakfast snack bar that cost slightly more than you could afford to spend at that time. At that precise moment, your net worth went negative."

"I promise I'll work that off starting with my next shift."

"All can easily be worked out if you help us on this minor matter. My accountants have struggled to reconcile our financial records and this is most unusual. When they finally identified when the discrepancies began, it was very disturbing. The fraud started precisely the day you and your lovely partner, Bree, entered town."

"I don't understand?" Gil worried that somehow his identity had been compromised.

"While your revenue-producing work efforts have been recorded correctly, very few of the costs incurred by your little partnership have been. You and Bree have been acquiring things without the cost of those transactions appearing on your ledger."

He had purchased nothing beyond necessities and their cabin was too small to hide anything. "You think we're stealing?" Then Gil remembered all of Bree's clothes.

Doris smiled. "Stealing? No. Such an unsophisticated transfer of wealth simply isn't possible here in Profit. You see, we match every transaction to every PID so whatever you do is automatically recorded. Now, fraud is far different than mere stealing. Fraud requires more planning and a great deal more sophistication. It is a far more evolved and interesting form of entrepreneurial endeavor than crass outright stealing. We know that your partner is blocking the electronic transmission of transactions into Profit's Enterprise Tracking system. Bree's effort, while clearly beneficial to her, defrauds Profit and its residents and the bylaws of Profit, the State of Ohio, and the Federal Interstate Commerce Commission considers such fraud a very serious crime, punishable by death."

"Death?" he asked, shocked. "No way. Bree's not . . . you can't . . . this is a joke, right?"

But Doris wasn't smiling. "The evidence is impressive and irrefutable. The problem we have is, we don't know how she's doing it. My best people are investigating, but haven't come up with a precedent or the technology someone like her would have access to that would allow her to do this and do it effectively. Bree is a very bright girl and we prefer to solve this without getting HomeSec involved but without your help, I'm afraid that we may be forced to send for them."

He tried not to be alarmed. "No, we don't want HomeSec involved."

"At least not yet. But this is most distressing and we must put an end to it."

"But certainly not death?"

"With forever as everyone's objective, the death penalty is a very effective deterrent against foul play. Now you don't need to be involved in this horrible business. Bree is who we want. It's clear she never involved you in what she's doing, so why allow her to take you down. Forever is more than long enough for you to forget all about her and find many better partners. We need your help and as her partner, after the execution, there will be benefits . . ."

"Execution?"

"Yes, what else? We'll see that you inherit her honestly accumulated wealth. However, if you don't help, when we determine she owes more than she's accumulated in value, well, you don't have the worth to cover your partner's debt and that means certain death for you, too. Help us and we will be there for you. Now is the time, Dan. Convince me you're worth it."

"I'll . . . I'll do what I can." He needed to be away from Doris so he could think.

"Good. We need you to discover how she's doing it. Once you tell us, all you have to do is stand aside and allow her to incriminate herself. After her trial, you'll receive a performance bonus, her wealth after expenses or failing that, a dispensation, if that's necessary, and a new administrative position worthy of a devout Morgan gentleman like yourself. What do you say?"

"But she's my partner," he pleaded.

"That is not the response an entrepreneur would offer at a critical time like this. Bree withheld important information from you, information that could have caused your execution. No partner does that, she had a fiduciary responsibility to you. You owe her nothing."

"Maybe she didn't know what she was doing or she didn't know it would mean death. Let me talk to her. If she stops and we agree to repay what she owes, everything can go back to normal. Is that acceptable?"

"We are not negotiating, but if you can provide us with the technology she's using, everything becomes negotiable."

"I'm sure I can get her to cooperate."

"That response is uncomfortable for me. It sounds like there is more than a business partnership and that is very concerning. Think hard on what I ask. Affection isn't cute; it is misguided and counterproductive every time. I will not unmake the law."

"No, I don't . . . It's just that-"

"Immortality implies a mistake-free life. I would be trivializing my religion, which is most important to me and my pursuit of forever, if I allow Bree Andrews, and you, to get away with this heinous crime. Think on it, Dan. What kind of world would it be if you could cheat death by cheating at life? Living forever can not be a casual endeavor and death is the cruelest, yet fairest way for others to learn from your errors."

"But-"

"This is a sad business, but it is business. You must put her interests aside; they are nothing now. She made her choice and is beyond your help. Work with us and we will make it worth your while and someday soon, you'll find someone who meets your standards far better than Bree Andrews. She may be even pretty like Bree, but your next partner will be someone who is economically viable and far, far more righteous. If it's love that drives you, sick as that is, you'll love again, there is time, I promise. But for a partnership to be successful, it must be above lies and yes, fraud. You deserve better. Profit deserves better. I implore you not to put your life at risk for an egomaniacal criminal like Bree." She stared at him as if trying to assess something. "And don't try to leave town, because security has been intensified during these difficult days."

What could he say? Reluctantly he nodded.

"Good. Say nothing to her about this. You've met Laurence Hilliard."

He nodded even though it wasn't a question.

"He'll instruct you. Basically, you have to convince Bree to transact business while Laurence is scanning with a special technology he is developing. That will give him the evidence we need to convict her, and

Profit will be indebted to you for your efforts. And we always pay our debts."

"Yes, ma'am," he said glumly.

"Go to Laurence's house, he is expecting you. Do this and you will have the gratitude of a grateful Mayor."

She left him standing in front of Merry Manor. As he trudged through the snow toward the veek's home, he was no longer angry with Bree for how she treated him, he was angry for what she had forced him to do.

Chapter 29

Profit — 2070

Gil stood outside Larry Hilliard's eerie-looking mansion for a short while, contemplating what would happen if he didn't go in. He knew that wouldn't happen; he just wanted to delay the inevitable for as long as possible. Eventually, he opened the gate and tramped through the unplowed snow to the front door. Hilliard was waiting.

"Good, we finally resolve this," Hilly said. "Please call me Hilly. Shall I call you Dan or Gil?"

"God, Hilly, Dan please. Doris told me I had to see you."

"Your partner, if that's who she really is, has gotten into some very serious trouble."

"Doris says she is to be executed."

"The law is very clear and although retribution is usually economic, more and more, death is the outcome from most business crimes these days. It's economical and unequivocally a deterrent. Besides, insuring confidence and trust in the system is paramount in a functioning capitalist economy and the death penalty reinforces that, in spades, and provides the community with assurances that business relationships are on the up and up. Yes, the criminal code is unambiguous."

"But it's not fair. If Bree truly did what Doris says, I'm sure she didn't mean to."

"Come inside," Hilly said. "It sounds like we have work to do."

Gil stepped into the foyer and kicked the snow from his work shoes. Hilly directed him to the living room where they sat and his host explained the situation.

"Bree Andrews, or whatever her name is, your partner, or girlfriend or more likely someone you met along the way, has broken the law. That is irrefutable. But there are two things Doris doesn't know. The first is how she's doing it and Doris is willing to pay dearly to discover that. The second thing is that I already know how Bree Andrews is doing it."

"You know?"

"Your partner is very smart, you know that." Gil nodded. "But how she is committing fraud is neither smart nor clever, she is more opportunistic. Ms. Andrews is modifying commercial transmissions by cloaking her identity and she does it through a top secret device, a very sophisticated and expensive personal cloaking mechanism that makes it impossible to pick up her personal information when it's turned on. I confirmed this when I traced transmissions emanating near her that were being disbursed unrecognizable into the void. Once I realized her device cloaks all PIDs within a certain perimeter, it was easy to track her. She uses it discriminately, turning it on and off as opportunities present themselves. Based on the discrepancies Profit's Auditor General provided, I suspect she turns it off when she works, but turns it on when she's transacting other business. The result is that goods and services change hands, but the economic transaction is never recorded when it isn't in her favor—it's kind of like single entry bookkeeping, which was outlawed year ago. It's evidence is unambiguous; she's committing a crime, a crime, unfortunately, but justifiably, punishable by death."

Gil put his head in his hands and stared at the dark, wood-grain floor. "Why doesn't Doris know what you know?" he asked, hopefully.

"Doris is very clever, too; she wouldn't be Mayor if she wasn't. Within days of your arrival, her auditors detected something because their books weren't balancing and that never happens. Then our logistics system started going haywire. Products were going missing that should have been available. At the tactical level, there was a small panic and when some of our merchants complained about irreconcilable shortages and lost revenue, it was kicked up to security because that just doesn't happen here. In a commercial world like ours, accuracy is paramount, when you lose it, commercial trust never returns.

"We thought our enterprise system was fail-safe so, at first, our auditors were confused. That isn't surprising to me because auditors aren't the brightest bulbs, they rarely have anything to audit. But Doris locked them in a room and threatened to hang them as accomplices and then they showed remarkable enthusiasm and insight. That's one of Doris' strengths, convincing people to align their interests with her. Anyway, Doris read their report and concluded she needed help from the *Federales*, but Doris prefers to go it alone, she considers the Chairwoman a rival and there's more profit to keep if you don't have to pay overhead. So, fortunately for you and possibly for your partner, I intervened. I don't usually take on projects like this but I was curious, because it involved you."

"But Bree wouldn't do anything illegal. She is a good person."

"It's nice that you believe that. My experience is that there are no nice people left in this world and obviously there are incontrovertible facts that indicate you are wrong about her. More important; what you believe is irrelevant. What interested me most was that every trail I followed turned into a dead end. That intrigued me more than the crime itself. I discussed it with my family and soon it became clear."

"What did?"

"Only someone with strong connections in the government could get access to this type of technology and it must be someone of consequence. Your partner, Bree Andrews, works for Chairwoman Brandt in some high-level capacity and if I were you, I would be very concerned."

Except for a groan, Gil was too stunned to comment.

"This is where, perhaps, you can enlighten me. I'm absolutely certain a cloaking mechanism like this device is utterly unattainable in any open or black market anywhere in the world so give that due consideration before arguing in her defense."

"It makes no sense," Gil tried to explain. "Bree hates the government. When I was hiding, she was hiding, too. She could have given me up countless times but she didn't."

"I don't doubt that, but it doesn't change the facts. Your partner has a personal cloaking device, a technology only highly-placed personnel in Tanya Brandt's government could possibly obtain."

Gil offered another possibility. "Maybe she's a rebel and stole the technology?"

"That's possible," Hilly said as he tapped on his glasses with his finger. "It's very unlikely a rebel could get close enough to steal that technology and if she stole it for the cause, why is she risking getting caught here? Why hasn't she given it to them or why isn't she using it for something more than buying little black dresses?"

"I don't know, maybe she was headed to drop it off before we met."

"Then why isn't she there? Certainly you weren't stopping her."

"I don't know. She was going to Detroit, but she couldn't get there because we were out of money and winter was approaching."

"Putting rebellion on hold because of winter, that isn't likely, but possible, I guess. A device like that would be very valuable to the revolution, but waiting would be risky and seems irrational, particularly for someone who had the audacity to steal it in the first place. And say it's true, explain why the government hasn't been more aggressive trying to find her or eliminate rebels if they believe they have this game changing device or are even actively seeking such a device? No, Gil, I mean Dan, whatever the reality; Bree is in the middle of something far too important for any alibi you're buying and, more importantly, you are at great risk because of it. Forget her, she's doomed. Fraud or rebellion, it doesn't matter. Both are punishable by death and the long tentacles of the government capture a great many peripheral people in the process."

Gil walked to a darkened window and stared at the broad, black brush strokes that covered it.

"Doris says you can do anything. If you can, then stop this. I don't want to lose her. Please help me."

"That's a pretty stupid thing to say. You don't know me. Suppose I report your request to Doris. Then where are you? The last time you were here I said I wanted to help, but you didn't trust me then. Do I assume you trust me now?"

"I'll do anything. I don't want her to die."

"I can't help you unless I know the truth about you."

Gil turned away. How could he trust Hilly or anybody with that information? But how could he not?

Hilly spoke again. "I know this is difficult. I work for Doris and she's not your friend. But if you don't trust me, I guarantee your pretty young partner will be executed and regardless what assurances Doris gives you, you will follow her to the gallows. You must tell me the truth. It is worth the risk."

Frustrated, Gil pressed his fingers into his eyes until he felt pain. He considered the alternatives, but the immutable reality of the situation overrode everything. In the past, he successfully avoided confrontation and decision, now it might be too late. Confronted with a whopper of a choice, he had no framework for deciding.

"Hilly," he began, cautiously, "I hear what people say is the truth from so many, enemies, business people, even friends and relatives, but everyone tells their truth, not THE truth and I've been fooled and disappointed before. How can I trust you when everyone I know lies? Why are you different?"

"It must have been very disappointing for you. This is why I spend so much of my life with family, people I trust. It's a difficult task, separating myself from all the others, the liars, cheating administrators, the capitalists, self-directed workers, all of them and more driven by greed to make the most, financially, of their lives at any cost. Why am I different? I'm successful, probably not as much as I would like, but as robust as the truth is, I believe that it is precious and unlike most, I won't give it up easily. I can't answer for your experiences. I trust my virtual family because they've never been disloyal, but in this situation, if I were you, I'd forget about truth, it's overrated, anyway. Trying to make something from the truth is a fool's journey. If you must trust something, trust yourself. Then experience truth from those you find trustworthy.

"It's far easier to consider truth as a matter of faith, though you're probably just as uncomfortable with faith so what can I say? I don't have a magic bullet answer, but I do have foolproof advice. You must live and die believing in yourself. Unless you're in the habit of deluding yourself, it's all you truly know, anyway. Do that and you will have a litmus test for everyone to prove their trustworthiness by their actions. Then, you play and learn. That's far more practical than treating everyone like a fraud. God, what must that be like? Anyway, that's the best advice I can offer."

"That's your fool-proof advice?"

Hilly smiled. "It works for all the fools I've met, but frankly, I haven't met every fool yet. Look, you're bright and sure, it's a gamble, but life's a gamble. In the end, it comes down to how good you guess and what you learn from your guesses that make you the person you want be, the person, going forward, you'll change least from. We're all flawed and nobody owns the truth or has the power to grant you faith."

Gil had an idea. "Trust me with an important secret."

"What?" Hilly asked.

"Trust me. You have a great set up here. Explain why you're risking it for someone you just met. Trust me. Do that. Then I will trust you."

"That's fair. I do know you. I've been deep into the Mesh core. There are strange things happening there, things that even my family can't explain."

"You said there are good people out there. If there are, why are you so dependent on the Mesh for relationships?"

"Truly, there are very few good people, people you can trust, people who aren't selfish and who wouldn't screw you for a buck, they're not here, or anywhere, anymore. I've accumulated impressive net worth, not just for me, but for many others in Profit, but I have never found someone who is more interested in me than in the value I generate for them. Never! I know that's how things are supposed to be, but it makes me sad. I know that it's me, but I don't find economics-based relationships satisfying and for the longest time, I was desperately alone. Oh I was cheered a great deal and people provided me with gifts and things, but they didn't want to know me or even try to understand me. In the end, it's easier to avoid them, to just stay home and do what they need, collect my bounty, and avoid disappointment.

"Maybe ten years ago, I did what more and more people are doing. I designed an Avatar and we became fast friends, real friends. I liked him so much that I designed more friends until I had this entire community of self-made friends. I know it sounds sad or deluded, but I'm not embarrassed by it. I even have a few wives and some children in the Mesh. It's not perfect, I have some ex's and I even have to pay child-avatar support. Some of my virtual friends made friends with other virtual friends and I learned to trust some of the real people who like me were building relationships in virtual. In time, some became like family, but only in virtual. Mostly it was me and my immediate virtual family. I never told anyone in Profit because it sounds weird and *Profiteers* pay for my loyalty and would consider this beyond that. They would never understand but you do."

"Why do I understand?" Gil said, becoming defensive.

"Hear me out," Hilly explained. "When I first designed my friends, they weren't quite right so I worked hard to improve them. By accident, I discovered that if you encode an Avatar with elements of empathy, it gets noticed—but at the time I didn't realize by whom. Two or three times my code was actually tampered with, yet I couldn't trace who did it or how they accessed my secure code.

"As I said, while developing my avatar family, I met others, equally lonely and dissatisfied, disappointed with real people, yet successful like me, people who resorted to living in the Mesh, trying to do the same thing I was attempting. We've never met in real life, yet we slowly grew into a community and as we helped each other, a feeling of family developed. These people are the ones who help me win proposals for Doris. Each of them has expertise in a great many disciplines.

"We explore the Mesh for answers and work collaboratively to improve ourselves, our virtual families, and our virtual environment. Wealth, time, and inclination have allowed us to become increasingly sophisticated. We discovered that someone is tampering with our avatars, but we could never get deep enough into the Mesh kernel to discover who. We still have no logical explanation although we have a working theory.

"There are other entities in the Mesh, not human, but with human-like thought processes and they use and control the Mesh at an entirely different level, far beyond our ability to understand or interact with other than in representations they provide when it's convenient for them to communicate to us."

"Entities?" Gil was uncomfortable with where this was going.

"Our best guess is that there are two. We've studied it extensively and determined there are really a great many entities, but primarily there are two main ones. I know this sounds crazy, but these two seem to rule the others. We call them the 'Parents' and to even get this far has been very taxing work because we're incapable of identifying their presence, so we're limited to working with their signatures or auras, for want of a better term. Each is very different and very, very powerful. Remarkably, we believe one is male and the other female; one is, for want of a better word, good, the other, I guess, evil. That's the best analog we can come up with."

Gil remained silent as Hilly continued. "You're not surprised. And it doesn't surprise me that this isn't news to you. You know them, don't you?" Gil sat motionless. Then, Hilly asked to see his glove.

Instinctively, Gil slapped his back pocket, "What glove?"

"The one you use to communicate with the Parents."

At this point, Gil couldn't think of a reason not to show Hilly, so he pulled out the glove and handed it to him.

Hilly handled it reverently. "Berne Thau? That makes sense, too."

"You know him?"

"I knew of him, but I never had the privilege of meeting him. He is a legend among my family. He did many things to help and protect the poor during those awful years of genocide. This glove explains so much.

To survive as public enemy number one for so long; Mr. Thau had to be assisted by the Parents, at least one of them. There's no other way. I assume that Berne Thau is a friend." Gil nodded. "Then so am I and so is my family."

Hilly put the glove on and flexed his fingers. Gil thought to stop him, but allowed him to continue. Hilly tried, without success, to turn access Joad.

"You communicate with the Parents using this. My family and I have been aware of their presence in the Mesh because they have limited our ability to expand our footprint. It was difficult and it cost us a great deal, but we traced their presence as far as we could and learned what we could. We don't have nearly the bandwidth and the power necessary to breakthrough, but we do know there's something critically important, some kind of contest or battle of wills going on in the Mesh. We lack the resources to determine what it is but many in my family believe it's a power struggle between the Parents, but that's just a guess."

Gil was intrigued and concerned. He wanted to learn more but Bree's problem was far more pressing.

"Hilly, this is all very interesting, but you haven't answered my question. Why are you risking so much?"

"The glove, Berne Thau, and what little we have deciphered in our searches tell us that you are somehow connected with the Parents and that is no small thing. We believe in you because of that."

"I don't know how to respond to that. You're mistaken if you believe that I'm some priest who has some magical access to God. You can't know me. And don't trust me because you believe that."

"We know what we need to know. You are important to them. That makes trust simple."

"But I'm not with them and you said one is evil. Suppose the evil one is the one I'm with. Can you still trust me?"

Gil wondered how much Hilly and his family really knew. And for whom did they know it? And this power struggle, the parents Hilly identified had to be Joad and Gecko but if Joad was defeated, what then? Gecko would know what Joad knew and the Chairwoman would know it too. His life was still in grave danger. What could possibly put him at ease and allow him to trust Hilly? Nothing came to mind except that Hilly might save Bree and that was important. Indecision and fear gripped Gil and he prepared to leave.

"No, don't go; there's more," Hilly said sharply. "Recently, for the briefest of moments, a parent communicated with me. It was the most astonishing thing I have ever been a part of. It was exhilarating, I truly felt like I was in the presence of god . . . and she was a lady!"

"I'm happy for you."

"Honestly, I don't know why I know this or if it's important, but here goes. There's a girl . . . a young girl who likes exotic places. She's sweet and kind and good and her name is . . . Andrea. And she loves you."

Gil felt for the nearest chair and grabbed it for balance. He tried to think. As staggering as this was, Hilly's statement proved nothing. Whether it was Joad, or Gecko, informing Hilly, it was clear the risk was great.

"Hilly," he said weakly, "I'm desperate. I need someone's help or Bree will die and then so will I. Before all this began, I would have believed you readily and with all my heart. I'm not that person anymore so I guess there's nothing you can say to make me trust you."

Hilly started to respond but Gil interrupted.

"I'm stunned that you know what you know. That you know about . . . her. But that alone doesn't open the heavens and allow truth to pour out and comfort me. I've learned that mean, evil people use the truth as a weapon to hurt the innocent and never give it another thought. I'm desperate. I need help, but I'm sorry, I can't trust you but I don't know what else to do."

He tried to think of something more to say but his mind was all jumbled up. Finally, in desperation, he just shrugged and begged, "Please, help Bree for me, please."

"Of course," Hilly declared. "It's obvious that you love her. Tell her what you know and listen to her explanation. What you learn from that will be important and if, afterwards, you still want me to help her, I'll do what I can."

"I will."

Hilly walked to a console and entered some information. "Right now, we have your signal captured so Bree isn't nearby. Do you know where she is?"

"She's at a sales party. Are you saying that when I'm near her, I can't send or receive?"

Hilly nodded. That explained Gil's earlier communication problems with Joad.

"But that isn't our only problem."

"What do you mean?"

"I understand why your signal gets blocked, but I lied to Doris when I attributed it to the amount of time you spend near Bree's device. It won't be long before Doris realizes that we've been receiving consistent yet false information from your PID that has nothing to do with Bree."

"How can you be sure of that?"

"My family has been in the Mesh a long time," Hilly said. "What is providing misinformation about you is significantly more intriguing than Bree's cloaking device. Our security protocols have been monitoring both yours and Bree's PID signals. We originally designed those protocols to track anyone who might be considering trying to escape without resolving their debts but, on Doris's command, we're adapting to solve the missing signal issue. We've developed an algorithm to interpret signal patterns to determine, based on what signals disappear, where the offending PID, the one blocking the signals, is located. We'll have the system debugged and operational by the end of the week and I can't be seen trying to delay development so we have to do something before the new algorithms go live. We only have a few days."

"What should I do?"

"My family and I have thought about it. Next Friday, you and Bree should host a sales party at one of the warehouses so she can invite as many Profiteers as possible. Leave it to Bree to determine what she wants to sell, but make sure everyone is invited. When she's ready to conduct business, have her cloak so every PID in the room ceases to transmit. As soon as Bree cloaks, Doris will have all the evidence she needs to arrest, convict, and execute her and you. That's when she will spring her trap. She will enter the warehouse and arrest you both."

"But-"

"You must trust me on this and you mustn't tell Bree anything other than what she needs to know about her sales party and that she must activate her cloaking device."

"You're asking me to—. Tell me what you're planning."

"You must trust me," Hilly smiled. "You said yourself nothing I can do could make you trust me. You lack faith and believe me, I understand. It might seem like I have a good thing going here in Profit, but I find what I am called on to do here, morally and ethically repulsive. Profit succeeds and another town must let innocent people die because they lose a contract and profits. They never consider how I feel and I detest what this place, and from what I can tell, the rest of the country has become. I'm trapped but I want to change it, to make it better.

So even though you can't trust me or my family, we do believe in you. We believe that you will play a significant role in making a better world and because of that, and in spite of your lack of faith, I'll do what is necessary."

With that, he ushered Gil out into the cold winter's day. Without the slightest hope of success, Gil dragged his feet through the snowdrifts toward home to face Bree, or Doris, or maybe even Ginger Tucker. What did it matter?

Chapter 30
Profit — 2070

Morose, anxious and conflicted, Gil waited restlessly in the tiny cabin for Bree to return. His mind developed and he pictured myriad hair-brained escape scenarios, including somehow shooting his way out of Profit in a spectacular gunfight, like he had read about in the Archive entries of the Old West. Mostly, he wanted to run, to try his luck on his own, but he stayed because of her. It was very late when she bounded happily through the front door. She stopped to take her jacket off and that's when she saw him lying on her verboten bed. She said nothing.

"Have a good day?" he asked.

She looked radiant in a short maroon dress. "Oh, Dan, I had a wonderful day. I'm sorry I was angry with you. My presents were well received and I stole some really good ones in a wild *Chrisnukkah* party game. It's a capitalist tradition they play in honor of the holiday season."

"You stole gifts?" Doris and Hilly's accusations were confirmed.

It surprised him when she laughed. Was she such a hardened criminal? How had he missed that?

"No, no, it's not what you think. It's a game, a tradition during *Chrisnukkah* and you are supposed to steal other people's presents. Everyone takes a gift from a pile or they steal one from someone who already picked one they really like. It's so fun to watch the apprehension on everyone's face while you're deciding who to steal from and then the disappointment when you take from them. It's so in the spirit of *Chrisnukkah*. You should have stayed. You would have enjoyed it. Where did you go?"

"It doesn't sound like my kind of fun," was all he could think to say. The fact that she wasn't angered by their earlier confrontation at the party surprised him. What he was about to discuss with her would be far more difficult than that.

"I'm really sorry," she sounded sincere, "about how I've been acting. I've been under a lot of pressure, but these past two days really helped. I'm so very, very, sorry. Please forgive me?" She smiled her best smile and stood with her arms open wide. He steeled himself and absorbed her embrace.

She realized something was wrong and pulled back to stare at him.

"I really did it this time, didn't I? You're mad at me. Please, please, don't be mad, I promise everything will turn out all right. Smile for me, please."

He smiled. "As your majesty commands."

Her face went pale. "That's cruel. I told you I'm sorry. What else do you want?"

"Bree, or whatever your name is, I'm learning to live with disappointment. What I want no longer matters."

"Is that what I am, a disappointment?" Taken aback by his unexpected resentment, she pushed him away. "If that doesn't piss me off. What? You don't like my choice of names, now? Suppose I don't like Dan, you don't own it, do you?"

He yanked her outside so they could talk without being overheard, but she resisted.

"Stop it!" she screamed. When she was finally outside and he closed the door, she remembered their need for secrecy and calmed down. "Okay, what's this all about? Excuse me if I don't see how my lies are any worse than yours."

"So you admit you've been lying to me?"

"Is that it? I lied to you. Did I miss something? Did I fail to read the new and revised book of Dan Stacey's rules on ethics? I know I haven't read anything about you earning the right to the truth."

That hurt. "That's not what I meant."

"So English is your second language now?"

"No. I don't want to fight about that. We have something far more important to fight about. I kind of hoped, after all this time living together, that you respected me at least a little. Apparently now that you're off sleeping around behind my back so you can earn enough money to get out, I have to find out the hard way. I know you're doing it. How did you expect me to react when I found out? What did you expect me to do?"

He dodged as her fist flew past his face.

"You bastard, you have no right to call me a . . . a whore." She looked around for something to throw but on the snowy porch, nothing was available so she removed her shoe and threw it at him, hitting him square in the chest. It stung. "I've had offers," she yelled, angrily, "plenty of offers from these hicks, but that's not who I am and you damn well know that. I can't believe this. You're nothing but a stupid loser and I hate you. How could you believe that I'd stoop to that? God, after living with me for so long, you believe I'd offer myself just to earn value, you . . . you have no faith, none whatsoever. I hate you, Dan Stacey or whatever your goddamned real name is. I wish you would leave, go to hell but go through *Wasterville*. I hate you." With that, she turned and stomped away, disappearing around the corner.

"Your shoe," he yelled, but she was gone. Frustrated, he sat on the porch step trying to figure out what to do next when he realized he couldn't let her go. They had important things to discuss. He found her shoe and ran across the small porch and out into the snow.

"Bree! Bree!" he yelled into the low-hanging mist that floated above the snow. "I'm sorry." but she was gone. Frantic, he searched for her footprints, but there were none. He was about to give up and go back inside when he turned to see her sitting on the glider on the other side of the cottage, hands on her shoulders, shivering.

She smiled sheepishly.

"I can't go far without a shoe. Dan, please don't be mad."

He tossed her the shoe. "I'm sorry."

"I'm sorry too. I know I've been difficult, but why would you believe some mean, stupid stories about me? I don't sleep around, I don't."

"Last night, when I called Steve Shea . . . he said, you know . . . what was I to believe? And then you didn't come back and this morning I saw you two at another party acting friendly."

She considered it. "Okay, I can see you had reason. But we've been living together long enough for you to trust me, at least a little. I don't sleep around—not with you, not anybody. When I was younger, there was a general . . ." She shivered, and he could see she was revolted by some distant memory. A tear welled in her eye. "Forget that. I never ever sleep around, that's all. It's just not true and it's simply not me." She offered her hand. "Let's you and I make a deal. I'll forgive you for what you were thinking if you forgive me for my recent bitchiness."

"What do you mean recent? You've been a bitch ever since I met you."

Her face started to turn red, but he smiled. "I'm kidding, yes, of course I forgive you."

She hugged him and he returned the embrace. He expected her to break it off quickly, but when she didn't, he closed his eyes, felt the heat rise as he enjoyed the experience. She gently pushed him back and although her violet eyes looked sad, she was smiling.

"What is it?" he asked.

"What?"

"Why are you smiling?"

"I've done it. I wanted to hold off telling you but I can't. Last night and this morning, I signed the contracts. When the sales are final in a week, on Nineteen Eve day, that's right before *Chrisnukkah*, I'll have more than enough to get us both out of here. Do you understand? By the end of next week, we can finally leave this hell hole."

When he didn't smile, her smile disappeared. "Please don't tell me you like it here and want to stay? If you say that I'll scream."

"No, they know about you."

Her shoulders drooped and her eyes went wide. She looked around, scared. "No. They . . . they can't. Nobody's come for me . . . have they?"

"Who would come?" he asked. She shrugged. "Doris knows about your cloaking device."

He was confused because Bree seemed relieved.

"My what? Is that something else you heard from the people who told you I was whoring around?"

"No, this, I have from a reliable source and you know that it's true and it's serious. What you've done, cloaking transactions and all, it's against the law and punishable by death."

"No way?" she was beginning to focus.

"Way. I met the mayor earlier and she told me. She wants me to set a trap for you. I'll be rewarded when they catch you, but you're going to be executed. Executed, Bree. It's the law. Why didn't you tell me what you were doing?"

"I don't know how to respond to that?"

"Don't give me that crap now. This is life or death for both of us. Why did you do it?"

She didn't answer immediately. When she did, it seemed honest. "I'm sorry. I really don't know how to respond. I had no choice, that's why. I needed to cloak for my protection and I really can't explain it to you without putting your life in danger, too."

"Can't or won't?"

"I mean it. If you know, your life will be in great danger."

"We're going to be executed. Our lives are already in danger."

"I'm sorry. It was wrong. Once I figured things out, I knew it would be impossible to earn the credits we needed to get out of Profit and I had to do something. You've seen your financial statements. Surely you realize that nobody can earn enough credits, honestly, to achieve anything substantive, including saving enough to get out. Forget about living forever. Profit is one big pyramid scheme that keeps the mayor and her cronies on the Board and in the Chamber of Commerce rich. The fact that she is arresting me for fraud is more than ironic. Dan, in Profit, it's the cheat they're looking for because it's the cheat they want. They don't say it in so many words, but cheating is the only way to advance in Profit, if you're lucky and good. The more cheats they discover, the more moneymaking techniques they have for themselves. Cheats run this town. They get rich on the honest, hardworking folks who believe in Morgan and capitalism and who work hard for what free markets and entrepreneurial effort are supposed to provide—at least until they get wise to the scam and are chased away to die as *Wasters*."

"If you knew, why didn't you tell me?"

"I didn't say anything because you're not one of them. You don't cheat, you care, you believe. And if I had told you this, what would you have done? Probably you'd have said something and gotten both of us in trouble and then we would never have had the money to leave. I couldn't take that chance."

"You took an awful risk. And you put me at risk by not telling me. Maybe we both would have been better off if you left without me."

"Honestly, Dan, when we first arrived, that was an option but after we'd been together a while, I tried to have it both ways. I thought I could cheat my way out, not tell you and get you out too. It was wrong and I'm sorry. But you're at fault too. You're too naïve. You believe that everyone thinks like you and Profit isn't for people like you. Profit sends people away and promotes people away, but nobody ever leaves of their own accord.

That's why, once I appropriated enough to escape, I realized, almost too late . . . I couldn't go without you."

"But how?" he asked.

"I'm bribing the security guards," she smiled sheepishly.

He searched her eyes for truth, honesty, kindness, anything he could believe in, but before he could evaluate what he saw, her eyes left him helpless to think at all.

"Hilly says you're with the government. You couldn't have a cloaking device otherwise."

"Please, Dan, I can't tell you how I got it. I want to, but I can't—at least not now."

"That's sweet. What is it you want me to believe? That you're helping me or using me?"

"I don't know. These feelings I have for you are new to me. I've never met anyone like you, not anyone. You . . . care. You care, not for value or advantage, but for no other reason, no other motive—you're just kind and you care and I don't know how to process that, what to do with it. And I don't know how to respond to it." She smiled at that comment, as did he. "I know it's not nearly enough but I really like how I feel and I really like you. I do, but-"

"Since I don't know anyone you dislike, what advantage is that to me?"

"Why are you so cruel? It's not you. Please don't try to make this hard. I'm not leaving without you. Can't you be happy for that?"

"Do I look happy?"

"Goddamn you," she yelled and pushed him. His feet slipped on the icy porch and he slid off into the snow. She was concerned, but then laughed at his partially submerged position.

"Doris is on to you. She's watching and won't let you escape."

"They can't stop me."

"They can and will unless you can make yourself disappear instead of just your identity."

She shrugged. "I'll think of something."

"Fortunately, I already have."

"I'm the idea person in this cabin."

He stood, grabbed some snow, and washed her face in it.

"Stop!" she yelled, "stop it, its cold." As she wiped the snow from her eyes, he moved forward, cautiously, and they kissed, and kissed. He pressed her close as she ran her hands through his curly brown hair. He wasn't sure for how long it was, but when she finally pulled away, breathless, Gil saw that for the first time her violet eyes appeared lost and without answers.

"We can't. The risk . . ."

"I know," he stared, willing himself to speak. "Listen, Bree, if we're going to get out, Laurence Hilliard is willing to help and he has a plan. This is what we have to do."

He told her some, but not all of Hilly's plan.

It was another hellacious week with Bon-Bon. It was so bad that he briefly considered Doris' offer of a better avatar. When Nineteen Eve arrived, the day started with a message from Doris that reminded him that, if all went well, as soon as the busy season ended, he would get his raise, a new assignment, and a new avatar. Bree worked hard all week on the party that she had agreed to host. Everyone from the large guest list confirmed their attendance for the grand sales party to be held at Gil's warehouse.

Gil spent the afternoon of Nineteen Eve preparing, cleaning out the warehouse, putting up the *Chrisnukkah* tree and decorations, and making other preparations necessary for the success of the evening. Fortunately, a winter storm was in the process of dumping a fresh foot of snow on the town and there were no shipments due in or out, so he moved one of the two delivery trucks outside and away from the warehouse, to make more room inside.

By eight o'clock, everyone was there except Doris and her Board, who were waiting out of sight until the right moment. Shortly after nine, Laurence Hilliard arrived and though the guests seemed uncomfortable in his presence, they cheered and made a fuss. Hilly avoided the well-wishers and ended up in a corner near the shipping dock quietly accepting greetings and congratulations from those few guests who overcame their discomfort and his.

After a hearty buffet dinner that Bree had paid top dollar to have catered, it was time for the commercial portion of the evening to begin. As was the custom, Bree, as majority partner, began by offering a presentation that she'd been working hard on.

"Thanks fellow *Profiteers* for coming," she began. "I asked you here tonight so I can present what is truly a once in a lifetime opportunity unlike all the rest. To get everyone into the spirit of the evening, I want each of you to consider this question very carefully before answering. My partner, Dan, is positioned at the keyboard." Gil raised his hand and waved. "Dan will enter your responses which will appear on the screen overhead. The question for the evening is, if you could invest in a lucrative ground-floor opportunity that had a high probability of appreciating beyond your wildest expectations and had only a small upfront risk, what dreams would this investment satisfy for you?"

One of the guests shouted, "How original!" Everyone laughed.

Smiling too, Bree raised her hands to quiet the crowd.

"Please, this is our first hosted party so go easy on us. To whet your financial appetites, I absolutely guarantee that the opportunity we're presenting here tonight has the greatest financial potential of any investment I've seen since I arrived in Profit. In fact, I guarantee that if you take advantage of what we present here; you will absolutely, positively satisfy your dreams. I'm serious about this."

The crowd, sensing the possibilities, quieted and Bree pushed her advantage. "Come on, *Profiteers*, let's hear from you and try not to be troglodytes. Allow your dreams to soar."

Gil yelled from his place under the overhead screen, "Someday, I'm going to own enough shares in Profit to become Mayor." He received mostly moans and a few half-hearted cheers for his response, but it opened the guests to the spirit of the occasion so Gil sat back, pleased with his contribution while Bree pointed to someone else.

"Nan, you and Drake are first," Bree said.

Nan, Nancy Cummings stood. She was a thin, austere-looking woman in a gingham dress and gray streaked hair pulled harshly into a bun.

"Well, first, of course, I would secure my new found wealth in a way that would insure I could fund forever."

"Of course," a few yelled. Bree added, "that's easy, Nan. Can you make it more unique and personal? Let your heart soar."

"I always wanted my own *Virtuoso* unit so I can talk to all the great religious leaders of the past, Jesus, Luther, Falwell, Saint Adam Smith and even our lord financial protector, Thomas Morgan, himself, you know, my all time favorites." Bree led the crowd as they cheered her on. "And I'd acquire a friendlier, more experienced Avatar, one with a better investment track record." There was laughter and a few more cheers.

"Nan, with your own *Virtuoso*," someone shouted from the crowd, "you can design someone for poor Drake here to play with." Laughter followed.

"Hey, I'm her partner and I can hear you," Drake shouted out.

While the crowd laughed, Nan was deep in thought. "Well, I'd love to have a large condo in those Morgan Towers; the ones that I read about near the Battery Levee in New York City. It would be a place where I can pray and get sanctified stock market advice, and maybe take in a Broadway show. That's enough for me, how about you, Drake? It's your turn."

Her partner stood up. "Of course I want what Nan wants," he said and the crowd booed. "No, really, I'd like my own *Virtuoso*, but not to design a lady friend." There were catcalls. "I always wanted to be a professional sports star. I can invest in a franchise and with *Virtuoso* be which ever star I want to be."

"Way to go, jock," someone yelled and there was laughter.

It went on like that until everyone except Bree, Gil and Hilly had spoken. Gil keyed in additions to the dreams list, keenly aware of and somewhat uncomfortable with the greed inherent in this activity. Not ever having been invited to one of these events, he was glad now that he'd been excluded. Finally, as the list of wants expanded, the crowd roared for Hilly to make his wishes known. At first he declined but the crowd insisted so he stood to face them.

"Everything of value is pretty much taken. Joe's got his yacht, Tim the MAG pass for whenever he visits other towns or takes vacations. Marsha's wish for a subscription to the *True Insider Trading Magazine* so she can make even more money is a good one too, I guess. I really don't know what's left. I'm not one for wishes so I'll just wish for peace on earth and maybe that everyone share good will, beginning with this *Chrisnukkah* season."

Though they revered Hilly, the guests booed his lack of true *Chrisnukkah* spirit. There were shouts of "boring", or "Christian", or "Socialist", heard above the laughter, but Hilly would offer nothing more and embarrassed he stepped away from the crowd and sat near a truck. Finally, the crowd calmed down and waited expectantly for Bree to present the prospectus that would make these Profiteers rich.

She stood below the overhead monitor and initiated a full motion audio-video presentation that supported her proposal.

"Picture a future," a deep male voice began, "where each of you owns a significant share of a real production town, a town very much like Profit."

"We do," somebody shouted.

To clarify, Bree paused the presentation.

"We're talking about owning real voting shares, real ownership—rather than the preferred, non-voting shares that provide dividends, some liability, and have limited marketability like the shares you earn now. We're talking about owning common shares, real stock in the town that would allow you to vote on real operations in your community and earn money when the town's performance causes that stock to appreciate. Wouldn't it be great to really own a town, together?"

"That sounds socialist." One person shouted.

"How can it be socialist," Bree explained. "We're a free market town. We're just broadening the ownership base, that's all. Operations go on like they always do—capitalism to the end."

"How could we do that?" someone asked.

"That's a great question," Bree answered. "Would it surprise you if I said it's already being done?"

"Where?" yelled an interested voice from the crowd.

"Right here in Profit. Doris and the other members of her Board own a stock called, *End Run, Incorporated*. It and similar stocks representing other production towns throughout the country trade on the Morgan Executive Stock Exchange in New York City and are great values."

The crowd quieted and the party atmosphere dissipated as the guests tried to assimilate this uncomfortable new information, unsure if Bree was joking at their expense.

It was here that Gil added his piece.

"According to Profit's founding prospectus, which is similar to the by-laws Doris and her Board ratified, the more effectively town costs are contained, and the more profit the town generates, the more likely Profit stock appreciates. This is not unusual. Towns like Profit have a history of providing significant capital gains due to their location and the effectiveness of their work force, but also because of the commercial support and security provided by the government."

More comfortable with the topic, Bree took over at this point.

"One of the reasons why so few Profiteers are promoted to locations outside Profit is that investors want continuity in operations to insure that quality and productivity remain high. It's equally important to Doris and the other stockholders that the citizens of Profit actively pursue every possible profit-making activity because Profit's common shareholders benefit directly from a Profiteer's constant and profitable hard work. The Profit Charter has been constructed so that chasing a fortune is paramount for us *Profiteers* and that diverts everyone's attention from the extraordinary distribution rights Mayor Doris, her stockholders, and the members of her Board of Directors receive. That is the reason why there are so many commercial events in town. These events generate more profits, of course, but the more distracted everyone is trying to earn, the easier it is for Mayor Doris to extract her profits from all of us without interference or protest. To protect Mayor Doris's wanton pursuit of capital appreciation and short term profits, she regularly threatens families with dissolution, she expels marginal performers and forces them to forfeit the rights to anything they've earned, and she refuses to hire certified professional accountants to audit town performance and bring to light some of her money making chicanery."

As the reality of what Bree was presenting became clear, Gil watched the reaction among the guests. Almost immediately, all the economic fun was sucked out of the party and a group near him began to grumble. An old plant supervisor shouted to be recognized.

Gil identified him.

"Bree, Sully has a question."

Tall and thin, Jason "Sully" Sullivan stood, looking awkward and uncomfortable as his body shifted from side to side.

"Ma'am, I don't know what you're trying to do here, but it isn't funny, productive, or right. Me and my partner have been working here in Profit, diligently for decades. We've almost saved enough to qualify to participate in the next mayoral elections–not that I want the job, mind you, or could even get elected. You two are new here so you haven't invested in Profit like most of us and what you're saying sounds real mean spirited, almost Commie-like. We trust Mayor Doris and her council. They've always been square with us."

Bree responded. "Yes, Sully, I am new, but you know the returns I've been getting on my commercial transactions, so you know I understand things. You and Sara are hard workers, sure, but look how you live compared to Doris and her Board. Rank has its privileges, certainly, but each of you here needs to evaluate your own personal situation and compare it to what you had when you arrived, how much you were told you needed to live comfortably, and what your expectations are. I believe most of you will find you're almost as far away from those goals as when you arrived."

Clearly agitated, Sully remained standing, swaying as he spoke. "Young lady, we've seen this before. New people come in here and they get impatient for the benefits of hard work. Some never get what we're all about. They're like you; they don't know how Profit works. Doris always warns us about new, young residents like you who come from other places and claim to know right and wrong and do exactly what you're doing now. You're disillusioned, that's all. Free Market Capitalism, like we have here in Profit, is the best way to live in the whole world. Ask anyone. Go ahead and ask them. Everyone in the nation and the world is envious of how we thrive here in Profit and that makes you nothing more than a communist malcontent who is trying to destroy the greatness we have here.

"Girl, why are you doing this? I think it's because you don't want to get in line or compete with your betters. It sure sounds like you don't trust the invisible hand of free markets to work magic for you like it works magic for us. Or maybe you don't want to invest the hard work because you think you're too damn privileged to start at the bottom like the rest of us good folks. If I were you, young lady, I'd apologize to everyone here and to the mayor herself when she arrives and then get the hell out of Profit." Some of the others applauded.

"You may be right, Sully," Bree said, "but have you ever considered who leaves and who stays and why?" Gil was proud of her for standing up. "I know it's a hard world outside of Profit, but that doesn't mean it has to be that hard and unfair, particularly economically unfair, inside. Sully, and the rest of you, before you judge what I'm saying, read our prospectus. Dan is transmitting it to each of your viewers. What we're proposing is a bit socialist, but it certainly isn't communist, I don't deny that, but it's capitalist too and what's more, it's fair for those whose efforts should be rewarded.

"Dan and I are proposing a reincorporation referendum that includes the entire community in the ownership of Profit. This is permissible, based on Profit's Articles of Incorporation. Our proposal won't redistribute wealth, if that's your fear of socialism; it just treats wealth more fairly, providing it more equitably to *Profiteers* who are working hard but seeing little appreciation. Each of you would have a say in how the Management team is selected, but the operation of Profit won't change from its current principles unless a majority of the stockholders vote for that change. That is the American way and it conforms to capitalist principles.

"I'm not talking a command economy here. I'm proposing changes in the ownership structure only, not in management or operation methods, which should be the responsibility of operations management. Each of you wants what's best for Profit, so why shouldn't you vote for it? I repeat, this isn't a simple redistribution of Profit's wealth, it provides every interested *Profiteer* with more involvement, more reward—and of course, more risk, but it's for everyone, those who create wealth, our workers and management, everyone. This is doable. We have a quorum here tonight, so after you read the prospectus, we can vote to put it on to the Board's agenda."

There was more grumbling, but soon everyone quieted as they began reading the prospectus summary. When they finished, there were questions, but it was clearer to the Profiteers that great wealth was being diverted to Doris. When they learned that, the guests seemed more interested in considering alternatives.

"Does anyone object to a vote?" Bree smiled at Gil, who nodded. Sully and most of the other attendees raised their hands but some Profiteers, though confused as to how much power they had, were in agreement. "Then let's vote."

Knowing that the vote wouldn't carry, Gil signaled for Bree to turn on her cloaking device. She did and then advised the guests on the next steps of their power play.

"On the back page of the Prospectus you'll find questions to ask Mayor Doris when she arrives. Keep in mind, there is great wealth here and you deserve to live better and insure the future of your partnership, your children, and your town, it is up to you and after all, isn't that what capitalism is all about?

"Ask Doris. But don't accept easy answers. She will try to overrule and overpower you. Don't let her. You work hard and you have every right to your own financial future. What we've proposed here is legal and more, it's right. It is up to each of you to force Doris treat you fairly and honestly. After all, we are all *Profiteers*."

As if on queue the shipping doors opened and Mayor Doris, along with members of her Board and an armed security force entered.

"Nobody moves!" she yelled. "I have an arrest warrant for Bree Andrews and Dan Stacey." When he heard his name, Gil smiled ruefully. She had intended to double cross him all along. This evening serves her right.

Gil took Bree's hand and moved to where Hilly was standing.

"Why are you doing this?" Gil shouted at the mayor. "We've done nothing wrong!"

Doris looked sternly at Hilly when she spoke. "This whore and her pimp here have been defrauding all of us. They've cheated Profit. She has a device that allows her to steal things without paying for them. They are crooks. Bree Andrews is the reason we haven't been able to reconcile our books and why there is missing inventory and revenue and we are losing money. Arrest them."

Facing security guards with pistols, Bree stared, frozen. Gil put his arm around her and slowly backed her toward the truck as the guests began shouting insults.

When they reached the truck, Bree held up her hands to quiet the quests and responded. "Doris is right! I did what she said and I'm sorry!"

"See," Doris shouted at the guests, "she confessed. Bree Andrews and Dan Stacey, you are guilty of fraud and theft and other economic crimes against Profit, and you will be executed tomorrow tonight." As the mayor spoke, her security force held their pistols at the ready and moved toward them.

Doris calmly spoke. "Don't do anything foolish or we will kill you right now."

"You're going to kill us anyway," Bree yelled angrily.

As planned, Gil took a gun that Hilly had hidden in his jacket pocket and pointed it at Hilly.

"If anyone tries to hurt us, I'll kill Hilliard," he said, acting as crazed as he could.

Per their script, Hilly begged, "Doris, save me, please save me. Listen, he's desperate and I don't want to die."

At that, Doris seemed unsure. "No, don't shoot them." She shouted at her guards. Then she stared into Gil's eyes and smiled. "You can't. You won't. You don't have the guts. And if you did-"

Gil grabbed Hilly's arm and twisted it behind his back. Then he pressed the muzzle of the gun hard against Hilly's neck.

"I'm warning you, Mayor, you're going to execute us anyway so we have nothing to lose. Let us go or we'll kill your cash cow here and then what'll you do? Profit will lose money and your portfolio will decline. Are we worth that to you? And without Hilliard, you can forget about your job in that manager's town, you can forget about your future and forever, Doris, because you'll be working the rest of your days here in Profit to make ends meet. Maybe you can take my job working with Bon-Bon in the warehouse." Doris hesitated.

Things were happening way too fast for Sully and the others in the crowd. They were confused, but had the presence to implore Doris.

"Mayor, we can't risk it," Sully said. "These people are desperate and Hilliard is too important to us. You have to let them go. We'll get them or somebody else will, later. We'll post a reward. They won't get far."

Hilly chose that time to speak to his neighbors who were acting as security. "Joe, Sammy, Pete, put your damned weapons down, don't make a mistake and get me killed."

Reluctantly, Doris motioned for the team to lower their weapons. Seeing this, Gil and Bree edged toward the truck, dragging Hilly along as a shield.

When they reached the truck's cab, Doris panicked.

"Not a step further, you two. We're not getting HomeSec involved in this. You're both guilty of fraud and you will be punished, here and now." Without taking her eyes off Gil, she addressed her security team. "You know him. You've seen his profile. He's an incompetent coward. He won't kill Hilly, he doesn't have the guts. Shoot him, but aim carefully, I don't want Hilly hurt."

Gil hadn't expected that, and a wave of fear washed over him. He looked to Hilly.

Hilly nodded. "It looks like you'll have to trust me now," he said and slowly put his hand on the gun. "Get in the truck and get the hell out of here."

Slowly, Bree opened the passenger side door and climbed in.

Doris screamed, "Stop her!"

One of the security guards fired into the side of the truck and the warehouse reverberated with the bark of the gun and again with the impact of the bullet. When the noise ceased and quiet reigned, Gil backed to the driver's side using Hilly as a shield.

"If he tries to get in, kill him!" Doris screamed.

Gil froze. He, Bree, Hilly, Doris and her security team stared at each other in a true stand off while the guests moved out of danger. It was going to end like an old west shoot-out, just like Gil imagined.

Hilly whispered again. "They'll discover my role soon enough. Shoot me now and go to Hamilton. Dan Burghe is a friend. Get in the truck and get out."

Before Gil could stop him, Hilly squeezed the trigger. His last words were, "Run," as a shot rang out. In horror, Gil watched as Hilly's body staggered toward the security team, blood spouting from his neck onto his crisp white shirt. Stunned *Profiteers* ran to save him as Hilly's lifeless body flopped dead on the floor.

"NO!" Gil screamed as he took one last look at the blood that had pulsed out of the wound in Hilly's neck, turning his white shirt red. He turned and bolted into the truck. With everyone frozen in disbelief, Gil started the engine, slammed it into gear, and stomped on the gas. As the truck lurched forward, he raised the truck's bed to hopefully deflect any bullets that might be fired at them. They sped out of the warehouse, demolishing the door as they left. He stared at the rear view screen, where light from the warehouse illuminated Hilly's crumpled body, lying lifeless on the floor, surrounded by the residents of Profit.

Bullets began dinging the truck bed as it fishtailed through the fresh evening snow. The truck skidded briefly, then the tires bit and they headed away. It wasn't until the lights of the warehouse disappeared in the distance that he took a breath.

"We are we going?" Bree asked, with tears rolling down her cheeks.

He couldn't answer, nor could he relax his grip on the steering wheel. "I . . . I killed him, Bree. I killed him. I shot him. Hilly's dead."

She put her hand on his. Startled, he jumped and the truck skidded in the snow. She screamed and he grabbed the wheel, braked slowly, and halted the skid. With the truck stopped, his head found relief on the steering wheel so he rested it there, wanting desperately to cry, but he couldn't.

"Hilly said to trust him, to have faith and now he's dead. He died for me . . . for us. Why? Why did he do it, Bree? How could he do it?"

He could hear her crying and was jealous. She squeezed his hand and rubbed his neck, gently.

"I don't know. I guess it was the only way. Dan, we're not safe yet. Are you okay to drive?" He nodded. "You're sure? I can do it." He nodded again. "Okay then, keep your hands on the wheel and your eyes on the road. Where are we going? Is there a map? Do you think they'll follow us?"

"No," he said. "While you were preparing for the party, I made sure this truck had good tires and I moved the other truck to the far side of town. By tomorrow all of the local *Tollers*, and probably HomeSec will be looking for us, so we'd better stay on the roads Hilly mapped out for us." He dug into his pocket, and pulled out a folded map.

"He . . . Hilly gave me directions. They'll take us far away from Profit. Why didn't I believe him? I should have told him."

She took the map from his trembling hand and unfolded it.

"That can't be helped now. Keep an eye on the road. We're taking Cedar all the way to Ninety, then we'll head west."

He was emotionally drained and drove silently, his eyes on the road ahead, but regularly checking the rear view camera for pursuit as well. He tried to shake the gloom that weighed on him, but all he could think about, dwell on, was that gunshot and the blood and Hilly toppling over. His only relief was in the monitor view of monotonous, mesmerizing snow rushing toward him illuminated by the truck's headlights. Bree clicked a button on the console and the flakes disappeared from the monitor, clearing his view but doing nothing for his mood.

He drove long after his eyes began to burn and his head ached. Even when Bree begged him to pull over, he refused because the weariness and pain somehow deadened the ache in his heart.

"You're exhausted," Bree insisted, finally. "Dan, it's safe enough. Please pull over." He ignored her.

Further on she tried again. "Take a break. I can drive. You need some rest. I promise I'll wake you in a couple of hours so we can figure out what to do next."

"How could I let it happen? I killed him, Bree."

"It wasn't your fault. He chose to die to save us."

"But why? He didn't know us, we were nothing to him. Why did he do it?"

"I don't know. You knew him longer than me; I had hoped you had an idea. I'm sorry he died but I'm glad he saved us. And honestly, until I saw your reaction, I thought shooting him was part of your plan."

He slammed his forehead into the steering mechanism.

"God, no. He never said anything about dying. If I'd known . . . he has family and how do you do that if you're going to live forever, God, what have we done? He was loved and he gave that up for me, for us and he barely knew us. Forever, he gave that up. I don't understand."

"Obviously, he felt it was more important for us to be alive than to live forever."

"Jesus, Bree, I don't want to believe that. How do you think that makes me feel? How do you repay a debt like that? He gave up everything, his family and forever for me. What could I ever do to repay that? And stop saying Hilly killed himself. I killed him."

"I saw it. He forced the trigger. It wasn't your fault."

He stopped the truck and looked at her. "We've been living together for months and you still don't understand me in any meaningful way."

She was hurt by that. "What can I say? I'm trying. Look, it's done. Nothing can bring Hilly back. I know you're sad, but you'll get over it. It won't be easy but you will. That's it. Change positions with me or I'm leaving right now." When she reached for the door handle, he stopped the truck, got out, reluctantly, and walked around the back of the truck while she walked around the front to change places with him.

"Now get some sleep," she said. "And don't talk anymore. People live forever but people die all the time. That's life. Some live for the wrong reasons and some die for the right reasons. At least he chose his death and it was pretty damned heroic if you ask me. Let's look to the future. We have the money we need and we're out of that horrid town. All in all, we accomplished what we set out to accomplish."

He slammed his fist into the console startling her. She stared defiantly at him while he spoke.

"I don't understand you. There were times back there when I thought I saw someone kind, someone nice, a good person. But you live in some kind of a shell. I see glimpses inside you sometimes and everything looks great, but it's only a glimpse. I don't understand. What are you protecting yourself from?"

"Whoa, big boy, you're saying that to me? Don't get all holier-than-thou with me. You described yourself just then. You're tired and upset and you need to sleep so I'm not going to argue, even though it seems that's what you think will help you get past this.

"I'm a bitch, okay, but believe me, I'm sad about Hilly, too. But I'm also thankful for what he did. You should feel good that there's something about you so compelling that he chose to give up his precious life to keep you alive. Live with it. He chose to die so you could live. I understand you being upset and confused, but how about loosening up and being grateful for what he did. Close your eyes and sleep. Things will be clearer when you wake up and we'll say a prayer for him."

"Who would we pray to?"

"Christ, I don't care." Annoyed, she gunned the engine, causing the truck to fishtail. She slowed down to gain control, turned on the windshield camera system and headed west into the night. He stared out into the white sky and under heavy eyelids, promptly fell asleep.

Gil woke startled and unsure where he was. It was a crisp, cold dawn and the truck was parked on a side street of a deserted town and there was no sign of Bree. Cautiously, he got out of the cab expecting Doris and others to be waiting for him, but all he saw were rows of one and two-story deserted homes covered with new fallen snow. He noticed footprints on the other side of the truck, and crunching through the snow, he followed them. When he reached the edge of the road, he saw a field. He took another step and slipped. As he slid down the embankment, he heard a loud shriek.

Embarrassed but laughing, Bree hurriedly pulled up her pants.

"Do you mind? I'm relieving myself here. Turn around." Gil turned and struggled back up the hill and to the truck. Moments later, she walked up to him and pulled him into her arms. He returned the embrace and they stayed cocooned as she gently messaged the back of his neck.

"What happened last night was horrible and I'm sorry. I feel bad about it and I feel bad about the way I've been treating you, too. You saved my life." Gil tried to interrupt but she gently put her fingers on his mouth to stop him.

"No, don't, please. You saved my life when there was no financial incentive to do it. Before I met you, if someone had done that or anything for me, immediately, I would have searched for their motivation. But now I know you and I'm confused but I'm starting to understand. There's something . . . . You and Hilly, you both . . ." She hesitated. "In . . . in my life, no one has ever done anything close to what the two of you did for me, and for no reason. If there was some quid pro quo I could understand, but neither of you asked for anything in return and I don't know how to process that. I know why you did . . . I know you like me, but to take such risks just for that, I . . . I'll never forget it and I promise you, I'll work at it. I will try to be . . . better."

"Bree, it was-"

"No, don't get all humble with me. I know you were just being you and that's the great thing. You're the one who doesn't understand. I've been around people all my life, but I've always been alone. I think, maybe everyone is, but since meeting you, I'm certain I was alone. No one ever offered to help me, but if they did I could depend on the offer being for reasons that would benefit them, not me. It's the way things are and I'm comfortable with that—or at least I was. I wish I could explain it better, but I can't because the more I tell you about me, the more your life will be in danger and I don't want that.

"Somehow, Hilly saw something in you that I wish I'd recognized sooner. You're good, a really good guy, and you're kind. In fact, you're the best person I've ever known even though I have no frame of reference for even saying that. I'm trying here. Please don't lose faith in me. Please don't give up on me."

Gil smiled and hugged her closer.

"I'm still here, aren't I? You're awesome too—a bit moody, maybe." She smiled. "Bree, I appreciate what you're saying but . . . it's not me. I wish it was, but it's not. I've done some very bad things, things I can't talk about, but I'm not good, or as kind as you think. I've hurt some people terribly." He paused, thinking back on Angel Falls, Annie, and then Hilly and he felt the cold on his face and knew it was his tears. He wiped them away and continued.

"I've done bad things to people who deserved far better. I'm trying to figure out why I did them, and who I am and, more important, who I want to be, but I have so little basis and it's hard and confusing. At least we're both trying. That's something." They stared into each other's eyes in silence and briefly, his fear and concern melted in her violet kaleidoscope. Finally, reality interceded and he stepped away. "Let me drive for a while."

Because of the heavy snow, instead of following Hilly's suggested path using back roads, he continued on the highway because it was a faster way of getting as far from Profit as they could. He hoped that after the storm, the *Tollers* who normally patrol Northern Ohio would be too busy plowing roads. And even though he was scared to meet up with them again, he had to take that chance. So they traveled on, mostly west and a little north, stopping at independent truck weigh stations where Bree's cloaking device allowed them to purchase fuel and food anonymously.

"What do you suppose the Profiteers will do about Doris?" he wondered aloud after they had pulled out of a fuel station.

"They're Americans so nothing," she responded. "At least we gave them something to think about, but they won't risk what they have to throw her out. Besides, Doris is a true entrepreneur so she'll find a way to prosper regardless of what they do."

"Someday, it might be interesting to come back to Profit to see how they fared."

She didn't even think about it. "No, I won't do that."

"You're right. My only friend there is dead. Still, I hope they do the right thing."

She smiled.

"What?" he asked innocently.

"The right thing? Don't count on it."

Through Ohio, the truck handled well on the unplowed highway, but with dark clouds threatening more snow, they felt safer knowing their tracks would soon be impossible to follow. They were more at ease now when they talked, but each stayed with safe subjects.

Soon, he would have an important decision to make. She was going to Detroit to find her father and although he wanted to go with her, to protect her, another option was preying on him. There was a stop he needed to make and Bree couldn't go. Without sharing their purpose, they agreed to head as far west as they could and when they saw that the sign for Angola was a different shape than the Ohio signs; he knew they were back in his home state of Indiana. They stopped for dinner at a local restaurant where he signed onto the Mesh at a public terminal and checked regional news. There was a report on the death of Laurence Hilliard on a blog site. Although Bree cautioned him not to, he left his condolences and clicked off.

They refueled, ate dinner and talked quietly. The restaurant was almost empty when they had first arrived, but slowly filled up as locals entered to eat and converse by the warmth of the fireplace. This relaxed, friendly environment seemed so distant from the intense world of Profit that it caused him to wonder how many towns in America were like this, and Angel Falls, as opposed to Aeden and Profit. At the end the day, they had closed more distance between themselves, but that made the coming decision that much harder.

It was dark now. "Bree, it's time," he said after a few hours of mostly silent driving. "To get to Detroit you have to take Route 69 north to Route 94 and then go east. It's the long way, but they won't be looking for you from that direction."

"You're not coming." She didn't argue.

"There's something I have to do. Afterwards, I'll go to Detroit. We can meet there."

She saw it in his smile and gamely matched hers to it.

"No, no you won't. But I understand. I hope I see you again, Dan, but if I don't, I'm a better person for knowing you and I owe you big time for that. Can you tell me where you're going?"

His heart ached. He pulled the truck over to the side of the road, next to a hip-high snow bank.

"I can't. It's something I have to do. I would go with you to Detroit but . . . I'll try, later, I promise."

"No, no promises," she said as she put her fingers to his lips. "You've thought this through?"

He nodded, opened the driver's side door, and hopped out. She watched him for a few seconds, then opened her own door and slid out. They met in front, illuminated by the headlights.

She began to cry but fought it. "Help me to understand. Why do you think we're going to see each other again? Tell me how we'll find each other when you don't know my real name and I don't know yours? And what about my cloaking device, it hides my whereabouts from surveillance and Detroit's a huge and divided city, with rebel communities, production towns, *Toller* refuges and lots of *Waster* villages. We could both be in the same place and we might as well be in different countries for all the good it would do us. So, tell me how will you find me?"

He took her hand and in the cold quiet evening, he faced her.

"We'll find each other. We'll just have to trust—not something either of us is very good at, I'll grant you. I have to find myself, first. Once I do, I'll find you, believe me, I'll find you."

"Is there any way?"

It hurt to speak. "I . . . can't . . . no. Bree-"

"Then tell me what I should do," she interrupted.

"You should give me a kiss and then go."

She looked down and her tears dripped into the snow. He touched her chin and gently raised her face so he could get lost in those mesmerizing violet eyes one last time. Like it was the first moment he saw her in the light, her eyes took his breath away. After a moment, she blinked and then closed them, denying him precious moments of happiness. Then she leaned into him and they kissed and held onto each other in a feeble attempt to freeze time.

For a brief moment, it worked and suspended in that moment, he changed his mind many times, but then, slowly, he broke the kiss and pulled back to see those eyes now red and glistening. He blinked away his own tears so he could see her better and kissed her on her eyelids and then her neck. She sighed and it sent a chill through him. Their mouths met and they kissed again. It pained him to break free.

"Bree, take the truck and go. I'll find my way from here," he handed her the key and the pistol that had taken Hilly's life. "I don't know who you'll meet . . ."

She smiled and took the pistol, closing one eye, aiming as if ready to shoot. "I know how to respond to that." She laughed and he hugged her one last time.

"You sure meet strange people on the road," he said as he helped her climb into the truck and waved as the truck rolled forward, easing back onto the road, heading north, toward Detroit.

He stared until the truck disappeared over the horizon and continued to stare long after.

The End

Gil's story continues in *Circle of Life*, Book 3 of the Joad Cycle